Kitty Ray graduated from St Martin's School of Art in 1968 and has worked as a designer, window-dresser, illustrator and even a stewardess aboard World War II DC3s for a regional airline. She lives in Suffolk, with her husband and two sons. She won the RNA Netta Musket best newcomer's award for her first novel, *Stoats and Weasels*. *A Peculiar Chemistry* is her third novel.

A Peculiar Chemistry

KITTY RAY

WARNER BOOKS

A *Warner* Book

First published in Great Britain in 1999
by Warner Books

A CIP catalogue record for this book
is available from the British Library.

ISBN 0 7515 2584 7

Typeset in Palatino by M Rules
Printed and bound in Great Britain by
Clays Ltd, St Ives plc

Warner Books
A Division of
Little, Brown and Company (UK)
Brettenham House
Lancaster Place
London WC2E 7EN

For Val

Acknowledgements

My thanks go again to Imogen Taylor and Rebecca Kerby at Little, Brown and to my agent, Sarah Molloy. Grateful thanks also to Barbara Saunders for proofreading the wartime sections of the book for me, to Janey Pirie, formerly of Thompson and Morgan, whose knowledge of the history of the seed industry was invaluable, and to Norfolk Lavender of Heacham, for providing technical help. I have drawn freely on Ipswich Library's newspaper archives, as well as historical and botanical publications too numerous to list, but special mention must go to Gavin Lyall's excellent *Freedom's Battle* (volume 2, *The War in the Air*), R. Douglas Brown's *East Anglia 1941*, and Froglet Publications' *Norfolk and Suffolk Weather Book*.

I came back late and tired last night
        Into my little room,
To the long chair and the firelight
        And comfortable gloom.

But as I entered softly in
        I saw a woman there,
The line of neck and cheek and chin,
        The darkness of her hair,
The form of one I did not know
        Sitting in my chair.

I stood a moment fierce and still,
        Watching her neck and hair.
I made a step to her; and saw
        That there was no one there.

It was some trick of the firelight
        That made me see her there.
It was a chance of shade and light
        And the cushion in the chair . . .

From 'Home' by Rupert Brooke (1913)

Chapter One

Ellis turned off the road and drove slowly along the green, bumpy track beneath the trees. She had been this way by car only half a dozen times, and her earliest memory was of walking, when she was less than five years old. She could still feel the moss, soft beneath her summer sandals, and the sun flickering against her cheeks as she moved in and out of the shade, holding tight to her mother's hand.

She brought her car to a halt at the edge of the clearing and stared out through the windscreen at the newly whitewashed cottage as she searched in her pocket for the key. *My* cottage, she thought, *my* key; the perfect hideaway for a pregnant single woman with more questions than answers.

The builders had cleared up well – apart from the yellow stains on the grass where their equipment had lain, a sandy patch by the front door where the plasterer had mixed his ingredients and the tyremarks where they had parked their lorries, taking up all the space in front of the house so Ellis had had to leave her car beneath the trees fifty yards away, it was neat and tidy. Over the past six months, she had been here only in the presence of workmen, surrounded by the noise of sawing, hammering and thumping pop music. She leaned back for a moment, closing her eyes and savouring the quiet, before opening the car door and swinging her legs to the ground. The turf felt springy beneath her shoes and she rocked on her toes, enjoying the sensation. The air smelled of damp grass and the late dog roses blooming among the brambles at the edge of the glade.

As she straightened up, she thought she felt a faint fluttering low down in her belly – her baby stirring for the first time? – and she laid both hands on her stomach, surprised yet again by the burgeoning voluptuousness of her own body.

Ellis Jones was a woman without conventional beauty. Her legs were passable enough, but the feminine curves men find so enticing were missing and she had known since childhood that her face would never launch a thousand ships. Ellis's features – intelligent, patrician, plain – owed nothing to her mother's delicate beauty, and the straight lines of her figure came directly from her father. She had never allowed her looks to get in the way of her ambitions though. Rather, she had always maintained it was to her advantage being plain and certainly she was taken more seriously by her male colleagues than some of the prettier women on the university staff. Her opinions were listened to, Ellis claimed, because there was no element of sexual tension there to distract from them – even the most cerebral of men, she would point out, are apt to be led astray by an appealing face, a curvaceous figure. Now, although her face remained as plain as it had always been and her thick, curly hair was as stubbornly uncontrollable and as boringly brown as ever, pregnancy was temporarily lending her body the curves of a Marilyn Monroe, a Sophia Loren; she was keenly aware of the irony.

She was early for her rendezvous. In an hour's time the removal van would arrive, bringing her bits and pieces. Frank and Eric would manhandle her fridge and her microwave through to the tiny kitchen, lug her bedding upstairs, unpack her crockery, her pots and pans, her files. They would arrange her sitting-room furniture, leaving only the books – she would sort through them herself in her own time – and towards the end of their labours they would manoeuvre her desk into place ready for her computer, then lean against it while they drank their coffee. They would remark upon the weather, the isolated situation of the cottage, the difficulty they had had finding the place. Then, when the van was finally empty and the house was full, they would take their cardboard boxes and their scrunched-up wrapping paper and bump away down the grassy track towards the main road, leaving her alone in her clearing in the woods.

Peace, she thought as she turned the key in the lock, swung the front door wide and stepped over the threshold into the cool, silent, paint-smelling interior. That's what I need just now, a bit of peace and quiet.

Chapter Two

She was standing by the open window when she first set eyes on him, in her office on an upper floor of the ivy-covered faculty building. It was the beginning of the Michaelmas term and she was slurping sherry with her friend Harriet as they watched the new student intake pour across the quad towards the refectory. They were picking out the radicals, the troublemakers, the virgins, the cool dudes, the sexpots, as they had done every year for the past five years, two thirty-something bluestockings, serious-minded, intelligent women whose lives were centred not upon husbands and children but upon the pursuit of intellectual excellence, sharing a tipsy ogling session which set them up for the academic year ahead and reminded them pleasurably of the time when they had been students themselves, before they acquired dignity, responsibility, gravitas.

It was Harriet who spotted him first. '*Corrr*,' she said, digging Ellis in the ribs and waving her sherry glass in his direction. 'Now *that* takes my Stud of the Year award!'

Ellis peered at the milling crowd of young men and women on the green below. 'Which one?'

'Which one?' Harriet was incredulous. '*That* one!' She pointed, jogging Ellis's sherry arm.

Ellis raised her glass and licked the sticky liquid from her fingers. 'Where?'

'There, standing next to the tall dark boy outside the Bursar's office, the fair-haired one wearing the red T-shirt and the bimbo bookends.'

Ellis spotted him immediately. Harriet was right; he stood out from the crowd, even taller than the tall boy beside him, tanned, well built, a blond Narcissus in a black leather jacket and well-cut black chinos. He was laughing, head thrown back, hands in pockets, enjoying his position at the centre of attention; a pretty girl hung adoringly upon each of his arms. Look at me, his body language demanded, aren't I just the most beautiful thing you've ever seen?

Repelled by his arrogance, Ellis moved on to examine the boy standing next to him, thin, pale, with over-long dark hair and intelligent angular features, inconspicuously dressed in faded jeans and a grey sweatshirt. Now you, she thought, leaning forward to see better, really *are* beautiful.

'Wow . . .' said Harriet, leering at her blond Narcissus.

'Wow . . .' echoed Ellis, gazing raptly at her dark nemesis.

As the group advanced, they fanned out into a procession and the dark boy fell back, allowing the jostling, skittering girls to flood past him, then came to a halt directly below her window. He pushed the thick hair out of his eyes then, slowly, deliberately, as if he was aware of being watched, he raised his head and looked straight at Ellis, standing by the window with her sherry glass frozen halfway to her mouth. Months later, after they had become lovers, he reminded her of that first encounter. It was then, he told her, that he fell in love with her. 'You looked like a Vermeer painting,' he said, 'standing at the window, framed by all that lush green ivy, with the sunlight falling across your face and a glass in your hand.'

He wasn't on her English Literature course and Ellis was relieved, in a way. Common sense told her it was ludicrous to imagine he might have felt the same over-whelming tenderness for her as she had felt for him in that first moment of eye contact. You are thirty-four years old, she reminded herself as she lay awake at night fantasising about him, you are practically old enough to be his mother; you are irretrievably plain and he is heart-stoppingly beautiful. *There is no such thing as love at first sight.* But over the ensuing weeks her secret passion, kindled by that one brief glance, fanned by every transient encounter in corridors and lecture halls, grew rather than receded. As a senior adviser, she warned herself sternly, it was her duty to provide pastoral care for her students, not lust after them; the Dean had made it perfectly clear when she took up her fellowship that intimate relationships between tutor and student were frowned upon, considered inappropriate by the university, even improper. She was uncomfortably aware, though, that it was only lack of opportunity which had so far prevented her from risking her career, her reputation and her dignity, for the sake of a mad adolescent crush on a boy not yet twenty.

Eavesdropping on student conversations, listening to the chat in the common room, gossiping with Harriet, on whose history course he was enrolled, she gathered information about him with the singleminded determination of a superannuated groupie. She discovered who he was – Joe Leavis, studying English and American History, scion of a northern grammar school, with a strong Yorkshire accent and a soft, low-pitched laugh. She watched him surreptitiously, noted (with a seething jealousy of which she had not thought she was capable) the girls he hung out with, which college residence he was in, the pubs he frequented.

She was careful to look away when he glanced in her direction, to feign indifference when he appeared at her table in the refectory and attempted to make conversation, or smiled at her as they passed in the quad. As a mature, intelligent woman she was aware how unsuitable, even ridiculous, her infatuation was, but she was gripped by an emotion stronger than anything she had ever experienced before, unable to help herself. He was out of bounds; he was nearly fifteen years her junior; how could he possibly feel about her as she felt about him?

When he materialised unexpectedly outside her office at the beginning of the Lent term she knew instantly, though, that he *did* feel the same, that it was up to her to stop it before it started, because he wasn't going to. But when he held out his hand she took it anyway, and as his fingers tightened round hers she knew it was already too late, that she would not, *could* not, stop it now, even if she wanted to, because once he had touched her she had no option, no choice in the matter at all.

He'd caught her by surprise, that was the trouble – maybe if she'd had some prior warning, if she'd known he was coming, she might have been able to get herself together, resist him. She might have pleaded a previous engagement, a headache, asked one of her colleagues to stand in for her. But she'd just opened the door and found him standing there. He looked even younger close-to than he did at a distance; the fresh, untainted quality of his youth left her breathless, rendered her incapable of rational thought.

He was almost as tongue-tied as she to begin with, stammering out some pathetic excuse about being unhappy with his chosen subject and wanting to switch. What were his chances of getting onto her English Literature course? he asked. Could she be his personal tutor? As he talked, he fixed her with intent, pleading brown eyes, hypnotising her.

She retreated behind her desk, almost scuttling in her haste to put a physical barrier between them, and settled tensely on the edge of her chair, arms folded across her chest as if she might thus ward him off. Then falling back on her briskest, most matter-of-fact lecturer's voice, she asked him what he thought he would achieve by changing tack mid-stream. He was already a term into his first year, she told him disapprovingly, surely he should have done something about it earlier if he was so unhappy? 'It's Joe, isn't it?' she queried, 'Lewis? Leavis?' as if she wasn't sure, as if his name hadn't featured in her dreams for the past three months, echoed in her head every time she glimpsed him across the quad. She was stern, dignified, as befitted an experienced thirty-four-year-old tutor dealing with an irresponsible nineteen-year-old student, but he persisted stubbornly until, desperate for something to do, she unfolded her arms and started fumbling through the papers on her desk with hands that shook so much it sounded as if she were conducting a whispering campaign. She had given herself away.

'Leavis,' he confirmed quietly, 'Joe Leavis,' and he leaned across the desk to still her twitching, trembling fingers with his own. Within twenty-four hours they were lovers.

Standing in the white empty room of her newly reno-vated cottage, with the sun streaming through the open door behind her, Ellis could see his thin, clever face as vividly as if he were standing there beside her.

Intellectually, objectively, she was perfectly well aware that it was *not* a particularly beautiful face, that its beauty existed only in the eye of one, besotted, beholder. But it was the only face which had ever moved her to tears, the one she had loved above all others. She had given him up because it was the right thing to do, but that didn't stop it hurting like an uncauterised wound. It hurt like hell, and she wasn't sure she would ever get over it.

By seven o'clock the removal men were done. Ellis watched them climb into their van and disappear down the track, then stood in the open doorway, listening. A blackbird clattered in the lilac tree near the pond, making her jump, and behind the house a pheasant chooked hoarsely in the undergrowth. A sudden anxiety gripped her, that she would not be able to cope all on her own in such an isolated spot. She had been a city dweller for years; she was accustomed to cars and buses, neighbours, street lamps, pavements. What if she couldn't manage the silence, the solitude? Unsettled by the thought, she strode back inside, shut the door on the quiet evening, and began to roam briskly from room to room, rearranging chairs, straightening rugs, counting the number of boxes she still had to unpack. She found sheets and pillowcases and made up the bed, hung temporary curtains, too long for the window, then, growing ravenously hungry, stopped to make soup, heating it in the microwave while she cut bread and cheese for sandwiches. When her hunger was assuaged she set to work unloading the rest of her provisions onto the larder shelves, rearranging the cupboards so she would know where to find the teapot, the frying pan, her favourite cafetière, making the place feel like home.

By nine o'clock she was ready for bed – seventeen weeks pregnant, she still tired easily – and, searching in the hall for the bag containing her night things, she disturbed a bluebottle, which buzzed irritatingly round her head. Snapping the overhead light off, she flung open the front door and flapped her arms at it until, attracted by the last of the daylight, the fly zig-zagged obediently into the dusk. Drawn by that wonderful scent of dog roses – or was it honeysuckle? – she followed it.

The sky was bruised with purple, the trees black against the glowing sunset. Ellis strolled into the middle of the glade, then turned back to examine the cottage, *her* cottage. Built originally for an estate gamekeeper, it was still known as Malletts after its first tenant. Once thatched, but now newly re-roofed with red pantiles and freshly whitewashed, with a chimney stack rising straight and solid from each gable end, it looked stark and pristine after its recent facelift. It needed a climbing rose – *Albertine*, maybe, with its blowsy salmon-pink blooms, or perhaps a fiery red *Danse du Feu* – to soften it. On the ground floor were two windows, sitting room to the left, storeroom (Ellis's study once she was organised) to the right, and upstairs a third window gazed out crookedly from beneath the steeply sloping roof. Behind the house a redundant brick privy, now housing Ellis's upright freezer, and a wide, still pond, lay half hidden amongst the trees.

Inside, it was tiny: two rooms and a small square hall at the front, a minute kitchen made out of the old scullery and a plain white bathroom fashioned from the lean-to wash-house at the back. A steep staircase made of tapering oak boards wound up from the hall to Ellis's quaintly crooked bedroom above the storeroom, all twisted rafters, uneven ceiling heights, and the newly renovated brass and iron bedstead she had inherited with the cottage. The place had no central heating, no mains drainage or water, no double glazing, telephone or television, but there was a new septic tank, mains electricity and a tank in the loft up to which a modern pump directed the water from the well outside the back door, an immersion heater to provide hot water.

This was where Ellis had chosen to wait out her pregnancy, plan her future. She would complete her current project while she was here – a treatise on the changing role of women in twentieth-century fiction, for which she had already received a hefty advance – but just at the moment she could raise no enthusiasm at all for the task. Later, when she was not quite so tired, she would make a start. She had a whole year to kill, after all.

It was thirty years since Nell, dozing in her armchair, had died here in a fire which had gutted the sitting room. One of Ellis's earliest memories was of being brought here by her mother to meet her.

Even at four years old she had been aware that she must make a good impression – Great-Aunt Nell had given Daddy his job at The Herb Garden a few years back, her mother said, when no one else was prepared to employ him, so she must be on her best behaviour. Ellis had clung tightly to Laura's hand as they walked along the grassy track, rigid with terror in case she said the wrong thing, then sat on a three-legged stool by the range while Nell fired questions at her: How did she like her name? Did she know that she, Nell, had chosen it? Who did she think she took after, her ma, her grandma? – an intense, frightening interrogation which left Ellis cowering behind her mother's skirts for protection.

'Are you clever?' Nell had demanded, leaning forward until her face was so close Ellis could see the tiny hairs on her upper lip.

'Yes!' Ellis had replied decisively. It was the first question to which she was sure she knew the right answer, but Nell had roared with laughter.

'Don't call me Auntie!' she had commanded imperiously. 'You can call me Nell, but don't you *ever* call me Auntie!' She smelled of smoke and fresh air, and when she bent to embrace Ellis the sharp, spicy smell made Ellis sneeze. But the scent she had carried away with her, the scent which after nearly thirty years still had the power to transport her instantly back to that day, was not smoke but the sweet, almost solid perfume of the large, beautiful lilac tree growing all alone between the house and the pond. In full glorious bloom, it was weighed down with heavy trusses of white blossom. A week after that first visit the old lady was dead, but that same tree had been in flower this spring when she made a flying trip to check on the building works.

Nell had lodged her will with a solicitor in Ipswich. She had left The Herb Garden, the plant nursery on the other side of the valley which she had built from nothing during the war and which had been the sole focus of her life for over twenty years, to her niece's husband, Ellis's father, as 'a reward for five years of loyal service', but it was not until Ellis was twenty-one that she discovered her great-aunt had left the cottage, its surrounding acres of woodland and a small legacy, to her. Until this year she had never given her derelict inheritance more than a passing thought, because she had never needed to.

Miraculously, the renovation of her bolt-hole, started on a whim (or had it been a premonition, that when her affair with Joe reached its inevitable conclusion she would need somewhere to hide?), had been completed in a little over six months. It was the only secret she had kept from him, apart from the biggest secret of all, and she was glad now that she had – it meant he wouldn't be able to find her, should he come looking.

The Tiffany lamp she had placed in the sitting-room window glowed yellow in the deepening dusk. It looked cosy, inviting, and for the first time in months Ellis felt a sort of tranquillity settle over her. Would Nell, she wondered, fierce, independent, intimidating Great-Aunt Nell, approve of the changes she had made?

A faint rattling came out of the night – the InterCity Express hurtling across the far side of the valley on its journey from Norwich to London – and, reminded of the outside world, Ellis shook her head at her own whimsy. There are no such things as ghosts, she chided herself, resisting the temptation to glance over her shoulder in case Nell might be watching her from the shadows beneath the trees.

The sky darkened to indigo and the air grew cooler as night settled over the glade. Ellis peered at her watch, trying to make out the time in the gathering gloom. Twenty past nine. The wine bar in Cutter's Lane would be gearing up for the second shift; the accountants, estate agents, secretaries, the university staff who congregated there for a quick drink after work, would have dispersed by now, and the night-owls would be starting to replace them. Harriet would be at home in her pretty Georgian town-house two streets away from Ellis's flat, tarting herself up to meet her married lover Malcolm for dinner or a drink. It was Malcolm, a History tutor at the university, who had spotted Joe arriving at Ellis's flat as he drove home late one night from an assignation with Harriet. He had wasted no time in passing on this most juicy piece of gossip.

'Have you gone stark, staring mad?' Harriet had demanded, barging into Ellis's office without knocking. 'It's obscene, messing about with a twenty-year-old at your age! And you'll get thrown out on your ear if the Dean finds out—'

'Who are you to criticise,' Ellis had countered, defensively furious, 'when you've been sleeping with

Malcolm Woolverstone, who has a wife and two children, for over six months? At least I'm not hurting anyone else!'

Harriet had flounced out at that, to return half an hour later with a box of sticky buns and an apology. 'You're right, of course,' she conceded reluctantly, perching on the edge of Ellis's desk to open the lid of her peace offering. 'But I mean it, Ellis, you'll lose your job if you're not careful; everything you've worked for will go up in smoke if the Dean gets wind of this.' She crossed her legs, waved a hand for emphasis. 'You'd be safer picking up a toy boy off the street if you fancy your meat fresh. Then at least you wouldn't be putting your career on the line.' She fished out a cream doughnut and pushed the box towards Ellis.

'Is that what you think I'm suffering from? A mid-life crisis?' Ellis chose an eclair and began to pick at the chocolate with her thumbnail. The cream oozed out at one end and she bit it off, then continued talking with her mouth full. 'His age has nothing to do with it—'

'Oh, come on, Ellis!' Harriet was scathing. 'Don't kid me you'd be messing about with a wet-behind-the-ears student if you could find a bloke your own age.' Ellis threw her out then, sticky buns and all, incensed by the accusation that she was cradle-snatching because it was the only way she could get a man.

Until Joe came along she had been perfectly fulfilled, living in a historic, pleasing university city, teaching a subject she loved, holidays spent walking in Tuscany, or exploring classical ruins in Greece, archaeological sites in Egypt, with her mother, who took a week off every year from what she called her 'domestic slavery' to keep her company. Ellis had always taken full advantage of the absence of those household ties her mother found so restricting, regarded the young woman who lived upstairs, who seemed to spend her life juggling pushchairs, shopping bags and grizzling babies, with pity rather than envy. She was entirely content with her life, she said when the inevitable questions about her marital state were asked, perfectly happy with her single status. And so she had been, until her neatly organised existence was thrown into turmoil by the advent of Joe Leavis. Their affair had started in January; it had taken her until July to summon the strength to end it.

'Stop it!' Joe had complained when she first voiced her misgivings. 'Stop *worrying* about it all the time. Why can't you just enjoy it?'

'Because this affair could ruin your future, and mine,' said Ellis. 'If you weren't so young and irresponsible, you'd be worried about it too.'

'If our roles were reversed,' he insisted, 'if I was thirty-four and you were twenty, you wouldn't be so paranoid. I'd be swanking about the place bragging that I'd managed to pull a babe and you'd be boasting about your sexy old man. Wouldn't you?'

'Don't be ridiculous.' Ellis dismissed the idea. 'I was never a babe. And if our roles were reversed the problems would be just the same, probably worse. You'd be accused of manipulating a gullible young woman just to satisfy your sordid middle-aged lusts and I'd be labelled a gold-digger, only after you for your power and influence. The problem is as much in other people's perceptions as it is in ours, can't you see that? And it's because I'm older than you that I can see the pitfalls. We can't just ignore them and hope they'll go away—'

'Why not?' Joe stuck obdurately to his guns. 'Times have changed, Doctor Jones. This is the nineteen-nineties – anything goes these days.'

They were sitting in Ellis's flat at the time, at her kitchen table. Joe leaned across and caught her by the back of her neck, pulling her face close to his. 'How old were you when you lost your virginity?'

'What?'

'How old were you when—'

Ellis felt the colour rising in her cheeks. 'You know how old I was. What does that have to do with anything?'

Joe grinned, triumphant. 'D'you want to know how old I was?'

'No!' Ellis was outraged now, as well as embarrassed.

'Fifteen.' He released her and sat back, watching her flushed face with amusement. 'Eh, lass,' he said in broad Yorkshire, teasing her, 'th'art reet canny when tha's flummoxed.' Then, pressing his point home, 'But you can hardly claim to be more experienced than me when I lost my virginity five years ago and you lost yours . . . how long's it been now . . .?' He tipped his head on one side and smiled, teasing again. 'January wasn't it? The seventeenth. Or have you forgotten?'

How could she have forgotten? After he'd been to see her in her office, trying unsuccessfully to wheedle his way onto her course, he had followed her home. He had stood outside in the pouring rain from five o'clock until nearly ten, when she had finally taken pity on him and let him in. He had been wet, bedraggled, absurd, and she had plied him with brandy because he was literally shaking with cold, then sent him upstairs to have a bath while she heated soup to feed him. He didn't get to drink the soup until the following day. By letting him into her flat she had let him into everything, her life, her bed, her body, unable to resist him. How could she possibly have forgotten?

Standing in the clearing outside her Suffolk cottage, gazing at the pool of light thrown by the Tiffany lamp, she missed him painfully, laid her hands instinctively on her belly to touch the unborn child which was all she had left of him. Hard to tell for sure, they'd said when she went for her scan, but they were pretty certain it was a girl. It was only after she'd turned down the amniocentesis test, because of the risk of spontaneous abortion, that she'd realised how much she wanted Joe's baby.

She hadn't told him about her pregnancy. This baby was the unplanned, accidental outcome of their affair, and it had made her more determined than ever that she must finish it before she ruined Joe's life. How could she lumber him with the responsibility of a child when he was barely more than a child himself? Without him though, the future seemed unimaginably bleak, the prospect of single motherhood dizzyingly complicated.

The youngest son of a large, close family, Joe had gone home to Yorkshire a month ago, to see his widowed mother. His mum got lonely now they'd all left home, so he couldn't put it off, he told Ellis, but he would be back. He had refused to believe her when she told him it was over. 'But we love each other!' he had protested, outraged. 'We can make it work, I *know* we can!'

'You'll change your mind,' he had added just before he left, attacking her with all the overweening confidence of youth. 'You won't be able to live without me, you'll see!' He had paused on the doorstep, searching her face for signs of doubt, waiting for her to call him back. 'Nowt else matters,' he had threatened her, his accent thickening as his temper thinned. 'Nowt but you and me, d'you hear?' Halfway down the path he turned back to face her. 'Call me,' he said. 'When you can't bear it a minute longer, call me and I'll come.' He took a step towards her, added, softer now, pleading, 'You don't even have to raise your voice.'

Ellis had already begun to close the door, trying to

shut him out, but she heard his parting words through the woodwork.

'You only have to whisper. I'll hear you . . .'

When he returned, he would find her flat empty, stripped of most of its furniture. When he enquired at the university he would discover that Dr Jones had taken a sabbatical year, leaving strict instructions that no forwarding address was to be divulged. By the time she returned he would have got over her. He would have begun to play the field, passed his twenty-first birthday. He would thank her for what she had done, eventually.

She glanced at her watch again but it was too dark now to see the time; nearly ten, she guessed. Somewhere in the distance she could hear a helicopter, the air-sea rescue patrol from the nearby airforce base, making its way home for the night. The leaves behind her rustled and she caught a faint echo from the past, a ripple of attention in the air around her. 'What was it like,' she addressed the shadows, 'living here all alone, pumping water from the well by hand, stumbling out in the early hours to the privy, cooking on that cumbersome range . . .?' She waited, holding her breath. Nothing. 'Nell?' she demanded, her voice ringing loud in the silence. 'What was it like?' The only reply was the rustling of a small bird, settling down for the night in the shadowy lilac tree.

At the Dower House, a mile away across the valley, her parents would be discussing her odd behaviour, her sudden decision to take a year off, so out of character for one hitherto completely wedded to her career. They would be mulling over her flimsy excuses (she had, after all, written numerous learned papers over the years without finding it necessary to give up all other aspects of her work), her stubborn refusal to let them see the cottage to which she had so arbitrarily decided to retreat, 'until it's finished'.

She had arrived at the Dower House the previous night with every intention of breaking the news of her pregnancy over supper, probably after they had imbibed a couple of glasses of wine. But when it actually came to it she had lost her nerve. William was so full of the plans he was working on for the patch of waste ground at the back of The Herb Garden, pressing a sheet of headed notepaper covered in sketches into Ellis's hand almost before she was through the door and monopolising the conversation all evening with his plans for a new plant section devoted exclusively to different varieties of lavender. As she was leaving this morning he had made another attempt to catch her interest, pushing the sketch at her for the second time with a hopeful wink and a murmured request to, 'Have another look when you've time, poppet, and see what you think. I'd be grateful for your opinion.' The Herb Garden, William's obsession as well as his business, was a subject guaranteed to infuriate her mother, and Ellis had found herself using William's preoccupation and Laura's irritability as an excuse to put off telling them about the baby until a more propitious moment. She was well aware that she was merely avoiding a difficult task; she had caught her father at intervals during the evening surreptitiously glancing at her, wondering what had *really* brought her back to Suffolk. After all, she had visited only twice since the builders started on the cottage and she had given no indication then that the renovations were anything more than a whim, a possible precursor to selling the place or at most using it as an occasional base for summer weekends. Sooner or later she was going to have to tell them both the truth . . .

She found the package, wrapped in heavy-duty paper and old-fashioned brown sticky-tape, as she made her way to bed, left on the storeroom windowsill by the builder with a note: *Dear Dr Jones, found this while we were demolishing the bread oven.* On the front of the parcel was inscribed, in a jagged, determined script which bit deeply into the paper, the one word, *Ellis.* Puzzled, Ellis sat down at the foot of the stairs and began to tear at the thick layers of wrapping. Inside was a cloth-covered book, battered and curled at the corners, with a stamp on the flyleaf scrolled in black round the edges. It smelled of damp and the page was spotted with brown stains. '*This Book Belongs To*' it said in printed gothic script at the top, and in the space below the same bold, spiky hand had written: *Eleanor Carter.*

Great-Aunt Nell. Once again it came, an echo from the past, an almost tangible presence in the air. Intrigued, Ellis changed her mind about going to bed, and began to flick through the pages.

Names, dates, places, scrawled notes in the margins, page after page of closely written text. Ellis's sense of Nell's presence grew stronger. She had asked what it was like, living here all alone, and the answer had been unexpectedly dropped into her lap. What she was holding was her great-aunt's journal, a first-hand account of a lost way of life. Turning back to the beginning, she leaned her head against the wall and settled down to read.

New Year, 1941, it began. *I am sick to death of Violet.*

Chapter Three

Walking up through the village towards the Dower House, Nell Carter hung back behind her companions, gloved hands in pockets, breath clouding in the freezing air. She was sick of the war, sick of the cold, but most of all, just at this moment, she was sick to death of Violet.

Her back ached and her face, and her palms tingled from an evening spent clapping in time to the Army band and smiling till her teeth hurt, pretending to enjoy herself while Violet cavorted around the village hall, doing the Gay Gordons, the Military Two-Step, the Polka, first with Laurence, then with a succession of eager young men, both in and out of uniform. She must, thought Nell, peering at her sister's jaunty outline up ahead, have stood for every single dance, and now she was slithering along in her high-heeled boots with Laurence's arm round her waist, giggling against his shoulder like an over-excited child. Given Laurence's background – public school, university, a promising career as a lawyer, cut short by the war – he and Violet had so little in common Nell had wondered when she first heard of their engagement what they could possibly see in each other. Tonight, during an evening when she had danced only twice (once when Violet kindly nudged Laurence into an invitation, and then again when he took pity on her wallflower state for a second time), the answer had been only too painfully obvious.

Violet was pretty. No, Violet was beautiful. Where Nell's lines were straight and angular, Violet's were lusciously curved; while Nell's hazel eyes were unremarkable and her thick, wayward hair was a dull mouse, Violet was a shimmering blue-eyed blonde. Nell's feet and hands were big, heavy-boned like Pa's, Violet's daintily small like Ma's; Nell had inherited Pa's prominent Roman nose, Violet their mother's pert retroussé profile. Where Nell was clumsy, ill at ease with her gawky frame, Violet was all grace and fluid movement. In competition with such physical perfection it was hardly surprising that Nell's greatest asset, her quick, intuitive intelligence, went almost entirely unremarked. Looks, in Ma's opinion, allied to a bright, uncomplicated personality, were the only things that mattered for a girl, and Violet had both in abundance. 'Brains?' Ma opined when asked. 'Who needs brains? Brains won't catch you a husband, will they?'

'Why can't you be more like Violet?' had been the recurring refrain throughout Nell's childhood, both at home and at school, a confidence-sapping accompaniment to everything she did, whilst Violet, four years her junior, had grown from charming babyhood through pretty child to ravishing young woman without for one moment having cause to doubt that she was unconditionally admired for herself alone. If Violet was sometimes a little condescending, if she was inclined to treat Nell with a sort of kind contempt, still Nell found it impossible to really dislike her dizzy, glamorous sister – after all, it was not Violet's fault she had been so very generously endowed.

Violet's had been a lightning courtship, as were so many in those dark days. She met Laurence Palmer on her twenty-first birthday, at a Tea Dance in the West End in 1940. She had pleaded for Nell to be allowed the afternoon off to help her celebrate, but Pa, in the middle of stocktaking, had been unable to spare his elder daughter, so Violet had gone with a friend instead. Laurence was on a weekend pass from Fighter Command, in town for less than forty-eight hours, and during the short time they spent together they decided they were made for each other.

'But Ma,' Violet pointed out when her mother queried the speed with which the wedding was being arranged, 'who knows how long we might have?' By the time Laurence took his new bride home to Suffolk at the end of October, he and Violet had spent only five days in each other's company.

Nell, her hopes of going to college firmly squashed by Ma, had been involved in the family drapery business for nearly six years, since she was nineteen. Starting at the bottom and making the best of her lack of options, she had moved steadily through the ranks from junior sales assistant to running one of her father's three shops. She was good at her job, took a pride in what she did, and she had a flair for the retail trade, Pa said, the knack of knowing what people would buy, a rare talent. She had done a bookkeeping course too, in order to understand the financial side, and Pa had been so impressed with her progress he had promised that once the war was over he would think about her going into business on her own account. Her sense of self-worth had increased with her responsibilities.

Why would she want to bury herself in the wilds of Suffolk when she was needed in London? she asked when Ma first broached the possibility, but her objections were airily dismissed. London was becoming more dangerous every day, Ma said, and Violet was lonely all by herself in the depths of the country without her new husband; surely it wasn't asking much of Nell to keep her company? 'Violet doesn't need me to hold her hand,' protested Nell. 'She's got her in-laws just up the road and there must be plenty to do in Suffolk.'

Ma was sharp. 'Don't talk so silly. She's terrified of her mother-in-law and she doesn't know anyone. You know what these country people are like – you have to live in a place twenty years before they'll even give you the time of day. What's she supposed to do, all on her own week after week?'

'Go for a land girl?' suggested Nell mildly. 'Learn to drive a tractor?'

Ma was shocked at the very idea. 'She's far too good for that sort of thing! Besides, she and Laurence've got two bedrooms; if you don't go, they'll have a spare room and the Ministry'll make them take in dozens of those dreadful evacuee children from the East End. No, this is the perfect solution. It's no good arguing, I've already told her you're going, and she's dying to see you. Don't be so selfish!'

Two days later Nell's shop took a direct hit from an incendiary bomb and was reduced overnight to a pile of smoking rubble. Tired of arguing, Nell gave in.

'Now do *try* to be a little more like Violet,' Ma reproached her as she bundled her onto the Ipswich train on a cold, dank November day. 'And remember, if Laurence manages to get leave over Christmas, keep out of their way. They've only been married a month and they've spent less than a week of that together . . .' As the train rattled through the wintry landscape towards East Anglia, Nell had wondered what was the point of her going at all, if she was supposed to make herself invisible every time the master of the house came home.

She had exchanged no more than a cursory handshake

with her new brother-in-law at the wedding, introduced by Violet outside the church just as the photographer was lining them all up for the family album; she hadn't paid him any attention until much later on, at the reception. The poor man had seemed dazed by the speed with which events were moving, and she had seen him once or twice during the proceedings staring perplexedly at Violet as if he had never seen her before, as if he was wondering how on earth he had come to be married to this beautiful, effervescent stranger. Or was it his upper-class parents' palpable disapproval of his choice which was causing him such obvious unease?

The Palmers seemed an ill-assorted couple. Sir Gerald was tall, handsome, with greying hair, cool, dun-coloured eyes and an iron handshake, a smoother, more urbane version of his only son with all the added confidence of a man completely sure of his position in society; although in his mid-sixties, his physique was still impressive, marred only by the pronounced limp with which he walked, the result of wounds sustained during a much-decorated stint of military service in the Great War. Laurence's mother, on the other hand, was plain, short and broad-beamed, with a square, pugnacious face and the brisk, no-nonsense air of a woman used to commanding respect.

'And you are . . .?' she had demanded as Nell shook her hand on the reception line, adding bluntly when Nell told her, 'Hmm, not much like your sister, are you?' But she had drawn the sting from the remark with a firm squeeze of Nell's fingers and a warm smile which quite transformed her otherwise unprepossessing face. 'And what do you think of all this?' she'd continued, waving a stubby hand at her son and daughter-in-law.

Embarrassed by the direct question, Nell had mumbled something about them making a handsome couple, whereupon Lady Palmer had snorted dismissively and said, 'Handsome is as handsome does, in my opinion!' from which candid remark Nell had guessed that a draper's daughter, however beautiful, was not what the Palmers, with their Suffolk estates and their aristocratic connections, had hoped for their son. War was changing the social order, sweeping away rules which had held for hundreds of years.

As for Laurence, when she had met him properly, he had made Nell wish, more fervently than ever before, that she could have been born pretty . . .

'All right, Nell?' came his voice from up ahead, and Nell caught the glint of his eyes as he glanced over his shoulder in the dark.

'Fine,' she called. 'Just watching my step,' and he turned back to Violet, whispering something in her ear which made her whoop with laughter.

They took a short cut through the churchyard, Laurence refusing to risk his torch so they were forced to grope their way between ghostly tombstones, then turned left into Post Office Row. As they moved onto the road, the heels of Violet's boots began to clack loudly on the tarmac and Nell saw the corner of Mrs Clark's blackout curtain twitch momentarily, then fall back into place.

She stopped at the end of the row, bending down to rub some life into her aching calves with fingers numbed by cold. Her breath was condensing in a white fog in front of her and she could feel the freezing air constricting her chest as it passed into her lungs. She thumped her woollen gloves together and stamped her feet hard, trying to improve the circulation. She should have stayed at home by the fire – would have, if Violet hadn't insisted.

'It's no good being stubborn, Nell,' she'd commanded.

'It's New Year's Eve and we're not going to the party without you!'

Like a fool, Nell had allowed herself to be persuaded, just as she had so foolishly allowed Ma to persuade her to come to Suffolk in the first place, seduced against all her instincts by the prospect of her brother-in-law's company. It had been a stupid idea. If she was dubious about Laurence Palmer's reasons for marrying Violet, Nell could see only too clearly why Violet had fallen for Laurence – he was a lovely man, big, gentle, almost as good-looking as his father, with thick, curly brown hair and the same athletic physique as Sir Gerald. The only features he had inherited from his mother were his bright blue eyes, which crinkled engagingly when he was amused, and Lady Palmer's ready laugh. He was quick-witted, good-humoured, articulate, and until tonight Nell had deliberately kept her distance because she had swiftly discovered upon her arrival that when he looked at her, when he smiled, stupid ideas drifted into her head, and she was tempted to harbour unsettling feelings towards him, feelings she shouldn't have . . . Serves you right, she told herself as she plodded along in the dark, following, as usual, in Violet's dainty footsteps, you should have stuck with your instincts and stayed in London, shouldn't you? Tonight, she had paid for not keeping out of the newlyweds' way with an evening of unalloyed humiliation, the only female at the dance who couldn't get a partner . . .

Violet and Laurence had stopped a little further on, by Charlie Bewson's piggery. Nell could see the outline of their heads, close together and wreathed with the white mist of their mingled breath. She straightened up, steadying herself against Mrs Beale's picket fence. The sky was cloudy and the wind was coming from the North East, sending gusts of sleety rain into her face.

During the evening the temperature had plummeted and a thin layer of ice was already forming on the puddles at the edge of the lane. The windows along the Row, dutifully blacked out with heavy felt curtains and stuck with strips of paper in case of bomb damage, gave no hint of the warmth behind them, but Nell could smell the wood-smoke; it drifted down from the chimneys to mingle with the sharp, pungent perfume of pig.

Straining her ears, she picked up the sound of the last few revellers from the village hall, homeward bound down the hill. Their New Year greetings carried on the fitful wind, mingled with an occasional burst of merriment from the soldiers manning the searchlight in the field behind Youngman's forge, celebrating as best they could while on guard for King and Country. The rest of their battalion were billeted at the Hall, the Palmers' grand, Italianate mansion on the far side of the valley, their duties split between the petrol dump down by the railway line and the cement works on the main road. Laurence's mother, Marion, was still in residence at the Hall, holed up in the servants' wing and muttering darkly about the necessity of 'doing one's bit' as she watched her prize roses dug up to make way for an anti-aircraft battery and her croquet lawn transformed into a rutted quagmire by a stream of black-belching trucks and army-issue boots. Sir Gerald, having left his wife to cope with this friendly invasion, was in London, planning strategies from behind a Ministry of Defence desk.

The men on the searchlight whistled when Violet walked down to Home Farm for the milk. When Nell passed they nodded and wished her a respectful good day, touching their caps as they did to the spinster schoolmistress, Miss Atnes.

Violet and Laurence were moving on. 'Do gee up, Nell,' complained Violet. 'I'm freezing!'

How could she be freezing? Nell had had nothing better to do all evening than watch her sister, flushed with exertion, whirl around the village hall with a dizzying succession of partners; she had seen Laurence take his wife's hand during a break in the dancing and lead her outside, returning her a full ten minutes later, even pinker and hotter and more dishevelled than before.

'Jealousy', Ma had reproached her once when she complained that Violet had got away with something at school 'just because she's Violet' – 'is a corrosive disease, my girl.' Especially, thought Nell, watching Laurence stoop to kiss his wife and wishing achingly that it could be her, when there's no hope of a cure. If she had known beforehand how she was going to feel about her sister's husband, she would not have been persuaded to move within fifty miles of him.

At least she was full of food, sausage and mash with onion gravy, the local Pig Club having generously slaughtered their porker to celebrate the birth of 1941. Oh, for the summer, she thought longingly, for warm days and short nights, when rationing won't seem so bad. Oh, for an end to this dreary war.

She had spent part of the evening standing next to a huddle of old men. They had been discussing, in rich Suffolk accents, local lads, lads Nell had never met and now never would – the Hawley boys, who had joined the Navy and whose parents had learned on Christmas Eve that they would not be coming back; Geoffrey Ware, the vicar's son, who had signed up for Fighter Command at the same time as Laurence Palmer and who, Nell had learned, eavesdropping reluctantly as she propped up the wall next to the beer table, had lost his way one night in thick fog and fetched up over Felixstowe instead of Great Yarmouth, there to fly into a barrage balloon and spin to destruction in the sea less than twenty miles from home. George Smith at Home Farm, crippled by polio and exempt from the call-up, had died too, along with his dad, when a lone Heinkel crash-landed on their barn; then in December the news came that George's elder brother Ben had been killed in North Africa, fighting the Italians at Sidi Barrani, and Betty Smith was left to run the farm alone. She had been told there was a six-week wait before she could get any Land Girls, the old boys said, shaking their grizzled heads at the iniquity of it, and her with thirty head of cows to milk and twenty acres of sugar-beet rotting in the ground. Nell, with her sharp, retentive memory, had found the names, *Hawley*, *Ware*, *Smith*, echoing in her head long after the old men had changed the subject and moved off to drown their sorrows in more beer. There seemed no prospect of an early end to the death and destruction.

Laurence and Violet had stopped again, waiting for her at the end of the lane. As she drew level with them, Laurence reached out and pulled her towards him, draping his arm round her shoulder.

'Poor Nell,' he said, bending his head so his cheek rested briefly against hers. 'You must be frozen too.'

The touch of his skin, rough with the beginning of tomorrow's beard, was infinitely comforting; it eased Nell's melancholy and she leaned gratefully against him as she had had no opportunity to do during their two vigorous polkas together; his greatcoat smelled pleasantly of fresh air and Players *Double Ring*, the pipe tobacco he had been smoking all evening.

Her pleasure was short-lived. As if aware that his innocent gesture might be open to misinterpretation, Laurence released her abruptly and she dropped back again, humiliated.

Their feet scrunched on the gravel as they turned into

the drive and somewhere behind them an owl hooted
eerily. Nell and Violet waited just outside the porch,
stamping their feet and blowing on their hands, while
Laurence searched in his pocket for the key.

'I'm whacked,' he said as he swung the door open
and stood back to let them pass. 'It's straight to bed for
me, girls. Happy New Year.'

As he bolted the front door, then moved past her into
the hall, Nell felt his hand brush against hers. She froze,
her knees weakened by the unexpected contact, felt his
breath, heavy with beer and tobacco, on her face, then
the touch of his mouth, hot and exciting against her
cheek. In the pitch-black she could see nothing of his
expression so she had no way of telling whether the contact was deliberate or accidental. By the time Violet had
found the light-switch and snapped it on, he was
halfway up the stairs on his way to bed.

Later, as she sat with her knees drawn up beneath the
blankets and her back propped against her pillows, with
the foolscap journal Ma had sent her for Christmas
spread in front of her, Nell heard him making love to
Violet, murmurs and giggles, then squeaking springs
and deep male groans filtering through the wall. Aching
with loneliness and that even viler disease, jealousy, she
turned to the first page and wrote in a stiff, angry hand,
I am sick to death of Violet . . .

Chapter Four

January began as December had ended, with squalls of sleet and snow and bitterly cold north-easterly winds; the temperature struggled to climb above freezing. Nell slept badly and rose early, tired of tossing and turning in her chilly bed reliving Laurence's fleeting kiss, and wishing she was back in London away from temptation. By the time Violet meandered downstairs in her dressing gown just after nine, she had already raked out the sitting-room grate and laid the fire, lit the kitchen stove and brewed a pot of tea; if her troublesome conscience rendered her less than usually communicative, Violet at least seemed to be blissfully unaware of any tension in the atmosphere.

Laurence was sleeping in, she explained. The poor darling was due to report back to his squadron tomorrow so he was catching up on the extra rest while he could. He had promised to take her into Ipswich this afternoon though, to see the Crazy Gang at the Regent. Would Nell like to come?

'No thanks,' said Nell, diligently stirring porridge and avoiding her sister's eye.

'It's no good being stubborn.' Violet, dear Violet, whose only crime was to be married to Laurence, was oblivious to Nell's discomfort. 'You'll come in the end, you'll see. If I can't persuade you I'll get Laurence to change your mind!' Then she whirled energetically out of the room, on her way to fetch the milk from Home Farm, leaving Nell to cope with the disturbing mix of guilt and pleasure the thought of Laurence 'changing her mind' had induced.

She needn't have worried. When Violet, at her most bewitching, begged him to use his powers of persuasion, Laurence glanced briefly at Nell, then turned his back and began to search his pockets for his pipe. 'If Nell doesn't want to come,' he said briskly, 'there's no point in forcing her. Now get a move on, Vi, or we'll miss the beginning.'

Nell, the colour rising hotly up her face at the calculated put-down, remembered an urgent task awaiting her in her room and beat a hasty retreat. As she crossed the hall, she could hear Violet complaining, 'You didn't have to be quite so rude, did you, darling?' and Laurence mumbling an ungracious apology through the stem of his pipe.

Sitting at her dressing table, resting her chin in her hands and examining herself critically in the mirror, Nell faced up to the unpalatable truth. 'Look at you,' she addressed her reflection bitterly. 'I ask you, why would any man give you a second glance?' Let alone one who was married to a woman as beautiful as Violet.

She stayed in her room the following morning, pleading a headache and pretending not to hear Laurence's peremptory goodbye, bellowed up the stairs in the direction of her door. She couldn't resist spying on him from her window though, standing behind the curtain biting her lip, as he kissed Violet, then climbed into his Riley and waved all the way down the drive to the lane. Was it wishful thinking that made Nell imagine it was her he was looking at as he backed the car round? Was it foolishness to hope that she might have been included in that last wave? Of course it was. Any idea that his fleeting New Year caress might have meant something had been dispelled by the touching scene she had just witnessed between him and Violet. Nell's corrosive disease seemed to be getting worse.

She knew what she ought to do – she ought to go back to London, leave Violet to settle down to married life in peace, and stop pining for something that was never going to happen. But when she broached the subject Violet was adamant.

'No! I won't hear of it! You've only just got here; how can you even *think* of leaving me out here in the sticks all on my own?'

'All right,' Nell agreed reluctantly, 'just so long as the minute you hear Laurence is coming home I pack my bags and catch the first train back to London. Two's company and three's a crowd.'

Gradually, they became absorbed into village life. Four days into the year Mrs Downes, who ran the village shop and delivered the papers, slipped on a patch of ice halfway up the hill and broke her arm in two places. Eager for something constructive to do, Nell offered to take over her round, just as Marion Palmer, an inveterate organiser, decided it was time Violet did her bit and set her to increasing the local knitting circle's output of Home Comforts for the forces. Violet, galvanised into action more by terror of her mother-in-law than by any natural enthusiasm, threw herself into the task with gusto, chivvying her 'troops' by day, and spending most evenings, while Nell read or listened to the wireless, clacking away at socks, balaclavas and gloves to keep up the quota Lady Palmer had set her. After hours spent wheedling and cajoling every female in the village into

Knitting for Victory, she was often speechless with fatigue by the time she and Nell sat down to their frugal supper, ready to fall into bed before ten most nights. She never missed writing to Laurence though, at least four times a week.

In exchange for trips to the outlying villages, taking it in turns to drive Marion's Morris 8 with a rackety trailer behind it, collecting old tins, kettles, saucepans, whatever scrap metal they could scrounge for the war effort, they were allowed to borrow the Morris for occasional trips into Market Needing, the nearest small town, or into Ipswich, to shop at Mason's and the Co-op, Footman's and Boots. They searched for bargains – satin-backed Bengaline at 6/11d a yard, Lifebuoy soap at 5½d a bar, Cadbury's Chocolate in 2½d blocks, when they had enough coupons in their ration books. While they were in town they scoured the shops for rare luxuries – oranges or nylon stockings, tinned peaches or condensed milk – but Marion was not a believer in pleasure for its own sake. For every purchase of their own there was an order from Lady Palmer – Service wool from the Modern Wool Shop (*knitting leaflets free to Working Parties*), Turkish bath towels from Footman's (*3/6d on special offer*), Bovril and Huntley-and-Palmer's breakfast biscuits from the Co-op. The last item on the list was always the same – Johnnie Walker whisky, the only thing Marion insisted, chuckling, that stood between her and complete despair. They grew used to the gas masks banging against their hips, to eking out the petrol, making every second in town count so they could get back before dark.

They became creatures of habit, tuning in to *The Kitchen Front* for domestic tips, to *Music While You Work* for Violet, and the evening concerts, Bach, Haydn, Schubert, for Nell – not Violet's cup of tea at all, 'but Laurence'll be listening, wherever he is'. They listened

avidly to the news and the war commentary, to *ITMA*
for Violet, the *Brains Trust* for Nell, and they eked out
their milk ration ('No special treatment for us, just
because we own the cows!' admonished Marion sternly)
so they could enjoy the delicious, guilt-tinged pleasure
of milky Ovaltine once a week. They sent off to the
Suffolk Mercury for Madame Doreen's dress patterns,
taking it in turns to use Violet's Singer sewing machine
to make blouses and a skirt for Violet from material
given to her for her trousseau, and a dressing gown for
Nell (who had inadvertently left hers in London), from
a cotton bedspread donated by Marion. They saw Joel
McRae in *Foreign Correspondent* at the Regent, Fay Wray
in *Lucky Partners* and Charlie Chaplin in *The Great
Dictator*.

The hall filled up with old newspapers, collected by
Nell during her rounds, then neatly tied into bundles
with string ready for the Market Needing Youth Squad.
The money they made, 1d for every three pounds
weight collected, was used to buy the ingredients for
buns which they took to Miss Ames to be distributed
among the children currently sharing the village
school – local kids in the morning, evacuees in the afternoon. With Laurence still away and no prospect of his
imminent return, Nell began to believe that she was
beating her disease, that her infatuation with her
brother-in-law had been the result merely of loneliness
and not having enough to do. If and when he came
home she would be able to face him with complete
equanimity, she told herself, now that she had other
things to occupy her mind. If she prayed for his safe
return every Sunday, as she knelt between Violet and
Marion in the Palmers' family pew at the front of the
crowded village church, it was out of sisterly concern
only, that he might not end up like *Hawley, Ware, Smith*.

The thought of his return no longer set her heart racing, or turned her stomach upside down. She could take him or leave him now. Easy.

Chapter Five

By the end of January Nell was beginning to feel settled at last, even glad that she had left London. Ma's complaints, rattled off at breakneck speed during their brief, once-a-week phone calls, about the bombings, the fuel shortages, the disgusting taste of the powdered egg which was all she could get nowadays, convinced Nell that life in the country had a lot to recommend it. 'Of course, *we've* got *real* eggs,' she found herself telling Ma, as smugly self-satisfied as if she'd laid them herself instead of getting them delivered from Home Farm, along with a steady supply of rabbits and plump woodpigeons.

'The Lunnon Girls', as they were dubbed by the locals, had grown closer over the past few weeks than they had ever been before. In the absence of Ma and Pa, or Laurence, when the drone of enemy aircraft set the air-raid sirens wailing in Ipswich, when the ack-ack guns began to fill the air with their staccato thuds, or even sometimes when she couldn't decide what to do for supper, Violet turned instinctively to her big sister to make her decisions for her. Should they hide in the cupboard? she would ask anxiously, or was the action far enough away not to bother? Should she blow a whole week's meat ration on a small joint of beef, or eke her allowance out? Did Nell think this new shade of lipstick suited her, or should she go for something a little more subtle? What do you think, Nell? What should I do, Nell? Which should I choose, Nell?

For the first time in her life, Nell felt equal – no, *superior* – to her beautiful sister, discovered that whilst Violet might be easier on the eye, in the face of ever-present danger she, Nell, was braver, more resourceful, more decisive. It was a good feeling, and sometimes she couldn't resist the temptation to abuse her position, settling Violet in the cupboard under the stairs as the air-raid sirens howled across the frosty fields, then making some excuse and tiptoeing up to the landing to watch the night sky light up over the coast, searchlights and anti-aircraft tracers, the red glow of burning buildings, whizzes and bangs and the heavy *crump, crump* of exploding bombs. With Violet tucked away below her feet, as safe as she could be from the worst the Luftwaffe might throw at them, Nell would stand all alone on the stairs feeling liberated, powerful, even – guiltily – exhilarated as if, detached from the reality of *Hawley*, *Ware*, *Smith*, by simply surviving she was actually becoming more alive . . .

She had even acquired an admirer. At least, that was what Violet, with a return to her habitual kind condescension, insisted on calling him.

Among the boisterous group of soldiers manning the searchlight in the field behind Youngman's forge, there was one who stood out, a quiet, serious young man who sat on the sidelines while the others joked and jostled, larking about like schoolboys in the playground as they brewed endless mugs of tea and polished their kit. Nell had noticed him when she first started delivering the papers, sitting with his back against a pile of sandbags and his nose buried in a book.

After a while he took to waving, then greeting her, 'Mornin', love,' in a thick Liverpudlian accent, as she passed by on her round. Occasionally he would call out, 'Spare us a paper?' and she would hunt through her bag for a discarded copy of the *Suffolk Mercury* or the *East Anglian Daily Times*. When one cold, damp morning he yelled after her, 'Gorra fag, love?' she finished her round, bought the last packet of Kensitas from the village shop, then plodded back up the hill and practically threw them across the sandbags, suddenly embarrassed by her own forwardness.

'Don't go,' he begged as she turned away, 'I could do with the company if you've gorra while.'

Nell hesitated, then sat down beside him on a damp sandbag. She could feel the hessian, cold and scratchy through the grey serge of her skirt, and twenty yards away half a dozen pairs of curious eyes watched them, the other soldiers whispering and sniggering and nudging each other like a bunch of cocky lads at a village social.

'Here.' He fumbled in his jacket pocket and counted out the 7½d for his fags, dropping pennies, ha'pennies and farthings into her hand. 'You've saved my life. I worr gaspin'.'

He offered her the packet, and Nell took one, then leaned across to the match he struck and drew the smoke deep into her lungs.

It was over two months since she had had a cigarette. Violet disliked the smell (although she could tolerate a pipe, she said at least once a day, gazing wistfully at the one Laurence had left behind on the mantelpiece), and Ma had never allowed smoking at home. It was Pa who had started Nell on the habit when she first began working for him.

'But not,' he warned, as he passed a Players *Navy Cut*

across to his elder daughter one evening after work, 'during opening hours'.

'Just isn't done,' he explained when she asked him why. 'Gives the impression you've a sloppy attitude, smoking in front of customers, particularly for a woman, makes you look tarty. Before or after but never during, that's the rule to remember.' When he put Nell in charge of her own shop she carried on his system, banning her staff from smoking on the premises and rationing herself to one in the morning before the girls arrived and one in the evening before she locked up to catch the bus home. Sitting on a damp sandbag in the middle of a muddy Suffolk field, the taste of that Kensitas cigarette transported her instantly back to London, to her drapery shop near King's Cross, now no longer in existence.

She could see it still, the walls, lined from floor to ceiling with custom-made wooden drawers, each with its own brass plate into which was slotted a label, *French knickers*, *Liberty bodices*, *Half Petticoats*, *Full Petticoats*, *Vests*, *Spencers*. The smell of axle grease and leather polish on the young soldier's hands reminded her of the wax candle she used every Monday morning to smooth the runners so the drawers would glide properly, of the Mansion polish with which she buffed the long wooden counter every night before she locked up. She drew in another lungful of smoke and closed her eyes, savouring again those rare moments of solitude at the beginning and end of the day, when a soft, still silence descended upon the premises and she would pace the floor, sorting, straightening, tidying. It was the only time she was completely on her own, and she took to guarding her 'quiet bit', as she called it, jealously, instructing her girls not to arrive too early or leave too late, lest they encroach upon her precious moments of peace . . .

'Good, eh?' her companion said, and she opened her

eyes and blinked at him, still lost in the dim quiet of a defunct draper's shop in London.

Arthur his name was, Artie Mulligan, eldest son of an immigrant Irish stevedore. He'd been all set to go to university, he told her, 'afore this lot started . . .' He waved his cigarette at the scene around them: the row of khaki tents, the billy-can bubbling over a Primus stove, brewing tea for the boys, the big, ugly searchlight. 'I worr goin' to college, fust ever in our family. Me mam were dead proud.' He said it wistfully, clearly sad that he had missed out on his life's ambition, and Nell, glancing at his earnest face, the round, tortoiseshell spectacles perched on the end of his beaky nose and the acne pock-marks dark against his pale winter skin, found herself wondering if he too suffered from being plain.

'You can always start later,' she pointed out, 'when this is over.'

'Dunno.' He shrugged, dismissing an insuperable problem. 'Da's bin invalided out, lost a leg at Dunkirk, so they'll need all the money they can get comin' in. Reckon it'll be the docks for me, if I make it through, humpin' crates for a livin'.'

They talked on about the bleak beauty of the Suffolk countryside, about the shortages, the difficulty of getting books; Nell promised next time she was in Ipswich to see if she could find him a few secondhand paperbacks. Artie was pathetically grateful, eager for anything she could get hold of. It was only when she rose to go home that she realised she had been sitting, chatting comfortably with a complete stranger for over half an hour.

On her return, Violet, wrinkling her pretty nose at the smell of smoke still hanging about her sister's clothes, wheedled her into confessing where she had been, then began to tease her unmercifully about her conquest. As

Nell's encounters with Arthur Mulligan grew quickly into an almost daily habit, Violet, refusing to accept that there was nothing more than friendship between the two of them, even offered to make herself scarce one night a week so Nell could do her 'courting' in rather more private surroundings.

'I think it's *so* sweet you've found someone of your own at last,' she told Nell as she set off with a pile of woolly scarves and gloves to see her intimidating mother-in-law. 'I do *so* want you to be as happy as Laurie and I are, darling Nell . . .'

Which generous, if somewhat patronising, sentiments were guaranteed to make Nell feel even more guilty than she already did, for her brief coveting of her sister's husband.

Chapter Six

It was after ten when Laurence arrived home. Violet was making Ovaltine in the kitchen and Nell was reading *Death on the Nile* in the sitting room, enjoying five minutes' respite from Violet's teasing.

She had been back less than half an hour, having gone for a farewell drink with Artie to the Rose and Crown in Market Needing. His unit was leaving tomorrow and he had wanted to show his appreciation for her company over the past few weeks. They had shaken hands, slightly self-consciously, at the bottom of the hill, because Artie was due back on duty for the last time at midnight. Violet, convinced her sister was keeping a romantic tryst, had been at her most irritatingly coy about the whole thing and Nell had struggled to keep her temper.

The first inkling she had of Laurence's arrival was the sound of the front door slamming and the thud as his kit-bag hit the hall floor. By the time he walked into the sitting room she was halfway out of her chair, on her way to see who was barging in unannounced at such a late hour.

He stopped dead in the doorway and stared at her. He looked dreadful, unshaven, hollow-eyed, exhausted, and he blinked in the light. His greatcoat collar was turned up but his uniform jacket was unbuttoned, his tie askew; as Nell froze, half sitting, half standing, he passed his hand across his eyes and staggered, had to reach out and steady himself against the wall.

'Nell . . .' He stopped, cleared his throat, started again. 'Sorry, didn't mean to startle you. Ran out of petrol. Had to leave the car down the hill. I . . .'

For weeks, Nell realised, she had been fooling herself. She wasn't over him at all, never would be. She opened her mouth, tried to speak, failed. What was there to say? She wanted to stroll casually across the room and welcome him home, inject some normality into the situation, but her legs refused to work. She wanted to disappear, before Violet came in and she was forced to watch her greeting her husband, settling him in his favourite chair, stroking him better. She wanted to be back in London, as far away from Laurence Palmer as possible. Worst, most shaming of all, she wanted to put her arms round him and comfort him, make that terrible haunted look on his face go away. Instead she slumped back into her chair, immobilised by emotion, and just gazed at him, with her mouth stupidly ajar and her heart thumping so loud she was sure he could hear it from the other side of the room.

He tried again. 'Violet . . .' he said. 'Where's Violet?' and Nell's stomach twisted with furious, unreasonable jealousy. She took a deep breath and pulled herself together.

'In the kitchen. You look worn out. Why don't you sit down and I'll go and tell her you're here?'

'No!' Laurence took a step into the room, stopped again. 'Don't! Nell, I . . .' He reached for the doorhandle and began to swing the door shut behind him. 'I have to talk—'

'Laurie?'

Laurence jumped violently, then turned, still clinging to the doorhandle. 'Oh,' he said. 'Hello Vi . . .' He hesitated, bent to kiss his wife's cheek. 'Sorry, short notice – didn't know myself till lunchtime . . .'

'Darling!' Violet, her hands fully occupied with two mugs of steaming Ovaltine, stood on tiptoe and kissed him back as best she could, missing his mouth. 'Whatever are you sorry for? What a *wonderful* surprise! We had absolutely no idea, did we, Nell?'

Nell shook her head obediently, cleared her throat, then rose and moved awkwardly away from the fire.

'Why didn't you let us know?' Violet continued, oblivious to her sister's difficulties and visibly bubbling over with delight at her husband's unexpected return. 'We would have saved you some supper. Have you eaten? Do you want me to rustle you up something? Let me get you a drink – you look exhausted, doesn't he, Nell?'

'Violet, don't *fuss*!' The words were expelled so angrily that Violet jerked backwards, spilling hot Ovaltine and squeaking with surprise and pain.

Laurence stared at her puckered face in horror. 'Oh, Lord. Vi, I'm so sorry! Take no notice of me, please, I'm just tired . . .'

He wandered across the room to Nell's vacated chair and collapsed into it, dropping his head into his hands and rubbing vigorously at his face. Nell made for the hall, shutting the door firmly behind her. This was nothing to do with her – whatever was going on, it was between husband and wife.

Her bedroom was freezing and she shivered beneath the blankets. After a while she heard them, Violet, interrogative, puzzled, then Laurence, gruff, monosyllabic and on his feet again by the sound of it, pacing the sitting room. Nell stared at the sprigged wallpaper and wished she had thought to bring her book up to distract her

from what was going on below. She rubbed her arms
and watched her breath clouding in front of her, then,
making a decision, flung back the covers, clambered off
the bed and pulled her suitcase from the top of the
wardrobe.

'Go now,' she muttered as she began to strip hangers,
fold blouses. 'Go now before you make a complete fool
of yourself.' There must be a train tomorrow; she would
phone first thing. Perhaps she could persuade Marion
Palmer to run her into Ipswich. She would have to think
of an excuse – Pa needing her urgently in the shop or
something – but Violet wouldn't mind her going now
Laurence was home. As for Laurence, he didn't seem to
be in a fit state to notice anything, let alone his ungainly
sister-in-law. She paused, a skirt dangling from her
hands, and closed her eyes, imagining. 'Stop it!' she said
aloud. 'For heaven's sake, just *stop* it!'

As she was folding her best white blouse she heard a
noise like distant thunder, and from across the fields
came the rising wail of an air-raid siren. Filled with sudden foreboding, Nell dropped the blouse and made for
the door. She reached the landing just as Laurence's
thundering footsteps hit the top of the stairs.

'Come on!' he snapped peremptorily, all his earlier
lethargy gone. 'Come on, quick!' He grabbed her clumsily by the arm, then propelled her towards the stairs,
practically pushing her down them. Nell could hear his
breath coming in short, staccato bursts behind her as he
bundled her along the passage, felt the heat of his hands
on her back as he pushed her, hard, into the cupboard.
She lost her footing, bumped into Violet, who was
already huddled against the back wall in the dark, and
sat down hard, jarring her spine. The noise was getting
louder now, more menacing, rumbling like an avalanche
roaring down a mountainside, and she wriggled further

into the cramped space, then twisted round and drew her knees up to her chin, making room for Laurence. He failed to materialise. Instead, above the uneven drone of aircraft engines, she heard the cupboard door slam, then another bang, fainter, further away, and realised that Laurence, not content with standing on the stairs, had chosen to walk straight out of the front door, directly into the path of danger.

The noise grew and grew, until all possibility of speech was squeezed out by the sheer volume of sound. The planes were almost overhead now, louder, lower than anything Nell had experienced before, even in London, and the exhilaration she had so often felt during previous air raids was washed away by a tide of fear, not for herself – it was difficult, trapped in her black, cacophonous prison, to believe in an outside world at all – but for Laurence, somewhere out there in the middle of it. She was peripherally aware of Violet, crouched beside her clutching her arm as if her life depended upon it, of the musty smell of old shoes, winter coats and furniture polish, but as the noise grew it began to beat inside her head, making her eyeballs ache and her teeth vibrate, until nothing else in the world existed at all.

When the kitchen window shattered, Violet screamed. Nell felt the impact through the soles of her feet, through her shoulders, braced against the wall, and was rendered momentarily deaf as the shockwaves battered at her eardrums. A cloud of thick, choking dust filled their prison, forced through the cracks in the staircase as the house shook from chimneypots to foundations, and Violet began to sob, gripping Nell's hand so tightly she had to bite her lip not to cry out with the pain.

Ten seconds (or was it ten minutes? – it was hard to keep track) after the first impact came another, and another, then two simultaneously, eldritch shrieks as they fell, almighty booms and thuds as they hit. In the kitchen something heavy crashed against the stove, which let out a hollow clang, like a bell tolling in some distant church.

The silence, when at last it came, was almost as deafening as the noise.

'Laurie?' came Violet's voice out of the darkness. 'Darling, are you all right?'

Nell swallowed hard. 'He's not here.'

'What?' Violet let go of her and leaned across, feeling blindly with outstretched hands. 'Don't be silly! Of course he's here, I heard him crawl in! Laurie?'

'It's all right, dear, I'm sure he's fine. I expect he decided there wasn't enough room for three.'

The necessity of talking, of soothing Violet's fears before they got out of hand, made Nell feel better, stronger. She could taste the grit on her tongue and as she turned her head towards her sister she felt the dust from her hair drifting across her cheeks. She brushed at her face, set another cloud moving, coughed. Stay calm, she exhorted herself; if you stay calm Violet will stay calm too. She struggled to her knees, set her shoulder to the door and pushed hard just as the catch was released from the other side. Attempting to force an exit against an unresisting barrier, she landed in a heap on the hall floor.

'Ow!' she exclaimed, relief rendering her furiously angry. 'What the *hell* did you have to do that for?'

It was as dark in the passage as it was in the cupboard, and she couldn't see a thing. She could sense him though, smell the scent of pipe tobacco that always hung about him. She could feel him too, his hands pulling her up so she was kneeling, his arms sliding round her, holding her tight, suffocating her. She turned her face, until his cold cheek was resting against hers, then repeated in his ear, whispering this time, asking a different question altogether, 'What did you do that for?'

She felt his mouth moving against her neck, heard her name, '*Nell* . . .' Then he muttered cryptically, 'Picked the wrong place to stand, didn't I?' and released her as suddenly as he had embraced her. 'Vi,' he called briskly, 'you OK in there?'

As he crawled into the cupboard to comfort his hysterical wife, Nell, plain, stolid, unemotional Eleanor Carter, who hardly ever cried, leaned her head against the wall and began, silently, to weep.

Later, after she and Violet had cleared up the worst of the mess and reassured the steady stream of concerned neighbours while Laurence boarded up the broken windows, Nell sat in bed in the dark, listening to her sister and brother-in-law talking downstairs. She couldn't pick out the words, only the inflexions, the rise and fall of their voices, but as the conversation went on Laurence began to sound agitated, Violet upset. After a while the sitting-room door opened and she heard their feet on the stairs, Violet first, followed slowly, reluctantly, by Laurence.

The argument continued next door, Laurence surly, vehement, Violet plaintive, clearly distressed. It began to sound as if Violet had managed to calm him down, and that was all right, just. But then it turned into something else, and Nell began to shift uneasily beneath the blankets, wishing they would be quiet. And then, as the unmistakable noises of love-making began to filter through the wall, she burrowed down beneath the covers and buried her head under the pillow, because listening to *that* was simply unendurable . . .

She was roused by the sound of distant fire engines and the floorboards creaking next door, heard

Laurence's heavy footfalls descending the stairs, then the clink of glass against glass as he helped himself from the whisky decanter, and the rattle of the poker as he prodded the fire back into life. By the time she finally closed her eyes just after four he still hadn't returned to bed. And very faintly, muffled as if she was trying not to make too much noise, she heard Violet through the wall, crying . . .

In the cold light of day, the damage didn't look too bad. The nearest bomb had landed some twenty yards away, demolishing the toolshed at the bottom of the garden and shattering the two windows on that side of the house. The heavy oak dresser was leaning drunkenly against the cold stove and there were still shards of glass and crockery littered across the kitchen floor. The sitting room, parlour and bedrooms were dusty, but otherwise unscathed. In the absence of Laurence, who had gone out almost as soon as it was light, the two women swept glass, mopped floors and wielded dusters all morning, then separated, Nell to go to her room and Violet to wait anxiously at the sitting-room window for Laurence's return. Violet was heavy-eyed, subdued, and Nell's conviction had grown all morning – whatever was going on between them they would sort it out better if she wasn't there.

'Nell?' Violet's lovely face, poking round the bedroom door, was crumpled with worry. 'Can I talk to you? What are you doing?'

'Packing.' Nell moved past her to the chest of drawers, picked out a pile of underwear. 'I'm going back to London.'

'Why?' Violet plonked herself down on the bed, setting Nell's suitcase bouncing beside her. 'Oh, please, Nell, don't go! I know you said when Laurie came home . . .'

Nell continued, doggedly folding and smoothing, tucking her last precious pair of nylons down the side of her case, piling her handkerchiefs – embroidered with her initial, *E* for Eleanor, and a Christmas present from Pa – neatly on the bed. 'Nell, you're not listening to me!'

Nell sighed, then moved the handkerchiefs out of the way and sat down heavily beside her sister. Sometimes, she thought, it was like dealing with a spoilt child. 'Violet,' she began, 'it's not right, a newly married couple sharing their home with a third party. Whatever was wrong with Laurence when he came home last night, if I hadn't been here you could've—'

Violet shook her head vehemently, setting her blonde curls dancing on her shoulders. 'No! No, you're wrong. It wouldn't have made any difference. He won't tell me anything, I've asked him and asked him.' She blushed. 'I asked him in bed, what was the matter, and he just said I wouldn't understand.' Her face puckered and she began to cry. 'He kept looking at me as if he'd never seen me before, as if I were a stranger . . .'

Nell picked a hankie off the pile and shook it out, then took Violet's chin in her hand and dabbed at her eyes. 'Violet,' she said gently, 'surely . . .' Oh, surely. I *heard* you. Even through three layers of blankets and a pillow, I heard you making love. I could have killed you both. 'Surely you sorted things out in the end? That's what double beds are for, after all.'

Violet blushed again. 'Well, yes, we did, but it wasn't . . .' She blew her nose on Nell's handkerchief, wiped it carefully, sniffed. 'It wasn't *right*. It was as if he was only half there, as if he was just going through the motions because I wanted him to, as if . . .' She dropped her blue eyes, brimming with tears, embarrassed to be talking about such an intimate subject. 'It was as if he was pretending I was someone else . . .'

All the conflicting emotions Nell had been through since the previous night, fear, love, longing, jealousy, desire, were swamped by pity for Violet's misery, poor, uncomplicated Violet who for the first time in her life was facing problems she couldn't solve, who was looking to her big sister to fix things for her.

'All the more reason for me to go back to London,' she said. 'If you and Laurence are having difficulties the last thing you need is me getting in the way while you sort them out.' She leaned across and kissed Violet's damp cheek, then tidied the remaining handkerchiefs away, snapped the lid of her suitcase shut and swung it from the bed to the floor. 'You're a married woman now, you know. It's Laurence you should be talking to about this, not me.'

'I don't even know where he is. He went off hours ago saying he was going to collect his car and he hasn't come back.' Violet stood up, twisting Nell's hankie anxiously between her hands. 'Nell, you *have* to stay.'

'No.' Nell felt better now her mind was made up. 'As soon as the phone's fixed I'll ring about train times and in the meantime I must get on with the papers. Mrs Downes'll be wondering where on earth I've got to and I'll have to tell her I'm leaving.' She leaned across and hugged Violet tightly. 'It's you I'm thinking of,' she said, her voice steady with the conviction of absolute truth. 'It's for the best, you'll see.' Then she went in search of her coat.

Violet, still tearful, followed her out onto the drive, protesting all the way that she wouldn't let her go. There was a strong smell of roast pork outside, and a thin column of black smoke was curling into the air from somewhere along Post Office Row. They could hear raised voices, the sound of pick and shovel, crashing masonry.

'Bewson's piggery,' said Nell, sniffing the air. 'Poor Charlie.'

'Poor pigs,' said Violet. 'Nell, you *can't* go . . .'

Nell sighed. Why must Violet perversely insist on trying to prevent her doing the right thing? 'Look,' she said, soothing, reassuring, 'I'll be back in an hour and there's no chance of a train before this evening, so we'll have the rest of the day together. Violet, dear, please don't make this harder than it already is.'

As she set off for the gate, Laurence's Riley turned into the drive.

'Laurie!' cried Violet, starting forward to greet him.

He had to brake hard to avoid running over his wife's foot. Nell could see his face behind the windscreen, as haggard as last night, as if he'd hardly slept at all. The car skidded to a halt, spraying gravel, and Violet rushed round to tap on the window.

'Laurie,' she began before he had wound it halfway down. 'Will you *please* talk to Nell! She's threatening to leave, and she won't listen to me . . .'

Nell made a clumsy exit, sidling past the other side of the car and practically running into the lane in her haste to get away.

Bewson's piggery was a pile of smoking bricks and all the windows on Post Office Row had been blown out. There was a crater five feet wide halfway down the street and most of the village, evacuees and all, were out and about, boarding up windows, sweeping glass, clearing debris, discussing the events of the night before, their first direct hit since the war began. Down at the bottom of the hill, the field behind the forge was a mess of mud, sand and metal, bits of khaki tent, hessian, and the mangled remains of the searchlight. Nell stopped, staring at the mounds of earth, soldiers and firefighters damping down, shovelling sand, loading piles of twisted metal and canvas onto a flatbed lorry.

'Three dead, thirteen wounded,' came a voice from

behind her. 'Poor buggers di'n't stand a chance. You off for the papers, miss?'

Nell's stomach lurched sickeningly. 'Do you know who . . . ?'

Ernie Beale was the only gardener left of the six who had worked at the Hall before the war; he had volunteered for the job of ARP warden despite his crippling arthritis. 'Your chap were standing over there so they say.' He pointed with a twisted, deformed finger at a morass of churned-up earth dotted with piles of sand and bits of sacking. Nell's stomach lurched again and she felt tears pricking at her eyes. 'Sorry, miss,' said Ernie. 'Can't keep no secrets in the country. You and him'd gotten close these past weeks, ha'n't yer?' He tipped his tin hat off his forehead, scratched his hairless scalp. 'At least it were quick,' he added. 'Poor bugger. You awright, miss?'

Nell blinked, gulped. 'Yes,' she said. 'Yes, I'm fine, thank you. I must . . . er . . . I must go and get on with the papers.'

Ernie patted her again, awkwardly. 'Wun't be none today. Them bastards, beggin' yer pardon, miss, got the depot last night. There han't bin no deliveries this mornin'.' He peered hard at her face. 'You sure you're awright?'

'Yes.' Nell nodded vigorously, noted the thick lines round his eyes and mouth and wondered irrelevantly how old he was. 'Really, I'm fine. It's just a bit of a—'

'Shock,' said Ernie helpfully. ' 'Course it is.' He adjusted his gas mask on his hip, coughed tactfully, glanced at her from beneath shaggy brows. 'Bit of a walk'll do you good. Clear the cobwebs.' He raised his face to the sky, felt in his pocket for cigarettes and offered her one. 'Nice day for it.'

'Mm.' Nell took the cigarette then, reminded suddenly

of Arthur Mulligan, said, 'No, you keep it. Thanks all the same,' and handed it back. She felt immediately churlish for rejecting the sympathetic gesture. Ernie Beale lived with his elderly mother on Post Office Row, pushing his bicycle across the valley to the Hall every day. He was no trouble to anyone. He was a nice man, kind, unassuming. 'I think I'll take your advice and go for a walk though. It looks like the sun's trying to come out, doesn't it?'

'Tha's the ticket.' Ernie straightened his tin hat. 'Well, best get on.' He turned away, stopped, turned back and thrust the whole packet of cigarettes at her. 'Dun't forgit your gas mask nex' time,' he said sternly, embarrassed by his own generosity. Then he shuffled off up the street without another word.

Nell watched him go, then set off in the other direction, walking for the sake of walking, with no idea where she was going. By the time Laurence caught her up she had already crossed the railway and she was on the main road, aiming for the humpbacked bridge over the river, and the woods which marched down the side of the valley, in search of something, or someone, on whom to vent her anger.

Chapter Seven

'He was only twenty!' Nell glared at him as if it were his fault Arthur Mulligan was dead. 'He was just a boy, he had all these plans for after the war! Why did they have to drop their bloody bombs here? What threat could we possibly be to them, out here in the back of beyond?'

Laurence walked beside her, adjusting his long stride to her shorter one, not looking at her. 'They don't need a reason. They probably didn't even know the area was populated. They were on their way home, getting rid of their load so they could make their fuel last longer. It happens all the time.'

'I don't believe you.' Nell dug her hands deeper into her pockets and increased her speed, trying to get away from him. 'They could have waited till they were over a town. Somewhere big that could defend itself . . .' It was an appalling thing to say, but she couldn't stop herself. She felt somehow as if it were her fault this carnage had been inflicted on the village; if she had remembered *Hawley*, *Ware*, *Smith*, if she had felt more fear and less exhilaration, Arthur Mulligan might still be alive. She was being punished for her bravado. Except that it was Arthur who had been punished . . .

'How will his mum and dad manage?' she demanded.

'His dad lost a leg at Dunkirk, you know. They were relying on him!'

'I'm sorry,' said Laurence.

'Sorry?' Nell's voice rose indignantly. 'What have *you* got to be sorry about? At least you're doing your bit! What am I doing? Apart from standing on the stairs watching it all happen, like some stupid child at a firework party.'

'What?' he said.

Nell shook her head. 'Nothing. Take no notice, I'm talking nonsense.'

She turned to look at him, found he was already staring at her, and stumbled. He reached out a hand and grabbed her elbow.

'Nell . . .' he began.

She shook him off. 'Don't!' she said. 'Don't, I can't *bear* it!'

'There's something I'd like to show you,' he said. 'Please?' He stepped sideways, giving her some space, and stared over her head at the heavily wooded valley as if, thought Nell, he knew how much he disturbed her and was trying not to make it worse.

'How long will it take?' She curled her fingers inside her pockets, feeling Ernie Beale's cigarettes, and examined her muddy shoes. 'I ought to get back.' She raised her head, challenging him. 'Violet will be wondering where I am.'

He accepted the challenge, meeting her gaze without flinching. 'It was Violet who sent me,' he said. He rubbed at his unshaven chin; Nell could hear his fingers rasping against the bristles. 'She told me not to show my face again until I'd found you. I'm supposed to persuade you not to go back to London.' He was wearing corduroy trousers and a lovat-green waistcoat under an ancient tweed overcoat. He looked, thought Nell, exactly what he was, what his father was when there wasn't a war on, an affluent country land-owner, solid, dependable, upright – except for the black rings under his eyes, the dark stubble on his chin. He cleared his throat, ran his hand across his mouth again, then said abruptly, 'Don't go, Nell. Please.'

'What did you mean?' asked Nell. 'Last night. What did you mean when you said you'd picked the wrong place to stand?'

It was he who walked away this time and Nell who followed, demanding an answer. 'Can't remember,' he said over his shoulder. 'I don't know what you're talking about.'

Nell skipped a step, trying to keep up as he strode along the road in front of her, refusing to let it drop. 'Why did you go outside when the bombs started? Why didn't you come in the cupboard with us?'

She was running now, shouting at him, and when he turned suddenly to the right and began to march along a green track beneath the leaf-bare trees she was taken by surprise, found herself slithering in the mud. 'Was it just bravado?' she yelled. 'Or were you trying to get yourself killed?'

He stopped so suddenly she almost cannoned into him, swung round and yelled back. 'What if I was? What's it to you?'

They stood face to face beneath the dripping trees, panting as if they had been running, and then Laurence's shoulders sagged and he shrugged. 'All right,' he said. 'Maybe I was. Maybe I was looking for an easy way out. I don't know.' He raised his hand, slid cold fingers across Nell's cheek, stroking stray curls of mousy hair from her eyes; his touch sent shivers of pleasure down her spine. 'I've mucked it up, Nell,' he said. 'I've mucked it all up and I don't know how to put it right.' He turned his back and walked on, more slowly this time. 'We're nearly there,' he said over his shoulder. 'Please, I want you to see it.'

'See what?' asked Nell, but he didn't answer. Unable to tear herself away, to do what she ought to do and go back to Violet, she gave up and followed him.

It was not so muddy off the road, and the leaves had drifted across the wide path so they waded ankle-deep in places, their feet shushing and shuffling, occasionally snapping twigs underfoot, moving gently uphill all the time. Nell could smell mushrooms, leaf-mould, a damp, earthy smell like nothing she had experienced before. It made her nose tingle and set her sneezing.

When they had gone a hundred yards she thought they must be nearly there, wherever 'there' was, but Laurence kept on going, two hundred yards, three, deep into the trees. A watery sun came out, filtering through the branches overhead and turning the leaves beneath their feet from brown to gold. 'Laurence,' begged Nell, 'I ought to go back.'

He stopped, waiting for her to catch up. 'We're here,' he said.

The cottage stood in a wide, flat clearing, basking in the winter sunshine. It was thatched, whitewashed, tiny, and it seemed to be floating on a green, white and gold sea, delicate nodding snowdrops and the glossy green leaves and yellow cups of winter aconite, hundreds, thousands of them, blooming exuberantly right up to the walls, untouched by war and death and destruction. Nell thought she had never seen anything so beautiful, or so obviously private, in her entire life.

'It's called Malletts,' said Laurence. 'After its first tenant. Up until five years ago it was used by the estate gamekeepers. Papa rears pheasant in these woods and he likes his chaps to be on the spot to keep an eye on things.' Watching his face, Nell thought she saw the tension ease a little. 'Mama persuaded him to give it to me on my twenty-first birthday. She thought I needed somewhere to . . . escape to.'

'And did you?'

'Yes.'

He didn't elaborate. Nell, uncomfortable in the ensuing silence, blundered on. 'I thought you owned the Dower House?'

'No.' Laurence fished for his pipe, then moved out across the sunny clearing, filling the bowl from his tobacco tin. 'That's still part of the estate, on loan until I come into my inheritance.' He struck a match, tamping the tobacco down with his thumb as he sucked at the flame. 'Mama thought we needed somewhere on our own when we got married. "No privacy at the Hall with all these military people about," she said.'

'Isn't this private enough?'

Laurence shrugged. He looked uncomfortable now, defensive. 'Vi would've hated it. There's no running water, no inside lavatory, no electricity. Besides, I didn't want—' He cut himself off. 'The snowdrops are late this year.'

Nell followed him into the sun, enjoying its warmth on her face, a presage of spring like the snowdrops and aconites. 'And did she?' she asked. 'Hate it, I mean?'

Laurence glanced sideways at her, appraising her with wary blue eyes. 'Violet's never been here.'

'Oh. Why not?'

Laurence, struggling with the latch, didn't answer. The door creaked on its hinges and he had to bend his head to avoid the lintel.

'Were you there?' he demanded as he disappeared inside.

Nell followed him reluctantly over the threshold. 'Was I where?'

'At that dance, when I met Violet.'

'Oh. No.'

'Why not?' He turned left from the tiny hall, busying himself with his pipe again, leaving a trail of aromatic smoke behind him.

'I was working. I couldn't get away.'

'You should have been there,' he said through the fog. 'If you'd been there I might not have—' He cut himself off again, and crossed the room to throw his spent match in the hearth.

'If I had been there,' said Nell before she could stop herself, 'you wouldn't have noticed. People don't, when Violet's around.'

He didn't answer – after all, what could he say in the face of such an obvious truth? – and, embarrassed by her revealing outburst, Nell turned her attention to their surroundings.

Everything was plain, the limewashed walls and cracked, uneven pamments, the uncurtained window, the sparse furniture. The wall at the far end of the room was dominated by a cast-iron range, an open grate in the middle with a hob each side and a brass rail at head height for drying clothes. To its left was an old-fashioned brick copper, to its right, set into the wall at chest height, the black-leaded door of what Nell guessed must be a separate bread oven. A sagging leather armchair sat next to the hearth, its feet resting on a multicoloured rag rug. There was a plain deal table near the door with an upright ladderback chair tucked beneath it, a makeshift bookcase made of bricks and planks and crammed with dog-eared books, a built-in corner cupboard and that was all, apart from the only ornament in the room, a model bi-plane with fabric wings and complicated struts such as a dexterous schoolboy might build, which sat, listing gently to starboard, on the deep windowsill. The room was silent, dim, and icily cold.

'It's chilly in here,' said Laurence, 'I'll light a fire,' and without another word he strode past her, bent his head under the lintel, and disappeared outside. Nell, left unexpectedly to her own devices, began to wander about the room.

She was drawn to the books: slim volumes of war poetry on the top shelf, Wilfred Owen, Siegfried Sassoon, Rupert Brooke, well thumbed and greasy with use; half a dozen *Biggles* stories, old, tatty and curled at the edges; then further down, *The Grapes of Wrath* and more poetry, Auden, Isherwood, Louis MacNeice, Ogden Nash and Hilaire Belloc; below that a still odder mix of titles, from *The Famous Five* to Nabokov's *Despair*, from *Winnie the Pooh* and *Just William* to Raymond Chandler's *Farewell, My Lovely* and Saint-Exupéry's *Wind, Sand and Stars*. There were books on wild flowers and birds, butterflies and aeroplanes, ancient Greek mythology. Nell's conviction that she was intruding upon something intensely private increased, and by the time Laurence returned with an armful of kindling she was on the other side of the room, standing in the scullery doorway examining the rough cupboards, the stone sink and the black-handled water pump protruding from the wall beside it. Laurence was right about Violet, she thought as he set about lighting the fire; she would never have coped with such primitive conditions.

He had clearly performed the task many times before; he was quick, skilful, snapping twigs between his hands then laying them across strategically placed lumps of coal gleaned from the scuttle in the hearth, tucking twists of paper fetched from the scullery, one here, one there. When he struck a match it caught immediately

'There,' he said, straightening up, 'that's better. What were we talking about?'

'I can't remember.' Nell's stomach lifted, turned over. It was time she left before she made an even bigger fool of herself. 'I ought to get back. Violet—'

'Damn Violet!' he said aggressively. 'I want to talk about you!'

Behind him the wood was beginning to catch. Nell could hear the creak of the front door, not quite shut, the skitter of some tiny creature above her head. 'Me?' she said, alarmed. 'What about me?'

Laurence leaned against the bread oven, folded his arms across his chest and stared into the fire. 'Violet told me about the boyfriend in one of her letters,' he said. 'And I've just seen Ernie Beale. The whole village seems to be talking about you.' He glanced up, frowning. 'This chap who's been killed. Was it very serious between you and him?'

Nell's temper suddenly flared again, and she advanced, cheeks flaming, towards the fire. 'For God's sake – I've had enough of this from Violet! Arthur was *not* my boyfriend, and even if he was it's none of your business!'

'Isn't it?'

'What?' She stopped, disconcerted.

'Isn't it?' repeated Laurence.

'He didn't fit in with the others, that's all,' she said defensively. 'He was different and they felt uncomfortable with him. He used to talk to me about his plans for the future, about Liverpool, how he didn't want to end up working on the docks like his dad. And we talked about books. He liked reading, so I got him a pile of Penguins from Ipswich. He needed someone to talk to because he was away from home and he missed his folks. He was lonely. Is that so bad?'

'No.'

In the ensuing silence Nell could hear the range crick-cracking as the metal heated up, was aware of the sun shining fitfully through the window, on-off, on-off, flashing a morse-code signal across the floor as it rode the thinning clouds.

'Are you lonely?' asked Laurence at last.

'Yes,' said Nell. 'Of course I am, sometimes. Aren't you?'

'Yes. If he didn't mean anything to you, why are you so angry?'

Nell flexed her fingers, beginning to ache as they thawed in the growing heat. 'Because I liked him. Because it's so *close*. Don't you get upset when your friends are killed?'

'Yes,' he said again.

He reached across to pick up the poker, hanging from a hook at the side of the range, then bent to prod the fire. Nell moved briskly out of his way and sat down.

'Tell me about standing on the stairs,' he said, but she shook her head, tired of all the questions, dizzy with heat after cold, with pipe-smoke and the sharp, sulphurous smell of damp coal.

'*Tell* me!' he repeated, squatting unexpectedly on his haunches in front of her and gripping the arms of the chair. 'Tell me about the fireworks, Nell, it's important!'

She told him more to exorcise the demons than because she thought he would understand. She told him about the guilty excitement, those solitary moments spent standing at the window, the awful exhilaration which churned and bubbled inside her even as she watched the bombs raining down on innocent civilians just a few miles away; she told him how beautiful the tracer bullets were, how the sparks from the fires leapt like red and gold rocket tails into the night sky, obliterating the stars. 'I made sure Violet was safe,' she said, excusing at least a small part of her behaviour, but she didn't look at him; she didn't want to see the disgust that must be stealing over his decent face, the disbelief that anyone, especially any woman, the nurturing sex, could be so unfeeling, so unnatural. When at last she raised her head and said bleakly, 'You see what a bitch I am?' he just stared past her at the wall and said nothing at all.

The silence seemed to stretch and stretch this time. Laurence straightened up, mended the fire, knocked out his pipe on the grate, set about filling it again, changed his mind and put it back in his pocket. Then, as if Nell's confession had opened some secret door, he began to talk.

He told her about his lifelong fascination with aeroplanes, how he had learned to fly with his university air squadron. He had signed up for the RAF, he said, as much so he could fly as to fight for his country. He described the early morning training sessions, with the mist hanging low over the airfield and hares boxing in the long grass on the perimeter, his first solo flight in a Tiger Moth, the thrill of popping out above the clouds into glorious sunshine, of weaving, awestruck, through the breathtaking beauty of towering white Cumulus. He recalled flying into the edge of a boiling black thundercloud, the anvil shaped Cumulo-nimbus, with his aircraft bucking and kicking beneath his hands like a wild bullock, scared witless that the flimsy structure would shake itself to bits and leave him sitting like a wingless angel in the middle of the sky. He described the rush of excitement as the wheels left the ground, the sensation, as the aircraft peeled off the top of a climb, that all his internal organs were trying to burst through the top of his skull, the thumping weight of gravity which glued him to his seat as he pulled out of a dive. He talked of coming off duty so intoxicated with adrenaline he thought his head would explode with the pressure, of drinking too much and sleeping with too many women, just to diffuse the energy which whirled constantly around in his brain.

'Is that why you and Violet have been quarrelling?' asked Nell.

'No! No, that was before I was married.' He shot her a swift glance, said, 'I've never been unfaithful to Violet,' then looked away and muttered, 'except in my head.' Then he crossed the room, his shoes leaving little drifts of mud on the stone floor, to fetch the ladderback chair, brought it back to the fire and collapsed onto it as if he was too tired to stand up any longer.

'Have you told Violet all this?' asked Nell. 'I'm sure she'd understand.'

'Have *you* told her?'

'Me? What should *I* tell her?'

'That you stand at the window watching falling bombs when you should be hiding under the stairs. That you get a thrill from—'

'*Don't!*' Nell covered her face with her hands, burning with shame. 'I wish I hadn't told you!'

'Who else would you tell?' Laurence leaned across from his chair and wrapped his fingers round her wrists, pulling them sharply down into her lap. 'Haven't you been listening? I'm the same as you. But how do I explain it to Violet? How do I break it to my wife, who thinks the sun shines out of my eyes, that every time I go up, every time I watch some faceless nameless German spinning down to destruction, I get such a thrill I laugh out loud . . .' His voice trailed away into silence, the silence of an awful confession made for the first time, and Nell became aware that they were both holding their breath, each waiting for the other to say something, anything, to break the spell.

'When I met Violet,' said Laurence at last, 'I'd been on stand-by for thirty-seven hours. I was out of my head.' He tightened his grip on Nell's wrists and leaned forward, intense, agonised, exhausted. 'I'd never seen anything so beautiful.' She tried to withdraw but he jerked her back towards him, forcing her to pay attention. 'I was drunk when I first set eyes on her and I stayed drunk for days afterwards. It was like reaching an oasis in the desert. Everything about her seemed so clean, so uncomplicated, so . . . so *simple*. But then it took on a momentum of its own. I wanted to tell her I'd changed my mind but instead I found myself rushing around inviting people I hardly knew to my wedding . . .'

Nell shifted uncomfortably on her chair. 'You shouldn't be telling me this,' she protested. 'It's none of my business.'

'Yes it is.' He leaned forward, until his face was only inches from hers and she could feel his breath stirring her hair. 'Until yesterday,' he said, 'I was resigned to what I'd done. I'd made my bed and I was prepared to lie on it.'

Nell leaned back, away from him. 'What changed your mind?'

He rose again and began to pace the room, hands in pockets, head down, speaking very fast. 'There was an accident. Yesterday morning. There's been some pilfering, some of the men pinching 100-octane to put in their cars, getting round the shortages—'

'100 octane?'

'Aircraft fuel. What we put in the Spitfires. This friend of mine, Harry – his girlfriend's been giving him a hard time and he'd been getting suspicious, thought maybe she'd found someone else. He was desperate to sort things out with her and he'd managed to wangle a pass, but he'd no fuel for his car so he'd sneaked a can of 100-octane. He was in a hell of a state when I bumped into him, imagining the worst, and I'd been trying to calm him down. I was about to go on my way when one of our ground crew came round the corner. He'd just come off duty and he was gasping for a smoke – there's no smoking on the airfield, or in the hangars, because of the fire risk. He'd got no matches so I gave him mine.' He stopped, took his hands out of his pockets and ran his fingers through his hair, resumed his pacing. 'He was only nineteen, even younger than your friend—'

'Arthur,' said Nell. 'His name was Arthur Mulligan. Go on.'

'He was talking, complaining about the roster for the following week. He lit his cigarette and dropped the match on the ground.' Laurence paused in the middle of the room, his feet resting in a puddle of sunlight, and stared out through the window at the white-gold carpet outside. 'I was on my way to the Mess by then, with my back to him, so I didn't see him go. There was just this thump, then a whooshing noise and Harry yelled. He'd been in a hurry when he filled up the jerry-can, and he hadn't put the cap on tight enough. He'd tripped running across the car park and spilt some petrol; the boy'd dropped his match right in the middle of it. He went up like a torch five feet from where I was standing.'

'Oh, God,' whispered Nell, clapping her hands to her mouth.

'I was like you,' said Laurence. 'I'd never been that close to real people dying, real people getting horribly mutilated. I've had the luck of the devil, came right through last year's carnage without a scratch. Until yesterday I thought I was invincible.' He fumbled for his pipe again, then suddenly dropped his head into his hands and shuddered. 'He started screaming, like a wounded animal. Harry and I just stood there, staring at him. Then Harry rushed at him and rolled him over and over on the grass, trying to put him out. I was frozen to the spot, useless, couldn't move, couldn't speak. He looked like a lump of raw meat, like a fox when the hounds have finished with it.' He glanced up, laughed suddenly, a forced, unconvincing attempt at humour. 'Can't stand hunting. I'm a great disappointment to Papa.'

'Didn't it make you angry?' asked Nell, reminded of Arthur, of *Hawley, Ware, Smith*, the sheer bloody *waste* of it all. 'Didn't it make you stinking mad?'

Laurence retrieved his pipe from his pocket, tapped it into his hand, then walked back across the room and dropped to his haunches in front of her again. 'No,' he said softly. 'It didn't make me mad, it made me sick.' His pipe tumbled, clattering, into the hearth and he fell to his knees, sliding his arms round her waist beneath her coat and dropping his head against her. 'I helped them put him in the ambulance,' he said into the hollow at the base of her throat. 'Then I walked round the back of the mess and threw up.'

Nell didn't think about what she did next until it was too late. She reached out instinctively to comfort him, wrapping her arms round him and stroking his hair.

'Nell . . .' he murmured, raising his head.

Just for a moment she tried to resist him, but when she turned her face away he turned her fiercely back, curling his fingers tightly in her hair and holding her still with both hands.

'Please, Nell,' he begged. 'I have to go back tonight. I've no time left for playing games.'

'I'm not playing games, I'm just trying to—'

'I *love* you,' said Laurence, and she gave in.

Chapter Eight

They walked along the track together, a foot apart, carefully not touching. Laurence had wanted to go straight back to the Dower House, tell Violet it had all been a terrible mistake, that it was Nell he wanted.

'You can't!' Nell had told him, at once entranced and appalled by the idea. 'She adores you. You can't just casually announce that you've changed your mind!'

Walking beside him through the woods, with dead leaves swish-swashing about her ankles and bare branches clashing above her head, she was visited by a swift mental picture of him after they had made love, sitting with his knees drawn up to his chin and his naked skin bathed rose-red by the light of the fire. She had wondered if she would ever see anything so perfect again, and now she didn't dare look at him, let alone touch, for fear it would remind her of what they had done, make her want to do it again. It was far worse, this new disease of wanting, than mere jealousy, it was all-consuming, painfully, wonderfully *awful*.

'How can I go on pretending?' Laurence came to a sudden halt, kicking the leaves into a heap in front of his feet and turning to face her. 'I can't do it, Nell, I haven't the time!' The sun went in as he spoke, and the sky overhead darkened. Laurence's face twisted and he reached for her.

'Don't,' said Nell, pushing him away. 'Don't make it any worse.'

'You love me,' he accused. 'You wouldn't have let me if you didn't.'

'My feelings don't come into it.' Nell pulled her coat closer about her, as if it might protect her from him, and walked on. 'Violet is my sister. She's your wife. We can't do this to her.'

Laurence, catching her up, glanced sideways at her. 'We already have.'

When Nell looked up, his eyes were blurred with tears and she turned hurriedly away, because she couldn't bear it.

He tried again. 'At least stay. If I have to carry on with this farce at least stay, so I know where you are.'

'How can I? How can I, after what we've done?'

'Easy.' Laurence stopped again and grabbed her arm, tugging her round to face him. 'Because if you don't stay I shall tell her. I shall walk out on her, right now.' He leaned close, so she could smell the smoke from his pipe, the scent of his skin. 'I *need* you,' he said. 'You're the only one who can keep me sane.'

'You've managed without me your whole life,' she said. 'Why can't you do it now?'

'Because I'm scared. I'm scared witless because now I have something to live for I'm more likely to die. I swear it, Nell, if you don't stay, I'll tell her all about us.' He released her, dropped his hands to his sides. 'I've nothing left to lose. I'll tell her everything: making love in front of the fire, how your skin tastes, the smell of your hair, that mole on your—'

'Stop it!' She clapped her hands over her ears and stepped back, away from him. 'All right, all right, I'll stay.' Laurence reached for her again. She snatched her arm away. 'On one condition.'

'Anything.'

'That you swear—'

'I swear, I won't do anything about it.' He hesitated, backtracked. 'For the moment.'

'*Ever!*' said Nell fiercely. 'If you breathe a single word of this to Violet I shall go back to London and you'll never see me again!'

'If you go back to London I shall follow you.' He grimaced at her, wiped his eyes with the back of his hand. 'All right, I won't say a word.' He turned sharply on his heel and waded on through the leaves. 'Did it mean that little to you?' he hurled angrily over his shoulder.

Nell stopped dead, watching him as he made for the road, striding out with his hands in his pockets and his head down, no longer waiting for her. 'Of all the *bloody* stupid questions!' she shouted after him.

She stood completely still for almost five minutes, watching her own breath clouding in the chilly air, imagining Violet's reaction. 'How could you, Nell?' she would say. 'How could you *do* this to me?' Her eyes, those big, beautiful blue eyes, would fill with tears. The question was unanswerable. How could she have done such a thing to her own sister? She raised her head and stared wide-eyed through the bare branches at the sky, deeper blue now and laced with indigo clouds tinged at the edges with pink. She wondered what the time was, remembered Laurence's hands, his mouth, the murmured endearments, and caught her breath, aching with longing for what she had only just found and could never have again. Then slowly, reluctantly, she began to move on, back to face the bomb-damaged field behind Youngman's forge, the walk up through the village to the Dower House, and Violet.

As she passed the smithy she glanced to her right. Already the signs were less, the worst of the debris had been cleared. As she moved further up the hill she was greeted by neighbours, people she had come to know well over the past few months, people who had seen her with Artie Mulligan and drawn the same conclusions as Violet. She was patted as she passed, offered sympathetic words and looks; her guilt increased, that all these kind people were feeling for her in her loss, a loss she could no longer feel at all, because of what had happened since.

She could see Violet waiting for her at the window, her face pinched with worry. 'Nell,' she cried, darting out to meet her as she walked through the front door. 'Where have you been? I've been worried sick!'

'Just walking, dear.' She followed Violet into the sitting room, where Laurence was already ensconced next to the fire, a large whisky in his hand. 'I ought to go and—'

'I've told Vi you're staying,' said Laurence, fixing her with over-bright blue eyes, daring her. 'That's right, isn't it?'

'Er . . . Yes, I . . . that is, I—'

'Darling Nell, I can't *tell* you how glad I am!'

Going to embrace her, Violet recoiled, wrinkling her pretty nose at the smell of smoke still clinging to Nell's clothes. Nell, her nostrils filled with the scent of Laurence's pipe tobacco, found herself feeling in her pocket for the cigarettes Ernie Beale had thrust upon her and mumbling a garbled explanation for their presence, guiltily excusing that which Violet had not even mentioned.

'And it'll be such a weight off Laurie's mind, won't it, darling?' Violet rambled on. 'Knowing I have you to look after me.'

Nell glared at Laurence. He glared back, then drained his glass in one gulp and stood up. 'I must go and shave,' he said. 'I have to leave in an hour.'

'Nell,' continued Violet, 'I'm so sorry about . . . you know. It must have been the most awful shock for you.'

'What?' asked Nell blankly.

'Why, poor Arthur Mulligan, of course . . .'

As he passed Nell, Laurence glanced down, straight into her eyes. His expression was defiant, unapologetic. 'I told Vi,' he said, taunting her. 'I told Vi about your boyfriend.'

'You had no right—' she began angrily.

'Would you rather she found out from someone else?'

'No, but I—'

'Well then.' He strode past her, making for the door. 'What the hell does it matter?'

'Laurie!' protested Violet, shocked by the snarled exchange.

Laurence stopped, took a deep breath, hung his head. 'Sorry,' he said. 'I'm sorry, Vi.'

'It's not me who needs an apology,' scolded Violet. 'It's Nell you should be saying sorry to, for being so horrible when she's lost her friend.'

Laurence turned slowly, locked Nell into a long, steady stare. 'I'm truly sorry, Nell,' he said. Then he turned his back on them both and walked out.

They heard him just before he left, retching violently behind the locked bathroom door.

Chapter Nine

The days dragged, and the nights were worse. As winter melted into spring, Nell's shame and guilt grew and the exhilaration she had once felt at the sound of an air-raid siren turned to revulsion and weariness. Violet, ascribing her sister's misery to the death of Arthur Mulligan, fussed around her until Nell thought she would go mad.

Laurence didn't help. Previously his letters to his wife, when he had written at all, had been perfunctory, businesslike affairs. Now, he took to writing almost every day, nothing particularly private, none of the dark secrets he had confided to Nell at the cottage, just day-to-day accounts of life in an RAF Mess. He wrote about the schoolboy pranks the men – *actually, only boys, most of them*, he corrected himself in the margin – played on each other to alleviate the boredom, about the camaraderie, the gallows humour which 'got the chaps through' when friends failed to return from a mission. He described the lucky mascots – everything from a moth-eaten rabbit's foot to the pair of purple silk pyjamas one pilot wore beneath his uniform every time he flew – the monotonous food, the difficulty of getting his pipe tobacco, the drinking sessions after which long, convoluted discussions would take place upon every subject under the sun, from how flies landed on the ceiling to whether tying one's scarf one way was more likely to prevent a stiff neck than tying it another. He described the layers of underwear, the thick sweaters and extra pairs of socks the pilots wore beneath their uniforms to combat temperatures as cold as minus 60°F, the smell of the oxygen masks, the restorative properties of off-duty beer. He mentioned the new CO's fury upon discovering the impromptu nighclub running in the mess, the lack of automobile tax and insurance to which the local police turned a blind eye. He was careful not to mention where he had been, the technical details of what he had been doing or how he had done it, but at the end of every letter he wrote, in a neat, even hand Nell quickly came to know almost as well as her own, *Are you looking after each other? Show Nell this letter and tell her I hope she is not too sad.* He signed himself, with unconscious (no, it *had* to be conscious) irony, *your faithful Laurence,* and Violet, dear innocent, trusting Violet, showed Nell every single one. Reading Laurence's letters was like listening to him talk; they made Nell's craving worse, which was, she suspected, exactly what he intended them to do.

His determinedly positive tone and the frequency of his communications convinced Violet that their problems during his last visit had been only temporary, his rejection of her attempts to get close to him due purely to fatigue.

'I know you two haven't always got on in the past,' she told Nell loftily, 'but you do see now, don't you Nell, how sweet he really is?'

It seemed to Nell that, on the contrary, Laurence was being quite unspeakably cruel; she wrote to him secretly to tell him so, posting the letter in Ipswich where the postmistress didn't know her, and begging him to please leave her out of his kind regards. Within days the letters ceased and Violet was plunged into a new round of self-doubt.

'Don't be silly, dear,' Nell reassured her. 'It just means he's too busy to write, that's all.' Why was it that whatever she did seemed merely to make things worse?

As the snowdrops faded and the crocuses started to push up through the sodden ground Nell began to wonder if she was sickening for something. She seemed to be always tired, and she was suffering from recurrent bouts of nausea, particularly on those evenings when Violet made Ovaltine. Sometimes the sweet milky smell made her feel so sick she would be forced from the room at a run, swallowing the sour taste of bile in her mouth. It was Violet who suggested that there might be a simple explanation for her sickness.

'Nell, don't take this the wrong way, but is there anything you want to tell me?'

Nell raised her head from her book. 'Like what?'

'Well, like . . .' Violet coloured prettily with embarrassment and rearranged her skirt neatly over her knees. 'Like, when did you have your last monthly?'

'What?' The implication took a second to sink in. 'No,' said Nell. 'Don't be so silly.'

'Nell—'

'I said, don't be ridiculous!' Nell felt suddenly dizzy with terror.

'I'm sorry, dear.' Violet began to tidy the room, on her way to bed. 'Tell me to mind my own business if you want. I just thought that maybe, what with that last evening you and Arthur spent together . . . well, it's on my mind, you see, because . . .' She folded the newspaper, tucked her knitting needles neatly into the skein, plumped a cushion. 'Well, because . . . I'm expecting a baby myself, you see.'

Nell stared at her sister's blonde head, bent over the armchair smoothing the antimacassar.

'Isn't it wonderful?' Violet straightened up, waiting expectantly for congratulations, flushed with pride and pleasure. 'Dr Hills confirmed it today. Laurie will be so thrilled when I tell him.'

Nell swallowed hard. 'Yes,' she said. She could hear her own voice, echoing in her ears. 'Yes, it's wonderful news, dear. Laurence—' She stopped, remembering his face, his voice, threatening her – *I'll tell her everything* – recalled the muffled sounds of lovemaking emanating from next door on the night of the bombing raid. Violet's news hurt so painfully she wanted to curl up and die. 'Laurence will be delighted,' she said. It would make up his mind once and for all that he must stay with Violet. Violet's question shouted in her head. *When was your last period? Why are you feeling so sick night after night? Oh, Lord, what a bloody mess you've got yourself into . . .*

The nausea that swept her now had more to do with fear than pregnancy. The signs had been staring her in the face for at least a fortnight – she had just chosen not to see them. She had thought if she pretended it wasn't happening she wouldn't have to face the consequences of what she – what they – had done. She rose awkwardly from her chair, crossed the room and embraced her sister. 'Violet,' she said, 'it's wonderful news.' Lies, lies, more lies. How had she got herself into this? Girls like Nell, good girls, *plain* girls, didn't get pregnant. It was fast girls who got themselves into trouble, pretty girls, girls who were no better than they ought to be.

The thought of having to break the news to Ma, of having to leave Suffolk and go back to London to face her wrath, appalled her. After Violet had gone to bed Nell sat on by the rapidly cooling fire, wondering what she was going to do, how she was going to deal with this crisis. Her cousin Molly had got herself into hot water a few years back; a pretty girl, she had had numerous boyfriends, but this time she had been careless. 'Little tart,' Ma had dubbed her. 'Girls like her deserve to be locked up. It's disgusting.' Nell's aunt, Molly's mother, had made arrangements, a filthy room above a dingy shoe-repair shop somewhere off the Commercial Road, a botched operation performed without anaesthetic or sterilised instruments. 'Best thing all round,' Ma had said after it was all over. 'Just *imagine* the shame.' Poor Molly had taken nearly six months to recover from her ordeal. She had been married for over a year now but she was still not pregnant and Nell had wondered more than once whether that back-street abortion might have had something to do with it.

Marion Palmer was brisk, irritable, in a hurry as usual, and she came straight to the point. 'Violet tells me you're not feeling quite the ticket, so I thought I'd pop you down to the doctor's, just to be on the safe side.'

Violet, refusing to believe Nell's vehement denial of her pregnancy, had decided that Nell's 'romantic interlude', as she irritatingly persisted in calling it, with poor Arthur Mulligan must be to blame for her condition. Nell had said nothing to disabuse her of the notion – it was safer than the truth, after all – but trying to fool Marion Palmer into believing that after a couple of hours in full view of the crowded snug at the Rose and Crown, Arthur Mulligan had persuaded her to accompany him back to his freezing tent, and that once there he had managed to seduce her in spite of the presence a few yards away of a dozen other soldiers, would not be so easy. Nor could she write to Laurence; she had done that once already and she had only made things worse.

'I'm fine,' she said, trying to sound buoyant and energetic. 'It was just the flu or something. I'm as right as rain now, honestly.'

Marion examined her, eyes narrowed speculatively. 'Hmm. Better safe than sorry in my opinion.' She glanced at the door, making sure Violet was still clattering about in the kitchen. 'Can't be too careful with pregnancy you know.'

'What?'

Nell's alarm must have showed in her face because Marion crossed the room to sit opposite her, then leaned over to pat her knee with a brisk, reassuring hand. 'It's all right, my dear, you can rely on me to be discreet.'

'Honestly . . .' Nell's heart began to thump with apprehension – 'honestly' was manifestly not the right word. 'It's not what you think. I'm fine, really I am.'

'Well,' said Marion drily, 'if you persist in putting on a brave face, I can't force you of course. But if you're not looking better by tomorrow I'll have the doctor up whether you like it or not. Can't have you fading away can we? What does your mother say about all this? Isn't it time you told her?'

'If you think,' said Ma, speaking slowly and loudly down the crackling line to make sure there was no misunderstanding, 'that I will allow you to bring your shame back here, you can think again. Your father has worked his fingers to the bone to build up the business and I will not stand by while you ruin his reputation with your filthy carryings on.' Then she hung up.

When Violet passed her in the chilly hall a couple of minutes later, Nell was shaking, but not with cold.

'What did she say?' asked Violet.

'Nothing,' said Nell, and ran for the bathroom.

*

Violet's pregnancy was proceeding without a hiccup. While Nell grew daily more pale and tired, was miserably sick every evening and began to suffer increasingly from lack of sleep, Violet positively glowed with health and vitality. She had never, thought Nell wryly as she watched her sister singing her way through the housework, looked more beautiful. When Violet reassured her, patting her kindly on the shoulder as if she were a rather backward child, 'It's all right, Nell, if the worst comes to the worst Laurie and I will look after you,' Nell was unable to think of a single thing to say, so she said nothing at all, not even 'thank you' . . .

It must have been her guilty conscience that had led her to misunderstand Marion's talk of pregnancy, she decided. She must have meant Violet when she talked about being careful with pregnancy.

'It's good news, isn't it?' she said brightly when Marion called back, as she had threatened, the following day. 'About Violet's baby, I mean.'

Unexpectedly, Marion snorted her disapproval. 'Frankly, I don't think Laurence could have timed it any worse, what with this bloody war going on ad infinitum and his father hardly ever here.' She straightened her tweed jacket, tugging vigorously at the hem. 'Gerald says I shouldn't interfere and of course he's absolutely right, but a more ill-suited . . . There, I've said it now. Violet's your sister and I'm very fond of the dear girl but – question is, when is your mother going to do something about you?'

'Me?' asked Nell, alarmed again. 'What about me?'

Marion tutted with impatience. 'My dear,' she said, 'you've lost weight, you're not eating properly, Violet tells me you've been sick every night this week—'

'Violet has no call to go—'

'Don't be silly!' Marion strode across the room, and

planted her broad rump firmly on the chair opposite Nell. 'My dear, I'm neither blind nor stupid. Have you told your mother yet?'

Nell, too tired and miserable to dissemble any more, nodded meekly.

'And what did she say?'

'She said . . .' Nell swallowed the lump that was rising in her throat. 'She said she wanted nothing more to do with me.'

'Hmm.' Marion sat back in her chair, placed her elbows on the arms and joined her stubby fingers in front of her nose. 'That rather puts the cat among the pigeons, doesn't it? And what about this chap, the father? Died in the bombing raid, Violet says. Are his family likely to be any help?'

'No!' said Nell, aghast at the thought of Marion Palmer confronting poor Arthur's parents on her behalf. 'I don't even know where they live.'

'I see. Up to us then, is it?'

'No,' began Nell. 'No, of course not. I'll—'

'You won't be able to stay here for ever, I'm afraid.' Marion became brisk, businesslike. 'It's one thing helping you out on a temporary basis – Dr Hills is a very discreet man, fortunately – but I was rather hoping your own family would have taken over . . . Still, let's look on the bright side; with your figure you won't show for a few weeks so I don't think we need to panic just yet. What about Violet – how does she feel about all this?'

Nell shifted uneasily in her chair. 'She's been wonderful. She says she and . . .' Laurence's name, she discovered, was beyond her. 'She says they'll do all they can to help. Marion, I'm so sorry . . .'

'Yes, well. Frightful mess, frankly, the whole thing, and you've been damned stupid, to put it mildly. But these things happen in war. It's the feeling that there's no tomorrow – makes people take risks I suppose. Most important thing is to make sure none of this rubs off on the family.'

Clearly, Marion's sympathy for her predicament, however genuine, extended only so far. Like Ma, no hint of a scandal must sully the family name.

But, thought Nell, what if Marion was to guess the truth, what would she say then . . .?

Chapter Ten

By the time Laurence arrived home for his next leave it was April and time would soon be running out for Nell to keep her pregnancy secret from the prying eyes of the village. He looked older than when she last saw him, the lines etched deeper into his face, his mouth grim where once it had been always smiling.

'He's twenty-five,' Nell remembered Violet telling her just after she first met him, 'but there's something terribly boyish about him. It's so attractive in a man, that spark. Oh, Nell, he's the one all right . . .' It was the spark, Nell thought, looking at him now as he stood in the sitting-room doorway, it was the spark that was missing. The tug of wanting him was joltingly physical, so strong she wondered if the baby could feel it too. The effort of resisting its pull rendered her weak-kneed and tongue-tied.

He was gentle with Violet, kissed her tenderly and told her what a clever girl she was. He had brought her a very beautiful bracelet, garnets and pearls set in gold. 'I called in to see Mama on the way here,' he said, 'and she agreed that you should have it. It's a family heirloom, left me by my grandmother.'

Violet was thrilled. She smiled up at him and said, her voice wobbly with emotion, 'Oh, Laurie, I'm so glad it's all right now. I've been *miserable* since you were last home.'

Nell was already halfway across the room, on her way out because she couldn't bear to watch them. Laurence turned away from Violet and stepped across her path.

'I've brought something for you too,' he said. 'Nell, I'm so sorry about . . .' It could have been a perfectly innocent remark, an expression of sympathy for the predicament his sister-in-law was facing. Except that as he spoke he turned his back on his wife and locked Nell into a blurred blue stare so she knew that he knew, that he was hurting as she was. He held out both hands and the heady scent of primroses, mingled with fresh soil, dew and pipe smoke, drifted up to her nostrils. 'I'll look after you,' he said. 'I promise.' He should have said, '*We*'ll look after you,' but he didn't.

She reached out and took the tiny posy he was holding, her fingers drifting momentarily against his. 'Thank you,' she said. She felt no inclination to cry with him; she didn't want to make him worse. She felt calm for the first time in weeks, strong. She could hear Violet somewhere behind his left shoulder, telling him what a good man he was to have thought of Nell and her troubles, but Laurence was gazing at her and Violet's voice seemed far away, as if it had nothing to do with her. His hands remained outstretched, as if still giving his gift, and the smell of the milky-yellow flowers was overpoweringly sweet.

It occurred to Nell that if she did not do something about it, he would stand there all day, just looking at her. 'I must go and put these in water,' she said and, turning her back on him, she walked out into the passage, making for the kitchen. Behind her she could hear Violet saying, 'Darling, that was *so* kind. I could see Nell was quite moved,' and Laurence answering huskily, 'We must make sure she's safe,' then clattering his tobacco tin and tapping his pipe.

Safe. What a funny word to use. Nell closed the kitchen door behind her, found a small brown milk jug, filled it with cold water and lowered her primroses gently into it. She took a long breath of fragrant air and felt so much better she wondered if she had accidentally happened upon a cure for pregnancy sickness. She was still standing by the sink when Violet found her nearly ten minutes later.

'Are you feeling ill again, dear?' she asked, peering anxiously into Nell's face. 'I ought to warn you, Marion will be here soon. She's called a family conference to decide what to do about your, er . . . problem, so I thought I'd put the kettle on in case she wants tea.' She bustled round the kitchen, chattering, stopping every now and then to examine the bracelet on her slender wrist, demanding Nell's attention, her admiration. Nell leaned against the dresser, half listening, thinking about Laurence, about primroses and pearls and how odd it was that the former should be so much more valuable than the latter, wondering about the nature of beauty and the peculiar chemistry involved in falling in love.

Marion didn't want tea, she wanted whisky. So did Laurence. Nell, feeling deadly sick again, didn't want anything, so Violet's tea went undrunk.

'Well,' said Marion, getting straight down to business. 'What have we so far? Clearly, the young man's family are going to be of no use to us. I've spoken to your mother on the telephone.' Nell's stomach heaved and she swallowed hard. 'She seems to think this is all my fault for not keeping an eye on you and she has made it perfectly clear that she will not have you back unless and until you have disposed of your problem.'

Her problem? Nell's hands went instinctively to her belly, as if she could shield her unborn child from harm by wrapping her arms round it, and she caught Laurence out of the corner of her eye, clenching his fists. He was standing in the shadows near the window. He looked out of place, uncomfortable. He looked as miserable as Nell felt. As she watched he straightened his back and turned towards the fire. She was gripped by panic, knew without a shadow of doubt that he was about to tell, and tasted bile in the back of her throat.

'Mama,' he began. 'Violet, there's something I must—'

'We'll look after it!' blurted Violet unexpectedly, cutting him off in mid-sentence. 'Laurie and I'll take Nell's baby, won't we, darling?' She rose to her feet, bursting with the idea, looking to Laurence to back her up.

'What?' Laurence frowned at her as if he were struggling to understand a foreign language.

'What?' said Nell and Marion in unison.

'Don't you see, this is all my fault!' Violet waltzed round the room in a graceful circle, waving her arms, trying to explain to everyone at once. 'If I hadn't asked Nell to come and stay, she wouldn't be in this mess, would she?'

'Don't be ridiculous!' Marion was dismissive. 'Since when does one have to live in the country to get into trouble? Laurence, for heaven's sake, tell Violet to stop being so silly!'

Nell, watching Laurence again, saw him briefly close his eyes and he turned away from the light, sagged. 'Violet's right,' he said. 'It's because of . . . us . . . that Nell's in this mess. If she'd never met . . . met . . .' He retreated further into the shadows, reached out to grip the back of a chair. 'So it's up to us to help her.'

'You see?' Violet was triumphant. 'The entire village already knows I'm pregnant, but look at Nell – she must be nearly three months gone and she doesn't show at all yet. Who's to say I'm not having twins?' She crossed the room to where Laurence was standing, still gripping the chair with both hands. 'Thank you for backing me up, darling,' she said, planting a kiss on his cheek. 'You're a truly generous man.'

Laurence winced and rubbed at his face; Nell could hear the faint rasping of his fingers against his chin.

'No!' said Marion stoutly. 'No, I absolutely forbid it!'

'But Nell's my sister,' protested Violet, made brave by Laurence's apparent endorsement of her plan. 'This is my niece we're talking about, or my nephew. What's the alternative? Adoption? Dr Barnardo's? I've always wanted lots of children. We can pretend both babies are ours. Can't we, Laurie?'

She was transparently delighted with herself; she'd come up with a solution to the insoluble, she'd saved her sister. Nell, listening to Violet excitedly mapping out her unborn child's future, felt as if the decision had already been taken out of her hands. She no longer dared so much as glance at Laurence, for fear of giving herself, and him, away.

'No!' repeated Marion. 'You can't possibly—'

'Yes we can,' said Laurence. 'Nell can stay here—'

'Absolutely not!' Marion was adamant. 'Imagine the gossip – Sir Gerald Palmer's son living under the same roof as two pregnant women! I will not have your father put in such a compromising position!'

'No one need know she's here.' At the mention of his father Laurence scowled. 'We can hide her until the baby's born, pretend she's gone back to London or something. It'll work, I know it will!'

'Don't be ridiculous! How can you possibly hope to hide her here? Do you seriously think no one will notice? I don't know what's got into you, Laurence! It's a crazy idea and I don't want to hear another word about it—'

'No it's not, it's . . .' Laurence faltered, then, as if suddenly aware that he was the centre of attention, changed tack. 'All right, if she can't stay here we'll find somewhere else for her to stay, somewhere close where we can keep an eye on her. There must be an empty house on the estate . . .'

Nell realised what he was about to say a split second before he opened his mouth.

'Malletts,' he said. 'She can have Malletts.'

'What?' Marion was astonished at the suggestion. 'But there's no electricity, no—'

'Spring's coming.' Laurence addressed Nell directly for the first time since Marion's arrival. 'You could manage, Nell, couldn't you?'

'I . . .'

'Malletts?' asked Violet.

'Gamekeeper's cottage in North Wood.' Marion dismissed the query with a wave of her hand. 'It's completely out of the question; far too primitive.'

'Beggars can't be choosers,' said Laurence. 'Besides, it's no worse than the sort of conditions most of our tenants live in. Would you rather have her up at the Hall?'

Unexpectedly, grudgingly, Marion capitulated. 'Very well. But on your own heads be it.'

She accepted the second whisky Laurence poured for her. She asked Violet if she would be kind enough to get her some water, and waited until she had left the room. Then she rounded on her son and demanded, 'What in God's name is going on, Laurence?'

'Don't ask,' said Laurence, fumbling in his pocket for his pipe. 'Don't ask, Mama. You don't want to know.'

Marion swirled the neat whisky round her glass and swallowed it in one gulp. Then she rose from her chair

and stalked across the room, stopping at the door to subject her son to another hard-eyed examination. 'I warn
you, Laurence,' she said, 'I will not tolerate a scandal.'
Then she turned on her heel and marched out into the
hall. They heard the front door slam, then the Morris
revving on the drive. By the time Violet appeared in the
doorway, holding a jug of water, the engine noise was
already fading into the distance.

'What's happening?' she asked, bewildered. 'Where's
Marion gone?'

'Home,' said Laurence. 'I don't think Mama approves
of your plan to extend our family. Vi . . .'

'Yes, darling?'

'You're a very generous girl,' said Laurence.

Violet's face lit up in a glorious smile. Her childlike
delight at having pleased her husband made Nell feel
sick again, with shame this time.

What have I done? she wrote in her journal that night,
as she sat up in bed trying not to listen to the murmur of
voices in the room next door, comforted by the absence
of squeaking springs which meant that, for tonight at
least, Laurence was not making love to his wife. *What
have I done to us all?*

Chapter Eleven

It took three days to get Malletts ready; three days during which Laurence spent all the daylight hours organising the cottage, fitting black-out blinds, stock-piling wood, coal and food, then borrowing his mother's trailer to take up extra furniture from the Hall under cover of darkness – a couple more chairs, a new mattress for the bed in the tiny attic room under the eaves, sheets, blankets, rugs salvaged from his old nursery.

While Laurence was busy at Malletts, Violet bounced around the village doing her bit for 'the conspiracy' as she persisted in calling it, spreading the word that Nell was returning to London. Pa Carter was seriously short of staff, she volunteered to anyone who would listen; with so many of his girls going off to work in the munitions factories he needed Nell at home to help him out. 'She's promised to come back in the autumn though,' she confided, blushing prettily, 'to help Laurie and me with our new arrival.' She returned from these outings glowing with the compliments that had been showered upon her – how well she was looking, how pregnancy suited her – and bubbling over with excitement at the clever trick they were about to play on their unsuspecting neighbours. It's all just a game, thought Nell, listening to her sister at supper, regaling Laurence with the clever subterfuges, the red herrings she had laid to throw the village off the scent, it's all just a game as far as Violet is concerned. When she broke the news to Mrs Downes that she would be leaving in two days' time, and apologised for the short notice, Mrs Downes patted her hand and said not to worry, young Mrs Palmer had already told her about Mr Carter's staff shortages.

'I shall miss you though, dear,' she said. 'You've been a good girl to me, you really have.'

The following morning when Nell arrived to do her last round, she was presented with a small fruitcake and a note which read, *To Eleanor, with grateful thanks for your willing help over the past few months and wishing you all the best for the future*. It was signed, *Sincerely yours, Grace Darling Downes*, and the little woman seemed as much embarrassed by the revelation of her rather eccentric christian name as she was by Nell's unexpectedly tearful acceptance of her gift. The tears seemed to be near the surface most of the time, these days.

Laurence was avoiding Nell as studiously as she was avoiding him. Walking into the kitchen and finding her there, he would walk straight out again. Passing her in the passage or on the stairs, he would press himself flat against the wall rather than touch so much as the sleeve of her blouse or the hem of her skirt, and turn his face away as if the sight of her was too much for him to bear. His studious adherence to the pact they had made hurt more than Nell would have believed possible. Any secret hope she might have harboured, that he would take things out of her hands, confess everything to Violet and to hell with the consequences, had slipped inexorably away with Violet's offer to adopt her child. How could he, in the face of such generosity, tell Violet that the baby she had so magnanimously promised to take on was his own bastard offspring?

So why, wondered Nell as she lay in bed, staring wide-eyed into the darkness, why, since their affair was over before it had even begun, did it matter so much that Laurence should *not* make love to Violet? Why did she strain her ears every night, then heave a sigh of relief when the giggles and groans, the unmistakeable evidence of private pleasure between husband and wife, failed to happen?

Violet came up each night as usual, just after ten, but Laurence stayed downstairs. Nell could hear him, the faint sound of his tobacco tin, the rattle of the poker, the whisky decanter. She longed to creep downstairs and comfort him, stop the miserable solitary drinking, ached all over with the effort of staying where she was. On that first night after the family conference, it was one o'clock when he finally staggered clumsily to bed, the night after that almost two. Laurence was being absolutely sweet, Violet told her confidentially as they washed up the breakfast things in the kitchen the following morning, so concerned about the baby he couldn't bring himself to 'you know what', just in case. Actually, she added, lowering her voice in case he came in at the wrong moment and caught them talking about him, she didn't feel much like 'that sort of thing' either at the moment, so it was probably just as well . . . Nell, despite the miseries of evening sickness, literally ached with frustrated longing.

Laurence was due to report back to his squadron on the day she moved into Malletts.

'Would you mind taking Nell across, darling?' Nell heard Violet asking him as she made her way towards the kitchen for breakfast.

'Do I have to?' came the reluctant reply. 'Can't you take her?'

'No, I can't.' Nell heard the thud as Violet set the iron back on its rest. 'If I don't get this pile finished you'll have no shirts to take with you. Please, darling, I know you're not feeling specially charitable towards Nell just now . . .'

Nell backed hastily away down the passage, then wandered into the sitting room and stood for a moment staring bleakly at her homely face in the mirror above the mantelpiece. One of Laurence's pipes was sitting there; he had three or four and he was always putting them down, then forgetting where he had left them. Violet had taken to rescuing them and returning them to the mantelpiece. Nell picked it up and cradled it in her hands, bending her head to breathe the scent of the tobacco. She could still feel the faint warmth left in the bowl.

'Right,' she heard Laurence say from the hall, and she jumped, then slipped the pipe guiltily into her skirt pocket. 'I'll put the cases in the car then, shall I?'

'Laurie,' came Violet's confidentially lowered voice, 'you're not having second thoughts about this, are you? Because if you are you have only to say and I'll tell Nell we can't go through with it—'

Laurence's reply was aggressively unequivocal. 'No, of course I'm not having second thoughts. For God's sake, Vi, give it a rest!'

Nell moved across to the window and stood there gripping the sill. She was not sure which was worse: the fear that Laurence might lose his temper and give away their shameful secret, or Laurence acting the faithful husband, behaving as if she and her unborn child were merely an inconvenient burden to be disposed of as neatly and speedily as possible.

She waited until he had dumped her suitcases on the back seat of the Riley, in full public view for any nosy neighbours who might be looking, then walked reluctantly out to the car. She submitted meekly to Violet's embrace, then took a deep breath, opened the door and climbed in beside him. He was making a big show of starting the Riley, revving the engine impatiently, and he didn't look up.

Violet appeared at his window and lowered her head to speak to Nell across him. 'I'll see you soon, dear. You're sure you'll be all right?'

'I'll be fine,' said Nell, nodding solemnly. 'Violet, I'm so grateful—'

'It's nothing. We're glad to help, aren't we, Laurie?' Violet leaned into the car and presented her face to her husband.

Laurence kissed her obediently on the cheek, said, 'Right, let's get on with it, shall we?' then put the car into gear and pulled smartly out of the drive.

He had to stop twice, once for the children pouring out of the village school for their midday break and again for Ernie Beale, pushing his bicycle up the hill towards Post Office Row. He touched his cap as Laurence slowed to let him past, then tapped on the window.

'Good luck, Miss,' he addressed Nell. 'An' I hope as that'll work out for you.' Then he touched his cap again and walked on

'He'll be cooking his mum's lunch when he gets in,' said Laurence, winding his window up. 'Although she's not nearly as helpless as she makes out. Poor bugger's so crippled he can hardly use his fingers at all, he's in constant pain, yet he never complains.' He glanced down at his own strong, healthy hands, tightly gripping the steering wheel. 'Makes you think, doesn't it, how lucky we are?' He leaned forward suddenly, resting his forehead on his clenched fists. 'Jesus Christ,' he murmured. 'Nell . . .'

'Don't,' said Nell, closing her eyes to shut out the sight of him and leaning her head on the window. She heard the scraping of gears and the car began to move again. The space between them, she thought, must be less than six inches, yet for all the good their closeness was, it might have been a million miles. Laurence was taking her to his secret hiding place, knowing that her presence there meant it would no longer be a secret, no longer a safe hiding place for him. She was assailed by a wave of terrible sadness, for what might have been, what *could* have been if they had met earlier, under different circumstances. She wanted to tell him that she loved him, in case she never saw him again, but she couldn't say or do anything that might upset his fragile equilibrium, tip him over the edge into confessing his sins to Violet. So they drove most of the way without exchanging a word, down the hill and across the railway to the main road, left past Home Farm towards Market Needing to follow the river for half a mile, then over the humpback bridge and along the edge of the woods, past the grand lodge-gates of the Hall. Only when Nell felt the jolt as they left the road did she open her eyes.

A faint haze of green was passing by her window, the smaller bushes already putting forth their first hesitant buds, a presage of spring like the snowdrops and aconites. The sun was out for the first time in days, dappling the track with bright spots of gold, and her spirits rose a little – she had always loved the spring.

'Warm weather's on the way,' said Laurence, echoing her thoughts as he brought the car to a halt on the edge of the clearing. 'You'll be safe now.'

Safe, that funny word again. 'And you?' asked Nell. 'Will you be safe?'

'Me?' He turned his head to look at her with haunted blue eyes. 'I'll be fine.'

'Don't you mind all this?'

'Mind? Of *course* I mind. What do you take me for?'

'I meant, don't you mind losing . . .' She waved her hand at the clearing, the tiny cottage basking in the watery sunshine, daffodils just beginning to open beneath its windows. 'All this?'

'I'm not losing it,' he said. 'I'm sharing it. You'll be here, seeing the summer in for me.' He fumbled for his pipe, failed to find it, and took his hands out of his pockets, resting them awkwardly on his knees as if he didn't know what to do with them. 'I love you,' he said.

Nell turned her face sharply away.

'It's all right. I shan't say it again.' He was already opening the car door, swinging his legs out. 'I just wanted you to know, that's all.' He flung open the rear passenger door, hefted the suitcases to the ground, then picked them up and strode purposefully towards the cottage, dropping them just inside the porch. Nell opened her door and planted her feet on the soft ground. Then she straightened up and followed him.

He had lit the range and the room was warm; there was a blackened kettle hanging from the ratcheted pothook to one side of the fire and a bunch of wild narcissi on the table, filling the air with their perfume. He had found an extra dining chair, a faded Turkey carpet for the floor, a battered rocking chair to go by the fire.

'You've been busy,' said Nell, keeping a safe distance, avoiding looking at the place on the rag-rug where they had made love.

The storeroom off the hall to the right, which she hadn't seen the first time she was here, was a repository for rusting gin-traps, old gunny sacks, empty feed bins, spades, forks and shovels, even an ancient cylinder mower; to the existing chaos Laurence had added a bag of potatoes, a heap of old newspapers (in defiance of government exhortations to save paper), a sack of coal, a pile of split logs, paraffin for the oil lamp, four boxes of candles and half a dozen bundles of kindling. As he moved around the cottage he became brisk, businesslike. He explained how to lay the fire, how to keep it in overnight by banking it up with the soft, shingly coal from the bottom of the scuttle then sprinkling it with cold water. He showed her the idle-back tilter which would allow her to pour from the hot kettle without having to lift its heavy weight off the ratchet, how to prime the well-oiled pump in the scullery with a cupful of water before setting it moving. It was the only improvement he had made to the place, he explained; he was here too little to waste time traipsing backwards and forwards to the pond as his predecessors had done, so he had had a well bored and the pump put in two years ago. He took her through to the wash-house, with its shallow stone sink, for which he had found a scrubbing board and a hand-cranked mangle, pointed out the tin bath hanging from a nail on the wall, then led the way up the steep, narrow staircase to the tiny bedroom, where they stood for a moment staring at the wide iron and brass bedstead before clattering hurriedly back down to the tiny hall, then out through the front door into the fresh air, as if the wide open space might evaporate the thoughts which had sprung simultaneously to both their minds at the sight of that inexpertly made double bed.

Laurence, casting about for something to ease the tension, fixed upon the privy and led her round to the back of the cottage. 'Have you ever used a bumby?'

'A what?'

'"Bucket and chuck-it" they call it in Norfolk. An earth closet.'

'Oh.' Nell nodded. 'When I was small we had an Elsan in the back yard, and when I was older I spent my summer holidays with an aunt and uncle in Essex. They had no modern conveniences at all.'

'Good, so you know about filling the bucket with soil after each visit then . . .' He waved vaguely at the woods, grinned. 'Just don't chuck the contents out in a high wind unless you're sure you're facing in the right direction.'

He caught Nell by surprise; grateful for the lightening of his mood, she even laughed. 'I'll manage,' she said confidently.

As they walked in single file along the path back to the cottage the wail of a distant air-raid siren carried faintly across the fields from somewhere on the other side of Ipswich. Laurence stopped short and began to search agitatedly in his pockets for his pipe.

'Here,' said Nell, holding out the one she had stolen from the mantelpiece at the Dower House.

'Thanks.' He glanced at the pipe, then at Nell, frowning, but almost at once the all-clear sounded, announcing a false alarm, and the frown became a smile; his face lit up with relief. 'You see?' he said, 'you'll be safe here,' and he ducked his head and disappeared into the scullery.

Nell stayed where she was, listening. The siren was dying away and she could hear a bird somewhere in the undergrowth, a series of liquid trills, then a couple of clear, single notes. A wood pigeon cooed softly to itself somewhere above her head, the sound of summer, of parched London parks, cotton dresses, hot pavements and petrol fumes. 'We'll be all right here,' she whispered to her baby, laying her hands on her stomach and taking a deep breath of untainted country air. 'We'll be all right, you'll see.'

She found Laurence in the bedroom. He had carried her suitcases upstairs, and he jumped when she appeared, then plunged his hands hastily into his pockets. One of her cases was lying open on the bed and he looked sheepish, defiant. He moved his pipe around between his teeth and puffed hard, hiding his face behind a wall of smoke.

'What on earth are you doing?' she asked.

'Nothing.' He took the pipe from his mouth and leaned across to place it on the chest of drawers behind him, the only piece of furniture, apart from the bed, in the room. 'Touching your things.' He leaned over the case again, feeling beneath the skirts and blouses, tugged. 'What's this?'

'My journal.' Nell started towards him, holding out her hand. 'Give it to me. It's private.'

Laurence held it up, out of her reach. 'So's this place,' he said. 'Share and share alike.'

'Don't—' Nell stood on tiptoe, stretching her arm towards it.

'Why?' He moved out of range then lowered it slowly, spreading his hand across the cover and curling his fingers along its edge as if to open it. 'Am I in it?'

'Please . . .'

He held it out instantly, full of remorse. 'Nell . . .' His voice was unsteady now, shaking with emotion.

'Thank you.' She snatched the book from him, wrapping her arms protectively round it. 'It's time you went. Violet will be wondering where you are.'

'Yes.' Still he stood, staring at her. 'Take care of yourself.'

'I will.'

'And the baby.'

'I will.'

'Whatever you need, Mama'll get it for you. You mustn't be afraid to ask, her bark's worse than her bite.'

'Yes.'

'Well . . .' He grimaced at her. 'Look after the old place for me.'

Nell could feel her resolution leaking away. 'For heaven's sake,' she begged, 'will you please just *go*?'

'Right. Take care.'

'You've already said—'

'Nell—'

'Take care yourself,' said Nell, and turned her back on him. She stood still, holding her journal, listening to his footsteps on the stairs. She heard the front-door latch, then the sound of his car starting. She moved slowly across the room to watch him from the window. She could see his face, but he didn't look up at her. He backed the car carefully round, found first gear, then bumped slowly away along the track. He didn't wave and he didn't look back. Nell lowered her journal to the windowsill, then leaned her arms on it and stared down at the clearing, where a faint blue haze of exhaust smoke still hung. The grass at the edge of the trees was dotted with creamy yellow primroses – it must have been here he had picked her posy, stopping off on his way home. She had brought the flowers with her from the Dower House, folding them between two sheets of brown paper and placing them in her journal until she could press them properly. They had begun to wilt a little in their jug and she had wanted to stop them dying before their time. Here in Laurence's secret place, it occurred to her, their companions would go on blooming year after year. She turned to face the room, straightened her shoulders.

'Come on, Nell,' she said. 'Get on with it. You're the strong one, remember?'

Chapter Twelve

Laurence was everywhere: in the sitting room, looking over her shoulder as she mended the fire or swung the kettle across it to boil; in the scullery, reminding her to prime the pump before she cranked the ice-cold water up from the well; in the tiny bedroom, his head bent low to avoid the crooked beams, the faint scent of his pipe drifting up to her nostrils every time she opened the drawers, wafting past as she settled his sheets and blankets round her and drifted off to sleep in his bed. The blackout blinds were crude affairs, just strips of heavy material nailed top and bottom to wooden batons which slotted into brackets either end of each window, so Nell could lift them off when she wanted to. On the first night, just before she climbed into bed, she blew out her candle, then unhooked the blind and bent her head to peer out at the glade. The moon was shining, draining the daytime colours into black and blue and silver and casting long shadows across the grass; a million stars glittered overhead and the war seemed far, far away. As she leaned forward, resting her arms on the cold stone sill, a deer stepped hesitantly from beneath the trees and sniffed the air, testing for danger. Nell watched, entranced, as it moved nervously out into the open followed closely by another, its dappled flanks merging and blending with the shadows, and a fawn, long-legged and unsteady on slender, gawky hooves.

You see, murmured Laurence in her ear as the trio lowered their heads and began to graze on the sweet new grass, *what a magical place this is . . .?*

She slept that night peacefully, dreamlessly, and woke the following morning to a calmer acceptance of her situation. From now on, she resolved, she must live for each day, stop worrying about the future until it happened.

The quiet took some getting used to – no wireless, no Violet singing or rattling pans in the kitchen, no village noises, no barking dogs. During the day the birds made up for the lack of human sounds, a hundred different calls Nell didn't recognise, as well as the rooks cawing hoarsely in their tall trees behind the Hall, the ubiquitous sparrows, as noisy and quarrelsome as their city cousins, and the seagulls, wheeling and crying over the fields on the other side of the valley, following the plough as it turned the heavy clay soil in preparation for sowing. The only time she felt the lack of noise was in the evenings – she missed her radio concerts then, and Laurence temporarily deserted her.

Still, at least as her pregnancy advanced her sickness abated, and the colour began to return to her cheeks. She moved around her new home with increasing confidence, discovered that the old-fashioned range was surprisingly efficient, that a bath taken in front of the fire using water heated by the copper was an unexpectedly nostalgic pastime, reminding her of those early years of childhood before Violet came along to steal her mother's affection. The soft well water suited her thick springy hair, gave it a sheen it had previously lacked, and her skin began to glow. She filled out, put on weight at last, acquired curves where none had ever been before.

Even using the bumby was less distasteful than she had expected it to be. It was much more basic than the one in Essex she had used as a child, which had at least had a flushing mechanism and been emptied by the honeycart once a week. This was just a thick plank with a hole in it and a galvanised bucket below which had to be topped up with soil after each visit and emptied when full by the user. The privy itself, a small red-brick sentry-box with ventilating gaps above and below the door, a shelf inside for a candle and a supply of torn newspaper threaded onto string, might be draughty and inconvenient, but like the tin bath it held unexpected pleasures – the ivy which trailed across its corrugated roof and curled its rich green tendrils into the interior, the spiders' webs jewelled with dew which sparkled in the corners in the early morning, the view of the stars at night, seen through the open door (no danger here of being surprised by unexpected visitors whilst sitting on one's throne), even the permanent carpet of leaves, blown back in however often she swept them out, rustled in friendly fashion round her ankles as she sat . . .

Marion, tight-lipped and short-tempered, drove Violet up after dark on Nell's fourth day at the cottage, to make sure she had everything she needed. Violet, with her cosseted London upbringing, was shocked by the primitive conditions in which her sister was living, appalled by the isolated situation of the cottage, its lack of neighbours, telephone, electricity. She refused point-blank to use the privy on the grounds that there must be all sorts of creepy crawlies in there, 'and what about rats, or spiders?' If she had known, she confided to Nell as she left, what Malletts was like, she would never have agreed to

Laurence's suggestion. 'But isn't it just typical of a man,' she added, 'not to notice these things?'

'Don't be so naïve,' Marion told her. 'This is how most country people live. Do you think all your neighbours in the village have phones and flush toilets and electricity? It's only people like us who can afford all the mod cons.'

Frightened of staying at the Dower House on her own, Violet was moving into the Hall for the remainder of her confinement. 'So I can keep an eye on her,' remarked Marion shortly. The Dower House was being turned over to an evacuee family so there would be no going back now, even if they wanted to.

The two women had come laden with bits and pieces: three pairs of Sir Gerald's trousers, generously pleated at the waist to accommodate Nell's belatedly expanding figure, typical of Marion Palmer's practical good sense, half a dozen of his old shirts and a couple of faded, old-fashioned maternity dresses which must have been Marion's when she was carrying Laurence more than twenty-five years ago. They brought more paraffin for the lamp, a loaf of fresh bread, tea and sugar, duplicating Laurence's donations, half a dozen eggs, the remains of a large, succulent ham and some dried split peas, so Nell could make soup from the bone once the meat was gone. Nell had no idea how they had managed to get the coupons together for such an embarrassment of riches, and she didn't ask. Grateful though she was for their generosity, when Marion's car finally disappeared into the darkness, casting ethereal pools of light beneath the trees from its taped-up headlights, Nell was glad to see them go. Laurence was everywhere, but to keep hold of him she needed solitude. She couldn't catch the echo of his voice, couldn't feel his presence when his wife and his mother were there.

There had been only one awkward moment, when

Violet, inspecting Nell's bedroom, had found Laurence's pipe sitting on the chest of drawers. He had put it down, explained Nell truthfully, when he carried her cases upstairs, and forgotten to collect it when he left. Violet smiled affectionately at it, then picked it up and put it in her coat pocket, 'for next time he comes home, bless him.' It was only after she had gone that Nell noticed the other pipe, still lying in the hearth between the coal scuttle and a pot of spills, where it had fallen the day Laurence made love to her. She retrieved it, placing it carefully out of sight in the unlit bread oven so she would know where it was. Then she fetched her journal from beneath her pillow and hid that as well, just in case Violet should stumble accidentally upon it and discover the guilty secret it contained.

Marion came back on her own the following night, knocking on the door just after midnight as Nell was thinking about going to bed.

'I've brought something for you,' she said, standing awkwardly in the sitting room doorway, her dumpy shape, vastly magnified, wavering on the wall behind her in the soft yellow light of the lamp. 'In case you needed some noise.'

Nell had been sitting by the fire, reading. She had found Laurence's note the previous night, tucked between the pillowslip and the ticking pillow on her bed, hidden, like her journal, in case of prying eyes. *This is a magical place*, it said, echoing the words she had prophetically put into his mouth as she watched the deer; *read my books*. He had not signed it, but she knew his neat, lawyer's handwriting and she had been profoundly touched by his generosity – she had wandered through the cottage after his departure, touching, stroking, but she had deliberately not taken a single volume from the shelves because of all the possessions Laurence had left in the cottage, more than anything else his books seemed to be part of his private space.

'Is that Laurence's?' asked Marion now. 'And if it is, do you have permission to touch my son's things?'

Nell noted her page number and closed the cover. 'Yes,' she said, 'to both questions. Would you like a cup of tea?'

'No.' Marion turned her back and disappeared outside again. Nell heard her grunting and puffing in the porch. 'Give me a hand,' she commanded peremptorily from the hall. 'Damn thing's heavy.'

Between them they manhandled the bulky, wind-up gramophone through the door, then Marion went back to her car to retrieve the horn from the boot, along with a pile of records. She assembled it on the table, stood back to inspect her work, then disappeared again, returning this time with a bottle of whisky clutched to her bosom. 'A glass, if you please,' she said. 'It's a bit damn much, in my opinion, being harangued over the telephone by one's own son!'

'What?' Nell was searching in the corner cupboard for a glass, still unsure where Laurence kept everything.

'Anything will do,' said Marion impatiently. 'An egg-cup if you can't find a glass. Laurence rang me this evening.' She dragged out a chair and sat heavily, resting her elbows on the table.

Nell emerged from the cupboard with a dusty glass and made for the scullery to wash it, playing for time. Had Marion come just to bring her a gramophone? Or was there some other motive for this unexpected visit? Had Laurence said something? About her? About them? He couldn't have, surely? He had *promised* . . .

She dabbled the glass in the enamel bowl in the sink, gave it a quick whisk round with her fingers, then wiped it dry and brought it back to her visitor. Marion was examining the book she had been reading, turning the pages and frowning. She poured herself a large measure of Johnnie Walker, then replaced the cap on the bottle and swilled the golden liquid round and round the glass.

'Don't you want to know what he was haranguing me about?'

'Yes—' Nell sat down, clasping her hands together to stop them twitching. 'No, I mean—' *Mama's bark is worse than her bite*, Laurence reminded her. *Don't let her intimidate you*. 'Marion,' she began, 'I really am grateful for everything you've done for me—'

'Yes, well.' Marion snorted dismissively. 'It's Laurence you should be thanking.' She settled her broad rump more comfortably on the hard chair and took an exploratory pull at her drink. 'This is his house you're living in, and that's his precious gramophone you've got. He was very insistent that you *must* have it tonight, so you'd better look after it.'

Nell's astonishment rendered her careless. 'How did Laurence know I was missing my music—?'

'Can't imagine,' said Marion drily, 'unless of course he assumed you'd need what he needs.'

Nell could control the expression on her face, but not the colour that flooded her cheeks. Marion placed her glass on the table and tipped it back and forth, watching the whisky coat its sides with a film of alcohol.

'I assume you know that this place belongs to Laurence, rather than to the estate?'

'I . . . yes. He told me when I moved in.'

'And did you know that since the day he took possession he has allowed no one . . .' Marion took another, rather unladylike pull at her whisky, dabbed a drip from the corner of her mouth with an index finger. 'I mean, absolutely *no* one, not even his own mother . . .' The pause was heavy with words left unsaid. 'To even cross the threshold?'

'No.' Nell lowered her head, overcome by embarrassment. 'No, I didn't. He's only letting me stay here for Violet's sake, you know. Because she asked him to . . .'

Marion harrumphed. 'Don't take me for a fool, my dear. So, how are you settling in? Beginning to feel at home?'

It was like a test, a test in which Nell knew neither the rules nor the correct answers. 'Yes. Yes, I'm getting to know my way around. It's a bit basic but it's—'

'It's my son's,' Marion finished for her. 'Which makes it the one place in the world where you would wish to be.'

This time it wasn't a question, it was a statement. Marion reached for the bottle and topped up her glass again. 'Violet doesn't know I'm here, by the way. Pottered off to bed just after ten. Does she always go up so early?'

'Pretty much.'

'Ah.' Marion swilled the whisky round and round. 'Getting her beauty sleep I suppose. Something you or I might need, my dear, but Violet – ridiculous! Laurence missed her, I'm afraid, but then he didn't phone until after eleven. Kind of him, wouldn't you say, to be so concerned about what his wife's sister might need in the way of an evening's entertainment, although why he thought it necessary that *I* should supply it rather than Violet . . . unless, of course, you know something I don't?'

Tired of playing games, Nell stopped trying to second-guess the little woman. 'What do you want, Marion?' she asked. 'If you have something on your mind, why don't you just come out and say it?'

'Right.' Marion rose from the table and began to pace

the room, her vast shadow following her round the walls. 'I am not a fool, my dear, even if your poor sister is. This baby you're carrying – it's Laurence's, isn't it?'

Whatever Nell had been expecting, it wasn't this blunt, full-frontal attack. She sat with her hands resting on the table, and stared at Marion in shocked silence.

'A simple question,' said Marion, 'requiring a simple answer. Is the child you're carrying Laurence's? And assuming it is, what are we going to do about it?'

Perhaps it was the whisky making her garrulous, or maybe it was the surroundings, the atmosphere created by lamplight and firelight and shadows. Whatever it was, by the time Marion took her leave over two hours later, Nell felt she knew her almost as well as she knew her own mother. She liked her a great deal more.

She had always thought of Laurence's mama as a 'type'. Watching her storming round the village, organising a bring-and-buy here, a cake sale or a raffle there, listening to her talk about the problems of running a large country estate or complaining about the troops cluttering up her home, Nell had assumed that Marion Palmer was a typical product of her age and class. She had met a dozen women like Marion since she'd been in Suffolk: strident county ladies with deep bosoms and booming voices, the backbone of the war effort, energetic, bossy women, bred to command, who spent their waking hours busy with good works, who formed committees so they could push their own often entrenched opinions onto others, who organised, cajoled and bullied their local communities into far greater efforts than they might otherwise have attempted. Despite their ability to get things done, to solve problems and foster a spirit of co-operation between neighbours, they were not the sort of women with whom Nell had ever felt at ease. She disliked the condescension which so frequently went with their self-confidence, the kindly contempt with which they so often treated those they saw as their social inferiors.

But Marion Palmer, Nell discovered during the time they spent together that night, was not just an overbearing upper-class matriarch. Nell had thought she knew how the top echelons of society worked – they intermarried within their own small circles and looked down on the lower classes, hence the Palmers' barely concealed disapproval of Laurence's choice of wife. When Marion spoke of her despair over her son's marriage, how she had warned him he was making a mistake, how, with typical stubbornness, he had gone ahead regardless, Nell's reaction was instinctively hostile.

'I told him it would end in tears,' said Marion, 'and of course it has—'

'What do you mean, *of course* it has?' objected Nell. 'Just because Violet's the daughter of a tradesman doesn't mean she's unfit to marry your son—'

Disconcertingly, Marion let out a loud bark of laughter. 'My dear girl,' she said, 'I never suggested she was. It would be completely hypocritical of me to do so, since I am the daughter of a tradesman myself.'

She had taken her whisky across to the fire, commandeering the leather chair and inviting Nell to sit on the rocking chair Laurence had brought from the Hall. She seemed highly amused by the astonishment with which Nell greeted the information about her antecedents, resting her glass precariously on the arm of her chair and chuckling richly. 'My pa was a self-made man, what you might call a rough diamond, and he built up his business from nothing, just like yours did. By the time he died he owned two textile mills just outside Halifax, and I was his only child. My pa had *brass* but no *class*,' she said, pronouncing 'brass' and 'class' to rhyme with 'lass', mocking Nell's accusation of snobbery, 'whereas Gerald,' reverting to her usual clipped BBC vowels, 'had *class* but no *brass*.' She leaned over the side of the chair and lifted the bottle from the hearth, poured another whisky. 'Just as well, to be honest – with a face and figure like mine, a girl needs all the help she can get. Gerald never made any secret of what he was looking for. When he inherited the estate from his father it was in a pretty bad way, run down, badly managed, short of capital. He was on the lookout, he told me the first time we met, for a rich widow.' She considered Nell for a moment, head on one side. 'And I hope you won't be insulted, my dear, if I suggest that you will know what I'm talking about when I tell you I took the opportunity because I didn't think there was likely to be another.'

Nell was slow to catch on. 'What opportunity?'

'To get married, of course; to get myself a husband. It was a straightforward business transaction. I had something Gerald wanted, and he had something I wanted.'

'Yes?'

Marion shifted her rump squeakily on the leather chair and sipped at her whisky again. 'It was a once-in-a-lifetime chance. I was a plain woman, the wrong side of twenty-five, in search of a husband. I was looking for what every woman wants – a home of my own, preferably one in the style to which I was already accustomed, and a family. So I proposed.' She chuckled again. 'Of course, Gerald wasn't too sure to begin with. Frankly, in the looks department I wasn't much of a catch.' Nell, on a wave of sympathy for the little woman, made deprecatory noises. Marion dismissed her pity with a cluck of impatience. 'But we came to an agreement in the end. He promised me a free hand to do as I pleased with the estate, and I promised him the freedom to do whatever *he* pleased, just so long as he didn't rub my nose in it.' She laughed again, but wryly this time. 'You see, my dear, if you have money, really serious money, you can buy your child almost anything her heart desires – the best education, the best finishing schools, the best clothes.' Her gaze drifted away from the fire into the shadows behind Nell's chair and her usual brisk, matter-of-fact manner momentarily went missing. 'But you can't buy her a pretty face. If he could have, my pa would have done it like a shot. But since he couldn't he did the next best thing. He bought me Gerald Palmer instead.'

'Sir Gerald got a bargain,' said Nell, feeling another rush of sympathy for the little woman.

'Yes, well, that's as maybe.'

Nell knew almost nothing about Marion's husband. On the one occasion she had met him he had, like most men, scarcely noticed her presence at all. Towards Violet he had been charm personified.

'Still,' she said, increasingly uncomfortable with the way the conversation was going, 'you get on pretty well together, don't you?'

Marion's glass seemed to be empty again. She reached for the bottle. 'My dear, we lead separate lives. Gerald prefers to spend his time in London and I'm quite happy to live in Suffolk, overseeing the day-to-day running of the estate.' She shrugged, sipped. 'Oh, it worked well enough when we were first married; he had plenty of money at last, and he enjoyed all the usual country pursuits. And of course, during the last rumpus he was in his element, had a good war, if you know what I mean. But then he was badly wounded at Ypres and invalided out. He was lucky not to lose his leg, and he came home after his stint in hospital to find he couldn't do all the things he had enjoyed before the war.' She stopped, sighed. 'Of course if Laurence had been . . . but all that's water under the bridge.'

'If Laurence had been what?'

Marion was slumped in her chair, sprawling inelegantly with her knees apart and the edges of her pale green bloomers showing. Her capacity for alcohol was prodigious – the bottle was over a third empty, but still her enunciation was clear, clipped, precise. 'Laurence is a misfit,' she said, 'born at the wrong time and in the wrong place. It's my fault, I suppose; just one of those things – took me ten years to fall for Laurence and I didn't manage any more. I should have liked a big family, and maybe if Laurence had had a sister, or a younger brother . . . No . . .' Her gaze drifted to the fire and she sighed again. 'An older brother would have been better, would have taken the pressure off him a bit. His father was thrilled with him to begin with, a big, strapping son, an heir to take over the estate, do all the things he could no longer do himself. He started him early, riding lessons from the age of five, bought him his own pony for his eighth birthday, just before he went away to school. Maybe if Gerald had been a bit more patient—'She stopped abruptly, shook her head. 'Still, doesn't do, does it, to apportion blame? And it was my fault too, of course, for not seeing what was happening and doing something about it.'

'And what was happening?'

'Laurence is a dreamer; only children often are, you know; even when he was small he was always off somewhere in his imagination, had his nose stuck in a book from the moment he could read. That pony, it was nothing special, just a little round barrel of a Shetland, but he loved it to distraction. It was the best present he'd ever had, he said, and that first year when he came home from school for the summer holiday he used to take himself off every day, wheedling a packed lunch from Cook and riding out all over the estate from morning to night.' Marion smiled, a fond, face-softening smile, looked, for a moment, almost handsome. 'Of course, he was as safe as houses really, but he thought he was Ivanhoe on his trusty warhorse. It became a bit of a game with the estate workers, seeing who could spot Master Laurence first each day, and how far away from home he'd fetch up. They used to flag me down in the pony trap to tell me what he was up to. Ernie Beale came across him one day right over at Arkenfield, jousting with a broomhandle at a half-finished hayrick.' More whisky was poured and Marion sipped again. 'But then the following year his father decided it was time to start him on more adult pursuits – after all, the shooting and fishing are a large part of what the estate is about, so he was going to have to learn sooner or later. Gerald bought him a gun, and taught him to shoot, clay pigeons to begin with, of course, you don't want to waste live birds on a novice. He was pleased with him, said the boy had a natural eye, and when he came home for Christmas that year Gerald decided he was ready for the real thing. They were getting along fine until Laurence bagged his first pheasant. Normally of course the beaters retrieve the birds, or the dogs, but because it was his first Gerald thought he'd put the damn thing right into Laurence's hands, give him the thrill of handling it while it was still warm. He was only ten at the time but I can remember his face when he got home as clear as day, even now. "It was so *beautiful*, Mama," he kept saying, "and I *killed* it." He was horrified by what he'd done.' She paused, staring into the shadows again. 'It was the pony that finished him, though.'

'The pony?'

'His beloved Shetland. He grew out of it quite quickly, of course. By the time he was eleven his legs dangled practically to the ground, so his father decided it was time to get him something bigger, something he could hunt on. He found him a bay, lovely animal, bit strong for him, but he was growing so fast it made sense. He was reluctant about the hunting; he'd already let his father down over the shooting, and as an ex-MFH—'

'MFH?'

'Master of Foxhounds. As an ex-MFH Gerald had a position to uphold, didn't want to be embarrassed again. Laurence knew what went on, of course, or he thought he did. He was terribly mixed up about the whole thing, attracted by the glamour when the meet was at the Hall, all those pink coats and magnificent horseflesh, handsome men and women, and he was desperate to make up for letting his father down, wanting to please him. But he was repelled by the thought of what happened to the fox at the end of it. He was nearly twelve by then, and. . .' Marion sipped at her whisky again. 'Well, to be honest, I'd put my foot down, said it was too dangerous, didn't want him breaking his neck going at a fence. Gerald saw the sense of it for a while – after all, with an only child, you have to think about these things. But when he reached his twelfth birthday, Gerald said it was time I stopped mollycoddling the boy.'

'He hated it,' said Nell, remembering. 'Hunting, I mean. He told me, said he was a great disappointment to his papa.'

Marion shook her head. 'Not to begin with he wasn't. For the first couple of weeks his father was thrilled to bits with him. He'd asked one of the whips to keep an eye on the boy, and he followed his progress from covert to covert in the trap, monitoring his performance; he was absolutely fearless, Gerald said, tackled fences even some of the most experienced riders avoided, always right there in the thick of things. He did as he was told, didn't ride over hounds, treated the whips with respect. Gerald was proud of him, bragged about him all over the county. I remember when Laurence came back after that first day he was scarlet in the face with excitement, told me hunting was the best fun he'd ever had in his life.'

'So what went wrong?'

'Ah.' Sudden, unexpected tears filled Marion's eyes and the whisky was gulped. 'They found, didn't they . . .'

'Found?'

'Put up a fox.'

'But don't they always?'

'No, not always. The previous winter had been hard, the spring was cold and damp; the fox population was down a bit, so on Laurence's first three outings they had an exhilarating gallop across country with nothing to show for it at the end but a cold hack home.' She stopped, not drinking now, just staring at nothing, holding her glass at a precarious angle and frowning.

'They found. . .' prompted Nell gently.

Marion jumped visibly. 'Mm, they found. And Laurence was in at the kill . . . I'm not sure I should tell you this.'

'Go on,' said Nell. Laurence's face came back to her, as he crouched in front of her. *Who else would you tell . . .?* and she knew suddenly what he'd meant when he said he hated hunting, knew what was coming even before Marion told her.

'He came home with blood on his cheeks.'

Nell grimaced.

'Oh, not his blood, he wasn't hurt or anything. It's

customary, you see, to blood the youngest member. His father got there just in time, so he was watching when Laurence was awarded the brush, a great compliment. Laurence humiliated him in public, in front of all his friends, his employees, in front of every hunt follower for miles around. He threw the brush down, charged right through the pack, practically a hanging offence in hunting circles, and galloped off into the blue. It was after midnight when he got home; Cook came to get me – she'd found him huddled over the fire in the kitchen, shivering with cold and sobbing fit to break your heart.' She glanced up, pulled a face. 'Lamp's going out,' she said.

The lamp was running low on fuel, the flame sputtering and dipping. Nell went to deal with it. She felt sick, sicker than she had felt for days. 'He got a thrill from it,' she said over her shoulder, 'didn't he?'

'And how do you know what goes on in my son's mind?' Marion's tone was belligerent, the whisky showing for the first time.

Nell turned the wick down a little, reached across the table to pick up the candleholder Laurence had left there for her, then returned to the fire and picked a spill from the pot in the hearth. 'It's the primitive hunting instinct,' she suggested as she held it out to the flames. 'Isn't it? A throw-back to when we lived in caves and had to kill to stay alive.' She lit the candle and placed it on the right-hand hob, then went back to the oil lamp and turned the wick right down, snuffing out what was left of the flame. A thin curl of paraffin-scented smoke drifted up towards the ceiling and the shadows deepened. 'He gets a thrill out of killing Germans. That makes him feel bad too.'

Marion was recovering her dignity, and her temper. 'I should have thought hating Germans was rather more appropriate these days than not,' she said briskly. 'I haven't told you the worst.'

Nell returned to the fire and sank down again on the rocking chair. She was exhausted; it was nearly two in the morning and talking about Laurence, about the secrets they had shared in this room, made her long for a sight of his face, the sound of his voice.

Marion drained her glass and put it down carefully in the hearth. 'The day after he disgraced himself he was summoned to see his father. He defied him, refused point-blank to talk about the incident, said he wasn't going to apologise and he was never going to hunt again. He was on his way to Home Farm to see his pony. He hadn't been to see it for over a week; it had been moved down to the farm to make way for his new hunter and that was all he could think about, that he'd been neglecting it.' She rose stiffly from her chair, rubbed her back, then bent to pick up her empty glass. 'His father told him there wasn't any point. The pony wasn't at Home Farm any more. He'd had it sent to the knacker's.' She straightened up, squared her shoulders. 'It'd been fed to the hounds that morning.'

The silence was profound. Nell tried to imagine what the revelation must have done to a sensitive child. She tried to imagine Sir Gerald perpetrating such a petty viciousness, but could summon only the urbane, handsome man she had seen at Violet's wedding, so like Laurence with his charming smile and commanding presence.

'How could he be so cruel?' she asked. 'How could he do such a thing to his own son?'

Marion moved across the room into the shadows, making for the door. For a woman who had imbibed almost half a bottle of whisky, she was remarkably steady on her feet. She stopped, turned, shrugged, but

Nell couldn't see her expression. 'I have asked myself,' she said, 'a thousand times, whether he did it deliberately. It's standard practice of course. When an animal reaches the end of its useful life it's turned into dogmeat; there's no room for sentimentality in the country. But all the same . . . I wish—' She cut herself off, leaving the words hanging in the air.

'What do you wish?'

'I shouldn't be saying this.' Marion sighed. 'Probably wouldn't if I hadn't drunk so much whisky. I wish Laurence had met you first. I think . . . all water under the bridge now, of course, but I think if he'd met you first, you might have been able to save him.'

'Save him? Save him from what?'

'From himself. Or what he imagines is himself. He thinks he's like his father.'

'Why? Why should he think that?' asked Nell.

Marion moved slowly back into the room and sat down heavily at the table. 'When Laurence was about four he started having bad dreams, waking up night after night screaming his head off. I told Gerald I was worried about him, but he said to leave him alone, accused me of treating the boy like a cissy, rushing off to comfort him every time he cried. I should stop fussing, he said, he'd soon get over it if I didn't take any notice. He wouldn't tell me what the dreams were about to begin with—'

'Who wouldn't?'

'Laurence. Said they'd get him if he told, whoever *they* were. It took me three months to find out what was going on . . .' Nell heard the chair scrape on the flagstones as Marion drew it closer so she could rest her arms on the table. 'Gerald'd taken to staying up late.' She paused, a thought occurring to her. 'Like Laurence. Like father, like son.' She turned her face, ghostly white in the shadows, towards Nell. 'Where was I?'

'Sir Gerald,' prompted Nell. 'Staying up late.'

'Ah. Yes. "Toughening him up," Gerald said when I asked him what was going on. "Don't want you turning the boy into a milksop." He'd been going to Laurence's room late at night, you see, and waking him up, telling him stories about the war. I caught them at it one night, Laurence sitting bolt upright in bed with his eyes like saucers and his hair all sticking up on end, watching his father demonstrate how to twist a bayonet so as to spill a man's guts with the maximum efficiency.' A piece of coal spat from the fire, and they both jumped. 'Why do men do that?' asked Marion. 'Why do they feel the need to prove themselves all the time? I swear Gerald got a thrill from it, terrorising his own child, reliving the war, sights he'd seen, deeds he'd done, a dozen different ways to kill the enemy, how the gases in a dead horse's stomach build up till the animal literally explodes with the pressure . . .' She petered out, began again. She sounded infinitely weary. 'It took me weeks to get it all out of Laurence. Sometimes he was physically sick talking about it. And yet part of him revelled in it – the excitement of sharing secrets with his father, his pride in what Gerald had done. His father was a hero. He had the medals to prove it, and Laurence wanted to be like him.'

Nell closed her eyes. So that was where it had all come from – Laurence's ambivalent attitude to his father, to hunting, killing Germans, the streak of cruelty he was convinced he possessed. *Hawley, Ware, Smith*; it was so easy to miss the connection, to feel the excitement and ignore the cost in human life.

Marion's revelations were over; she was on her way home. She pushed her chair back and moved out into the hall. 'Some time soon,' came her voice, 'we're going to have to decide what to do about you and your baby. But not tonight, eh? Sleep well, my dear.' Nell heard the creak of unoiled hinges, the clatter of the latch, and she was gone.

Nell slept late the following morning, waking to the sun on her face and a discordant tumult of birdsong. Lying in bed with her hands resting protectively on her stomach, she went over the previous night's conversation again and again. For the first time she began to think about her own child, to *really* think about it, not just as a vague, almost spiritual entity, but as someone real, a potential human being with all the vices and virtues that entailed. She wondered whether she was carrying a boy or a girl, decided, instinctively, that it was a boy, then moved on to imagine what he would look like, whether he would take after her or Laurence, whether he would be tall or short, fat or thin, obedient or wilful. Padding downstairs in her nightgown to make tea, she grew by turns impatient that it was taking so long for him – yes, it was definitely a him, it *felt* like a boy – to grow, curious about the partially formed person she was carrying around inside her, exhilarated at the prospect of seeing him for the first time, then unbearably sad, that she would almost certainly have to give him up before she had a chance to get to know him. Moving about the sitting room in her bare feet, reviving the fire, filling the kettle and setting it to boil, fetching the tea caddy and warming the pot, she grew more and more angry, that the rules made it impossible for a woman to bring up a child alone. While she waited for the kettle she fetched her journal and sat at the table to put down her fury in black and white.

In fifty years' time, she wrote, scoring the words hard into the paper, venting her spleen on the page, *it will*

have ceased to matter whether children are born in or out of
wedlock. In fifty years' time we will have grown out of judging
so harshly. Why is it always the women who suffer?

When she had got it all off her chest she put her journal back in the bread oven and went upstairs to get
dressed.

Chapter Thirteen

The anger was hard to sustain. Gently, subtly, the cottage subsumed her. Cut off from the outside world, without up-to-date newspapers or wireless, it was easy to lose her grasp on reality. The place, the fabric of its walls, the floors she walked on, the very air she breathed belonged to Laurence. Sometimes Nell imagined he was there, watching her as she made the tea or scrubbed Marion's faded maternity dresses in the wash-house sink, that he had left part of himself behind specially to keep her company. She didn't tell Marion – she would have told her not to be such a romantic fool – but as the days passed she grew more and more convinced that she was becoming part of a living, breathing entity. Sometimes, placing her hand on the wall, she thought she could feel the plaster vibrating faintly beneath her fingers; perhaps it was her condition, playing tricks on her mind, but she became convinced that the house was alive, even that it was benevolently aware of her presence, that it was keeping her safe as Laurence had promised it would.

With the warmer weather came damp and fog. Sometimes, on those mornings when the mist was heavy along the river at the bottom of the valley, she would look out early to blue sky above, a wide bowl of milk where the grass should be and the trees, bereft of their lower limbs, floating at anchor in the white sea like green, arboreal islands. She would lean out over the stone sill of her bedroom window and dabble her hand in the mist, bring her fingers up dripping with moisture, then lick the cold droplets from her skin and imagine herself adrift in a thatched, whitewashed Noah's Ark. She grew enamoured of the fancy that she and her unborn son were the only souls in the world with their heads in the sun, that somewhere down below, the rest of the human race was blundering about in the dark, waiting for the daylight to get through; she had to keep reminding herself that beyond the trees, only a few hundred yards down the green track, life was going on without her, that war was still being waged, crops planted, children attending school, workers toiling in factories and fields, shopgirls polishing counters.

Only Laurence was real; somewhere out there, she told her unborn son as she sat on the windowsill in her nightgown, he was sitting on an island of his own with the sun warming his face, just like them . . . and although she thought about him constantly she missed him hardly at all, because he was still there with her. Every night now she sat by the fire, reading his books and listening to his records, Beethoven's *Pastoral* Symphony, Schubert's *Trout* Quintet, Debussy's *Prélude à l'après-midi d'un faune*, Mozart's *Requiem*, soft, dreamy music which further increased her sense of unreality. As the days passed, the world outside slipped inexorably through her fingers, until it seemed less solid than the world inside Laurence's books; even the air-raid sirens, the drone of aircraft overhead, the occasional distant explosion failed to dent her sense of detachment. None of it was anything to do with her anymore.

Which was probably why, when she saw what looked at first glance exactly like a leprechaun, she was not as surprised as she might otherwise have been.

She was hanging out the washing when she spotted him, hovering under the trees like a crumpled goblin. His lined face was shadowed by the bright new growth around him, his clothes, browns and tans and greys, melded with the background so if she hadn't seen him move out of the corner of her eye she wouldn't have noticed him at all. She had been living at the cottage for less than two weeks, but already she had practically ceased to worry about the prurient interest the village might be taking in her. She had no idea how long he had been standing there, but there was no way of escaping – it was far too late for that.

'Morning, Mr Beale,' she greeted him, and he touched his cap, then moved hesitantly out into the clearing. Nell could see his bicycle behind him, leaning against a tall, rangy sapling, up which a climbing plant was merrily leaping.

'Mornin', miss.' He touched his cap again with twisted, lumpy fingers, and smiled tentatively. 'I hope I'm not intrudin', only Lady P, she said she thut that'd be awright, seein' I already knowed . . .'

'Knowed?'

'That you was here.'

As he drew closer he removed his cap altogether, revealing a pale, shiny bald pate surrounded by a fluff of silver down. Nell dropped the pegs she was holding back into the basket and straightened up.

'How did you find me?'

He shuffled his feet and twisted his cap awkwardly between his crippled hands. 'Mr Laurence, when he's away, he like me to keep a' eye on the place, make sure tha's awright. I come up unce a week, just to check like, so when I see car lights up the drift—'

'The drift?'

Ernie pointed towards the green track to the road. 'The drift, tha's what folk call it round here. Anyhow I thut I best have a look. But then I sin Lady P gettin' out at the door, and I knowed she dun't hardly niver come here, so the next day I asks her . . . and she say there's a lady livin' here secret like, so I thut mebbe I best kip away for a bit . . .'

'Ah.' Nell pushed her hair out of her eyes and bent to heft the wicker washing basket onto her hip. She was wearing one of Sir Gerald's old shirts, and a pair of his trousers, held up with a length of binder twine she'd found in the storeroom. Ernie was trying hard not to look, but her condition was now beginning to show, the bump exaggerated by her odd clothes. He would draw the same conclusions, she was sure, as Violet had, but she wondered whether he had told anyone else she was here; if he had it would no doubt be all round the village that Violet Palmer's unmarried sister was pregnant and living all alone at Malletts. After that, it was only a question of time before someone more meddlesome than Ernie Beale put two and two together and linked her with Laurence. 'Would you like a cup of tea?' she asked, trying to ease the awkwardness. 'Come inside and I'll put the kettle on.'

The little man seemed shocked by the very suggestion. No, he said, he dursn't. In the four years he'd been looking after the place, he explained, he'd not been inside once. Mr Laurence wouldn't like it.

'I'm sure he wouldn't mind,' Nell persisted, but Ernie refused to budge. 'Well, then,' she said, 'I'll bring you one out, shall I?'

He seemed a bit happier with that. It was a warm

morning, almost the first, after a long, hard winter, when one could actually believe that summer might be just around the corner. Beneath the trees a patchy carpet of blue was spreading as the bluebells came into flower, and the green fuzz of a fortnight ago was now an explosion of exuberant new growth.

Nell carried out the dining chairs and invited Ernie to sit down. He was uneasy and immediately started making his excuses – he hadn't meant to stay, he'd just popped over to see if there was owt she needed, he didn't want to put her to no trouble. It took all Nell's limited diplomatic skills to persuade him. The tea seemed to relax him a little, but it was only when she began to question him about their surroundings that he unbent a little.

'Best time o' year, this,' he told her, sitting bolt upright on the edge of his chair with his cap tucked in his pocket and his short legs planted wide apart so he could make a run for it if he had to. 'When the blackthorn and the bullace comes into flower you can reckon as spring's well and truly here.'

The country education of which Nell had bragged to Laurence, actually gleaned during an annual fortnight on her aunt and uncle's farm near Saffron Walden when she was lent to Pa's sister as an unpaid kitchen skivvy during the hectic weeks of harvest, was limited at best. 'Bullace?' she queried.

'Cherry plum we call her,' explained Ernie. 'Like a yaller plum but roundabout the size of a grape. She make a lovely jam. Now that over there, tha's the Blackthorn, you make sloe gin with her, and tha's a wild cherry, Gean we call her. The one next the cherry, she's a Guelder rose, Wayfarin' tree. Smell grand of a evenin', she do.'

Nell rose from her chair and strode across the glade towards the spot where Ernie had left his bicycle, talking over her shoulder. 'What's this climbing plant?'

'Clematis. Old Man's Beard. Come the autumn he's covered in grey fluff, like on a old gent's chin.'

'And this, with the tight buds?'

'Hawthorn. She wun't be out for another month yet.' Ernie glanced sideways at her and chuckled, his eyes creasing with sly amusement. 'Even you Lunnon girls must'a heard of the May tree.'

Nell smiled back at him. Now that she was nearer she could see the narrow path, winding into the distance towards the Hall, barely visible unless you were looking for it. She touched the sapling against which Ernie's bike was leaning.

'And what's this?'

Ernie came closer and peered short-sightedly at the pale, narrow-leafed specimen Nell was indicating. 'Ah,' he said. 'That there's Gatteridge, that is. Spindle, you'd call her.' He fumbled beneath the foliage with clumsy fingers to reveal a spray of tiny, tight-shut buds on a straight, graceful stem. 'She dun't put on her best bib and tucker till autumn, this lady.' He went to grip the thin, whippy branch but his fingers, welded together by arthritis, skated ineffectually past. He tried again, managed to grasp it this time, nudged the insignificant cluster of buds with his other hand. 'She have berries then, lovely things they are, like pink sugar buttons off a lady's dress. She's my favourite.'

He looked up, shyly offering her his enthusiasm, and Nell smiled at him again. 'I can't wait to see it,' she said. 'Mr Beale . . .'

'Ernie,' he said, finally at ease now he was dealing with matters he understood. 'You call me Ernie, miss. Mr Laurence do.'

'And my name's Eleanor,' said Nell, 'but everyone calls me Nell.'

Ernie shook his head. 'No, miss, that wun't seem right, not with you bein' Mrs Laurence's sister.'

'Ernie, have you told anyone else about me?'

No longer on the subject of plants Ernie grew wary again. 'No, miss,' he said. 'I reckoned if Mr Laurence tucked you away up here, that were 'cause he wunt to keep you private.'

Nell nodded. 'Has Lady Palmer said anything to you about . . .?' She gestured at the bulge beneath her voluminous shirt and Ernie's already tanned face darkened further with embarrassment. He moved past her, making for his bike.

'I better be on my way . . .'

Nell persisted. 'Ernie, it's important this doesn't get out.'

He had reached his bicycle by now, grasped the handlebars and hefted it away from its resting place. Having something solid to hold on to seemed to restore his confidence a little. 'I wun't tell nobody, miss.' He leaned the saddle against his hip and fumbled in his pocket for his cap. 'I've knowed for weeks now, that you wus . . .' He blushed again. 'You know whut, but I han't breathed a word to a blessed soul.'

'Oh, *Ernie*!' Nell's voice was squeaky with alarm. 'If you've noticed, the rest of the village must have noticed as well! And the whole point of moving here was so that no one would find out. Lady Palmer agreed to let me stay only if I kept out of sight. The last thing she needs is a scandal—'

It was Nell's turn to be agitated, Ernie's turn to play the soothing uncle. 'Now then,' he said, plonking his cap back on his head, 'don't you go gettin' yourself in a tizz. I'm tellin' you, ain't nobody in the village know bar me. And I wun't say nuthin' to no one.'

'But if no one else has noticed how did you guess?'

Was it her imagination, or did Ernie's already lugubrious face take on the mournful aspect of a man bereaved? I knowed a . . . lady once,' he said at last. 'There's things you notice, if you're a noticin' sort of chap, a look what hangs about a . . . lady when she's . . .' He gazed determinedly into the middle distance, embarrassed again. 'But you dun't wunt'a worry. There were a mite cagmag in the village over you and that young Mulligan chap, but there ent nobody sayin' nuthin' about you now.' He wheeled his bike a bit further, turning it in a narrow circle so it was pointing along the winding path away from the clearing. He touched his cap again, said, 'Best get on,' then stopped, half turned. 'Mr Laurence,' he said, 'he trust me not to blab.' He rubbed his cap backwards and forwards across his head, scratching at the sparse silver hair above his left ear. 'I put the word about when he fust took this place over, as there was ghosts. Laid it on with a trowel, I did, flickerin' lights, strange noises, all sorta carryin's on. So folks dun't come near now. She's a haunted county, Suffolk, and we dun't like to take chances with the supernat'rul. Tha's the ghosts as kip 'em out. Can't stop folk talkin' a'course, but what you got to remember is them round here either lives on the estate or works on it, most times both. We need the Hall for the roofs over our heads and the food on our tables, so tha's not for us to go blabbin' the family's business about, is it? You like flowers?'

'What?' The abrupt change of subject caught Nell by surprise. 'Yes, I suppose so. Why?'

'Got some beddin' plants left over, tha's all,' said Ernie. 'Might bring you some up.' He considered her for a moment. 'Mr Laurence allus said if he got the time he'd grow his own spuds like, and a few carrots and stuff, somewhere to empty the bumby bucket. Might dig you a veggie patch – if tha's what you'd fancy?'

Nell, touched out of all proportion by the offer, found her eyes filling suddenly, stupidly, with tears. 'Yes,' she said. 'Yes, I should love it. Thank you, Ernie.'

Over the ensuing weeks Nell became accustomed to the sight of Ernie Beale's bent figure lurking on the edge of the clearing. He never came to the door, never made an appointment. He just turned up, leaned his bicycle against a tree, and stood patiently watching the back door until Nell appeared to hang out the washing or beat the mats. Only then would he approach shyly to ask if miss was busy today, or would she like him to lend a hand?

Nell, aware that he was giving up almost all his limited spare time to come and see her, was doubtful to begin with, but he seemed so keen that it grew easier with each visit to say yes. He dug flowerbeds for her beneath the cottage windows, planted pansies, forget-me-nots, lupins, nasturtiums, and next to the porch Black-eyed Susan and Morning Glory. A woman of city pavements, of tarmac and concrete, Nell watched them grow with all the fascination of a small child. Ma had never taken an interest in gardening – the two-up-two-down in which Nell had spent the first five years of her life had had a backyard, not a garden, and when Pa's business began to flourish and they moved to a bigger, better house, Ma's first act was to call in the builders and have them put crazy-paving down. 'Far too much trouble,' she said. 'All that weeding and tidying.' A couple of floribundas at the front to keep up appearances with the neighbours were quite enough for Ma. Nell found Ernie Beale's assertion that flowers were something no one should have to manage without a revelation.

As spring advanced her enthusiasm increased. After

the bluebells came buttercups, and ox-eye daisies which glowed with ghostly phosphorescence at dusk like pale miniature reflections of the moon. Around the edges of the glade swathes of cow and dog parsley blossomed about the feet of sycamore and beech, fluttering in the breeze like fine lace curtains at a bedroom window, and tall mullein thrust up between them. Pale mauve wood-violets opened along the edge of the pond; later in the year, Ernie said, after they had finished flowering, they would hide from the summer heat beneath the dark, glossy leaves and white, frothy flowers of meadow-sweet. Ernie knew the names of them all, celandine, wood-spurge, selfheal and yellow rattle, delicate white wood anemone and pale pink columbine, which twined itself relentlessly round whatever it found in its path. The forget-me-nots burst into flower beneath the cottage windows and the lupins thrust up green spikes tinged with pink or purple. Each day now Nell woke with a new sense of anticipation, wondering what she would find that had not been there the day before.

Some things she discovered for herself, the hard way. When the elder which leaned over the pond at the back of the cottage produced an abundant mass of sweet-smelling blossoms, she picked armfuls of the stuff for the sitting room, only to discover that what smells sweet on the tree can smell foul when picked. The house reeked of tom-cat for days afterwards and it was a lesson she did not forget.

She grew physically stronger, and her skin began to glow with the fresh air. She soaked up like blotting paper all the information Ernie could provide and stored it in her memory for future reference. She watched the birds, noted their characteristics, pored over Laurence's reference books searching for them or begged Ernie to identify them: the jay with his fancy peach-coloured weskit and blue and white arm-bands, the green wood-pecker with his swooping, dipping flight (the wet-bird, Ernie called him, or the yaffle-bird, because of his curious croaking cry), the gang of itinerant long-tailed tits which visited briefly, hanging upside down in the silver birches twittering and snickering like garrulous circus acrobats, then decamping as suddenly as they had arrived for pastures new. Pudden-e-pokes, Ernie called them. She learned how to tell a chaffinch from a bullfinch, discovered that the wren nesting in the ivy just outside the privy door had a loud, decisive voice and an outsize personality distinctly at odds with its tiny pert body; she learned to tell the difference between the song thrush, long familiar from London parks, and the shyer, more beautiful mistle thrush, with its loud, hissing alarm call. She became impatient to *do*, instead of just watching.

The wildflowers had already caught her imagination, a hundred different species from the diverse environments of woodland, water and meadow, all thriving together in a few acres of Suffolk countryside. They had kept her fascinated for weeks, until she discovered the herbs.

Ernie had taken to bringing her seedlings in clay pots which he wedged into a wooden box strapped to the back of his bicycle, vigorous green shoots of chive and basil, applemint and thyme, marjoram, and borage with its hairy stems and rough grey-green leaves. He brought her cuttings too, bay and rosemary, sage and sweet, lemon-smelling southernwood, also known, he told her, as *garde-robe*, after its use in the Middle Ages as a moth-repellent. He didn't mention its other name, Maiden's Ruin, presumably out of a gentlemanly concern for her tender feelings, but she found out anyway, when she looked it up after he'd gone.

She should have been concentrating on vegetables, of course, doing her bit for the war effort. But tucked away in her secret glade, cut off from the outside world, who was to know what she was growing for her own pleasure?

At last, she had found something to occupy her mind.

Chapter Fourteen

This was just a flying visit, Marion announced when she arrived on foot along the path from the Hall, bringing Nell a wide-brimmed straw hat, 'to stop you getting so frightfully brown,' and a book she thought might come in handy, a battered, 1931 edition of *Sanders' Encyclopaedia of Gardening* she had found when clearing out a box room.

Now that the weather was better she seldom came inside. She wasn't comfortable indoors, she said when asked. 'Frankly, my dear, I feel as if I'm intruding, and I don't like feeling an intruder in my own son's house.' All Nell's efforts to reassure her that she was welcome had been to no avail. 'It's not you,' she had explained. 'It's the house. It's too private, too . . . *secret*.' She had shrugged apologetically, and Nell could see she was trying hard not to blame her, but then she had added, unable to quite keep the resentment out of her voice, 'Luckily, you seem to be able to manage it quite easily . . .'

'What are you going to do with that?' she asked now, pointing at the garden fork leaning against the porch wall next to Nell's heavy outdoor shoes.

Nell had been suffering badly over the last couple of

days, from lack of sleep. Two nights ago she had woken in the early hours, convinced that Laurence was somewhere near, then lain awake for the rest of the night, listening for him. She had even got out of bed at one point, so sure was she that he was close by, and gone to the window to peer out into the glade. There had been nothing there except a solitary badger, snuffling in the shadows beneath the trees, but she had been sleeping badly ever since.

'I'm going to make a herb garden,' she said, 'over there.' She moved past Marion into the open, indicating the spot she had chosen, to the right and slightly back from the gable end of the cottage towards the pond, where it would get the sun all day. 'It's so sheltered here, so warm, and the soil is wonderful . . .'

'Two 'undred year a' shit and leaf-mould,' Ernie had told her gleefully as he began to turn the sods for the vegetable patch on the other side of the cottage, to the left of the privy. 'Just you tak' a sniff o' that.' He had thrust a handful of crumbly black mulch under her nose, and Nell had caught a whiff, vividly remembered from the first time Laurence had brought her here, of that smell, rich, mushroomy, almost spicy. She had had to turn away, tears blurring her eyes, the reminder was so strong.

'Ernie's given me some seedlings to start me off,' she said, 'and some cuttings, so I thought I'd—'

'Have you asked Laurence?' demanded Marion.

'No, I . . .' Nell, carried along by her enthusiasm, had thought no further than the doing. 'I'm sorry, Marion, it didn't occur to me. Do you think I ought—?'

Marion snorted irritably. 'Of course not. You're absolutely right. What's his is yours, and what's yours is his, eh?'

'No. No, that wasn't what I—'

'Which means, of course, that you don't need to ask his permission for any changes you might wish to make.'

'I could write to him, if you think it would be a good idea?'

Marion snorted again. 'Oh, no you don't! Leaving aside the waste of time and effort involved, when you and I both know what his reply would be, I think the less you two have to do with each other from now on the better, frankly.' She examined the square, studded with daisies and buttercups, where Nell's herb garden was going to be, already marked out as Nell had seen Ernie do with the vegetable patch, with a stake at each corner, then said briskly, changing the subject, 'It's time we talked about the baby. About what you're going to do.'

Nell brought out the dining chairs plus, at Marion's request, the whisky bottle, and they sat in the sun with their backs to the cottage. It was obvious now that Marion had not come merely to bring straw hats and encyclopaedias and Nell was assailed by a creeping apprehension, found her hands growing damp with nervous sweat.

'Laurence has been home,' said Marion, pouring whisky, 'and he has agreed . . .' She looked tactfully away, pretending not to see the tears which had sprung to Nell's eyes at the news that he had been so close and not been to see her. 'He has agreed that he cannot, *must* not, let Violet down. Whatever I think of him marrying her in the first place it's done now, and he cannot, *must* not, abandon his wife and his legitimate child just because he thinks he's made a mistake. She's not too well at the moment, poor lamb – Doctor Hills thinks she's been overdoing it and he's prescribed bed-rest for a few days. So . . . the only thing we have to decide now is what we're going to do about you.'

Nell could hear a blackbird tuning up in the hornbeam near the pond, and her Jenny Wren, perched on an old tree stump, trilling an ebullient warning to the world that she was on guard for her fledglings, hatched less than a week ago. Somewhere near her feet a cricket clicked its legs together in the grass.

Marion cleared her throat and sipped at her whisky. 'I had a telephone call from your mother yesterday.'

Nell's head came up sharply. 'What did she want?' she asked. Then, wistfully, 'Did she – did she ask how I was?'

'Well . . .' Marion took another pull at her whisky and stared at the trees on the other side of the glade. 'In a manner of speaking, I suppose.' Nell clasped her hands tightly across her stomach and waited. The apprehension was spreading, a hard, solid lump of suet beneath her ribs. 'She thinks she's found a way of solving your – our – problem.' It came out as a brusque pronouncement, as if Marion knew Nell wasn't going to like it and she wanted to get it over and done with as quickly as possible. 'She's found someone to take on your baby and bring it up as her own. She feels it's the best solution—'

'No!' Nell clapped her hands over her ears. 'No, I won't listen!'

'It's an answer.' Marion persisted, raising her voice so that even through her tightly clamped hands Nell could still hear what she was saying. 'Not a perfect answer, I grant you, but then nothing ever could be under the circumstances, could it?' She reached across, patted Nell's knee with her free hand. 'It won't do to get your hopes up, you know,' she said, more gently. 'You can't possibly keep it. And you can't take up Violet's offer either. Look at Laurence and his father – even when Laurence was small the resemblance between them was obvious to everyone who saw them together. What if your baby looks like Laurence? What if Violet guesses? It would be too cruel—'

'What's *this* then?' Nell burst out. 'If it's not cruel? I can't have Laurence, and now you want to take away my child as well! What does that leave me?' She flung her arms out angrily. 'What's left? What's the point of hiding me away here if at the end of it I'm going to have to give my son away to a complete stranger?' For weeks now she had been slipping further into the dream, further away from reality. She had been living in a world of make-believe, pretending the real world didn't exist. And now the real world was going to take away her child.

'Eleanor, dear, if you'd just listen to what I have to say—'

'You're asking me to give my son away to a stranger.' Nell's eyes filled with tears. 'At least if he'd gone to Violet I'd have been able to see him.'

'That's what I'm trying to tell you, if you'll just let me get a word in. It isn't a stranger; it's someone you know. Doesn't that make it a bit easier to bear? Your cousin Molly has been trying to get pregnant for nearly eighteen months, so your mother tells me, and now the doctors say she's damaged inside, so she'll never be able to have children of her own—'

'*What*?' Nell shouted, sending a shower of birds clattering from the trees at the sudden noise. 'My *cousin*? Marion, do you know *why* Molly can't have children? No? Well, I'll tell you! Molly can't have children because a few years ago she had an affair, not her first, I might tell you, she just happened to be unlucky this one time, and she got herself into trouble. So she and her mother between them decided that killing her baby was better than having to suffer the shame of an illegitimate child! And her husband, who she met long after her little accident had been neatly swept under the carpet, doesn't know that she skewered her first-born on a dirty knitting needle so it wouldn't ruin her chances of getting a ring on her finger. He doesn't know anything about her past, he probably thinks, poor fool, that she was a virgin on her wedding night. And Ma . . .' She leaned closer, waving her arms around, still shouting. '*Ma* actually *congratulated* my aunt when she heard what she'd persuaded Molly to do. My cousin murdered her own child and now as a reward for her bad behaviour, I'm supposed to give her mine!'

'My dear . . .' Marion was scarlet in the face with shock and embarrassment. 'My dear, I'm *so* sorry. I didn't know. It seemed like a sensible solution, that's all, and your mother said – oh, Lord, don't cry, come along, Nell dear, crying won't help.'

Nell had dropped her face into her hands. She was shaking, heaving with sobs of impotent rage which wrenched her stomach and left her fighting for breath. She shook Marion's comforting hand off her arm, and barged past her, making for the cottage, for her sanctuary. If she could just get inside, was the only thought in her head, it would be all right again; the magic would start to work again, and this would go away.

It was only after she had slammed the door and collapsed against it that it hit her – whatever she had subconsciously hoped, that Laurence would *somehow* make it all right, that she would *somehow* be able to keep her baby, that they would *somehow* manage to be together eventually, it wasn't going to happen. There wasn't any magic, no one was going to come along and make it better. She had lost Laurence, and as soon as he was born she would lose her son.

The guilt she had so successfully put on one side over

the past weeks came flooding back. Poor Violet wasn't well, and she was carrying Laurence's baby too. Violet had done it properly; she had got the ring on her finger, the piece of paper, those two essentials that alone entitled a woman to a man's love and loyalty. As Laurence's wife, Violet had the right, a right which Nell had never had, to expect Laurence to look after her. So Violet's needs, Violet's feelings, must take precedence over Nell's. She ought, it occurred to Nell, to have got used to Violet taking precedence by now.

What if, she thought, clutching at straws, what if she went away, started afresh somewhere where no one knew her, attempted to bring up her child alone? But then, how would she support herself? What would she and her son live on? She could expect no help from Ma; Pa would go along with whatever Ma decided, as he always did, and she could hardly ask Laurence for support, or his family – Marion was not, *could* not, be on her side in this. There was no alternative, no way out of the pit she had dug herself into.

So maybe this was for the best, a blessing in disguise? Maybe, once she had got used to the idea she would see that it was the best solution. She did not particularly dislike her cousin, had even felt rather sorry for her during all her troubles, and the husband was a pleasant enough young man, what Nell could remember of him. They were comfortably off, too; her baby would be well cared for if they took him. Without him she would be free to start over, she could take up Pa's offer to set her up in business on her own. She would hand her son over as soon as he was born, then get right away, begin again somewhere far from Suffolk . . .

She fumbled in her trouser pocket for her handkerchief and blew her nose. Feeling the embroidered initial, *E*, beneath her fingers, she was reminded suddenly of

Violet, sitting on the edge of her bed at the Dower House sobbing as she told her about the problems she and Laurence had been having. It would make it easier for Laurence if she went away. He would be able to get on with the life he had chosen, concentrate all his energies on Violet and his legitimate child . . . They would be cousins, her boy and Violet's . . . was Violet carrying a boy or a girl? Their pregnancies had been quite different so far – all Nell's problems had been at the start and Violet's seemed to be only just beginning; did that mean Violet's baby was likely to be a girl? A niece, she thought. I'm going to be an aunt. Auntie Nellie. Cold comfort.

Face facts, she scolded herself. You must face facts, be practical. You owe it to your son to make the decision that's best for him. The tears welled again; she closed her eyes, clenched her fists. When she had herself under control, she straightened up, and blew her nose again, hard. Then she turned, grasped the latch, and went back outside to Marion, now standing in the middle of the glade, staring into the shadows under the trees and sipping at her whisky.

'All right,' said Nell. 'You can tell Ma I agree. But Marion . . .'

Marion inclined her head but she didn't turn round. 'Yes, dear?'

'Not yet, please. Can you wait for a few more weeks before you make it definite? Just for a while, so I can go on pretending a little longer . . .' She stopped, unable to trust her voice.

'If that's what you want.'

'Thank you. And could you – would you – give my love to Violet and tell her I hope she feels better soon?'

'Yes, of course. Well . . .' Marion began to walk towards the narrow path which wound through the woods to the Hall, then turned back, holding out her empty glass for Nell to take. 'I'd better be getting along. I'll see you tomorrow.' She moved on again, stopped. 'And could you, do you think, do something for me, my dear?'

'Yes,' said Nell. 'Whatever you want.'

'I would be most awfully grateful . . .' Marion cleared her throat, then rubbed her hands vigorously up and down her arms, as if she was chilly. 'I would be most awfully grateful if you would try to remember . . . that the child you are carrying is also my grandchild. Which makes all this rather painful for me too.' With that, she marched briskly away across the grass towards the trees, and Nell stood still, watching her progress, her free hand pressed hard against her mouth to silence the sobs which were rising again to overwhelm her. Why hadn't she thought about Marion's feelings? What must this be doing to her – she, who had confessed to wanting a big family? How many people have we hurt? she wondered, Laurence and I. And how will we ever put it right?

Chapter Fifteen

She must find something to do, she resolved, find something to occupy herself, fill every minute of every waking hour with activity. She mustn't allow herself time to pine, mustn't be tempted to stand with her palms pressed against the wall, trying to recapture the magic. The magic was gone, shattered by Marion Palmer's visit, by the decision she had made to give her child away and the news that Laurence had been home and not been to see her. She mustn't wallow in self-pity either. It wouldn't do her, or her baby, any good. She must just get busy.

Easy to say, even easier to do. She dug the ground. She got brown and fit, developed powerful muscles in her arms and legs, and an aching back; she worried her friends (because Ernie was a friend too now, like Marion, a steady, reliable source of comfort and support) with her determination to do things pregnant women are not supposed to do. 'I'm fine,' she reassured Ernie when he confided his fears for her health. 'I need to keep myself occupied,' she told Marion when she accused her of overdoing it. 'Hard work never killed anyone.'

Only at night, when the blackout curtains went up, when she lit the lamp and the silence closed in, did her courage desert her. Then the music, Laurence's music, helped a little; and the faint tingle she could feel through her skin as she pressed her hands against the walls gave her much-needed strength. For a few hours she retreated from reality, allowed herself to dream. The deer helped, and the moonlight which filled the clearing on cloudless nights. Sometimes she sat on the cold stone windowsill until three o'clock in the morning, with her knees drawn up to her swelling stomach and her chin resting on her arms, watching the silent glade outside, losing herself in the unreality of moonlight and mist, and pretended he was coming home. She knew she shouldn't, that imagining what she wanted would not make it happen, that sooner or later it would instead, if she allowed herself to believe in it, break her heart. But she did it anyway, because she needed a reason to carry on.

The herb garden grew. Its sides, straight and neat to begin with like Ernie's vegetable patch, began to curve, because Nell found curves more pleasing than straight lines, more in harmony with the wildness all around her. She wheedled Marion into providing more books, filling in the gaps in Laurence's library, then pored over them for hours, finding out what sort of soil each plant needed, whether they preferred shade or sun, good drainage or poor, learning the Latin names, not because she needed to, just because it kept her brain busy as well as her hands. She started a second bed, near the pond where the ground was damp, then a third, for those plants her books said liked partial shade. She dug up clumps she had already set out and moved them around, putting a chive in front of a bronze fennel Ernie had brought up one morning with a big smile and a 'just tak' a look at this gre't ol' beauty!' so the rich lilac chive flowers were thrown into dramatic relief against the feathery golden fronds of the fennel, and she replanted a tall lovage, with its thick stalks like giant celery sticks, right at the back of the biggest bed, lest it swamp every other plant in the vicinity. She put an applemint, with its green-and-white stippled leaves, at the front, then backed it with comfrey, lush, hairy-leaved, with dainty, delicate flowers which uncurled from tight spiral buds into rows of hanging bells in every shade of blue from palest sky to deep purple, all on the same stem. She begged extra pots from Ernie and divided the most prolific specimens – parsley, thyme, marjoram, basil – then donated them to Marion to sell at the forthcoming Summer Fair, a Hall tradition going back almost two centuries. This year it was being set up in the walled kitchen garden, currently (with the exception of what few vegetables Ernie was still managing to keep going) lying fallow due to the lack of gardeners. Laid out some distance from the house at the behest of the fourth Baronet, who had had a particular aversion to seeing cabbages from his bedroom window, it was the only part of the estate gardens not yet overrun by the army. It was the fourth Baronet who had built the Dower House on the far side of the valley too, for a particularly domineering dowager.

Nell heard about the preparations secondhand from Ernie who, assisted by occasional off-duty soldiers, had spent days laying plank walkways across the derelict flowerbeds, erecting trestle tables, clearing clay pots, garden tools, watering cans and wheelbarrows from the abandoned Orangery to make a refreshment room. All proceeds this year were going to aid the war effort.

'You should set up in business,' Marion reported back to Nell the following day. 'I could have sold twice as many plants as you gave me!' She brought her a present, a leggy, pot-bound white lilac, which Nell planted in the open space between the herb beds. It would make a nice spot to sit, she thought, once it took.

Ernie, feeding Nell's enthusiasm, sent off to Ipswich to the seed merchants, Thompson and Morgan, and ordered a lucky dip of threepenny packets to surprise her, savory and purslane, hyssop and horehound, tarragon and dill. Like Mary, Mary Quite Contrary's, Nell's garden grew, and with it the strength to cope with the situation she was in. She delighted in the feel of the soil between her fingers, loved to rub the leaves of common thyme between her finger and thumb, then move on to compare the lemon variety with its sharp smell of citrus, or roll the soft, grey-green needles of aromatic rosemary between her palms. She became drunk on smells, intoxicated with textures, dazzled by the picture she was painting, a pallette of greens and greys, yellows, pinks and blues, which changed and shifted every day against their backdrop of woodland green.

On 4th May the temperature plummeted. Vaguely recalling something Ernie had said about tender young plants and frost, Nell spent the last hour of daylight frantically trying to protect the herb garden with the old gunny sacks from the storeroom. When she woke the following morning to her breath clouding in front of her and ice on the inside of her bedroom window, then looked out at the hoarfrost coating the ground and riming the leaves of every tree, she felt a sense of real achievement, that she had somehow beaten the system, caught out Mother Nature at her own game. The potatoes, completely forgotten in her anxiety to protect her favourites, were not so lucky – she lost almost half the crop, along with all the May King lettuces Ernie had planted only a week previously, and most of the Fisher's Early Wonder runner beans. The white lilac, already in bloom, turned brown overnight and dropped every single flower.

There was another hard frost on the 11th, and again

she managed to second-guess the weather, this time remembering the poor vegetables as well, although it was too late for the lilac. 'Dun't you worry, duck,' Ernie reassured her. 'Tha'll come again next year. You're a nat'rul, you are. Green fingers.'

She wheeled Ernie into sharpening the mower blades, taking it to pieces herself, then putting it back together when he had finished and oiling every nut and bolt before mowing meandering paths from both back and front doors to her garden. Then, having pushed and rattled her way round the edges of the herb beds and the vegetable patch so she could see what she was doing, she left the rest of the glade to grow as it pleased.

The grass in the middle, away from the trees, was tall and feathery now, and thick with wildflowers – purple selfheal, tiny scarlet pimpernel, white meadow saxifrage, cotton-thistle and white campion, batchelor's buttons as Ernie called it. Beside the privy door a wild chicory shot up almost overnight, opening its azure blue petals until midday, then closing them tight as a spinster aunt's mouth until the following morning. By the middle of June the glade was buzzing with dozy bumblebees and shimmering with butterflies; the pond hummed with green and brown Southern Hawker dragonflies and the air was thick with pale drifts of pollen.

Yes, Violet was much better now, Marion said when Nell asked.

'Then why hasn't she been to see me?' asked Nell. 'Is she angry with me? Has she . . . I mean, does she suspect . . .?'

'No, I don't think so.' They were sitting in their usual spot at the front of the cottage. Marion was brisk, reassuring. 'Laurence is writing regularly, phoning once a week, playing the model husband in fact.' She glanced at

Nell's face, then busied herself pouring whisky. She was well into her third bottle now, a tot or two consumed every time she visited. 'She's got a bee in her bonnet, silly girl, about this place.' She waved her glass at the cottage behind them, then sipped slowly, savouring the taste.

'What do you mean?'

'Hard to explain. She's gone all fey on me, says it doesn't like her.'

'What do you mean, it doesn't *like* her? How can she imagine a *house* would dislike her?'

'You tell me.' Marion leaned forward, resting her arms on her well-upholstered thighs and holding her glass between her hands. 'She says she felt unwelcome when she was here, as if she was intruding.' She swilled the golden liquid round and round. 'And I have to admit, fey or not, I know what she means.'

'But that's not my fault!' protested Nell. 'I can't help the way the cottage is, but I would never deliberately make Violet feel unwelcome. It's just . . . just . . .'

'Mmm,' said Marion drily. 'Funny thing about houses, isn't it? The way some feel like home the minute you walk in and others are, well, *unfriendly* for want of a better description. This place is *private*, and I think Violet sensed it. It made her feel uncomfortable, like an outsider. I shouldn't think it's a sensation she has experienced too often in her short life, should you?'

'Does she know Malletts belongs to Laurence?' asked Nell.

'I don't think so. It's hardly common knowledge and *I* haven't told her; Ernie Beale certainly wouldn't without asking me first, not that she's seen him. She hasn't seen anyone lately. She's not . . .'

Nell was alarmed. 'Not what? Not well? Not happy? What's the matter with her?'

'Not *concentrating*,' said Marion. 'She seems to have retreated into a little world of her own since Laurence's last visit, just sits at her bedroom window all day watching the soldiers drilling and knitting endless bloody scarves.' She laughed suddenly. 'Frankly, I wish I'd never got her going on Home Comforts. Now she's started she doesn't seem to be able to stop. Dr Hills says she's all right in herself, nothing clinically wrong. She's just a bit lethargic, he says. Pregnancy takes some women like that.' She glanced across at Nell's brown face, her long, unkempt hair, her tanned arms and legs. She was wearing one of Marion's faded maternity dresses and she looked like a gypsy, or one of the dark-skinned diddicoy women who arrived every year for the harvest, then moved on as soon as it was done. 'Certainly hasn't taken you that way, has it? Anyway, she won't come. I've tried to persuade her, but she just says, "Say hello to Nell and tell her I hope she's well." What can I do?'

The nights grew shorter; Midsummer's day came and went and the war moved on, but Nell took little interest. Laurence had been home again, Marion reported, a flying visit of less than forty-eight hours, which Nell already knew about because working in her garden one afternoon she had experienced that same feeling of anticipation she had had during his last visit home. This time though, she had known he would not come and see her, so she had not been surprised when he didn't. Sad, but not surprised.

As the summer wore on the heat increased, became more difficult to bear. Despite all Nell's efforts with Jeyes Fluid, and the fly papers which caught at her hair every time she ventured in, the privy was permanently smelly, infested with obscenely shiny blowflies which buzzed angrily around her face however often she brushed them away; often when she went to empty the bumby bucket she found it crawling with fat white maggots, and the rustling around her ankles was more likely these days to be a fat, glossy brown rat than last year's dead leaves. The sitting room, even with the range only just ticking over, was stiflingly hot and the milk Ernie brought up every other day was on the turn almost before Nell had taken it from his hand.

Only the ice-cold well-water gave her some respite. On the hottest nights she would lug the tin bath outside, fill it with basin after basin of water, then balance the oil lamp on the wash-house doorstep and wallow naked by its light, splashing her breasts and her swollen belly until she was cool enough to attempt sleep. Whatever was left went to water the plants the following day.

Despite all her efforts, by the end of August the herbs were beginning to look tired, exhausted, like her, by too much sun and the oppressive heat of the glade where only the briskest of breezes made a difference to the still air. Some of them were annuals, she discovered, and would not survive the winter to flower again. Ernie showed her which ones she could take seeds or cuttings from, which could be left out to fend for themselves, which would over-winter in pots in the warm sitting room. Moving Laurence's model aeroplane, still sitting on the stone windowsill where he had left it, to the chest of drawers in her bedroom, she filled the space where it had been with young plants – basil, chives, thyme. Touching the canvas wings each night on her way to bed, she thought she felt a faint vibration beneath her fingers, and it made her feel better, just a little.

Still, as the harvest was gathered in across the valley, she began to long for it all to be over. It was more than four months now since she had last seen Violet, and during that time she had undergone profound changes: she had grown older, grown up, lost hope and found a passion for growing things; she had gained a small knowledge of herbs and how to tend them, and a love of solitude. It was almost done now, her brief time in the country. Another couple of months and she would be back in London, her son would be rocked to sleep in someone else's arms and she would be exactly where she had been in October 1940, living with Ma and Pa and quietly nursing a hopeless, long-distance passion for her sister's husband.

She had ceased to expect anything from Laurence – he wasn't hers to take and she had no right to try and hold on to him.

Chapter Sixteen

The war receded still further from Nell's small corner of Suffolk. The air raids were few and far between now, the aircraft which droned occasionally overhead mostly friendly. Cut off from the gossip which filtered out to the villages from Ipswich, Nell began to slip back into her dream world.

The early part of September was dry and mild, with thick fog in the mornings and sometimes at night. Nell no longer had the energy for heavy digging; the glade was close and stuffy, the soil was like dust and she was restless, on edge all the time, waiting. Violet was the same, so Marion reported; the last few weeks of pregnancy took most women like that, she said.

After days spent mooning about the cottage, not in the mood for gardening or reading yet restless for something to occupy her mind, Nell sat down to pore over the Thompson and Morgan catalogue Ernie had brought her, planning next year's garden. She was aware that by next year she would not be here but the mental exercise at least kept her mind concentrated, stopped her brooding over the future. A garden can be grown anywhere there is space and soil; there was nothing to prevent her starting again elsewhere, she told herself. Marion's throwaway remark had stuck in her head – maybe later, when this endless war was over, she would ask Pa for the money to set up a business of her own, growing and selling herbs.

She sat up late, drawing plans, playing with colour-schemes, putting off going to bed. All day, despite her recent lethargy, she had been aware of a growing excitement, a rising tide of almost feverish anticipation. It was the same feeling she had had a couple of times before, only much, much stronger, so strong that by the time she put her pencil down just after midnight she was practically suffocating with it. It must be the idea of starting up on her own she found so exhilarating, she thought. Thompson and Morgan were offering in their catalogue over three thousand flower varieties, a quite astonishing range to provide in the middle of a war, and that was excluding the herbs, pages and pages of vegetables – parsnips to peas, melons to mustard, carrots to curly kale, as well as a dozen different seed potatoes. There must be a market out there, she thought, even if it was only for the more mundane varieties. She banked up the fire, sprinkled water on it to keep it in overnight, then extinguished the oil lamp, removed the blackout and stood still, listening.

It was quiet outside, windless, and she could hear faint pattering noises beneath the window, water dripping steadily from the thatch onto the flowerbed below. She cupped her hands and peered into the gloom but she could see nothing. It must be foggy tonight. She waited until her eyes had grown accustomed to the dark, then wandered out into the hall. She was so used to the place by now that she could find her way around blindfold, but she had grown heavier over the past few weeks and the oak steps had begun to seem steeper, the narrow opening to her bedroom more difficult to negotiate. She was slower than usual, tonight, dreamy. Perhaps she was catching Violet's torpor she thought, except for this curious excitement, still squeezing her chest.

She had left the bedroom window wide open that morning, and she could hear the trees across the clearing, sighing and rustling, some animal scuffling close to the front door. Everything in the room seemed to be out of focus; even to her night-adjusted eyes the chest of drawers looked blurred and the bed was fuzzy round the edges, indistinct. She could hear the water trickling from the stone sill, but she couldn't see the window. The air felt thick, cool and wet against her face.

She felt her way past the bed, her swollen stomach and heavy breasts making her slow and clumsy, then sat on its edge in the fog. The mattress creaked and she heard the staircase behind her creaking too, the boards expanding in the damp. The excitement she had been feeling all day was constricting her throat, making her heart thump too quickly. She began to undress, enjoying the cold air on her bare skin after the heat of the range in the sitting room.

By the time she had pulled her nightie over her head and buttoned it up her eyes had adjusted to the mist which swirled around the room and drifted in wisps through the window. She pushed herself up and went to lean on the sill. Outside she could see nothing, just a soft grey soup, but underneath the fog she knew what it looked like. The grass, so green and vivid in the spring, had gone to seed now and it lay flat, as pale and dusty as straw; on the other side of the glade, where the drift ran away under the trees, the leaves hung heavy and lifeless, waiting for autumn to turn them red and gold when they would drop to form another carpet, like the one she and Laurence had waded through all those months ago. She could hear noises in the fog, dripping, pattering, the faint sound of a lorry on the main road, its engine note muffled by the thick grey blanket. She leaned further out, trying to pick out the nearest trees, but the fog was impenetrable. The vibration beneath her hands, spread on the sill to take her weight, was even stronger than usual. Don't be a fool, she mocked herself, he won't come back here until you've gone, but still she strained her ears, listening.

'I've broken the news to Laurence about the arrangements for your baby,' Marion had told her the previous week. 'And I've warned him not to think of seeing you again before you go back to London. It would only make things harder for both of you, and he's agreed it's best if he stays away.' She had drunk a lot of whisky that day, as she always did when she knew what she had to say was going to wound. Nell bore her no ill will for her determined efforts to keep Laurence from temptation. For all her bluff manner Marion clearly found it difficult, even painful, keeping them apart. 'It's not a question of whether I think it's fair or not,' she said, over and over. 'It's simply a question of what's right and what's wrong.'

A sudden current of warm air, carrying with it a faint whiff of sulphur from the fire downstairs, wafted past Nell's face towards the window. It stirred her hair on her shoulders and sucked a swirl of fog past her into the night. The excitement had settled down to a steady rapid pulse, a void behind her breastbone which rendered her short of breath and slightly light-headed. She leaned across and pulled the casement towards her, meaning to shut the window just a little, but the iron catch was wet and slippery; it swung in too quickly, banging against the window frame.

'Don't shut it,' came Laurence's voice from behind her. 'I can't sleep with the windows shut . . .'

He was standing in the doorway, a vague, looming

shadow wreathed in mist. His head was bent beneath the sloping ceiling, just as she had imagined him in wistful dreams. He took a step nearer, momentarily dispersing the fog which hung about him, and before it rolled back she saw that he was in his shirtsleeves, hands in his trouser pockets, and he was wet, his curly hair slick on his forehead, his shirt clinging to his shoulders. She couldn't pick out his face in the gloom but she could tell he was smiling, she could hear it in his voice when he spoke. She could hear him breathing too, so he must be able to hear her, taking short, panicky gulps of air to fill the vacuum in her lungs.

Now that he was here she felt no surprise. Needing to hear him speak again, still not sure whether he was real or just an apparition, she cast around for something to say and discovered that her mind was so cluttered up with happiness there didn't seem to be any room left for rational thought. She could think of nothing at all.

'You're here,' she managed at last, stating the obvious. 'I've been waiting for you.'

'Yes.' He was still smiling, she could hear him. 'I know you have.'

She moved back to the bed, wrapping her hands round the brass knob at the top of the iron frame and resting her chin on her hands, in need of support. 'You promised your mother you wouldn't come.' She tried to sound stern, but she was smiling too, she couldn't help it; she was grinning, beaming so hard it was making her face ache. Not that she was in danger of giving herself away, she thought, because he couldn't see her, she had her back to the window and there was too much mist in the room. Either way, she went on doing it, because she couldn't help herself. 'You shouldn't be here,' she told him.

'I know.' He moved forward and copied her, curling

his fingers round the knob on the other side of the bedstead and resting his chin on his hands. 'You'd better
tell me to go away.'

'Go away,' said Nell.

'No,' he said. 'You don't mean it. I can hear you smiling.'

Of course he could, how silly of her to think she could
hide it when he couldn't. 'So I am,' said Nell. 'You'd better stay then.'

'All right.' He was laughing now. 'Nell, I'm awfully
tired. Can we go to bed, please?'

He undressed clumsily, struggling with his wet shirt and
muttering over his shoelaces. Nell climbed into bed and
waited for him, watching his shadowy figure as he
hopped and muttered and banged his head on the
beams, the mist swirling about him as he fumbled in the
dark.

He smelled of pipe smoke and wet hair, damp skin
and carbolic soap. Nell took deep breaths, reminding
herself. He dropped his head to the pillow and sighed.
He was still smiling; she could feel him now even
though she couldn't hear him. He settled heavily against
her and hugged her tight, the chill of his skin penetrating
her cotton nightgown. He laid his cheek against hers,
murmured, '*Ahh, Nell . . .*' and fell instantly asleep.

Nell, wide awake, lay listening to the water dripping
off the thatch, to her own heart beating and Laurence's
steady breathing. She had no idea where they went from
here, but it didn't seem to matter any more. She felt
relief, that he was safely back where he belonged, but no
regret; it had gone too far for that. Tomorrow, they
would talk about what to do next. Tomorrow . . . she
dozed, woke, moved his hand so it was lying on her
stomach. Her son, who had been quiet for the past few

weeks, was restless, wriggling and squirming against her. Laurence spread his fingers over the kicks and she felt his mouth move against her shoulder. 'Oh,' he murmured, 'hello, you . . .' and then he drifted off again. Tomorrow, thought Nell, tomorrow we must . . . She turned her head so she could smell his wet hair, then she too fell asleep.

Chapter Seventeen

She woke to a pale grey morning. Shreds of mist still hung in the air above the bed, and Laurence's head was resting heavily in the hollow of her neck. Sliding out from under him, then propping herself on one elbow, Nell examined his face minutely.

The lines were etched heavily round his eyes and mouth, white against brown where he had been squinting into the sun. His eyelashes were dark and luxuriant but his curly hair was already flecked with grey, and even in repose he looked older than his years, far older than when she had first met him. His mouth was curved in a half-smile, softening the harsh grooves running down either side of his nose and, as she leaned across to touch, his eyes opened.

'Mmm, dear girl,' he said, and his smile widened.

By tacit consent they didn't make love. They didn't even kiss, at least not on the mouth, not anywhere that might lead to something more. They touched though, tracing lines, stroking, caressing, arms, shoulders, faces, interlacing fingers, leaning against each other, skin to skin. They looked too, long, steady exploring glances, drinking each other in. It was after ten by the time they roused themselves to get up, and when Nell planted her feet on the cold floor she found that she was dizzy with happiness.

'I was all set to go to the Hall,' Laurence told her, 'but somehow I didn't get round to phoning to let them know I was coming. Then yesterday I mislaid my uniform jacket, so I had to come here instead.'

'Why should mislaying your jacket mean you had to come here?'

'Because I've lost my lucky mascot. I always carry it in my jacket pocket and I can't go flying without it.'

They were sitting by the range. Laurence, wearing one of his father's collarless shirts and his own, badly crumpled linen trousers, was browning toast on a long-handled fork; Nell, barefoot and dressed in one of Marion's maternity dresses, was sipping tea and watching his face over the top of her steaming mug.

'I stole one of your handkerchiefs,' he confessed, 'while I was going through your things. It has your initial embroidered on it.'

It made sense now, the guilty jump when she had caught him in the bedroom going through her suitcase, the furtive way he had plunged his hands into his pockets, his discomfort when she'd asked him what he was doing. She hadn't even noticed it was missing.

'I need a replacement. If I go flying without it, you see . . .' He left the rest of the sentence hanging in the air.

'All right,' said Nell. 'Just to be on the safe side. But then you must go. Your mother will be over later. She comes every other day to bring me provisions and make sure I'm all right. You don't want her to find you here, do you?'

'Doesn't matter.' Laurence examined his toast, then turned it over. 'She'll have to be told sooner or later. So will Violet.'

'Laurence, you agreed. You said—'

'Yes.' He tested his toast again, decided it was done, picked it off the fork and dropped it on the plate sitting at his feet. Nell caught a whiff of it, pleasant, slightly nutty, a little burnt at the edges. Normally the smell of warm brown toast would have made her feel hungry but the empty space which had opened beneath her ribs was not fillable with food. 'I know what I said, but I've changed my mind. I'm going to tell Violet I can't stay with her any more.'

'No. You can't. We agreed—'

'Yes, I can.' He impaled another piece of bread and held it out to the fire, then forgot it and let the toasting fork drop, trailing in the ashes which had collected there. 'I've thought it all through, gone round and round in circles night after night for months now. It's the only way I can see to make it work.' He turned to face her. This was not like the last time, when he had been so distraught. This time he was confident, sure of himself. 'Whatever I do, whatever I decide, someone is going to get hurt. Either you or Violet. And in the end, if I stay with Violet I shall hurt both of you. So I'm going to finish it now, once and for all.'

He made more toast, a pile of it, but he didn't eat it; it was as if the activity itself was the only point of doing it, like the ritual of his pipe. Nell was reminded that she still had one of his pipes, hidden away in the bread oven. She must give it back.

'I've gone over it a thousand times,' he said, 'round and round in endless circles. I know I'm responsible for the whole bloody mess, but I still keep coming back to the one thing that matters in all this. I love you. And I can't stay with Violet because I don't love her.' The piece of toast he was holding began to smoke and a small yellow flame licked at the corner. He snatched it from the heat, then dropped it, fork and all, in the hearth. 'I've tried and tried these past few months. I thought without you there to complicate things it might be better, but it isn't, it's worse. And Violet's not happy either. She's not so stupid that she can't tell something's wrong. She just doesn't know what it is, that's all.' He raised his head, met Nell's dubious gaze straight on. 'I've tried, Nell, I swear I've tried. But I don't love her, and she can tell.'

'She's your wife. And she's going to have your—'

He reached across to stop her mouth with his hand. 'She's going to have my baby. Nell . . .' He took her tea away and set it down in the hearth, half resting on the scorched toast. 'Do you remember what we did here? Do you remember how it felt? How *we* felt?'

'Yes,' Nell whispered, tears suddenly close to the surface.

He leaned forward, taking hold of her hands and gripping them tightly. 'The night before I made love to you I slept with my wife – no, *listen* to me.' He tugged at her wrists, demanding her attention. 'She was miserable, accused me of not loving her any more. I should have told her then that I never had loved her, that the whole thing, our marriage, was just a terrible mistake but instead . . . I'm not proud of what I did that night. I persuaded myself that being close, being intimate, would put things right, but it didn't, it just widened the gap, and then by the next day I had something to compare it with, I'd had the real thing with you. And now . . . now it's like a bloody great chasm between us, and I'll never be able to cross it. When you and I . . . when we . . .' He closed his eyes, opened them again, raised his head. 'When you and I came here that day, that was when I knew I couldn't go on kidding myself any longer.'

'When?' asked Nell, the age-old question. 'When did you realise that you loved me?'

Laurence smiled, a gentle, wistful smile, fit to break

your heart, thought Nell. 'Oh, long before then. On my wedding day, when Violet introduced us. Do you remember? You didn't even look at me. The photographer was trying to get us organised so he could take his pictures, and you were too anxious to get out of the way to notice me at all. You were embarrassed, uncomfortable because everyone was waiting for you, and in your rush to escape you kept getting in the way. I knew then.'

When did the lightning strike? How did you know? What did you feel? Tell me. Tell me everything, every tiny nuance, every glance, every touch. All lovers need to be told they are loved. They long to hear the exact details, so they can store the information, hug it to themselves, warm themselves in the glow of mutual passion. It is part of the peculiar chemistry of love.

'And you; when did you know?'

'At the reception.' Nell had given up, stopped fighting it. 'That was the first chance I had to really look at you, really listen to you talk. Halfway through the evening – you were dancing with Violet at the time and you looked across and smiled at me – I worked myself into such a temper I had to leave the room or I would have kicked you both as you passed. I actually hated my own sister.'

'Why?'

'Because I was jealous.'

'I couldn't tell. Every time I looked at you, you looked away. I thought you didn't like me.'

'Then you're blind, Laurence Palmer.'

'Is that why you were so reluctant to come to Suffolk? Violet was terribly hurt, you know. Every time she asked, you kept coming up with all sorts of excuses, she said, and it was only when your shop was bombed that you changed your mind. Was it because you loved me even then that you didn't want to come?'

'No,' said Nell. 'Yes. I don't know.'

Laurence dropped his head until his forehead was touching her hair, stroked her palms with his fingers. 'And I persuaded Violet she needed you, pretending it was for her sake when really it was for me, because I wanted to see you again. I should have been telling her it was finished, before I did too much damage. I couldn't have got it any more wrong, could I? What a bloody fool . . . I haven't touched Vi, you know. Not since you and I—'

Nell reached across to silence him with her fingers, as he had just done to her. It didn't need saying, not now. They'd said it all, both of them, confessed their sins. But confessing your sins does not always lead to absolution. Despite Violet's adamant refusal to visit the cottage, she was there in the room with them, whispering a silent rebuke every time they touched, every time their eyes met; she would continue to haunt them until it was all out in the open, until they had confessed their sins to her as well as to each other.

'I have to finish it properly,' said Laurence, reading her mind. 'I owe it to Vi to tell her face to face. But I cannot, *will* not, go on living with her, pretending something I don't feel.'

'Laurence—'

'Not now though. Today, and tomorrow, I want to be here with you. Nell . . .'

'Tell me again.' said Nell.

'I love you. Now you. You've never said it.'

'I love you.'

'If you love me, tell me I can stay.'

She said yes. She no longer had the strength to say anything else. She had wanted him so badly for so long and now he was here she was too tired to fight it any more. So she said yes to everything, because she was weak and he was irresistible.

He rambled on, holding her hands in his, outlining his plans for the future, their future. They should get away, he said, start a new life. As soon as this bloody war was over they should emigrate, to Australia, or Canada maybe. 'This Canadian chap on my squadron,' he told her, 'reckons there's a good living to be had out there for someone with the right qualifications. Once this show's over they'll be starting up more and more new companies, civilian airlines like BOAC, carrying passengers all over the world.' The possibilities were endless, he enthused, air transport was going to be huge one day, the only way to travel, and they would be crying out for good people after the war. He would be in at the beginning, a pioneer of commercial aviation. 'Imagine,' he exhorted her, gripping her tight, bringing her hands up to his face so she could feel his breath on her fingers. 'Imagine, Nell, a new start, a new country, no more having to pretend, no more Papa breathing down my neck, *expecting*, no more having to work in some stuffy law practice while I wait to come into my inheritance . . .'

Nell was reminded of Marion's words, 'Laurence is a dreamer . . . Ivanhoe on his trusty warhorse . . . jousting with a broom handle at a half-finished hayrick . . .' but she nodded and smiled anyway, and she didn't ask any of the awkward questions that flitted through her mind as he talked. Laurence took her silence as a sign of acquiescence. 'Then you'll come?' he begged. 'Nell, that's *wonderful*!' and she found herself beaming, laughing, crying, all at the same time, swept along by his enthusiasm, by the fact that it was *her* he wanted to share it with.

She agreed to everything. He had thought it all out, he said, how he would make sure Violet was provided for. 'I don't want to hurt her,' he said, returning again and again to his decision, worrying at it like a dog with a wound that refuses to heal, 'but in the long run I'll hurt her more if I stay with her. She won't want me to stay, once she knows I don't love her . . .'

Nell swallowed her misgivings and told him he was doing the right thing, the kindest thing. It was so easy to give in, to believe that they could make it work. Tomorrow, she thought, tomorrow I will suggest, gently, that maybe it's not as simple as you think, that if Violet is offered the choice, she will opt to hang on to you. Tomorrow I will remind you that it is not only Violet you are contemplating leaving, but the child she's carrying as well. But just for today I'm spinning out the magic, allowing myself to dream.

So she ate the toast Laurence finally remembered to butter for her, poured more tea, and played at Happy Families.

Later, when they had cleared the breakfast things, she took him outside to show him her herb garden, and explained to him that it was Marion who had sown the seed – Laurence laughed, amused by the unintentional pun – of her idea for growing herbs on a commercial basis.

Yes, he agreed, it could work; why not? There'd been a knot garden at the Hall until the last war, he told her, planned by the first Baronet and laid out by the second. There were lithographs depicting it in the library. They wandered from bed to bed, Nell showing him what she had done, boasting of her hard work, apologising for the present air of lethargy which hung over everything. 'They're tired, like me.'

Those species nearest the pond, sweet cicely, cress, spearmint, wild garlic and angelica, were suffering most; planted less than three feet from the water's edge to take advantage of the damp ground, as the weather had continued warm and sunny and the water level had sunk by nearly two feet, they were left high and dry. The brown tidemark round the edge of the clay bowl showed how full it had been at the beginning of the summer. Nell, her grip on reality still tenuous, picked a stick from the undergrowth and leaned precariously over the edge to draw a heart in the mud. Then she stood back and watched as Laurence clambered down the slippery slope to inscribe in neat capitals, NELL IS MY OWN TRUE LOVE. As he turned to climb out his foot slipped and he had to grab her hand to stop himself tumbling into the brown, stagnant water.

'Ellis?' demanded Nell, playing the outraged girl-friend. 'And who, might I ask, is Ellis?'

He had trodden on the 'N' of Nell, so the tract now read, '–ELL IS MY OWN TRUE LOVE.' He looked down at it, laughed, then said, 'Ellis . . . That's it! We'll call our baby Ellis. It'll do for a boy or a girl, won't it? What do you think? Ellis Palmer. It has a good ring to it doesn't it? Nell?'

Nell, who had spent the past few weeks trying to get used to the idea of giving away her child, found her eyes filling with tears.

'Nell, darling,' Laurence was horrified, 'don't cry. Please, don't cry. It's going to be all right, I swear. Truly it is.'

Meaning to comfort, he put his arms round her, as best he could with her awkwardly bulging stomach coming between them, and held her close. Nell raised her damp face to his and smiled.

'Sorry,' she said. 'Just being silly.'

Laurence smiled back. Then he bent his head and kissed her, for the first time since his arrival, on the mouth.

The only trouble was, once they'd started, they couldn't stop.

When Marion walked, unannounced, into the sitting room late that evening, they were seated side by side at the table. They were fully dressed, and leaning their elbows on Nell's garden plans, discussing the possibilities of buying land in Canada, wondering how they could go about starting a market-garden and where they would need to apply for emigration papers. When she slammed the door behind her they jumped as guiltily as if they had still been lying together in the big iron bed upstairs. She brought the chill wind of reality with her.

'My feet are soaked,' she announced belligerently. 'I thought I'd drive over for a change, but your car,' glaring at Laurence, 'is parked under the trees, blocking the way. I've just had to wade through the grass in the dark,' Nell's turn for the basilisk stare this time, 'and it's sopping wet.'

'It's the fog.' Nell stood to attention, hands behind her back, head down, an errant schoolgirl caught misbehaving. 'Can I get you a—?'

'Whisky,' said Marion tersely. 'I'll have a large whisky, if you'd be so kind.' She moved the chair Nell had vacated, then sat down opposite her son. 'Does Violet know you're here?'

'No.' Laurence rose and moved away across the room to the fire. 'But I might as well tell you now, it's finished, Mama. I'm not playing any more.'

'I see.' Marion accepted the whisky Nell handed her with a curt nod, ordered her to bring the bottle. 'And have you told Violet about your decision?'

'Not yet.'

Nell hovered in the background, watching them, mother and son, so unlike yet so similarly obdurate, minds as stubbornly set as their expressions. She was still recovering from an afternoon spent making love, exhausted by a curious mix of overpowering emotion and the sheer physical effort of finding ways round her advanced state of pregnancy, which had lent an edge of hilarity to even the most arousing moments. She was still suffering from the guilt, which refused, despite all her attempts to ignore it, to go quite away. The contrast, between Marion's uncompromising view of the situation and the vision of happiness she had tasted with Laurence, left her muddled and uneasy. She couldn't blame Laurence for what had happened – she had wanted it just as much as he had – but that didn't make it right. Maybe if the decision to be together had been made months ago, before everything got out of hand, it might have been less hard on everyone. But it was too late now to go back and put things right. What a mess, she thought, leaning against the wall listening to Laurence sparring with his mother, what a bloody awful mess.

'I hope you don't expect any assistance from me?' Marion was saying, furiously angry at Laurence's stubborn refusal to listen to reason.

'No.' Laurence ran his fingers through his hair and scowled at her. 'I don't even expect you to understand, let alone help. But I can't stop it. I *won't* stop it, I won't give Nell up.'

'And what about your child. Your *legitimate* child?'

'I will do my best to support both Violet *and* my legitimate child, but I won't go on living with her.'

Marion poured more whisky and tried a softer tack. 'You haven't thought it through. You haven't considered the consequences of what you're doing.'

'Yes I have.' Laurence leaned against the bread oven and fumbled in his pocket for his pipe, his substitute for the whisky bottle. 'I've done nothing else *but* think it through. I've been considering the consequences of what I've done, what I'm doing, for months, how I could sort things out so no one got hurt, how I could keep both the children I have so thoughtlessly sired, how I could be with the woman I love without letting down the woman I'm married to.' He found his tobacco tin, filled his pipe, tamping it down with his thumb, then bent to pick up a spill from the hearth. 'I can't come up with a solution. I don't think there is one, not one where no one gets hurt. But at least if I stay with Nell . . . ' He turned towards the fire, lit his spill, then sucked the flame into the tobacco, sending a cloud of aromatic smoke drifting up towards the ceiling. 'At least if I stay with Nell she can keep her baby.'

For a moment Marion seemed to be at a loss. 'And what about your other child? Don't you care about her?'

'Her?'

Marion shrugged, annoyed by the question. 'You know perfectly well what I mean. Violet's convinced her baby's going to be a girl. She thinks that's partly why you've been so distant lately, because she might not be able to give you a son and heir.'

'Surely you don't believe all that claptrap?' said Laurence.

His mother bridled. 'No, *I* don't, but Violet does and it's making her miserable. Besides, her, him, what does it matter? She – he – will still be your legitimate child, still be the heir to the estate.'

Laurence turned back towards the room. His face was set, closed. 'And what if I don't want the estate?'

'What?' Marion stared at him with undisguised horror. 'What do you mean, you don't want the estate! Of *course* you want it! Why do you suppose I've been keeping it going all these years, if not for you? Laurence, you cannot, I will not *allow* you to throw away everything I've built up for you, just because you think you've fallen in love—'

'I don't *think* I've fallen in love.' Laurence moved back across the room towards his mother. 'I *know* I have.' He sat down again, facing her, then leaned across the table and took her hand. 'Don't you remember, Mama?' he said. 'Don't you remember what it feels like to be in love?'

Marion snatched her hand away, slapped it down hard on the table. 'This has nothing to *do* with love. It has to do with duty, with morality, with right and wrong.'

'And are you honestly telling me, Mama, after thirty-five years of living with my father, that I must go on living with Violet when I love someone else? Is that how you want me to treat Violet? You of all people ought to know what it feels like to be on the receiving end of—'

Whatever point Laurence was trying to make, it touched a raw nerve. Marion's bull-dog face crumpled; she went first scarlet, then white in the face with anger. She swallowed the remains of her whisky, slammed the glass down, then stood up and leaned across the table. 'How *dare* you!' she hissed. 'How *dare* you blame me for all this! How *dare* you talk to me like that about your father!' Unexpectedly her eyes filled with tears and she stood up, knocking her chair flying. 'You'll get no help from me!' she hurled at her son. 'If you persist in this perversity I will fight you every inch of the way!' She turned in the doorway, holding on to the jamb for support. 'And if you expect me to do your dirty work with Violet—'

'I don't,' said Laurence. 'I'll do my own dirty work.'

'Damn right you will!'

He tried one last time. 'Mama . . .'

'What?'

'I'm sorry,' he said. 'I'm truly sorry.'

She did not deign to reply. They heard the front door latch clatter, and she was gone.

Her car started up in the distance and Laurence retreated to the fire, clutching his pipe. 'Handled that one well,' he said, 'don't you think?'

Nell pushed herself away from the wall. 'What did you mean about your father? That seemed to upset her even more than the prospect of you leaving Violet.'

'I should never have mentioned it.' Laurence tamped the tobacco and sucked, attempting to resurrect his pipe. 'I was trying to make her understand but I shouldn't have said it, it's too close to the bone.'

'What's too close to the bone?'

'Papa.' He sat down heavily in the leather chair, dropped his head back and grimaced at her. 'You know why he married her, don't you?'

'Yes,' said Nell. 'Yes, she told me. It was a business arrangement; she had something he wanted—'

'And he had something she wanted. True, but not the whole story. She didn't marry him, as she would have you believe, for the prestige of his name and the big house. She married him because she loved him, absolutely adored him. I remember when I was small, he was away practically all the time, he had invested a large chunk of Mama's money and he used business as an excuse to spend time in London, staying the week in town and just coming home at weekends. He was getting bored with the whole charade even then; Mama was showing no sign of producing any more children, and I suspect she annoyed him by running the estate better than he ever had. Every Friday night she'd be like a kid on Christmas Eve. She'd get all togged up in her best frock, then spend the evening darting from window to window, listening for his car. Sometimes he'd change his mind, or something would crop up – tickets for the theatre, a long-winded meeting on the Friday night – and he wouldn't turn up until the next day. Or he wouldn't turn up at all. Mostly, he was with his mistress. He still is.'

'Oh,' said Nell, shocked.

'He's been with her for years, but when they could have married she had no money and neither did he. She's married too, of course, to a rich and rather complacent banker. It's common knowledge in the City, such an old scandal no one really takes any notice any more.'

'And Marion gave him permission,' said Nell. *I promised him the freedom to do whatever he pleased* . . . He had taken her at her word. No wonder she was so angry with Laurence – she was putting herself in Violet's shoes.

'So you see, she'll never come round.'

'No.' Nell followed him to the fire and sat down on the rocking chair. 'Laurence, I'm not sure I can go through with this.'

'Yes you can.' He sounded weary, tired of going over and over the same ground. 'Because regardless of what you and I decide, I can't live with Violet any longer. Why ruin both our lives for the sake of a principle? It's not you who's guilty, it's me. I shall just have to learn to live with it.'

Nothing further was said that night. They put the subject on one side and went to bed. They avoided it the next day too. They spent the morning wandering in the glade, inspecting the vegetable patch, the herbs, the state of the grass. Laurence lifted two rows of potatoes and a row of carrots, then found gunny sacks in which to store them while Nell made potato and carrot pancakes for their lunch, to a *Kitchen Front* recipe she had first tried out at the Dower House the previous February. It seemed like a hundred years ago, a million miles away, another life altogether. It was hard to remember now what it had been like: neighbours, noise, electricity, telephones.

They spent the afternoon lying in the warm, Indian-summer sun on a tartan rug Laurence unearthed from the back of his car, staring at the blue sky above their heads through narrowed eyes and talking quietly about the progress of the war, how long it would go on, what it would be like coming out the other side. It was only an errant bee, blundering across her face, that made Nell sit up just in time to see Ernie Beale wheeling his bicycle hurriedly away along the path towards the Hall. Laurence was unconcerned.

'He won't tell,' he said, sitting up. 'I know him. He won't breathe a word.' He wrapped his arms round his knees and rested his chin on them, turning his head sideways so he could look at her. 'He was in love with someone else's wife once.'

'Ernie?' Nell was disbelieving. 'Don't be silly—'

'Why is it silly? Because he's crippled with arthritis? Because he's not twenty-one years old and easy on the eye?'

Nell grimaced. 'If being handsome was the only requirement for being loved, you wouldn't be here. You'd be up at the Hall with Violet.'

Laurence professed astonishment. 'You are infinitely more beautiful than Violet.'

'Don't be ridiculous.'

'I'm not being ridiculous. You have something *extra* about you, a quality of . . .' He petered out.

'Ah,' said Nell. 'You see? You can't think how to put it because you know it isn't true.'

'No.' He uncurled himself and leaned across, pulling her close. 'Just because I'm not good at putting it into words doesn't make it untrue. I love your face.' He bent his head and kissed her. 'I love your great big, fat belly . . .' He laughed, ducked the hand she swung at his left ear, then rolled onto his stomach and began to pick at the dry brittle grass on the edge of the rug. 'I *recognised* you, the first time I clapped eyes on you. The set of your mouth, the way your hair curls round your face, your eyes, everything. When I was in my teens it used to be the first thing I looked for in a girl; if she didn't have a pretty face I wasn't interested. But then you start to notice that what comes out of a woman's mouth is more important than the mouth itself. Once you've grasped that, conventional ideas of beauty cease to count for anything. They're like pictures in a book, pleasing to the eye, but they don't touch any deeper than that.'

'So why did you marry Violet?'

'Below the belt,' he said. 'Because I was drunk. Because I wanted someone to come home to, someone to live for. Because I was frightened. Ernie had a different problem . . .' He touched her face with a chaff-dusty finger. 'Or not so different. By the time he met the woman he wanted to spend the rest of his life with, she was already spoken for.'

'The poor man.' Nell stretched out again, closing her eyes against the glare of the sun. 'Go on.'

'It was during the last war. Ernie has a younger brother, Bill his name is, lives somewhere in Yorkshire now, but they both worked on the estate in those days; Bill was ploughman at Home Farm, and Ernie was an under-gardener at the Hall. Anyway, in the summer of nineteen fourteen Bill went on a charabanc outing to Southwold . . .'

'How do you know all this? Surely, you weren't even born in nineteen fourteen?'

Laurence chuckled. 'Correct. Sharp little miss, aren't you? I was born the following year, and I was told the story by my old nanny when I was fifteen years old and just beginning to take an interest in girls; a cautionary tale, she called it, a warning of what could happen to young men if they fell into the path of temptation.' He reached across to tickle Nell's cheek with a feathery grass. 'Actually, I just thought it terribly sad.'

Nell batted the grass away with a languid hand. 'Go on.'

'Where was I? Yes, well, Bill went on this charabanc outing, and he came back full of this girl he'd met on the promenade. It was just before war was declared, and he married her in a hurry, within less than three weeks Nanny said, and brought her back straightaway to live with old Mrs Beale and Ernie. Ernie was almost thirty, a confirmed bachelor and his arthritis was already quite bad even then. Bill, on the other hand, was a big handsome lad of twenty-two, all the girls for miles around were after him, so Nanny said, and he'd obviously swept this one off her feet. She was a pretty little thing, apparently, but painfully shy, wouldn't say boo to a goose, and from the day she moved in old Mrs Beale ran her ragged. Anyway, don't ask me what a nineteen-year-old slip of a girl would see in a poor cripple like Ernie, but she certainly saw something, because she and Ernie fell in love.'

'How do you know?' Nell rolled over, dipped her head closer to Laurence's. 'Did they run away together?'

'No. They were seen, sitting on the bank down by the river, holding hands and whispering sweet nothings to each other.' Laurence shrugged. 'Unlike you and me, they had nowhere private to go, and you know how gossip spreads in the country. I think they must have tried hard to do the right thing – Ernie went to join up the minute war was declared – and the strain of it must have been intolerable, the four of them all living hugger-mugger in that tiny terraced house on Post Office Row. But the army turned him down because of his arthritis, and then, as the war began to get going in earnest, Bill was called up. He was quite happy to go. He'd never taken the gossip seriously, refused to believe that his shy, demure, pretty little wife could possibly prefer crippled, ugly, middle-aged Ernie to him. So off he went to war, and there they were, Ernie and his little girl, living with old Mother Beale. That was when the gossip really took off, because the girl was pregnant, you see, and with Bill not there the rumour began to sweep the village that the child was Ernie's.'

'And was it?'

'I don't know. I don't think anyone does to this day, but it seems pretty unlikely; with old Mother Beale as chaperone I'd defy anyone to manage an illicit love affair in that house. But the whole village sent the poor girl to Coventry anyway, made life so unbearable for her that after a couple of months she fled home to her parents in Yorkshire. And when Bill came back from the war he saw the writing on the wall, the choice between living on Post Office Row with his dear old mum and Ernie, working on the estate for the rest of his life, or moving up north with the prospect of eventually inheriting his in-laws' farm and being his own master. So he followed her to Yorkshire. He took over her parents' farm when they retired, his wife had a son, then two daughters, and for all I know they're still there. Ernie never talks about them, and I don't think they keep in touch.'

'Oh,' said Nell. '*Poor* Ernie.'

'Mmm.' Laurence plucked another grass and began to bend the brittle stem over and over between his hands. 'Poor Ernie. I asked him once, when he first started keeping an eye on this place for me, whether if he could live his life over he would do things differently.'

'And what did he say?'

Laurence began to tear the bent straw into tiny sections, trickling them between his fingers. 'He said, "If I had my time again, I'd bugger off while I had the chance."'

'Oh . . .'

Laurence swept the pile of cuttings into his hand, then poured them back out onto the rug. 'That was all he ever said. I'm not even sure if he knew I knew about her. But I think that given a second chance, he would have just taken his lady love and disappeared, and to hell with the consequences.' He rolled onto his back again, propping himself on one elbow, then leaned across, shadowing Nell's face so she could no longer see the sun. 'And that, my darling,' he said softly, 'is why he won't tell on us . . .'

They went to bed early because Laurence had to be up at dawn the next day. Before she undressed for bed, Nell rummaged in the top drawer of the chest for a handkerchief, a replacement for the lost lucky mascot; Laurence shook his head. 'I lied,' he said. 'It was just an excuse to come, because I couldn't bear to stay away any longer.' He fumbled in his trouser pocket and produced Nell's monogrammed handkerchief, neatly folded, and surprisingly clean considering what it must have been through over the past few months. Then he replaced it carefully and began to shed his clothes. 'Next time,' he said, as he climbed into bed beside her, 'next time I come back, I'll be coming home.'

He woke her in the middle of the night, wanting to make love. She responded sleepily until he bent over and began to suckle at her. Her breasts were heavy, voluptuously swollen at this late stage in her pregnancy, the skin threaded with blue veins and the nipples distended;

with every tug she felt an answering pull between her thighs.

'I can *taste* you . . .' Laurence's voice was hoarse with astonishment and when he kissed her mouth his lips were still sticky with her milk. 'Say yes,' he murmured. 'Once and for all, Nell, say yes.'

'Yes,' she said.

Chapter Eighteen

Nell lay awake, with Laurence sleeping beside her. She could feel his skin, warm against hers, and she could hear his breathing above the distant rustle of leaves, the hooting of an owl. If she were to move her hand a little to the left she would be able to feel his heart beating, a slow, steady *thud, thud, thud*, beneath his breastbone. She resisted the temptation though, in case he woke; he must leave in less than three hours and he needed his sleep. There was time to think now, now that the declarations of love had been made. They had burned their boats, committed themselves body and soul, and there was no going back. They could no longer claim, 'It was only the once – the circumstances were exceptional – we got carried away.' They had made love for the fourth time tonight; she could still feel where he had been, warm and slippery between her thighs.

For almost all of her life Nell had been second best, the dutiful daughter, the plain one. At twenty-five she had long been resigned to her allotted role: Eleanor Carter, spinster of this parish, working for her father, living at home. All Ma's ambitions, all her hopes, were for Violet, not for Nell, and she had made no secret of her expectation – when she and Pa grew too old to look after themselves it was Nell who would take on the task. No one had ever asked if that was what Nell wanted, whether that was how she wished her life to be; it was simply assumed. There were thousands of women like her, Nell knew that, especially since the Great War, from which so many men had not returned. For them, marriage, children, a home of their own, were pipe dreams. Don't get your hopes up, she had been told when she was seventeen and off to her first grown-up dance, don't expect too much – you will only be disappointed. With the best will in the world, you're not pretty, and men don't look twice at plain girls . . .

She turned her head to gaze at Laurence, still sleeping peacefully beside her. There was no fog tonight; the sky was clear and the glade was bright. How could she have let it go this far? She was not a wicked woman, and Laurence was an upright, honest man, a gentle man, not by nature given to deliberate acts of cruelty. Yet that was what his love for her had already driven him to, that was what he must perform if they were to be together. Would he have the courage to do it? Or would he lose his nerve when confronted with Violet's beautiful, trusting face, change his mind? It was still hard to believe he cared more for her than for her infinitely more alluring sister.

The thought of Violet revived the guilt. It was unforgivable, what she had done. But I couldn't help it, she excused herself, truly, Violet, I didn't mean to . . . There ought to be an honourable way of ending things when a mistake has been made. Men and women fall out of love all the time. Look at Pa, poor henpecked Pa, who gets no peace in his own house from ambitious, shrewish Ma, who keeps him in place as ruthlessly as she keeps her house in order. Had Pa, Nell wondered, never considered leaving? Or Marion Palmer and her philandering husband – had she never been tempted to walk away?

Which question brought her back to the beginning again, to Violet and the guilt. She had no answers, no glib solutions, only Laurence, only keeping her child, having what she had thought she would never have. She couldn't give him up now.

The following morning the fog was back. They said goodbye on the front doorstep, Laurence back in his crumpled shirt, Nell in her dressing gown, and they both cried. Then Laurence waded out through the wet grass and disappeared into the mist. Nell heard him trying unsuccessfully to start his damp car, then the sound of the cranking handle, the rattle of the engine, loud at first, then fading as he bumped away along the drift. She listened until all she could hear was the water dripping from the trees and the faint sound of the milk train rumbling through the valley on its way south to London. Then she closed the door and went back to bed.

Chapter Nineteen

Nearly there now, heavy, uncomfortable, more ungainly than ever. Nell's back ached constantly. She sweated beneath her heavy breasts and she needed to pee every hour.

The weather continued warm and the trees showed no sign of turning. Violet was unwell, Marion said, her wrists and ankles were swollen and she was suffering blinding headaches. Marion was cold, disapproving, but still she came, punctilious in her concern for Nell's welfare, bringing fuel and food, taking away what rubbish could not be buried or composted. It was all bearable, even Marion's disapproval, now that Nell had a future to look forward to, but still she was impatient, waiting for news of Laurence, who had promised to get leave as soon as possible so he could put things straight with Violet. Until that was done she would not believe he was really hers. She felt as if she had spent her whole life waiting for this, for him.

September was over now. The brambles were laden with ripening blackberries and the wild geese were flying overhead, their wings creaking eerily, on their way south for the winter. Ernie had already put the vegetable patch to bed, leaving only the Brussels sprouts and a few winter cabbages, turning the soil, fertilised by the bumby bucket, ready for the spring. He had brought her a gift the last time he was here, a brown paper bag full of soil-encrusted corms. 'Cyclamen,' he said. 'Flower in January, they will, lovely pink blooms jus' when you need cheerin' . . .' Watching him wheel his bicycle away along the narrow path towards the Hall, Nell had wondered where she would be next January – in Canada maybe, starting a new life? She, *they*, would have a child by then, a son. She found the thought astonishing, exciting, amazing and the guilt was lessening a little every day as she grew used to the idea. She slept badly that night though, waking suddenly in the early hours to such a sense of impending disaster it left her literally shaking with terror. After a while the fear subsided, but she was left with a profound melancholy, which refused to go away. The following night she was reluctant to sleep in case that awful sensation returned, and the sadness remained, undefined, unfocused, but with her all the time.

When Marion appeared in the doorway Nell was sitting at the table poring over Laurence's ancient school atlas, tracing the rivers and mountains, the boundaries of Canada, chanting the names out loud, 'Alberta, Saskatchewan, Manitoba, Snare River, Great Slave Lake, Goose Bay . . .' Marion made her jump.

She didn't say anything at all. She just put the piece of paper down on the table, patted Nell awkwardly on the shoulder, then left, closing the door quietly behind her. Puzzled, Nell leaned across the table to read it. It was addressed to Violet, and she didn't take it in the first time; she had to read it again before it registered properly.

Once she was sure she had understood, she pushed it away and sat back in her chair, staring at nothing. Of course, she thought, how stupid she was; she should have guessed. The sadness, focused now, settled over her like a black, suffocating blanket.

Long afterwards, she wondered how many hours she had been sitting. The light in the room had changed and the fire was almost out. When she stretched her legs she found she was stiff from staying in one position too long. She rose to mend the fire, then changed her mind and went instead to the bread oven to fetch her journal.

She sat for ages, trying to think how to put it, how to record the ruin of all her hopes, but in the end it was too much, her brain simply wouldn't function sufficiently coherently. So she pulled the paper towards her and began laboriously to copy it, word for word.

When she had finished she closed the book and put it back in the bread oven. Then she felt around with her fingers until she found Laurence's pipe, the one she had placed there all those months ago. She took it across to her chair and sat down, cupping it in both hands. That was all she had left now, a faint smell of stale tobacco and a tatty piece of paper, the contents of which would stay imprinted on her mind for the rest of her life.

Chapter Twenty

Ellis was wandering from room to room, calling Joe's name. She was crying, sobbing with loneliness, but when she saw him coming across the glade and rushed to open the door, it wasn't Joe, it was Laurence standing in the porch. She knew it was him because his shirt was wet and his trousers were crumpled, but his face was blurred, like one of those television reconstructions when the villain's or the victim's features are distorted on the screen to prevent recognition. 'I know who you are,' she accused him, screwing up her eyes in a vain attempt to get him into focus, 'Nell's told me all about you.' Laurence, ignoring her, stretched his arms wide, pushing her back against the wall and when she turned to look, it was Nell he was trying to reach, as shadowy and indistinct as he, recognisable by her thick mousy hair and her faded maternity dress. 'What are you doing here?' complained Ellis, angry that they had come instead of Joe. 'And why must Laurence push and shove when I've already let him in?' As she moved forward to bar Laurence's way, he wavered, then dissolved, and the door swung shut. *Thud* . . .

Startled peremptorily out of sleep, Ellis jerked upright and stared blankly around her. She had been half sitting, half lying on the stairs, her legs drawn up beneath her,

her head resting at an awkward angle against the wall
and Nell's journal open on her lap; now it was face down
on the floor at her feet. The light filtering into the hall
from the sitting room suggested early morning rather
than late evening and when she looked at her watch she
saw that it was almost seven.

Flipping through Nell's journal she found her place,
then stared down woozily at the capital letters, scored
deeply into the page in Nell's distinctive, jagged handwriting.

> *Telegram OHMS*   *02.10.1941*
> *IMMEDIATE FROM AIR MINISTRY KINGSWAY*
> *REGRET TO INFORM YOU THAT YOUR HUS-*
> *BAND ACTING SQUADRON LEADER*
> *LAURENCE PALMER DFC IS REPORTED MISS-*
> *ING AS A RESULT OF AIR OPERATIONS 30TH*
> *SEPTEMBER 1941 ENQUIRIES ARE BEING MADE*
> *THROUGH INTERNATIONAL RED CROSS*
> *GENEVA AND ANY FURTHER INFORMATION*
> *RECEIVED WILL BE IMMEDIATELY COMMUNI-*
> *CATED TO YOU LETTER CONFIRMING THIS*
> *TELEGRAM FOLLOWS.*

She had read those words in the early hours, then sat,
too shocked to go on, too exhausted to make herself
climb the stairs to bed. Sometime after three she must
have fallen asleep, but even in her dreams Nell and
Laurence had refused to leave her alone. Struggling to
stand on stiff, uncooperative legs, as she reached out to
steady herself against the wall she could have sworn she
felt a faint but tangible humming, the barest whisper of
a vibration beneath her fingers and, startled, she
snatched her hand away. Don't be ridiculous, she
scolded herself, it's just a trick of the mind, the result of

sitting up too late reading. You're still dreaming, you fool. But touching the wall again she felt it a second time and she had to sit down, so shaky were her legs.

If it was just a trick of the mind, why did it feel so *real*?

She ate a frugal breakfast, still suffering from lack of sleep and not thinking straight. She must get out of the cottage, she decided, do something constructive to take her mind off the mental images whirling about her head. By eight o'clock she was ready to go, and pausing only to find her keys, carelessly dropped on the sitting-room table and hidden from sight beneath the sketched plans for the lavender garden her father had given her – was it really only yesterday? – she made for the hall. As she stepped out into the warmth of the morning sun, she stopped short, and shivered.

The room she had just left was furnished simply enough – a pair of traditional armchairs, chosen for comfort rather than elegance, a small pine table and two rush-seated dining chairs. White-painted bookshelves filled the spaces either side of the cast-iron range, where the bread oven and the copper had been before the builders did their work, and Ellis had made plain cotton curtains for the window, brought a couple of pretty rugs from her flat along with a few pictures, soft, gentle seascapes in blues and greys and greens, currently leaning against the walls waiting to be hung. The room was littered with piles of books and the sun was slanting through the window onto the newly repaved floor.

But just for a moment, as she glanced back over her shoulder, she had seen not her freshly painted walls and comfortable furniture, not her rugs and pictures and the chaos of unpacking, but cracked, uneven pamments, a rough deal table, an ancient leather armchair and a makeshift bookcase of bricks and planks. And as she'd stepped out into the sunshine from the darkness of the tiny hall she had found her nostrils tingling, not with the clean, fresh smell of early morning dew, but with the sharp, spicy scent of pipe tobacco . . .

That's what happens, she thought as she picked her way across the sodden grass towards her car, when you stay up half the night delving into other people's secrets. Reading Nell's journal had been like eavesdropping on a crossed line, one of those ones when you pick up the receiver and realise you are listening to a complete stranger confessing their most intimate secrets; you know you should hang up but instead you hang on, guiltily indulging in the voyeuristic fascination of prying into someone else's private life. Why hadn't she just left the damn thing alone? She would put it away when she got back, she decided, resist the temptation to delve any further into the past . . . Yet Nell had scored her name, *Ellis*, so decisively on that parcel. She had chosen the name herself, she had told Ellis all those years ago, so clearly she had intended her to read it. But why?

When she went to put the key in the ignition Ellis found her hand was shaking. She pulled away too fast, forgetting how uneven the ground was and set her teeth chattering as she bounced along beneath the trees. Slow down, she told herself, get a grip, you're just tired, that's all, your brain's playing tricks on you . . . but what had happened to the other Ellis? Why would Nell have given her the name she had chosen for her own, illegitimate son?

The sun was climbing into a hazy blue sky; it promised to be a lovely day. She would go shopping, she decided as she pulled out onto the road, she would stock the larder, then go and see her mother, tell her about the pregnancy and explain why she was not going to marry the baby's father. She would break the news to William later, catch him on his own at The Herb

Garden – the prospect of having to explain to her beloved father, to whom she had always been so close, the predicament she had managed to get herself into, was too hard to face just now.

Driving along the dual carriageway towards Ipswich, she felt oddly detached from the speeding traffic, caught herself examining the countryside along the way, searching for clues to the past, peering at houses and hedgerows, fields and barns, and wondering what they might have looked like in 1941. She must put Nell's journal away, Ellis resolved again; she was in danger of becoming obsessed with it.

It occurred to her that Joe would probably be back from Yorkshire by now. Would he go straight round to her flat the minute he arrived? And when he found her gone, with no clues left behind as to her whereabouts, would he shrug his shoulders, heave a sigh of relief that she had made it easy for him and get on with his life? Or would he wish it might have ended differently, feel, just for a moment, a pang of regret? She screwed up her eyes, trying to conjure his face, and that feeling stole over her, the warmth only Joe could generate. You're better off on your own, she told herself. Before Joe your life was ordered, neat, *reliable*. She had already started planning for the baby, both financially and logistically, making sure she could continue to work and bring up a child without neglecting either. After all, there were plenty of women less smart, less materially secure than she, who managed to work full time and run a family without a man to support them. If only, she thought as she turned into the supermarket car park, if only organising one's emotions were as easy as organising one's shopping . . .

She shopped in a daze, then loaded her purchases into the car and made for the middle of Ipswich, aware that she was wasting time, putting off going to see her mother. She drove aimlessly for a while, then turned north towards Christchurch Park and slowed to examine the row of tall Victorian mansions, once the fiercely academic girls' school, her Alma mater, which faced out across the wide expanse of grass and trees. The school was gone now, and the buildings had been sold to a developer for conversion to an upmarket complex of town-houses and apartments. She stopped opposite the entrance, reliving the smell of sweaty adolescent girls and school dinners, the clatter of a hundred pounding feet on the stairs, the massed thunder of Junior Gym . . .

Ellis's best friend at school was Grace Helliwell. Grace was not only pretty, she was also extremely bright, and she and Ellis had been the shining stars of their final year, the girls destined for great things. They were both ambitious, determined to make their mark on the world, but while Ellis had taken up her university place, had gone on to fulfil all that had been expected of her and more, Grace had opted instead for marriage and children, for a narrow, comfortable world of cleaning ladies and nannies, dinner parties for her husband's clients and two foreign holidays a year.

She still lived in Ipswich; her husband was a successful man, head of his own company with branches in Diss and Bury St Edmunds. He and Grace had two children and they lived in an elegant grey-brick house a stone's throw from Ellis's old school. It had struck Ellis the last time they met that Grace had traded life for lifestyle; she had lost her edge, the sharp, inquiring mind she had once possessed, had lapsed into smug, middle-class, middle-aged passivity. Grace had been equally contemptuous of Ellis's solitary academic life, her lack of that ultimate status symbol, a husband, but as Ellis pulled slowly away from her old school, it was the thought of her erstwhile friend that lifted her spirits. At least I'll never get like Grace, she thought, smug, complacent, dull. She was doing the right thing going it alone, for herself as well as for Joe. If only she didn't *miss* him quite so much . . .

It was after ten by the time she took the road out of Ipswich and the heat was increasing, the sun shimmering on the tarmac and the air heavy with traffic fumes. William would be at work by now, making it easier to break the news to her mother about the baby. She branched off onto the road, familiar from a thousand childhood school-runs, that ran along the other side of the river, cut off from the Hall by the dual carriageway which had sliced the valley in two when it was built in the eighties. It was time to face the music.

Approaching the church at the top of the hill, she was overwhelmed by a wave of that curious lethargy pregnancy brings, and, pulling onto the verge opposite the iron gates leading to the churchyard, she cut the engine, leaned her head back and closed her eyes. She would just sit for a few minutes, she thought, until her energy returned.

It was a long time since Ellis had been to church. Even before she left home at the age of eighteen her attendance had been desultory, limited mostly to Christmas and Easter and the odd Harvest Festival when William put his foot down and insisted on her company. Ellis's father had the sort of faith she occasionally longed for but had never found – a solid, unquestioning belief which sustained him through whatever life could throw at him, which comforted and supported him twenty-four hours a day and nourished him when things went wrong. As she grew older and the twentieth century moved towards its close, it seemed to Ellis that the church was becoming more and more a relic of England, not as it was now, but as it had been in the past, when habit and tradition had informed the everyday pattern of rural life. Today though, for the first time in years, she felt a need for that peace which only the silence of an empty church can bring, and rousing herself with some difficulty she left the car, crossed the road and entered the churchyard.

Her shoes scrunched on the gravel path and snippets of Nell's journal drifted back to her – taking the shortcut through the churchyard to Post Office Row after the New Year party to usher in 1941, praying for Laurence's safety in the Palmer family pew before they became lovers, pretending to herself that she cared for his welfare only because he was her sister's husband. Pausing to rest her legs, still stiff from her night on the stairs, Ellis looked for, and found, the narrow path, worn down by the feet of generations and clearly still used, that wound up through the long grass towards Post Office Row.

The church was unlocked, unusual in these days of thieves and vandals, and as she lifted the latch the noise echoed loudly in the hollow interior. The air inside felt cold on her sun-warmed skin and her shoes squeaked as she moved towards the altar. The chill revived her a little, but she was not prepared for what she was about to find.

His name was on the scroll of honour, one of nearly sixty young men who had given their lives for the village in two world wars. The wooden plaques hung side by side on the whitewashed wall, halfway along the aisle, with a wreath of silk poppies resting on a plinth below. Thirty-five names on the first list, six from one family alone, lost in the Great War – *Sharman, Jarret, Overton, Bishop*, almost an entire generation wiped out – and on the second twenty-four more, the same surnames again and again, killed in the 1939–45 conflict. The numbers seemed impossible for such a small community to sustain even once; yet twice within thirty years the sacrifice had been asked for, and made.

Hawley, *Ware*, *Smith*, they were all there, no longer merely bit-part players in someone else's history, but real men who had left behind real mothers, real fathers, brothers, lovers, wives. The shock when Ellis found her grandfather's name, cut in neat capitals into the wood, was so intense it rocked her back physically on her heels; *Palmer, L.*, halfway down the last column between *Overton, J.* and *Smith, B.*, just one more casualty of war.

Standing in that simple country church, with one hand gripping the back of a wooden pew for support, Ellis struggled to comprehend the sheer scale of the loss, not just Nell's, but all those others; Violet and Marion Palmer, the Hawley boys' mother, Geoffrey Ware's father, the parish priest comforting his parishioners every Sunday while grieving for his own dead boy, Betty Smith from Home Farm, whose husband and both sons had been taken from her within the space of a month. Emerging into the sunshine from the dim, dark quiet of the church, Ellis had to turn back for a moment because she couldn't see for the dazzle of tears in her eyes.

When she was sufficiently recovered she took a deep breath, and waded into the long grass to search through the faded names on the gravestones.

She didn't find Laurence, but she found other names familiar from Nell's journal, Ernie Beale and his mum, buried side by side and sharing a headstone, Mrs Downes from the village shop, Charlie Bewson, whose pigs had been prematurely roasted by a German bomb, Miss Ames the spinster schoolmistress and poor Arthur Mulligan, Nell's Liverpudlian friend, buried in a country churchyard hundreds of miles from his one-legged da and his mam. Where was Laurence's last resting place? wondered Ellis. Was he buried somewhere in France? Did he lie at the bottom of the North Sea, or deep in a remote Norfolk bog? She was reminded of the other Ellis, the child Nell had conceived and carried at Malletts. He would be her first cousin once-removed, in his mid-fifties by now, if he was still alive. Or had Nell, all alone in her primitive cottage, been delivered of a stillborn son and bestowed his unused name on Ellis in his memory? It was like opening a Russian doll, she thought – for every puzzle solved there seemed to be another hidden inside.

Marion was buried in the Palmer family plot. *1880–1960*, her dates proclaimed, *Marion, Faithful Wife of Gerald, Loving Mother to Laurence. Requiescat in pace.* Sir Gerald's death, two years earlier, was recorded on the other side of the monument, maintaining his distance even in death, and they were fenced in, with previous generations of Palmers, by rusty iron palings. Their tomb, a stone sarcophagus embellished with scrolls and curlicues, was one of the grandest monuments in the churchyard, but Violet had no grave there – Ellis checked every single name. There was no Ellis Carter either, but then it was hardly likely that Nell's illegitimate son would be buried in the Palmer family plot, Ellis supposed.

She stumbled upon Nell almost by accident, as she was picking her way back through the long grass towards her car. She was tucked away in a dank, weed-infested hollow near the north-eastern boundary of the churchyard, and her grave, marked only by a small decaying stone and a straggling briar rose, was almost invisible among all the larger monuments to the departed. Ellis crouched over the crumbling stone, leaning close to decipher the words, *Eleanor Mary Carter,*

1915–1965, RIP. Only fifty when she died, yet to Ellis's four-year-old eyes she had seemed as ancient as the cottage she lived in. The letters were barely legible, worn away by time and weather and neglect; soon there would be nothing left to mark Nell's passing except a forlorn, drunkenly crooked slab, indented with meaningless hieroglyphs and almost completely obscured by rank vegetation.

'Are you resting in peace?' asked Ellis, tugging at the weeds in a futile, sentimental attempt to tidy her great-aunt up. 'Or are you turning in your grave now that you've confessed your sins, wishing you'd kept your guilty secret? Are you trying to tell me something?'

She was reminded of the vibration she had felt beneath her palm when she touched the cottage wall, that brief, startling glimpse of Nell's sitting room, the whiff of tobacco as she'd left the house. Had they been merely figments of her imagination, products of too little sleep and too much reading, or were they more significant than that, clues left deliberately for her benefit?

There was no Ellis here either, no extra name added to Nell's stone, no marker for a stillborn baby. So Nell must have given her son away, sent him to her cousin Molly as she had promised Marion she would . . . Picking her way slowly back towards the gravel path Ellis reviewed what little she knew of her family history.

On her father's side there were no secrets – Thomas Jones, son of an impoverished Welsh hill farmer, had come to Suffolk in the 1920s, attracted by low agricultural rents and the strong non-conformist community in Ipswich. He had married a local girl, gone to war, come back to Suffolk and settled down to raise his family, then later, growing homesick, he had moved with his wife and two younger children back to Wales, leaving his eldest son, William, behind. Granny and Grandpa Jones were respectable, devout, and distant. Now in their late eighties, they lived just outside Llandudno, and Ellis kept in touch with thank-you letters at birthdays and Christmas and the occasional duty telephone call. They had never returned to Suffolk and she had seen them no more than a dozen times in her life, brief, strained visits to Wales in the course of which there had been no disguising their disapproval of both their eldest son and his wife; Ellis, included in the general opprobrium, had wondered what she could have done to deserve such pursed lips and coldly pious glances.

She had known for a long time that Laurence, her maternal grandfather, was dead. She must have been six or seven the first time she asked about him. It was just before Christmas and they were making cards at school, sticking down messy bits of coloured paper and tinsel and writing uneven messages of love to parents and grandparents. The child next to her was already on her third card –she was quicker than Ellis, who was finding the whole exercise tedious in the extreme and would rather have been reading a book.

'You've done too many,' Ellis remarked, leaning across to examine the other's wobbly handwriting.

'No I haven't.'

'Yes you have,' insisted Ellis. 'You've already done a Granny and Grandpa one, look.' It was a particularly lurid example, a glue-sodden holly leaf, the green dye from the tissue paper smeared across the white card. Ellis pointed to the seasonal message: *To Grammy and Grampy B, a happy Xmas wit love form Jennifer.*

Jennifer regarded her with contempt. 'That's my *Burton* Granny and Grandpa. This one's for my *Hancock* Granny and Grandpa, stupid.'

Ellis had gone home and demanded to know why she had only one set of grandparents when Jennifer Burton had two. Her mother had been oddly evasive, suddenly terribly busy with the mince pies she was making.

'Your other grandfather died during the war,' she said reluctantly when Ellis persisted. 'I never knew him.'

'And what about my other granny?' asked Ellis. 'Did she die in the war too?'

Laura was silent for such a long time Ellis thought she hadn't heard her and repeated the question. 'No,' she said at last. 'We just don't see each other, that's all.'

Clearly, as far as Laura was concerned, that was the end of the conversation, but her mother's reticence served only to fuel Ellis's curiosity; Laura never talked about her own childhood, never mentioned her mother, or her grandparents. The more Laura prevaricated the more she nagged and wheedled; the more Laura attempted to divert her into more important matters, such as what she wanted for her tea, or whether her homework had been done, the more wilfully determined she became to get an answer. Over the ensuing weeks she refused to let the matter lie, bombarding her mother with questions and stubbornly resisting all attempts to sidetrack her. As Ellis's curiosity grew, Laura's discomfort became more and more marked, until Ellis had only to mention her grandmother for her mother to leave the room, on more than one occasion in tears.

Being thwarted merely fed Ellis's craving. In the end she became so insistent that her father took her to one side. A mild, unassuming man, William intervened only rarely in the disciplining of his only child and the ensuing conversation was so unusual Ellis could remember it almost word for word.

'Ellis, I want you to stop badgering your mother right now.'

'But Daddy—'

'But nothing, young lady. It's upsetting her and I

won't have it. She doesn't want to discuss the subject so I would be grateful if you would just let it drop.'

Ellis, going through a mildly rebellious phase, was disposed to sulk. 'But it's not *fair*. It's not as if I'm asking anything unreasonable, I just want to know where I come from, that's all. Why won't she tell me? Is my granny a murderess or something?'

Her father had smiled then, amused, as he so often was, by his daughter's precocious verbosity. 'What a funny child you are; the only seven-year-old I know who would be so grammatically correct as to use the word murder*ess*. No, your granny is not a murderess. Now just leave it, Ellis, before I get seriously annoyed.'

Ellis was a daddy's girl; the thought of her father, who had never lost his temper with her in his life, seriously annoyed, was enough to give her pause; the subject was reluctantly dropped.

As she entered her teens, and settled down to pursue her academic ambitions, the mystery faded into the background. She would come back to the subject one day, she promised herself when some minor incident rekindled her curiosity; when the right moment presented itself she would demand more information, refuse to take no for an answer . . . but gradually over the years her interest had faded. She had moved on, become immersed in her career, left her roots behind.

There had been a few small nuggets of information dropped unwittingly over the years, mostly by William. Ellis had known for instance since she was quite small that the walled kitchen-garden from which her father ran The Herb Garden was once owned by her great-grandfather and that Old Hall Country Club, the grand Italianate mansion perched on the steep wooded hillside across the valley, had been the hub of that same great-grandfather's agricultural estates, known for miles around simply as the Hall. She knew that the Dower House had been left to her mother by her great-grandmother, Lady Marion Palmer, and that Laura had come to Suffolk for the first time specifically to take possession of her inheritance. She had discovered, studying local history for a school project, that Sir Gerald Palmer, the sixth, and last, Baronet, had gone broke in the late 1940s and that the estate had been broken up and sold piecemeal to pay his debts. She knew it was Great-Aunt Nell who had started The Herb Garden, that it was William who had helped her build it up into the thriving specialist plant centre it was now, and it was Laura herself who had told her about Nell's generosity when no one else would give William a job. But Ellis, busy pursuing her own agenda, had paid scant attention to these small snippets of information, had never got round to forming a coherent picture of her family history. Until Joe came along to distract her, her career had taken up all her energy, all her attention.

Yet here she was, consumed once again by the curiosity that had gripped her so hard as a child. Abandoning her car, she left the churchyard by way of the worn path which wound up between the graves and strode out onto the lane, following in Nell's footsteps along Post Office Row towards the Dower House.

She would break the news about the baby first, get the difficult bit out of the way first. But then . . . oh, *then*, she would demand some answers.

Chapter Twenty-One

Ellis had never felt quite comfortable with her mother. As a child she had thought maybe it was her lack of conventional prettiness Laura found so disappointing, had worked even harder at school to compensate for her physical shortcomings, but it hadn't helped. Her mother had commended her achievements, praised her diligence, but Ellis had looked in vain for the warmth, the everyday banter, the jokes and teasing most of her contemporaries seemed to enjoy with their mothers. It was not that Laura didn't love her – Ellis assumed that she must – it was just that, in those early days at least, sometimes she seemed not to *like* her very much.

She was closer to her father. The Methodist background from which William sprang was male dominated, an enclosed, insular society with a fiercely puritan chapel-going ethos and fixed views about 'a woman's place', but William was not remotely like his dour, stern father. A ruddy-faced, bumbling bear of a man, Ellis's father was genial, affectionate, and completely devoted to his wife and daughter.

Sadly, although Ellis thought the sun shone out of his eyes, the harder he tried to gain Laura's approval, the more she pushed him away. The clashes, while Ellis was growing up, between her mother's restless discontent and her father's clumsy attempts to please, had been conducted behind closed doors, and it was not until much later, after she had left home, that she was able to step back and view her parents more objectively, begin to notice how much Laura resented the daily routine of her life, how hard (and mostly unsuccessfully) William had to work to keep her happy. Although punctilious almost to the point of obsession in her domestic duties, Laura took no pleasure in her role as homemaker and clearly resented William's heavy-handed attempts to win her favour. His presents, flowers, trinkets, chocolates were received either with indifference or with outright irritation, and in revenge for some imagined slight she would often sulk for days on end. It was many years before Ellis realised that her mother's early coldness towards her had stemmed from frustration rather than dislike; unhappy in her marriage and stuck on her own all day with a small child, she had vented her spleen on the nearest available person – her daughter. They were closer now than they had ever been when Ellis was living at home, but Ellis still found it difficult to talk to Laura about intimate matters. It was not that she didn't trust her; it was simply the habit of reticence forged during those early years.

The list of questions grew with every step. Why did Violet take Laura back to London as soon as she was born? Had she found out about Nell and Laurence? How had Nell acquired the walled kitchen-garden with its handsome Orangery, from which she ran The Herb Garden until her death? Malletts might have been Laurence's to dispose of as he pleased but the kitchen-garden would have belonged to the estate. Nell's first home-grown herbs had been auctioned in aid of the war effort from that garden – why had she left it to William, rather than to Laura, her own sister's daughter? *Where was the other Ellis?* Why hadn't she asked all these questions long ago, Ellis wondered – why hadn't she dug her heels in, insisted upon answers?

Nell wouldn't recognise the village any more, it occurred to her as she walked along the lane towards the Dower House. In the fifties the spaces between the original cob-walled, thatched cottages had been filled in with modern housing and a small council estate built; a neat row of bungalows had replaced the terrace on Post Office Row. Even during Ellis's lifetime the place had changed out of all recognition. The shop at the bottom of the hill had been demolished to make way for a garage selling secondhand Fords, and every property in the village – including the council houses, sold one by one during the Thatcher years – was now in private hands. Ellis doubted if there were half a dozen residents left who could still remember the place as it was in the forties and fifties, and it was too late to start asking questions now – she should have done it when she was younger, when local memories were still fresh of those years during the war when Nell was building up The Herb Garden from nothing.

Nell and William had worked side by side in the business for five years before Nell's death – Nell had given William a job when no one else would employ him. *Why* would no one else employ him? Had Nell put pressure on her niece, demanding in return that Laura take sides between her and Violet?

Ellis slowed, daunted by the myriad questions buzzing in her head; maybe she should leave well alone, not risk stirring up a hornet's nest of family conflict. But now she knew some of Nell's story, how could she let it rest? She had to get to the heart of it now, otherwise she would have eavesdropped on Nell's life for nothing.

She met Laura coming out.

'Darling!' her mother exclaimed, offering a smooth cheek for her to kiss. 'What a lovely surprise. I wasn't expecting to see you again so soon. Is everything all right?'

'Yes, of course,' said Ellis, pecking dutifully. 'Everything's fine. I just thought I'd pop across and say hello. Have you time for a chat?'

'Yes, I think so.' Laura consulted her watch, then tucked her head on one side and examined Ellis with wide-set blue eyes – Violet's eyes? wondered Ellis, recalling Nell's wistful description of her sister's physical charms, or were they Laurence's? His were blue too, the only feature he had inherited from his mother . . . Even now, in her fifties, Laura was a good-looking woman. Her skin was unblemished, her blonde hair thick and glossy, her figure slim and svelte. It must be pure luck, thought Ellis, examining her mother with newly educated eyes, whether one inherits one's genes from the right parent.

'I was just off to Market Needing,' Laura was saying, 'but it's nothing that won't wait. Coffee?'

Nell wouldn't recognise the Dower House either, thought Ellis as she followed her mother inside. Over the years the place had been extended to almost twice its original size, a new, more spacious sitting room with a third bedroom above it, a double garage, a shiny new kitchen, a conservatory for the fuchsias William had developed an interest in during the eighties, diversifying from the herbs. During one of his more prosperous years he had bought a parcel of land at the bottom of the hill and laid out a knot garden, based on the lithograph which sat over the mantelpiece in the Dower House sitting room. Ellis knew now where that lithograph had come from – it was mentioned in Nell's journal, part of her family history. Had it been handed down through the generations? Kept in the family after the loss of the estate? The knot garden was open to the public from April to October as a living advertisement for the business, but until last night Ellis had had no inkling of the connection between her father's beautifully landscaped showpiece and the bomb-cratered field behind Youngman's forge where poor Arthur Mulligan had breathed his last. The questions surged again, swamping her.

Laura was as immaculately turned out as ever, her make-up perfect, her fair hair as stylish and biddable as Ellis's was wild and untameable. Today she was in her usual uniform of neatly tailored blouse, straight skirt and elegant court shoes – a habit of tidiness formed, Laura always claimed, as a defence mechanism against years of living with her chronically disorganised husband. 'William uses all his energy keeping his tiresome herbs tidy,' she was apt to say. 'At home he's a complete shambles.' Ellis took after her father in this as in so many things – her filing system was a standing joke, her lecture notes almost indecipherable, yet somehow the work she managed to produce out of the chaos was always meticulous. Even when working she lived in trousers and long-tailed shirts, and sometimes when she was younger she had wondered fancifully whether she and her mother were actually related at all, so little resemblance did they bear to each other. At least now she knew where Laura had got her looks from, she thought ruefully, even if she hadn't inherited them herself.

Laura moved about the kitchen, finding the coffee filter, measuring grounds, pouring water, organising biscuits, plates, sugar, milk. When everything was laid out to her satisfaction she picked up the tray and led the way back through the house.

The conservatory, a luxurious blend of exotic green-ery, brass fittings and faux-gothic arched windows, was William's most successful innovation. Despite the heat outside it was pleasantly cool, shaded even this early in the day by heat-resistant blinds, and the flowers of William's fuchsias, lilacs, pinks, purples and reds, were alive with bees and hoverflies. Ellis, weary again, sank gratefully into the nearest chair.

'So, how are you settling in, darling?' asked Laura, laying out cups and saucers, teaspoons and milk jug, as formal, thought Ellis, as if she were entertaining an acquaintance from the local Bridge Club rather than her own daughter. 'And how long will you be staying, do you think?'

'For a while, at least. Mum,' began Ellis, 'there's some-thing I have to—'

'Biscuit?' Laura handed sugar, placed coffee, milk jug, plate, at Ellis's elbow.

'No thanks. Mum, what I want to—'

Laura straightened up and examined Ellis's face, flushed from her explorations in the churchyard, the cot-ton shirt bunched round her waist, her legs, encased as usual in denim jeans. 'You look well, darling,' she said. 'Positively blooming, in fact. You've put on a bit of weight, haven't you? It suits you.'

'Yes.' Ellis tried again. 'Yes, I have. Actually, Mum—'

She was too late; Laura had already moved on. 'I should think Malletts looks a bit different now from the first time you saw it, doesn't it?' She bent down, busying herself with her own cup, then settled back opposite Ellis and crossed her legs. 'It couldn't have been much worse, could it?'

Ellis spooned brown sugar into her coffee and made an effort to relax. 'No, it couldn't,' she agreed. 'But it looks terrific now. You must come and see it soon.'

They had walked across from the Dower House on Ellis's twenty-first birthday. Enticed home from university one sunny May weekend by the promise of a 'surprise present', Ellis could still remember the shock when she emerged from beneath the trees to confront her inheritance. Since Nell's death the cottage, hidden from the outside world, had been left untouched except by wind, rain and nesting birds. One end, almost completely gutted by the fire, was a stark skeleton of blackened beams and smoke-scorched walls, only the cast-iron range, the brick copper and the bread oven, built to withstand the heat, intact. The other end had escaped the flames, but the thatch was gone and the walls, open to the elements, were green with damp, the window frames rotten and the glass missing. Climbing the rickety stairs to investigate the tiny bedroom, Ellis had found Nell's brass-and-iron bedstead still incongruously in position beneath the open sky, its rolled-up mattress oozing mildewed stuffing and a robin's nest perched precariously among its springs. The storeroom, piled with charred, mouldy clutter, was permeated with a strong smell of mice and soot and the only cheering note during an otherwise thoroughly depressing tour of her newly acquired property had been the white lilac in full, glorious bloom near the pond. Its blossom had filled the air with heavy, exotic perfume and, breathing its scent, Ellis had been reminded of that first visit to Nell when she was four years old. Its fragrant beauty seemed almost miraculous in the midst of such ruinous decay.

'Very quaint,' she remembered remarking to her mother as they walked back towards the road, 'but I hope you don't expect me to live there.'

She had felt no curiosity at the time as to why Nell had left Malletts to her rather than to her mother, only frustration that she had been dragged away from her studies on a wild-goose chase. She was nearing the end of her final year at university, working flat-out and completely preoccupied with her approaching exams; if anyone had told her then that she would end up living in that sad wreck of a house, she would have laughed. Not knowing its history, she had kept the brass-and-iron bedstead, had had it repaired and a new base put on. She would sleep in it tonight, if she was able to sleep at all, and wake in it tomorrow morning, just as Nell had done during the long, lonely months of her pregnancy.

'Do you remember that bedstead?' she asked Laura now. 'The one with the robin nesting in it? I've had it renovated and it looks wonderful.'

'Only vaguely.' Laura sipped at her coffee, frowning with concentration. 'Nell used to settle me by the fire in the sitting room when I visited and I never went further than the scullery. I didn't feel comfortable there, to be honest. I always had the feeling that she was expecting something from me, only I hadn't a clue what it was so I couldn't provide it. She used to stare at me all the time, then turn away as soon as I looked at her – terribly disconcerting. And she was so *fierce*. D'you know, she even told William she would take him on only if we named you after some long-lost friend of hers. And that time I took you to see her – you can't have been more than four, yet she bombarded you with questions, as if she were conducting some awful intelligence test. She did it to me the first time I met her, then told me there was no doubt whose daughter I was and sent me packing! She scared me a bit actually, what with her gypsy face and that awful pipe—'

'Pipe?' interrupted Ellis. 'What pipe?'

'Didn't you know?' Laura glanced at her in surprise. 'It was the pipe that killed her. She'd been smoking for years, took it up during the war, I think, and the fire people said she must've dozed off in her armchair while it was still lit. There was an old rag rug in front of the range and it would only have taken one spark. Falling asleep while smoking is one of the most common causes of domestic fires apparently . . .'

Ellis listened with rising excitement. Laura talked so rarely about personal matters, yet here she was offering information, even mentioning names, without prompting. The questions came thicker and faster, tumbling through her mind. What did Nell and Laura talk about as they sat by the fire at Malletts? Did Nell talk about her affair with Laurence, mention the other Ellis? Don't interrupt, Ellis chided herself, don't push too hard. She probably knows nothing about Nell and Laurence . . .

'That day we went there,' Laura was saying, 'on your twenty-first birthday, was the first time I'd ever been in the bedroom. Your father did all the clearing up after the fire—'

Hungry for more information, Ellis forgot her resolution. 'Tell me about it,' she commanded. 'Did you see much of Nell when you were growing up? Did Violet take you there when you were small?' Almost before the words had left her mouth she knew she'd made a mistake.

'No.' Laura's cup rattled loudly in its saucer. Caught off guard, she had been reminiscing as if it were a natural pastime, but now Ellis had reminded her; even after all these years, it seemed, the mention of Violet's name was capable of upsetting her. 'No, I didn't meet Nell till I came to Suffolk, when I was nineteen.'

Too far in to stop, Ellis ploughed on. 'But didn't you ever come to stay at the Hall for holidays? Didn't Vi— I mean, didn't your mother ever bring you to visit your granny?'

'No.' Laura was growing agitated. 'No, I've just told you.'

The questions teemed in Ellis's head – she could see that Violet might want to cut her daughter off from Nell, but what quarrel could she possibly have had with Marion? Marion was on her side, wasn't she? After all, Laura was a Palmer, Laurence's daughter, Marion's granddaughter.

She was getting too close, too personal; Laura's discomfort was visibly increasing. 'Tell me about Malletts,' she said, changing tack. 'Why did Nell leave the cottage to me?'

Laura shrugged. 'It was hers to do with as she pleased and she took a shine to you, that's all. She said you reminded her of herself. She thought you were quick.'

'Quick?'

'Mmm, quick. You know, smart, bright, clever.' Laura cleared her throat, made a stab at a smile. 'Actually, you told her so, when I took you to visit her. I don't suppose you remember, but Nell was highly amused at the time.'

'How did she come to own Malletts in the first place?'

Another shrug. 'She must have bought it from my grandfather I suppose.'

The reply answered one of Ellis's questions: if Laura thought the cottage was in Sir Gerald's gift, she couldn't know about Nell and Laurence. But it posed another: had Laurence made a will, leaving his most precious possession to his mistress? Was that what had given the lovers away?

Laura was fiddling with her coffee cup, picking it up, putting it down, rearranging her skirt.

'How did Nell get started with The Herb Garden?'

'I've no idea. Does it matter?' Laura was staring sullenly out of the window; Ellis began to beg.

'Please, Mum. Tell me about the estate. Tell me about

Nell. Tell me . . .' Her brain still spinning with unanswered questions, she ran out of patience. 'Tell me about *everything*. I *need* to know.'

'Oh, *Ellis*!' Laura's composure deserted her completely. 'Why must you drag it all up again? How many times do I have to tell you I don't want to talk about it!'

It was like being seven years old again. Ellis leaned forward in her chair. It seemed desperately important suddenly, as if she could come to terms with the baby growing inside her only if she could place it in context, give it a history to be part of. Nell and Laurence's affair, the quarrel which had kept Violet and Laura apart for the whole of her lifetime, her namesake, Ellis, Nell's missing son –somehow, in some way she had not yet fathomed, they were all connected. 'Please,' she begged again. 'Please, Mum, why won't you talk to me? I really, really need to know.'

Laura moistened her lips and stared straight ahead. 'No,' she said. 'No, I can't. I *won't*.' Then she dropped her head in her hands and burst into tears.

In the end Ellis lost her nerve. When her mother began to cry she told her it didn't matter, that she was asking only out of idle curiosity. She was sorry, she said, soothing ruffled feathers, she hadn't realised that the subject would still be so sensitive after all this time. When Laura, elegant even in distress, gazed at her dolefully with blue, tear-filled eyes and said, 'I'm sorry Ellis, I simply don't want to discuss it,' she said she quite understood, then began meekly to talk about other things, unimportant things like the sand the builders had left, the difficulty the moving men had had getting her desk through the front door, the sort of trivial conversation she and her mother had been conducting for as long as she could remember. Then she made her excuses, apologised again for any upset she had caused, and made her way back along the passage to the hall – probably the only part of the house, she thought as she passed the cupboard under the stairs, Nell would still recognise. Before she departed she issued an invitation for both her parents to come to supper the following evening. The news about the baby would have to keep until then.

She ought to find it easier than this, it occurred to her as she walked across the drive, to talk to her own mother.

The car was stifling. She wound down the windows, letting out a little of the heat, then sat staring out through the windscreen and thinking about Nell's journal. She would have to finish it now; now that she'd begun, she had to know the rest.

Chapter Twenty-Two

The most important element in William's life, after his wife and daughter, was The Herb Garden, and every single family holiday during Ellis's childhood had been spoiled by her father's ill-concealed impatience, from the moment the car was loaded and they set off down the drive, to get back as soon as possible. None of his staff could be trusted to understand his beloved herbs as he did and his lack of interest in whatever resort they were staying at, his twitching anxiety to be done with Broadstairs, or Barcelona or whatever location Laura had set her heart on that year, always sent Ellis's mother into such a towering rage it had been a relief when the attempts to get him away from work were finally abandoned as being not worth the aggravation. But it wasn't until Ellis was in her mid-twenties that she had begun to realise how like her father she had become, how far her work dominated her life.

At university she had immersed herself totally in her studies, and as she moved up the hierarchy within the enclosed academic world she had chosen, those friends she had made at university had drifted away almost without her noticing. Most of them had gone into commerce, become journalists or advertising executives, stockbrokers or captains of industry. All of them were married, most had children, and, although she kept in touch with a handful of her contemporaries with cards at Christmas and the occasional phone call, it was not the same, *they* were not the same, as in the old, carefree student days.

The annual week's holiday with Laura had been Ellis's idea, an attempt to get closer to her mother, find some common ground. Maybe, she had decided, if they could get away together they might learn to talk to each other. After all, who else did she have, if not her family?

It had worked, up to a point. Laura had been pleased to be asked, flattered that her daughter wanted to spend time with her. Over the ensuing years they had visited some spectacular places, seen sights neither of them would have seen on their own, and they had grown closer too – Ellis rang her mother more often, kept her informed of her progress, saved amusing stories of university life to tell her when she visited, and in return Laura had become noticeably warmer towards her. But still, during those annual vacations spent touring Greek ruins or Egyptian tombs, ancient Inca cities or primitive French cave paintings, their conversation never strayed beyond the superficial, never touched any subject more serious than the picturesque qualities of the view, the shortcomings of the local cuisine, the anticipation of tomorrow's excursion. Whenever Ellis threatened to turn towards the personal, her mother would deftly change the subject. And now, thought Ellis, guiltily reviewing what had just passed between them, she had pushed Laura too far again, upset her, exactly as she had when she was seven years old.

It was only when she began to unload the shopping that she realised how tired she was. She lugged the bags through the house, then stacked the ready-meals to which she had so lazily succumbed in the freezer in the old privy. Then she wandered back to the kitchen to unpack the rest of the shopping, flour and bread, butter, soft and oozing in its packet, wilting lettuce, sweating mushrooms and some strong crumbly cheddar from Tesco's delicatessen.

Since Joe's departure she had struggled to come to terms with her situation. Lately, she had started to talk to her unborn child as if it – she – were a real person, confiding her fears, discussing her plans. 'The first thing we have to do is get the place shipshape,' she told her now as she stashed new potatoes and onions in the tiny larder at the end of the kitchen. 'Really it was daft to invite your granny and grandpa for tomorrow. I'll pop up to The Herb Garden this afternoon and see Dad, explain that I'm not ready for visitors yet.'

You're putting it off, her conscience intruded, you're finding excuses. You're scared of what they'll say. You've already made it more difficult for yourself, upsetting Laura. The look of relief she had caught on her mother's face when she'd taken her leave, and the hesitation before Laura had agreed, reluctantly, to come to supper were proof enough of that.

'Of course, from a purely practical point of view, whether they approve or not doesn't really matter,' Ellis reassured her daughter. 'We'll be fine with or without their approval. We've got money in the bank, a roof over our heads, and now . . .' – stashing stock cubes and olive oil on the top shelf – '. . . we've got food in the larder.'

She placed her hands over her stomach where she thought the baby was lying, and squeezed gently. And what about Joe? demanded her conscience. Where does Joe fit into this cosy little scenario? This is his baby too. Doesn't that give him rights? Responsibilities?

'Coffee,' said Ellis, quelling the thought. 'Now where did I put the coffee?'

She ate her lunch in the glade, setting up her deckchair in the shade between the pond and the lilac tree and carrying out salad and cheese, chunks of crusty french bread and a glass of orange juice. In front of her the cottage, still littered with stacked books, unhung pictures and unsorted files, basked peacefully in the sun. What would Joe make of this place? she wondered. Would he love it as she already did? Or would he shudder at the isolation, hate the lack of modern facilities, demand instantly to return to the noise and bustle of the city? How little she knew about him, she thought, chewing her bread and cheese without tasting. They had never talked much about their respective backgrounds – it had been books and plays, arguments about politics, favourite poets . . .

She took a long pull at her orange juice, then settled herself more comfortably in her deckchair and shaded her eyes with her hand. Would he feel Nell's presence here as strongly as she did? And what would he make of Nell's journal, still lying on the stairs waiting for her to summon the nerve to pick it up again?

She had tested the wall when she stepped inside, resting her shopping bags against her legs and spreading her hand on the plaster next to the sitting-room door. There had been no vibration, just cool, solid wall, and she had felt . . . what? Relief mostly, she supposed, but it was a relief tinged with regret. There, she had admonished herself sternly, you see what a fool you've been? There's nothing here, it was just a figment of your imagination. But the knowledge that she was really, truly alone had made her feel surprisingly lonely, as if Nell, having confided her innermost secrets, had now abandoned her to sort out the resulting mess by herself.

Of course there was a perfectly logical explanation for what she had experienced this morning – she got shocks from her car sometimes, and from the carpet in her office at the university. It wasn't dangerous, just inconvenient, a build-up of static electricity. 'That's all it was,' she told herself as she finished the last crumbs of bread and cheese. 'It was nothing to do with Nell. It was just too much static.'

It was evening when she woke. The shadows had lengthened and her bare arms were glowing where the sun had caught them. An angry wasp was buzzing in the inch of orange juice she had left in the bottom of her glass, half drowned but too sticky to climb out. She stretched, then glanced at her watch. Twenty to seven. If she was going to postpone tomorrow's supper she must go and see her father now, or it would be too late to catch him before he went home. For a moment she regretted not having put in a phone, until she remembered that the phones at The Herb Garden were switched off at five-thirty every night so William could do his books in peace.

She examined the glade. Over the years the trees had encroached upon the open space, an ash here, a sycamore there, a young oak in the middle of what must once have been Nell's vegetable patch, like Birnam Wood coming to Dunsinane. There were brambles and wild roses dotted about, mounds and hummocks beneath the swaying grasses. She must ask her father the best way to tackle it, she thought, whether she should clear the ground completely or just take out the biggest trees and leave the rest.

The sun threw its last rays across the clearing and she

shaded her eyes against the glare. Was that rosemary, that bush over there? And across to her left, was that the pink spire of a self-seeded lupin? This, it occurred to her, the very spot where she was sitting, was the site of Nell's first herb garden, the place where it had all started. She felt a buzz of excitement, then a rush of apprehension, the same daunting weight of responsibility she had felt as she walked along Post Office Row to see Laura. What if she didn't like what she discovered? What then?

She stood up. She could still catch her father – he worked late most nights at this time of year. Maybe she would tell him about the journal, ask him what to do. He was so down to earth, so sensible. He would help her get things in perspective. Perhaps she would ask him some of the questions she clearly still couldn't ask her mother. Or maybe she would just sit in his office, drink his awful tea, and enjoy his unflagging enthusiasm for The Herb Garden.

She rescued the wasp, then cleared up the remains of her lunch, and strode back, through grass already wet with evening dew, to deposit the tray in the kitchen. Then she picked up her keys, tucked them in the back pocket of her jeans, and made for the front door.

She avoided touching the walls, and as she threaded her way through the piles of books littering the floor she stared fixedly straight ahead. But she paused in the hall and glanced back, unable to resist. There was no sudden, startling glimpse of Nell's ancient leather armchair, no smell of tobacco. You see? she mocked herself, there's no one here but you. Whatever it was that had caused her mind to play tricks on her, it was gone now.

Nell's journal was still sitting on the stairs. She ought to put it somewhere sensible, Ellis thought. She bent to pick it up. She would put it away, leave it for a few days until she had calmed down a bit—

Clack!

The latch rattled against its hasp and Ellis stepped sharply backwards, seized momentarily by the insane notion that it was Laurence outside, her grandfather returning fifty years too late to reclaim his mistress. 'Who is it?' she demanded. 'What do you want?' Don't be ridiculous, she scolded herself, it's just Dad, calling round on his way home to see how you're settling in, or the builder, dropping off the final bill for the renovations. So why didn't whoever it was say something? Her nervousness increased. She drew Nell's journal tight against her chest, folding her arms across it as if it might shield her against . . . what? 'Who is it?' she repeated. 'Dad, is that you?'

'Me. It's me.'

Joe? Ellis stared intently at the door. She was shaking, her heart thumping violently, her mouth suddenly dry. His voice conjured vividly that moment, all those months ago, when she had stood at her study window and picked him out from a crowd of milling students; the mental picture increased her confusion, rendered her dizzy with mingled delight and distress. Reaching out to steady herself against the wall Ellis felt it – a faint vibration, barely perceptible, spreading beneath her fingers.

'Joe?' Panicking, she snatched her hand away. 'Joe, is that you?'

'Who the bloody hell else would it be?'

Ellis found Nell's words on her tongue. 'Go away.'

Joe seemed to be working from Laurence's script. 'No,' he said. 'You called me.'

'No I didn't!' Her dream came again, wandering aimlessly through the cottage calling his name. Surely, crying out in one's sleep didn't count, did it? 'How did you find me?' she demanded. 'I left strict instructions—'

'Not strict enough, obviously. Are you going to let me in?'

'No.'

'Then I'll huff and I'll puff and I'll blow your house down.'

Ellis, smiling involuntarily, put her hand up to straighten her cheek muscles and heard it again – Nell's tune, still playing in the recesses of her mind. 'Go away,' she repeated.

Silence again, then, softly, '"*Is there anybody there?" said the Traveller, knocking on the moonlit door . . .*'

Poetry. How ridiculous, how ludicrous, how *typical* of Joe to start quoting poetry at a time like this . . . How could she ever have thought she might be over him?

'I'm still here.'

Ellis struggled to marshal her scattered wits.

'I'll wait then, shall I?'

'No, I've told you—'

'Open the door, Ellie. I can't hear you.'

Ellis took a step nearer, drawn inexorably. 'How did you find me? I told them in the office not to release my address.'

'I asked around.'

'Around? Around who? Who did you ask?'

'Your friend Harriet. Let me in, Ellie.'

Ellis closed her eyes – Joe was the only one who ever called her Ellie. Get your act together, she told herself. This is what you didn't want, remember? Joe Leavis standing on your doorstep demanding to be let back into your life; this is the scene you've tried so hard to avoid, the reason you went to such lengths to cover your tracks. 'You're lying,' she said. 'Harriet doesn't even know this place exists. You've been talking to my mother, haven't you?'

'Funny woman, your mam.'

'What do you mean?'

'Didn't seem too chuffed to see me.'

'Then how did you get her to tell you where I was?'

'Ah . . .' He actually had the gall to *laugh*. 'Easy. I told her you were expecting my kid.'

'*What*?'

'I told her—'

'All right, I heard you.' He must have known all along. What a fool she was, to think she could keep it from him.

'Let me in,' repeated Joe stubbornly, 'or I'll kick the door down.'

Ellis watched her hand move towards the catch of its own volition, pulled it sharply back. 'On one condition.'

A long pause, then, truculently, 'What?'

'No funny business.'

'No *funny* business? You sound like a bad movie.'

'I mean it.'

'Yeah. All right, OK. Whatever you say. No funny business.'

Ellis snapped the catch and swung the door open, then backed into the sitting room, tripping over a pile of books in her anxiety to put some space between them, still clasping Nell's journal to her chest.

'So, Dr Jones.'

He stopped in the sitting-room doorway and leaned against the jamb, watching her. He was wearing faded jeans, a navy-blue T-shirt, a pair of heavily scuffed desert boots. His face and arms were tanned, as if he had spent most of the past month out of doors, and in the weeks since she had seen him he'd had his hair cut short. His features looked older beneath the close crop, harder, his chin was rough with three days' growth of beard and he was crumpled, untidy, as if he'd been sleeping in his clothes. Ellis opened her mouth to comment on his appearance, then shut it again – she must keep her distance, stay cool. She could hear her own breathing and the faint sound of Joe's boots shifting on the stone floor.

'When were you going to get round to telling me?'

'Telling you what?' Shut up, Ellis scolded herself, don't treat him like a fool.

'Don't treat me like a fool,' said Joe, advancing into the room.

Ellis had forgotten how tall he was, what he was capable of doing to her knees. Her reserves of courage sapped by a sleepless night, a confusing day and too much sun, she simply wasn't equipped to cope with him. 'Look . . .' She backed further away. 'I'm . . . er, you've caught me by surprise. I wasn't expecting . . .'

'You called me,' Joe persisted stubbornly. 'So I came. And now you want me to go and sit in the long grass and meditate till you're ready to receive me, right?'

'No! No, that's not what I want at all.'

'Good.' He was brisk, dismissive. 'Because frankly, I don't fancy it much. It's sopping out there and I've never been a great one for getting my bum wet.'

'Joe, will you please stop—'

'Thought you'd never ask.' He grinned. Ellis had forgotten how disarming his grin was; she could guess how he had charmed Laura into giving away her hiding place. 'I've got my gear outside,' he said, 'shan't be a tick.' Then he ducked his head beneath the lintel and disappeared.

Ellis closed her eyes. The minute he returned, the second he walked through the door, she would tell him to go. She should never have let him in in the first place. She wasn't in command of the situation, didn't have the upper hand; unless she could wrest the initiative from him he would walk all over her.

She heard rasping noises in the hall, then Joe reappeared, dragging a large, delapidated rucksack which he dropped at his feet. 'Sorry,' he apologised, 'all my worldly goods. It's a hell of a weight.'

Ellis stared at him in disbelief. 'Joe, you *promised*. No funny business. I thought I'd made it clear—'

'Yeah. But I've nowhere else to go – Mam's slung me out.'

'Why, what have you done?'

He bent to fumble with the straps of his rucksack, talking over his shoulder. 'Where would you like me to start? I'm having an affair with a woman fourteen years older than me, who also happens to be a senior lecturer—'

'*Were*.' Ellis frowned at his back, infuriated by his use of the present tense, by his self confidence, his arrogant refusal to accept that it was over. 'You *were* having an affair with a senior lecturer. Past tense—'

'I'm having an affair with a senior lecturer,' continued Joe imperturbably. 'I've put her up the spout, as my dear old dad used to say, I've jacked in my university place—'

'*What?*' Ellis sat down on the nearest chair and stared at him in horror.

'I've jacked it in.' Joe straightened up, stretched like a thin, wiry cat, shrugged. He looked unconcerned about what he had done, even pleased with himself. 'I handed in my letter of resignation two days ago. I've spent the last couple of nights in my car. I could do with a shave.' He moved across to the window and stood with his back to her, staring out at the last rays of the sun slanting across the glade with his hands thrust deep into his jeans' pockets and his shoulders hunched, the only sign that he was not completely at ease. 'Nice spot, this. So now there's no reason why we can't carry on where we left off, is there?'

Ellis struggled for words. How could he? How *could* he have been such an idiot as to throw away his entire future on her account? She dropped Nell's journal on the table, slapped its battered cover for emphasis. 'You must go back and tell him you've changed your mind,' she said. 'Now, before it's too late. Tell him you were drunk or something. He'll understand, he's seen it all before. Students often make mistakes in the throes of—'

'Oh, *shut up!*' said Joe.

It was only then, as he folded his arms and glared at her across the piles of books, that Ellis realised just how furiously angry he was.

She panicked again. Rising from her seat she fumbled in her jeans' pocket, removed the front door key from the ring and placed it on the table, on top of William's plans for the lavender garden. Then she made for the door.

'I thought you'd got the message,' she said, speaking slowly and clearly, as if he were deaf or stupid. 'It's over, Joe. We had an affair. I'm sorry if you thought it was more than that, but I can't be responsible for you reading something into our relationship that wasn't there. I'm going out now. You can have a wash and a shave, but when I get back I shall expect to find you gone. If you've any sense you'll go and see the Bursar first thing tomorrow, tell him you want your place back before he reallocates your room. I must go and put things right with my mother. You can leave the key . . .' That reminder of the past came again, Nell's tune playing insistently in her head. *It's called a bumby . . .* 'You can leave the key on the shelf next to the bumby.'

'Next to the what?'

Ellis shook her head, attempting to clear the debris cluttering her mind. 'There's an old privy out the back. There's a shelf just inside the door.' . . . *for a candle, a hook for the torn squares of newspaper* . . . 'You can leave the key there.'

She went to pass him, but he stepped in front of her. 'D'you know what your mam said?'

'Excuse me.' She moved to one side but he moved with her, blocking her way.

'Is it true, Ellie?'

'Is what true?'

'I told her it was an accident, the kid. And you know what, Ellie? She said, "Don't be stupid, no woman gets pregnant these days unless she wants to." She said if you're having a baby it's because you want a baby, because you intended to have a baby. She said . . .' He moved out of her way, but he kept on probing, trying to guess what she was thinking, what she was feeling. 'She said lots of women these days opt to have a baby without wanting the hassle of a father to go with it. I told her it wasn't like that with us. It wasn't like that with us, was it, Ellie?'

Ellis couldn't bring herself to look at him. 'What does it matter what my reasons were?' she said, staring fixedly at her feet. 'What difference does it make whether it was deliberate or not? I shan't change my mind.' It was true – what did it matter what Joe thought of her? The affair was over. In a way it was better for him if he thought the worst; if he thought she had merely used him as a means to an end he would get over her more quickly. Whether she would ever get over him was another matter.

'Don't forget to lock up when you leave,' she said.

She seemed to have caught him by surprise – he made no further move to detain her – and she strode out into the hall, anxious to escape before he could recover sufficiently to challenge her again. It was not until she had waded through the wet grass to reach her car, then struggled past his rusty Ford Fiesta, parked so close she had to climb in via her passenger door, that she began to get herself under control. It was so easy when he wasn't there to believe that she was doing the right thing finishing it, so *hard* when she was with him. Sometimes over the past few months she had even thought about giving up her teaching career, resigning from the university and trying to make a living from her writing. Then Joe could get on with his degree and they could be together without looking over their shoulders all the time. But then the cold light of reality would creep in. Ellis had spent her whole adult life working towards what she had now; she adored teaching, loved the university – even the decision to take a year's sabbatical had been hard enough. Sooner or later she would regret giving it all up, resent Joe's part in the sacrifice of everything she had worked so hard to achieve. And how would Joe live with the knowledge that she had made herself miserable for his sake?

But now Joe had done it instead, given everything up for her. 'And it still won't work,' she said out loud, gripping the steering wheel with one hand and wiping her brimming eyes with the back of the other. 'It simply won't work, you bloody fool.'

She drove slowly along the drift, calming herself down, then turned left onto the side road which would take her under the dual carriageway and back along the other side of the valley to the Dower House. She must apologise to her mother, explain that she had tried to break the news about the baby that morning, that she hadn't intended her to find out like this. What must Laura think of her? How could Joe have *done* such a thing? Working herself into a self-righteous rage, she began, perversely, to feel better.

*

She meant to go straight to the Dower House, but, approaching a pretty lodge-house, flanked by a sweeping curve of wall and a pair of impressive stone gateposts, she made a quick, cowardly decision and turned off the road. She bumped over the cattle grid, passed the signs for *Old Hall Country Club* and *The Herb Garden*, and drove on into the park. Quarter past seven. The final parting with Joe had taken less than twenty minutes. She might still catch her father.

The sun was low now, and on either side of the road groups of black-faced sheep lay beneath the trees, already settled down for the night. At the top of the rise the Hall, with its ornate towers, finials, balconies and balustrades, was silhouetted against the deep blue of the evening sky, its windows already illuminated against the approaching dark. Ellis could hear the sound of tinkling glass and china coming from the open dining-room windows which faced towards her across the raised terrace and, as she swung left past another sign announcing *The Herb Garden*, she caught the noise of clashing pans and the raised voice of the chef bellowing orders at his minions in the kitchens in the north wing – the servants' quarters when the estate was still owned by the Palmers. This was where Marion lived during the war, she thought, where Violet waited out her pregnancy, where Laura was born . . .

The board hanging beneath the sign said CLOSED, but that meant nothing – William was always the last to leave, long after his staff had packed up and gone home, and his employees had instructions to flip the board on their way past. Ellis drove on for another hundred yards before her way was blocked by the high red-brick wall of the old kitchen-garden, then followed the road round to the gravel car park at the back. She parked the car, then climbed out and leaned against the bonnet, staring across the close-cropped grass towards the wide expanse of woodland which ran along the steep-sided valley. Somewhere at the heart of the green swathe sweeping down the hill towards the river, Malletts was hidden, and she strained her eyes in the fading light, searching for a clue – a chimney pot, a glimpse of tiled roof, even some faint trace of the narrow path along which Ernie Beale had once pushed his bicycle on his way from the Hall to see Nell. Was Joe still there, waiting to start the argument all over again? She was assailed by loneliness, and doubt.

William's battered estate car was parked on the other side of the car park, next to the patch of waste ground at the end of the propagating units. She recalled her father's bubbling elation the other night as he talked of his plans for the site – which varieties of lavender he was going to plant, how he would lay it all out. He had been planning it for over two years now, buying in new varieties, taking cuttings, dividing stock, potting up, so when the time came he would have all the bushy, healthy plants he needed. She should have brought his plan back, it occurred to Ellis, but it was still lying on the table at Malletts, with her key resting on top of it. Where was Joe now? she wondered. Was he standing in the sitting room, staring out of the window with his shoulders hunched? Or was he in the bathroom, shaving? She had always loved to watch him bathe, his hair, slick and black with water, his body, pale and lean and surprisingly hairless for such a dark-haired man, his long legs . . . only now, all that was over. She was here because of Joe's big mouth, not because of his body, his habit of quoting poetry at inappropriate moments, his ability to make her laugh even when she was trying to be serious. It was no good looking back, it was the future she had to face up to now . . .

The propagating units, wood and glass set on brick plinths, with their own irrigation and feeding systems and automatic vents, had replaced Nell's original flimsy half-hoop, plastic-covered structures only about fifteen years ago. They had doubled the space available for bringing on young plants and William had had to take out a hefty bank loan to get them built, Laura having refused point-blank to contemplate a mortgage on the Dower House. 'This is my house,' Ellis remembered her telling William at the time, 'and I have no intention of putting it in hock just so you can indulge your silly fantasies!' When William returned, grinning from his mission to the bank, Laura's reaction had been entirely predictable. 'We could have gone on two world cruises for that sort of money,' she had complained angrily, 'but of course your stupid *herb* garden has to come first!' The lavender garden was already becoming a bone of contention, before it was even started.

As Ellis locked her car she made a quick mental calculation: assuming Joe had driven straight to Malletts from the Dower House it would have been too late for Laura to phone William – the phones would already have been switched off. At least, since Joe had already broken the news to her mother, she ought to have the courage to do her own dirty work with her father. She took a deep breath, then shoved her keys in her back pocket and strode across the gravel towards the arched iron gate. As she entered the garden she quickened her pace, eager to see her father.

Dad would make her feel better. He always had, ever since she was a little girl.

Chapter Twenty-Three

The place was quiet, tranquil; the last members of staff, always there for at least an hour after closing time, watering, dead-heading, tidying up abandoned trolleys and straightening pots knocked askew by over-eager customers, had gone for the night. This was the best time, when the garden was empty, when the shadows began to stretch across the herb beds and the heat inside the high walls had been dissipated by the cold water from the hoses – the watering was always done in the evenings, so the sun wouldn't burn through any dampness and mark the leaves.

Ellis walked slowly, enjoying the rich scent of wet earth and the other, more pungent smells the watering had unleashed. The rubber hoses lay coiled like neat black snakes along the edges of the concrete paths, ready for the next day. Here too, she thought as she strolled towards the brick lean-to at the far end of the main path, once a potting shed but now William's office, here too there had been changes since Nell's time. William had planted a wisteria walk to draw the customers in, and another knot garden to show off his wares, a miniature facsimile of the one on the other side of the valley. He had raised the gravel display beds so people didn't have to stoop to see what they were buying, installed a round pond at the crossroads in the centre of the garden, with waterlilies and a fountain to provide a soothing background to the hum of conversation, the rumble of trolley wheels on the paths and the constant *ting-ting* of the tills at the entrance to the Orangery, where all goods were paid for. The front half of the Orangery had been turned into a shop selling peripherals – jars of local honey, boxes of fudge, coloured candles, remedies for pests and funguses, seed packets (William's own brand, emblazoned at the top with *The Herb Garden* logo in swirling gold letters), clay pots, watering cans, garden furniture – loungers and parasols, plastic tables and canvas chairs – even coal by the bag and bundles of kindling. At the back, where the great expanse of glass roof swept down to join the garden wall, William had created a room within a room for the fuchsias, his latest passion. The windows were darkened now, the glass glimmered in the last of the daylight and the goods inside were just vague shadows. This place was part of Ellis's childhood, woven into her earliest memories, and she was aware that it was her father's greatest regret that she had displayed no aptitude for his abiding love, no instinct for the growing and nurturing of plants despite all his attempts to pass on his enthusiasm.

The light from the open office door spilled out onto the path and an electric fan was whirring busily to itself in a corner. Everything was comfortably the same as it had always been. A Victorian sideboard, its surface ringed and scored with the marks of years of careless use, sat solid and ugly against the back wall, anchored by the weight of its own squalor. One door hung drunkenly from its hinges and the other was missing altogether; its top was cluttered with used coffee cups, a battered kettle, an open bag of sugar, two cartons of milk, one empty and lying on its side, a box of tea bags and a jar of coffee with the lid missing. An assortment of sticky teaspoons lay face up amidst the mess in little pools of liquid. Next to the sideboard two ancient filing cabinets squatted like fat, broody metal hens beneath a sagging shelf laden with gardening encyclopaedias; piles of pots and gardening magazines spilled untidily from beneath a broken wooden bench littered with an assortment of mismatched gardening gloves. Despite the noisy efforts of the fan, the room was stuffy and airless.

Ellis's father was sprawled in an elderly kitchen chair in front of a cheap peeling plastic-veneer desk, with his shirtsleeves rolled up and the top of his head shining in the light from the window above him. William was almost completely bald, but the remaining fringe above his ears and his pepper-and-salt eyebrows seemed to get bushier and more untidy every year. He was mopping his forehead with a large grubby handkerchief and his hands were grubby too, the fingernails encrusted with soil. Drifts of dirt had accumulated on the untidy pile of paperwork he was working on, more plans for the lavender garden sketched on everything from old invoices and receipts to brand-new headed notepaper and the backs of used postcards. Every horizontal surface in the long, low room was covered in a thick layer of dust and Ellis paused in the doorway, struck as always by the contrast between the immaculate public display and the private shambles behind it that constituted her father's business life.

'Ellis!' William lumbered to his feet, performing an awkward sideways ducking movement to avoid hitting his head on the ceiling. 'What a lovely surprise. Kettle's just this minute boiled, poppet. Cup of tea?'

'Mmm.' Ellis returned her father's rib-crushing embrace with enthusiasm, then perched on the edge of his desk and watched as he moved around the cramped space, dunking tea bags and dropping them carelessly next to the kettle, scooping sugar straight out of the packet with a spoon still wet from stirring then dropping the spoon back into the mess where he had found it. Comparing her father's slapdash preparations with her mother's methodical efforts earlier in the day it was no wonder, Ellis reflected, that her parents muddled along so indifferently – they were chalk and cheese.

'Thanks.' She took the chipped mug William handed her and sipped gingerly, grimacing at the taste. William could never remember how anyone took their tea, so everyone got it the same, sweet and milky as he liked it himself. Such was his unstudied charm, nobody ever had the heart to complain, and he remained in blissful ignorance of his incompetence.

'Right,' he began, flopping back into his protesting chair, 'what can I do for you, pet? All well at the hide-away?'

'Mmm.' Ellis lied. 'Everything's absolutely fine. Still a shambles of course, but once I've got it shipshape . . . " She sipped again, eyeing him over the top of her mug. 'Dad . . .'

'Absolutely fine, eh?' William blew loudly on his tea and lowered it to the desk. 'So what's bothering my pop-pet, then, that she has to come all the way over here just to tell me everything's absolutely fine?'

'Is it that obvious?' Ellis settled herself more comfortably on the desk, resting her feet on the side of William's battered chair. 'I've upset Mum.'

'Oh, dear,' said William. 'And you've been getting on so well lately.' His ruddy face crumpled. 'Nothing too serious I hope?'

Ellis hesitated. Blast Joe and his big mouth. Why couldn't he have let well alone? She put her tea down on William's plans and folded her arms protectively over her stomach. 'I asked her about my granny,' she said, putting off the most serious news. 'I asked her about Violet and I made her cry.'

'Ah.' William leaned back in his chair and rubbed his chin, sprinkled at this end of the day with silver stubble. 'Whatever did you do that for, pet? I thought you'd got all that curiosity-kills-the-cat stuff out of your system years ago?'

Ellis shrugged. 'I just—' Oh to hell with it, what was the point of putting it off? He'd know soon enough anyway, thanks to Joe, and it would be better coming from her than from Laura. 'I'm pregnant,' she blurted, 'and I need to know where I come from.'

William was drinking his tea; he didn't even pause.

'Well?' pleaded Ellis. 'Say something. Dad?'

'Biscuit?' William rose clumsily and moved across to the sideboard, his bald head hunched sideways to avoid the lightbulb dangling from the ceiling. He fumbled around in the left-hand cupboard. 'Ginger nuts,' he said, bringing out a battered Quality Street tin and peering inside. 'Scrummy. They were your favourites when you were little, d'you remember?' He returned to his chair, held out the tin, helped himself. 'Good for dunking. Julia – that's my new girl, don't think you've met her yet, have you . . .?' He bit off a chunk of biscuit, masticated thoughtfully. 'Dear little thing, you'll like her. She gets them for me on her way to work, spoils me rotten, bless her. It was jaffa cakes yesterday.' He dropped the tin on the desk. 'So what did your mum say when you told her?'

Ellis nibbled uncomfortably. 'I haven't told her yet. I did try but she wouldn't listen. You know what she's like.'

'I'm sure it wasn't deliberate,' said William, typically loyal. 'She probably didn't hear you. She's getting a bit deaf, you know, although she won't admit it.' He finished his tea and put his mug down next to Ellis's. 'So, what now? Don't worry about breaking the news to your mum – I'll do that when I get home.'

How typical of William. No questions about how she had come to be in such a mess, just an immediate offer of help. 'No need,' said Ellis. 'Someone else has already done it. That's why I'm here, because I'm too cowardly to face her.'

'Eh?' William scratched his head, leaving a grubby mark. 'I'm not grasping this too well, poppet. If you haven't told her, who has?'

It all came flooding out then, Joe's unexpected arrival at the cottage, the gist of his conversation with Laura at the Dower House, as well as Ellis could remember it sec- ondhand. William listened in silence, his eyes focused on the darkening sky framed by the window above his desk, and his fingers tapping a gentle rhythm on the sides of his mug.

'So,' he said at last. 'And was it deliberate?'

'Getting pregnant? No,' said Ellis. 'Just a stupid acci- dent, bad management on my part. And "it" is a girl, by the way. They told me when I had my scan a couple of weeks ago. I'm keeping her, in case that's your next question.'

'Ah.' William flicked the lid off the biscuit tin, helped himself to another ginger nut. 'And what about the . . .?'

'The father?' Ellis reached across to the tin and munched for a bit. 'No, I'm not keeping the father.'

'Ah. And have you told him yet?'

'Yes.'

'Uh huh. And he's quite happy about that, is he?'

'Yes,' Ellis lied, then recalling Joe's fury just before she left the cottage, 'no, not very.'

'Ah.' William crunched his ginger nut, then fell back on his usual cure-all. 'Fancy another cup of tea?'

'No thanks, I haven't finished this one yet.' Ellis imagined Joe driving away from the cottage, and was swept by another wave of loneliness. 'I wouldn't mind a shoulder to cry on, though.'

William nodded. 'Whenever you like, pet.'

She told him everything. She told him about Joe, about the age gap, the impossibility of sustaining a relationship between tutor and student under the disapproving eye of the university authorities. She told him how hard she was finding it to be sensible, how much more difficult Joe had made the situation by refusing to accept that it was over. The relief, talking about it for the first time to someone other than Joe, was enormous. 'But you needn't worry about me, Dad,' she said, leaning across the desk and dropping biscuit crumbs all over William's sketches, 'I've thought it through and I shan't ask you for any financial help, I promise. You mustn't think you have to—'

'I don't suppose you've considered getting married?' said William.

'What?'

'Getting married. The university couldn't complain if you were legal, could they? But I suppose people don't any more, do they? Get married, I mean.'

Ellis sighed. 'Dad, Joe is fourteen years younger than me. How long do you suppose it would take for it to fall apart? What would be the point of getting married knowing before we even start that it was bound to fail?'

'Ah . . . ' William nodded sagely. 'Is that what all this frantic activity has been about then? Renovating Malletts, taking a year out?'

'Mmm.' Ellis swilled the remains of her tea round and round. In all the time she and Joe had been together, marriage had never been mentioned – she had assumed from the beginning that it was not an option. 'Dad—'

'Do you love him, poppet?'

A straightforward question, requiring a yes-or-no answer. 'Dad . . . '

'Well, poppet?'

'Tell me about The Herb Garden,' said Ellis. 'Why did Nell leave it to you and not to Mum?'

'Eh?' The sudden change of subject caught William by surprise. He leaned back in his chair, tipping it onto two legs and resting his feet on the bottom drawer of his desk, then raised his face to the cobweb-threaded ceiling. 'Because I wanted it. No, because she knew I loved it.' He clasped his hands behind his head, turned to look at her. 'Why? You getting enthusiastic at last?'

He sounded wistful, as if he still nursed a faint hope that Ellis might change the habits of a lifetime, discover – how had Nell put it in her journal? – *a passion for the soil*, give up the academic life and come home to learn the ropes so she could take over when he retired. Over the past couple of years he had grown increasingly anxious about the future. He was nearly sixty-four now, but he had yet to find a successor, someone with that extra something, the instinct for growing things Nell had had, the instinct he possessed himself. 'I can't go on for ever,' he had reminded Ellis when she came home for Christmas last year. 'And if you don't want it, what will happen to the poor old place when I'm gone?'

She pushed herself off the desk and squeezed past him to the sideboard. 'The thing is . . . ' How to put it? How to explain without raising hopes she could never fulfil, why it was so important to her? 'The thing is, sometimes I feel as if half my past is missing. In a few months' time I'm going to have a baby and I still don't know where I've sprung from, where I belong.' She moved along the sideboard, sorting dirty mugs from clean, retrieving teaspoons, folding the neck of the sugar packet. 'Oh, I know a bit about my Welsh side. I know that Nell was my great-aunt and that she gave you a job, but I don't know about Nell's family, about my grand-mother, my great-grandmother.' She waved a hand at the window and the garden beyond. 'I don't know how Nell came to acquire this place, or why she took you on. I don't know why my mother doesn't talk to my grand-mother. Was it because of Nell?'

'Huh?' said William. He seemed surprised that she might think there was a connection. 'No, it was nothing to do with Nell. It was . . . why should you think that?'

'But if it wasn't anything to do with Nell,' persisted Ellis, 'what *did* they quarrel about? Mum won't tell me. Why can't you?'

'Because I promised . . .' William heaved his feet off the desk. He looked uncomfortable, embarrassed. His chair-legs thudded onto the floor and a small cloud of dust rose from beneath his feet. 'Sure you won't have more tea, poppet?'

'All right, go on.' Ellis returned to her perch on the desk, making herself small so William could squeeze past her to the kettle. 'Well, if you won't talk about my grandmother, will you at least tell me about The Herb Garden?'

'What do you want to know?' William glanced at her over his shoulder, spilling hot water.

'Everything. Begin at the beginning, with how Nell started all this, and go on to the end, to how you took over.'

'Fair enough.' William settled down with his second mug of tea and attacked the ginger nuts again. 'Can't do any harm, I suppose, talking about The Herb Garden. Start at the beginning, eh? Um . . . Well, Nell first came to Suffolk during the Blitz, got friendly with one of the gar-deners at the Hall. Then, when she came back—'

'Came back?'

'Uh-huh. She was recalled to London early in forty-one by her father.'

'Who told you that?'

'Mmm?' William frowned. 'No idea; can't remember, poppet. Um . . . Lady P, possibly. Nell came to Suffolk to keep your grandmother company at the end of nineteen forty, returned to London the following spring, then came back after your mum was born, to help with the baby.'

Ellis was sure he was telling the truth, or at least whatever truth he had been fed by Marion. Which meant that Nell's secret was known only to a handful of people, all dead now except for Violet and maybe, Nell's missing son. 'But didn't Violet – my grandmother – take Mum back to London straight after she was born?' she asked.

William shrugged. 'Um . . .' He was looking uncomfortable again. 'Maybe she thought Nell was being too bossy or something. Anyway, with or without her sister, Nell decided she wanted to stay. It gets you like that you know, Suffolk, gets under your skin . . . and as soon as she was settled at Malletts she started growing a few herbs, potting up seedlings to sell in aid of the war effort – you know, plant sales, local markets, bring-and-buys – and then she got carried away.' William chuckled, spreading his hands to encompass his herbal empire. 'As one does, you know?' and Ellis laughed too, sharing the joke. 'She was one of those people who couldn't bear having nothing to do, and there can't have been much else to keep her occupied, a Londoner stuck in the depths of Silly Suffolk in the middle of a war. After a while she decided she might as well turn an enjoyable pastime into a proper job, but of course to produce plants on a commercial scale she needed more room, so she talked Lady P – Lady Palmer was your great-grandmother, by the way, your mum's granny on her father's side—'

Ellis nodded. She probably knew more about Marion Palmer, it occurred to her, than William did. 'Go on.'

'So she talked Lady P into letting her use this place. It was practically derelict when she took it over, what with the war and everything, but once she had the space there was no stopping her. By the summer of forty-three she was advertising in the local paper, calling herself The Herb Garden, and by nineteen forty-five she was running a thriving business and taking orders from all over the country. Of course, even commercial nurseries had to grow mostly vegetables during the war – no more than ten per cent flowers was the rule, I think – but she managed to persuade the man from the Ministry that her herbs had some culinary value, so he turned a blind eye when she slipped in more than she was strictly allowed between the cabbages. She showed at Chelsea in forty-seven, the first year it was held after the war and by the time the estate went under the hammer in forty-eight she had enough money saved to buy both the kitchen-garden and the plot of land next to it, where the two propagating units and the car park are now. She was way ahead of her time, a single woman running a successful business . . .'

He took another gulp at his tea, and Ellis waited, longing to ask about the estate, how and why it had come to be sold, what part Marion had played in the disposal of everything she had worked for, but not daring in case, like Laura, he clammed up completely.

'The Herb Garden was the most important thing in Nell's life,' he went on. 'All the energy most women expend on their families she poured into tending her plants. Mind you,' he added, 'there's a limit to what one woman can do, however energetic. By the time she took me on she'd been running the place virtually single-handed for over ten years. Ernie Beale, the chap who started her off on the whole thing, was long gone by then, and although she'd half a dozen young lads work-ing for her she didn't trust any of them to tackle more than the most menial tasks, so she was doing practically all the skilled jobs herself, potting up plants, propagating seedlings, taking cuttings, keeping the books. She was one of the strongest, fittest women I've ever met, but the strain was beginning to tell . . .' William peered at Ellis's mug, still sitting on the desk surrounded by a damp ring of milky tea. 'Tea all right, pet? You haven't touched it yet.'

Ellis drank obediently, then cradled the mug between her hands, breathing in the steam. 'Did Nell confide in you?'

'Good lord, no.' William chuckled. 'Nell never talked about anything personal, wasn't her way. It was Lady P who told me how it all started. She was rather proud of Nell I think, although to hear them spat you'd never guess how fond they were of each other.'

He paused.

'Go on,' prompted Ellis, hungry for more.

'Of course, Nell wasn't prepared to take me on trust. Wouldn't let me loose on my own till she was sure I knew what I was doing.'

'Did you know lots about plants?' asked Ellis.

William slurped more tea. 'Absolutely nothing. She was just doing your mother a favour. Didn't take long to convince her she'd done the right thing, though – I took to it like a duck to water . . .'

Nell took your father on when no one else would employ him. Why would no one else employ him? Ellis sipped her tea and curbed her tongue. Don't ask, she reminded herself, look what happened with Mum.

'And she left me The Herb Garden because she knew I'd look after it, because I loved the place as much as she did.'

'Wasn't Mum hurt, at being left out?'

'A bit.' William shifted in his chair. 'But she already had the Dower House . . .'

Why? If Marion wanted to keep the Dower House within the family, why skip a generation? Why not leave it to Violet? Ellis bit her lip. So many questions . . .

'There was no snub intended,' William was saying. 'It was just that The Herb Garden was too important to Nell to let family loyalty get in the way. She was a middle-aged spinster; she didn't get on with her mother, she'd fallen out with her sister . . .' He stopped, glanced across at Ellis, pulled a wry face. 'Don't ask me why, poppet, that's one of those family secrets I know nothing about – she had no husband, no family of her own. The Herb Garden took the place of the child she'd never had.'

'Oh . . .' The reply confirmed what Ellis had already guessed. Over the last few years of Nell's life William must have been closer to her than anyone else in the world, *yet he didn't know about the other Ellis*. It gave Ellis the oddest sensation, the realisation that she was in possession of information even her own father did not have.

Violet must know though. Violet must know what had happened to Nell's son. Assuming she was still alive . . .

'Mind you,' William was saying, 'she was annoyed about Malletts. Nell changed her will, you see, the day before she died. It was after your mother took you to see her, remember? Her original will left Malletts to your mum but she took such a shine to you that day she changed her mind. She took the morning off – unheard of for her – to go into Ipswich specially.'

Outside, the evening was advancing and the square of

sky visible through the window had turned a deep, velvet pink. William peered at his watch. 'I must get off, poppet. Your mum'll think I've had an accident.' He heaved himself clumsily out of his chair. 'Leave your tea; one of the kids'll deal with it in the morning.' He shuffled around, stooping to turn off the fan, switching internal lights off, plunging them into fusty darkness, then outside lights on, turning the room acid blue. 'Ready?'

Ellis slid reluctantly from her perch on the desk. It was like being terribly thirsty, then turning on the tap and finding that the water will come out only in drips. Here were more drops of information, cut off almost immediately at source. It was *so frustrating*.

William rattled the doorhandle to make sure it was locked, then led the way along the broad central path towards the fountain. The garden was bathed in harsh white light, the colours bleached to neutral and the shadows banished to the furthest corners by the floodlights placed at intervals around the walls. 'Two minutes,' warned William as they set off, 'before the lights go out. Funny, now I come to think about it. She had something else for you, Nell said, but she hadn't wrapped it yet. She was going to bring it in the following day for me to look after, in case something happened to her – must've had a whatdya-call-it, a presentiment, don't you think? I was to keep it somewhere safe for you until you were older, she said. She was very insistent about it. "You mustn't show it to anybody else," she said, "not even Laura. It's for Ellis, and if she doesn't want it then she must burn it." But when I asked her what it was she just said, "Mind your own business," and sent me off to spray the greenfly.'

'What happened to it, this something else?' Ellis felt a tightening in her chest, a prickle of excitement at the back of her neck.

'I don't know.' William scratched his head again, leaving another dirty mark. 'It must have been in the cottage somewhere but I searched all over for it when I was clearing the place out and I didn't find anything. Mind you, I hadn't a clue what I was looking for – it could have been three inches square or three feet for all I knew. Whatever it was it must've been destroyed in the fire.'

Except that it wasn't. Nell had hidden it in the bread oven, the only place, with its brick walls and iron door, where it was protected from the flames. And when she wrote *Ellis* so decisively on the brown paper wrapping, Nell *had* meant it for her.

'Did she say what she wanted me to do with this . . . something?' asked Ellis, raising her voice as they neared the fountain, to make herself heard over the sound of running water.

'No.' William bent down to straighten a crooked pot, missed earlier by one of his assistants. 'Just that if you didn't want it you were to destroy it. But that's not important, poppet. It's your baby we've got to worry about now.'

They had reached that part of the garden where William had laid out his miniature knot garden – four triangular herb beds, culinary and medicinal, separated from each other by low, neatly clipped box hedges, forming a symmetrical diamond pattern with the fountain at its centre, 'so folk can see how to put it all together'. This was William's personal fiefdom. Here the customers could wander at will, sniff the plants, ask questions, seek advice, and it was here that William was almost invariably to be found during opening hours. He was never too busy to stop what he was doing and talk plants; Ellis had watched him over the years, persuading, encouraging, sharing his knowledge, expecting no other reward than a smile or an exclamation of pleasure. People bought their herbs from William because his enthusiasm rubbed off on them, because he made them believe they would get the same delight from growing plants that he still got after almost thirty-five years in the business.

They were close to the fountain now and the sound of trickling water was loud. The rising jet was black and silver in the stark beam of the floodlights and the ripples in the pool beneath glittered coldly as they spread. Ellis could feel the mist spraying from the thin column of water, like soft summer rain against her face. 'Don't you worry about your mother, pet,' said William, linking her arm through his and patting her hand. 'I'll smooth things over with her when I get home, and then we can get down to the practicalities.'

Ellis knew what that meant – her father would take the flak for Joe's untimely appearance, and her failure to break the news about her pregnancy, by redirecting Laura's hurt and anger to himself. She reached across and patted him back. 'It's all right, Dad,' she said. 'I'm old enough to carry the can for my own mistakes. Just tell her I'm sorry and I'll see her tomorrow.'

Something wet brushed against her jeans and she trailed her fingers down, then picked a dripping leaf, holding it up to her nose to sniff. The scent was lemony, sharp and fresh in the damp air. 'What's this?' she asked, holding it up for William to identify.

He took the feathery spray and crushed it gently between his fingers. 'Southernwood. Used to be known as *garde-robe*.'

Because of its use as a moth-repellent. Also called Maiden's Ruin . . .

The lights went out, depriving them momentarily of sight, and the smell of the herb seemed to grow more pungent. Ellis was enveloped in a lemon-scented haze of images: Nell and Laurence, Joe's angry face when she left him at Malletts. When her father's voice came prosaically out of the dark she jumped, startled back to the present.

'*Artemesia abrotanum*,' quoted William. 'Funny thing about Nell. She knew the Latin names of every single plant she'd ever come across, but she only ever used them if she was specifically asked. She liked the old names, the local names Ernie'd taught her, Batchelor's Buttons, Pigs-Toes, Cuckoo Flower . . .' He took Ellis's arm again and began walking her slowly along the concrete path. Despite her temporary blindness Ellis felt perfectly safe; William knew these paths better than he knew his own back garden.

'What was Nell like?' she asked, emboldened by the dark. 'I can hardly remember her at all. Describe her to me.'

'Well . . .' William weighed each word carefully, in case, Ellis guessed, he revealed something he shouldn't by accident. 'I got her completely wrong when I first met her – I thought to begin with she was a bit simple, but actually it was just eccentricity, that wild, unkempt hair, and those clothes, men's trousers held up with bits of twine, baggy woollen shirts, winter and summer alike.' Ellis squeezed his arm, encouraging him. 'People used to take her for a man, or assume she was one of the assistants and ask her where they could find the boss. She was funny about Malletts too, didn't like visitors, guarded her privacy fiercely. When I first visited in nineteen sixty she was still living in the most primitive conditions.' He chuckled, enjoying the memory. 'I spent years trying to persuade her to put in mains water and a proper septic tank but she wouldn't hear of it, said if Malletts was good enough for the previous tenants it was good enough for her. She'd already turned the Water Board down once, Marion told me, when they connected the rest of the village in fifty-three and at the time of the fire she still had no electricity, no inside lavatory, no mains water.'

They walked on towards the Orangery, just a dark, indistinct mass now at the end of the path. 'She had the most extraordinary hands. Not elegant – you could never describe Nell as a dainty woman – but big and capable, with knobbly fingers and heavy bones that stood up proud out of the skin like the ribs of a fan. Man's hands. Yet she had the most delicate touch with a seedling – it was as good as watching a skilled surgeon at work. Her skin was brown, cracked and wrinkled like old leather, and she didn't say much, opened her mouth only when it was absolutely necessary. She didn't suffer fools gladly either – she could be quite fierce if you got on the wrong side of her – but she would rarely look you straight in the eye, even when she was tearing you off a strip.' He slowed, squeezed Ellis's hand affectionately. 'Sometimes, you know, you have a look of her, must be something in the genes, I suppose . . .'

He led her on, taking the long route up the wide central way, then turned right at the Orangery to double back along the narrower path which ran parallel with it towards the garden entrance. The air felt warm on Ellis's face, damp, almost sticky, and as her eyes adjusted she began to pick out familiar landmarks again. Why didn't Nell look anyone in the face? she wondered as they progressed slowly towards the exit, stopping every now and then so William could bend to say goodnight to his plants. Was it because she was plain?

When she had first started teaching, Ellis had had to force herself to look at her students. Direct eye contact was essential in her job, she had realised early on, an integral part of asserting her authority, but it was a skill she had had to learn rather than one which came naturally. Nowadays, professionally at least, she was outwardly at ease, confident, authoritative; privately she had never been that sure of herself. Was that a trait common to all plain women?

When she left home to begin her university studies, she had determined to be more sociable, less of a blue-stocking. 'Too much work makes Ellis a dull girl,' her friend Grace told her as they said their farewells the day before she went up. 'For goodness' sake, Ellis, get yourself a boyfriend,' and she had made an effort to mix. She had gone to all the parties, to the pub, the disco, the university bar, but she had found the experience embarrassing, even painful. Men, she had quickly noticed, looked past her, smiled round her, talked through her. She was surrounded by girls who were prettier, sexier, more appealing than she, girls who knew how to fascinate, intrigue, seduce. She stopped looking at men when she was introduced because she didn't want to see the message in their eyes – the swift appraisal, the disappointment, the loss of interest. And after a while she decided enough was enough. She went back to her books, and found it a relief. She stopped bothering about the world outside her academic studies, stopped trying to compete, and the world went on without her. Why make the effort, she had concluded, when making the effort merely made her feel inadequate? If she was lacking in all those qualities of sex appeal a woman was supposed to have, she would make up for it by being cleverer than anyone else. And because she worked so hard at it, she was.

She'd looked at Joe though. She'd looked at Joe because he had looked, *really* looked, at her, because she could see reciprocated in his eyes all the pleasure, all the delight, she took in him. And sometimes, when he stopped whatever he was doing just to stare, when he smiled – no, *grinned*, ear to ear, face-splitting stuff – or when, in the middle of making love, he would stop moving and just gaze at her, transfixed, she would know that he had been waiting for her, as she had been waiting, all her life, for him. It had been a unique experience. No, not quite unique. How did Nell describe it in her journal? *The peculiar chemistry of love . . .*

'Nell liked this time of night best of all.' William pressed Ellis's arm against his ribs. He was worrying again, Ellis could tell, about what would happen to The Herb Garden when he was too old to carry on.

'You'll find someone,' she encouraged. 'Sooner or later the right person'll come along. What if you trained up your new girl?'

'Julia?' William grunted. 'Far too silly, poppet. You know what girls are like at that age, hardly an idea in their heads apart from boys and discos. I should have started looking for someone years ago. I'm sixty-three. How long have I got, d'you think, before I get too old to carry on? Five years? Ten if I'm lucky?'

They had reached another crossroads. William stopped again, staring out over the sleeping herb beds, the fountain murmuring to itself across the way, the Orangery glimmering at the far end of the garden. 'You don't think, if I passed it on to you, you might learn to . . .?'

'No,' said Ellis gently. 'If I had the feel for it I'd give it a try, Dad, but you know as well as I do, I couldn't do it justice. You'll recognise the right person when they come along, just like Nell did.'

She stood watching the sky while William set the security lights, then preceded him through the arched gate and waited while he locked up. 'Maybe you should advertise,' she suggested. 'See if you can find a manager, someone older with a bit of experience who could take some of the burden off you straightaway.' She felt a rush of affection, reached up to kiss his cheek. 'You do far too much for a man of your mature years.'

William chuckled, already recovered from his moment of doubt. 'What else would I do, poppet?' he asked, flinging his arms wide to take in the garden behind him. 'But you're right, of course. It's time I gave things a shove in the right direction.' He kissed her in return, then walked away towards his car. 'Drive carefully, poppet,' he called over his shoulder, 'and don't worry about your mother. I'll sort her out.'

Ellis saw the internal light come on in his car and his bulky figure appeared in the driver's seat. The engine rumbled and the headlamps leapt into life, illuminating the patch of ground where the lavender garden was going to be, before arcing round to face the road.

It was getting misty, strands of white hanging in the air like silk cobwebs. William slowed as he passed, then stretched out a hand to give her one last squeeze. 'Dad,' she said, leaning down to plead through the open car window, 'I really do need to know where I come from. It's terribly important, can you understand that?'

She could just make out her father's bald head, bobbing up and down. 'All right, pet,' he said. 'I'll see what I can do.' He drove on a little way, slowed, then backed up and leaned out of the window. 'There was something else,' he said, 'but I'm blowed if I can remember what it was.' Then he drove on again. Ellis watched his rear lights disappear round the corner then turned towards her car, facing west towards Malletts. The woods were dark now, and there were no lights twinkling between the trees, no clue to where the cottage lay. Too late, she thought, too late to change your mind now. Joe's gone for good this time.

A knot had formed beneath her breastbone, and it was growing into a physical pain.

The fog along the bottom of the valley was patchy, quite dense in places, and she almost missed the entrance to the drift. She drove slowly, reluctant to confirm what she already knew – that Joe's car, and Joe, were gone. The blank cottage windows, caught briefly in her headlights, mocked her with their emptiness. Ellis switched off the engine, then sat with her hands on the steering wheel, waiting for her eyes to get used to the dark.

Sleep, she thought as she fumbled in the darkened privy for her key. What I need is a decent night's sleep. I shall feel better in the morning.

The hall was silent, empty. Ellis stood for a moment listening, then reached out tentatively to touch the wall beside her. It was cool beneath her fingers, no vibration, no humming against her skin. She switched on the light. Static electricity, that was all it had been.

Everything was as she'd left it, except for the faint smell of soap hanging in the air. She turned right into the study, then walked through it, avoiding the packing cases still littering the floor. The bathroom was neat and tidy, only the fogged-up window, a small pool of lathery water in the bath and a few black speckles in the basin betraying the fact that Joe had ever been there. She picked the towel off the rail and held it to her face. It was damp, but cold; it must be a while since he had used it. Did it smell of Joe, or was it her imagination playing tricks on her again? She dropped the towel on the floor, made her way back to the hall, then carried on up the stairs to Nell's brass and iron bed, and sleep.

She woke with a start in the early hours and lay for a while, staring at the pattern of beams above her head.

Then, drawn by the night air drifting in through the open window, she rose and went to look out at the glade. The mist had cleared, and the deer were there, Nell's deer or their descendants, grazing fitfully near the lilac tree, tearing at the grass and raising their heads while they chewed, sniffing the air for danger. Ellis settled on the sill to watch, drawing her knees up and curling her toes against the cold stone. There was no vibration beneath the soles of her feet.

This was where Nell had sat, waiting for Laurence to come home. *In fifty years' time, women will be able to choose* . . . It must have sounded so simple when Nell wrote it. But it wasn't as easy as that. Practicalities – finances, logistics, a supermarket trolley full of disposable nappies – that was the easy part. Attitudes might have changed towards unmarried mothers, but that didn't make the rest of it any easier, facing up to being on one's own, taking sole responsibility for another human being.

The stone sill was hard beneath her buttocks and she was getting chilly; it was time to go back to bed. As she swung her legs to the floor she caught the casement with her elbow and it rattled. The brown heads came up sharply and the deer scattered, white tails flashing as they raced for the cover of the woods. Tomorrow, Ellis determined as she burrowed down beneath her duvet, tomorrow I'll make a fresh start, stop pining after what's gone.

She woke to strident birdsong and the sun slanting through the window. She was up by eight, her breakfast finished and cleared away by twenty past. She inspected the morning outside, sorted a pile of washing and set the machine running in the bathroom. She must go and see Laura today, she decided as she pushed buttons and twisted dials. She must sort things out, explain, apologise. It was time she dealt with the piles of books still cluttering the floor too. She wandered back to the sitting room and stood in the doorway surveying the mess. Nell's journal was lying on the table where she had left it. She was putting it off, she realised, surprised by her reluctance, now it came to it, to touch the thing. Was she frightened of what it might contain? Or was she scared that once she picked it up Nell might not let her put it down again?

She cleared a wide space on the floor, filled some shelves with books, rearranged them twice, added a few more, and made herself a cup of coffee. When she finally plucked up the courage to face the journal it was after ten. She half expected to find it humming with static, and it took the musty smell that rose from it as she turned the first few pages to remind her how far in the past, how irrelevant to her present circumstances it actually was. It was pointless to get so involved, ridiculous to get so overwrought about it. She left it on the table and went to make herself another cup of coffee.

She found the marker when she returned. Joe had used William's headed notepaper, her father's sketch of the lavender garden, turning it over to scrawl in angry black biro on the blank side: *Next time you call, I shan't be listening.* Then he had slipped it into the journal for her to find. There was nothing else, no contact address, no last plea for her to rethink her decision. He had taken her at her word. Far more angry than she had been when he was here, Ellis slammed the book shut and left the room. Fresh air, that was what she needed. As she flung open the front door her father's car appeared at the entrance to the drift.

William was uncomfortable, pink with embarrassment, and he wouldn't come in. 'Got to get on, pet,' he said, standing awkwardly half in, half out of the porch with his head bent to avoid the lintel. 'Just thought I'd pop over and let you know what's happening. Your mum wants to see you.'

'Yes. I'm sure she does. How did she—?'

'Take it?' William flapped his big hands helplessly. 'Better than I expected, on the whole. Of course, she was . . . disappointed, not to hear the news from you in person, and she doesn't think, under the circumstances, it would be a good idea for us to come to supper tonight. But she does want to see you, talk things over. You know.'

He looked tired. He looked old, thought Ellis, worn out, and it was her fault.

'I've brought you something.' He fumbled in his jacket pocket and brought out a crumpled envelope, slit untidily along its edge. 'Don't know whether I'm doing the right thing or not; probably not, but you did say . . .' He held the envelope out. 'Your mum doesn't know.' He tapped his finger against the side of his nose. 'But it's gone on far too long and if it's left much longer it'll be too late to put it right. It's up to you. You don't have to do anything about it if you don't want to.'

'Dad,' protested Ellis, 'what on earth are you talking about?'

William shrugged. 'You said you needed to know where you came from, but I gave your mum my word so this is the best I can do. Just promise me one thing.'

What was he on about?

'Promise me if you get to talk to her you won't make any snap judgements.'

Who? If she got to talk to who?

'There're two sides to every story.' William's face was puckered with worry. 'I wish I could be sure I'm doing the right thing . . .'

Two sides to what story?

'Of course, it's pretty unlikely she'll still be there after all these years, in which case there's no harm done, is there? Most likely outcome, I should say. Always meant to do something about it myself, but you know how it is – bit of a coward when it comes to that sort of thing, and time flies by. Best not to mention our little chat last night either, don't you think? I must get on, poppet, the contractors are delivering the topsoil for the lavender garden today and I'm still not happy with the layout. Doesn't seem to have the right *feel* to it, somehow.' He took a deep breath, planted a hearty kiss on the top of her head, then backed out of the porch before Ellis had time to collect her wits, and walked away. She watched him lumber across the open space to his car, leaving a trail of flattened grass, then stood listening until the purr of his engine was absorbed into the faint general hum of the traffic on the dual carriageway.

The crumpled, battered envelope was addressed to *William Jones Esq., The Herb Garden, Old Hall Estate*, and inside it were two letters held together by a rusty pin. The first was typed but the second was handwritten, in a neat, round, schoolgirl script. The ink was faded and the paper was yellow and brittle. The documents were dated less than a week apart, and the address at the top of the handwritten one was: *Rosemount, 14 Lyford Road, London N13*.

It was signed: *Yours sincerely, Violet Palmer.*

Chapter Twenty-Four

Dear Mr Guthrie,

Re yours of the 15th June, I am sorry your letters to Miss Carter have been returned by the Post Office. I can only suggest you write to Mr William Jones at The Herb Garden, Old Hall Estate, Ipswich – if my sister has indeed moved away from the Ipswich area she may have left Mr Jones a forwarding address. As you know, I am anxious to put my mother's affairs in order as soon as possible and I would be grateful if you could deal with this matter without delay.

Yours sincerely
Violet Palmer

It was dated 17 June 1965. Ellis turned to the other, more official-looking letter.

Dear Mr Jones,

As you will see from the enclosed, we are anxious to establish the current whereabouts of Miss Eleanor Carter, and any assistance you can render in this connection would be greatly appreciated. We understand from her sister, Mrs Violet Palmer, that Miss Carter's last known address was Malletts, The Drift, Old Hall Estate, Ipswich, Suffolk. Perhaps you would be kind enough to confirm this, as well as her present address, if known.

Yours sincerely
Leonard E. Guthrie
Guthrie, Booth and Taylor,
Attorneys at Law

It was dated 23 June 1965. Ellis closed the front door and returned to the sitting room, then took the letters to the window and stood staring across the sunny glade. She had forgotten to get the deckchair in the previous night and it was still sitting beneath the lilac tree.

The lilac tree . . . She screwed up her face, trying to recall the dates on Nell's headstone. *1915–1965, RIP.* The day Laura took her to see Nell, when she was four years old, the lilac was in full bloom, and five days after that visit Nell was dead. Lilac bloomed in May, didn't it? And later, on her twenty-first birthday, 11th May, it was flowering then too. So when Violet's solicitor tried to contact Nell that June, Malletts was already a burned-out shell. I *am anxious to put my mother's affairs in order.* Was that why Violet was trying to get in touch? To let Nell know that their mother had passed away? But surely, Nell would have known, wouldn't she? Just as Violet would have – *should* have – known about Nell's death.

Except that, with Nell and Violet not speaking to each other, the one person who would under normal circumstances have acted as go-between, the one who would have broken the news of Nell's death to Violet, relayed the message about her grandmother's passing to Nell – Laura – was no longer speaking to her own mother.

Rosemount, 14 Lyford Road, London N13.

'Nell?' said Ellis. 'What do I do now, Nell?' Tentatively, she reached out a hand to touch the wall, spreading her fingers wide and pressing her palm against the plaster. 'Tell me what to do. Please.'

It was there, so faint it was barely detectable, but *there*. Ellis dropped the letters and the torn envelope onto the windowsill, then raised her other hand, stretching her arms wide and closing her eyes. Behind her lids she could still see the lilac tree. It was so close she could almost reach out and touch it and it was laden with heavy trusses of white blossom. She took a deep breath, expecting to smell its sweet perfume . . . and found her lungs filling instead with the sharp, spicy scent of tobacco.

'All right,' she said. 'If you're sure.' She dropped her arms, opened her eyes. The glade was just as it had been before, hot, still, and the lilac tree was casting its shade towards the house. It wouldn't bloom again until next spring. 'But I warn you,' Ellis addressed the empty air. 'Don't blame me if it all goes horribly wrong.'

She retrieved the letters and returned them to their envelope. She had a lot to do, if she was to get going before lunchtime.

In the end she just went, snatching up her keys and leaving the house without even pausing to change her clothes. She stopped at a Link machine to get some cash, and then again to ring William from a phone box.

'Hello? Dad, it's me, Ellis. Listen . . .'

'You all right, poppet?' asked William. 'Look, I've been thinking, probably better to ignore those papers wouldn't you say? No point in stirring things up just for the sake of—'

'That's why I'm ringing.' Ellis tucked the phone into her shoulder and searched through her purse for another

10p piece. 'Dad, can you tell Mum I won't be able to pop round today? Tell her I'll come and see her as soon as I can. Tell her . . . tell her I've left some vital files at the flat or something and I have to go and get them.'

'Ellis—' began William.

'And Dad . . .'

'What, poppet?'

'Thanks,' said Ellis. 'I won't abuse your trust, I promise.'

'Ellis, what are you—?'

Ellis stopped searching for coins and took the phone back into her hand. Really, the less time William had to think about this the better. 'Dad, I have to go now or I'll miss my train.'

'Train? What train?' William sounded bemused. Ellis tightened her grip on the receiver.

'The train to London. I'm going to see Violet. Now, today.' Then she cut him off, before he could talk her out of it.

She picked up her purse, then pushed open the door, walked back to her car and climbed in. Get on with it, woman, she told herself. She placed both hands on her stomach, and patted it. 'This is for you,' she told her daughter. 'So you'll know where you come from.'

She parked in the shadow of the railway embankment and ran across the car park. She paid in cash for a day-return ticket, then marched out onto the platform.

There was no hurry, despite what she'd said to William – the London train wasn't due for another half an hour. Frustrated by the delay she bought a paper, then sat on a bench in the sunshine not reading it, trying to keep calm. How much do other people care about their family history? she wondered as commuters and tourists strolled back and forth in front of her. Do they take their nearest and dearest for granted, never stop to think about their ancestry? Or do they treasure their parents' memories, mine them as a rich seam of history? Struck by a sudden idea, she rose from her seat and strode back to the booking hall to find a telephone.

'Directories,' said the woman on the other end. 'Which town, please?'

'London,' said Ellis. 'The name is Palmer, Violet Palmer, and the address is Rosemount, 14 Lyford Road.'

There was a pause, then a click, then a recorded voice, sing-song, impersonal, unemotional. 'The number you require is . . .' Ellis put the phone down. You knew, she challenged Nell. You knew she was still there.

So now she *had* to go.

Chapter Twenty-Five

Lyford Road was lined with neat, affluent, suburban Edwardian villas. John Betjeman would have loved it, might even have been moved to write a paean of praise to its confidently jutting bay windows, the exuberant coloured lights above its carefully refurbished front doors, its tidy shrubberies and garish hanging baskets. At least Violet isn't living in an inner-city slum, thought Ellis as she walked slowly along the wide pavement.

She had asked the taxi driver to drop her on the corner, wanting to approach Rosemount, and Violet, at her own pace, only to discover that Number 14 was right at the other end. It was a long road, uphill all the way, and by the time she was halfway along she was wishing she had asked to be dropped right outside. Her feet, bare inside her soft canvas shoes, were beginning to rub, her skin felt grimy and her tongue was gritty, sheened with the dust of a London heatwave. The palms of her hands were damp too, but that had more to do with nerves than with the ambient air temperature.

She counted as she went, *ninety-eight*, *ninety-six* . . . *seventy-two*, *seventy* . . . *sixty*, *fifty-eight*, and the houses grew more affluent as she progressed, the cars parked outside – second cars, Ellis guessed, used mostly for school-runs and shopping – more up-market, Range

Rovers, Shoguns, BMWs. *Twenty-two, eighteen, sixteen . . .*
She stopped in the middle of the pavement.

Number 14 was like a boil on the smooth, pretty face
of the neighbourhood. The low wall fronting the pavement was cracked from top to bottom and a large section
had broken away to lean drunkenly towards the road. A
single rose bush, spotted with black and yellow blisters,
drooped apathetically over the path leading to the front
door, in the last throes of some terminal disease, and the
space in front of the house, laid drearily with crazy
paving, was pocked and pitted, the edges of the slabs
blurred by the nettles and dandelions which had forced
their way up through the cement grouting. Ellis recalled
the description in Nell's journal: *Ma had the builders put
crazy paving down . . .* and confirmed another piece of
the puzzle.

This was Ma Carter's house. This was the house
Violet had run to after Laura was born. The front gate
hung crookedly from its hinges, the remnants of long-
ago applied blue paint still adhering grimly to its rotting
carcass. An estate agent's board was nailed to the post;
SOLD said the sticker slapped diagonally across its face.
Ellis stared at it in dismay. Was she too late?

The house looked as sad as the garden – paintwork
peeling, wooden casements crumbling away, tiles missing from the roof. Grey nets hung limply at the upstairs
windows and the guttering had pulled loose from its
moorings and been left to dangle precariously in thin
air. Downstairs, dreary mustard-coloured curtains were
drawn across the right-hand window, their hems stained
brown with condensation, and the bay on the left had its
two side panels blanked out by more of the same, leaving only the central section to let in what light could
manage to filter through the grime.

Ellis walked slowly up the path, then climbed the two

steps to the front door. The brass knocker was welded to its base, pitted with verdigris. Raising her hand, she took a deep breath, then knocked loudly with her knuckles on the glass.

'Yes?'

The woman was in her early fifties, Ellis guessed. She was thin, with greasy grey hair drawn back into a sparse ponytail, and she was wearing a dirty pink nylon overall with an inch of cotton petticoat showing beneath it, and a pair of rubber flip-flops. She kept the door half shut, holding it with a Marigold-clad hand so Ellis couldn't see past her into the house. Cleaning lady? Housekeeper? Whoever she was, with her mean, down-turned mouth and suspicious little eyes, she wasn't Violet. Caught by surprise, Ellis found herself momentarily tongue-tied.

'Wotcha want?' The voice was impatient, coarse.

'Er . . .' Pull yourself together, Ellis scolded herself. 'I'm here to see Mrs Palmer.' BT Directories thought Violet still lived here, and so did Nell. She looked the woman straight in the eye, as she had trained herself to do with countless students. 'Mrs Violet Palmer. Perhaps you'd tell her I'm here?'

An expression of sly cunning crossed the woman's face. 'Dunno,' she said. 'You from the social?'

Ellis returned the beady, speculative glare until the woman looked away. 'I'm Mrs Palmer's granddaughter,' she said. 'Now if you would—'

'Who?'

The woman was clearly startled by the information, and none too pleased either, judging by her beetling frown. She began to close the door, mumbling through the narrowing gap. Ellis, suspecting that once shut out she would stay that way, stepped forward and pushed hard.

' 'Ere!' Caught by surprise, the woman lurched backwards into the dingy hall, her sandals flapping stickily on the floor. ' 'Oo joo fink you are, bargin' in 'ere?' The front door swung shut behind them.

'I've told you who I am,' said Ellis. 'I've come to see my grandmother. Where is she? In here?'

She went for the door on the left, the room with the bay window, because she could hear a television burbling away faintly inside, but it wouldn't budge. The woman folded her arms and watched. ' 'S not right,' she volunteered, 'leavin' the poor old cow in this dump. I do me best, but there's a limit—'

'Is it locked?' asked Ellis, rattling the doorhandle again.

'Nah,' said the woman, resigning herself to the inevitable. 'Sticks, tha's all, like everyfink else in this 'ouse.' She unfolded her arms and flapped across, then set her scrawny shoulder to the door and pushed. Ellis could see the light from the television, flickering against the wall. 'Visitor for you, dear. 'Course,' she added over her shoulder to Ellis, 'some days she ain't wiv us at all, poor cow.' She raised her voice. 'Are yer, Vi?'

The room smelled strongly of human excrement. The cleaner, housekeeper, whatever she was, saw Ellis's face and sniffed. 'Why d'yer suppose she's goin' into a 'ome?' she said. 'Can't manage on 'er own, can she? I do me best.'

'I'm sure you do,' said Ellis, quite sure that she didn't. All she could make out in the half-dark was a vague, hunched shape in a big wing chair by the window, illuminated fitfully by the television. 'But now I'm here she won't need you any more, thank you.'

The woman bridled. 'You can't come waltzin' in 'ere takin' over,' she said indignantly. 'I bin looking after 'er nearly a month now. Where was you all that time? *And* I ent bin paid yet neither. She owes me.' The arms were folded again, with an I'm-not-budging-till-you-pay-up air of finality, and the shape by the window began to stir in its chair, raising a pale moon-face towards the disturbance.

'Out!' hissed Ellis, yanking hard on the woman's arm.

She caught her off balance, and their momentum carried them out of the room to land in a huddle in the passage. Ellis moved across to close the door.

'How much?'

Her eyes were growing more accustomed to the light, so she caught the sly look the woman flung her. How much can I get away with? it said. How much can I sting you for? 'Well, there's the four weeks' wages . . .' A hesitation, while she gauged how much Ellis would swallow. 'Two hours a day at . . . three pound . . .' – another pause – '. . . seventy-five an hour. An' there's the shoppin'. I dun 'er shoppin' every week, and she never give me nuthin' . . .'

Ellis made a quick calculation, subtracting what she had spent so far on trains and taxis from what she had taken out of the Link machine, and bluffed. 'I've not got much cash on me,' she said. 'You'll have to take a cheque.'

'What?' The arms were folded again, the expression even more mulish than before. 'Over my dead body! I ain't leavin' this 'ouse till I git my money!'

'Then you'll have to make do with what I've got in my purse.'

' 'Ow much?'

Ellis subtracted her taxi fare back to the nearest tube station, plus a bit for emergencies and something for a cup of coffee at Liverpool Street. Then she took off ten pounds just because she didn't like the woman's face. 'Sixty-two pounds,' she said. 'Take it or leave it.'

The woman hissed through her teeth, but she didn't argue. Blast, thought Ellis, she could have got away with even less. She turned her back to count out the money, three twenty-pound notes and a couple of coins, then placed it in the woman's outstretched hand. 'Mrs Palmer won't be needing you again,' she repeated. 'So you'd better get your stuff.'

' 'S in the kitchen.' The woman flounced off down the passage, and returned carrying two bulging carrier bags. 'I'm entitled,' she said defensively as she passed. 'I paid for it, din' I?'

Ellis held the front door open. She watched the woman flap down the path, her back a poem of outraged virtue, and waited until she was out of sight. Then she closed the door. It could have been worse, she thought, she might have been a live-in housekeeper, much more complicated. A bluebottle was buzzing lazily against the coloured glass at the top of the front door and she could hear the television muttering to itself in the sitting room. She had done it now, made herself solely responsible for the old lady. She waited until the panic had subsided, then put her shoulder to the door and pushed.

The figure by the window was slumped again. The room was cluttered with furniture: a chest of drawers with a couple of silver-framed photographs on it, a one-legged table, plastic-and-steel on wheels, designed to slide across a bed or a chair, with a set of shiny false teeth glimmering pinkly in a plastic beaker and a pair of glasses with tortoiseshell frames. There was a double wardrobe with mirrored doors, a wash-basin on a stand, and a single bed, covered untidily with a worn candlewick bedspread, against the back wall. A heavy round dining table littered with bits and pieces – a box of Kleenex, tissues spilling from its open mouth, a huddle of pill pots, a jug of water with a glass up-ended on its neck, a tray with the remains of a frugal breakfast on it and a toilet roll – sat bulkily in the middle of the room with two high-backed chairs and a one-bar electric fire tucked beneath it. Next to that was an old-fashioned commode. Its lid was up, and the chamber pot slotted into the seat was full.

There was an Australian soap on, all primary colours and twangy antipodean accents. Ellis skirted the table, then bent down to peer at the old lady. A trickle of saliva dribbled from the corner of her mouth and her chin was sunk on her chest. She appeared to be asleep, but her left hand trembled in her lap as if it had a life of its own and her breathing was laboured. Ellis turned to the commode, grimacing with distaste.

She found the bathroom on the first floor – black and white tiles, a high-level cistern, a cracked wooden loo-seat, its varnish long since worn away. The bath was enamel; its surface, dulled by years of scouring, and stained with green where the cold tap had dripped, was littered with dead flies. Ellis flushed the contents of the pot down the lavatory then rinsed it out and turned to the basin to wash her hands. There was a dead moth lying on its back in the bowl and there was no plug, no soap, no towel. When she turned on the tap the water was brown and rusty-looking, as if it had been sitting in the pipes for months. She gave up and went back to the landing.

It was quiet up here, the noise of the television so faint she had to strain her ears to hear it at all. She moved across to the nearest door and turned the handle. It wouldn't budge. Stuck, she thought, like the one downstairs. She moved on to the next, and the next. Not stuck, she realised – locked. The only item of furniture on the landing was the chest of drawers sitting opposite the top of the stairs. Its drawers were half open, as if someone had rifled through the contents in a hurry, but there was nothing of any interest inside, just piles of bed linen – sheets and pillowcases wrapped in bags made out of what must once have been white damask tablecloths. Some of the sheets were neatly darned and patched and one of the drawers was almost empty, nothing but a couple of scrunched-up handkerchiefs and an ancient lavender bag which smelled as musty as the drawer – the cleaner must have found something worth stealing apart from food, Ellis guessed.

She tidied up and closed the drawers. She was wasting time, she realised, putting off going downstairs. Yet she'd come all this way to see Violet. She retrieved the chamber pot, took a deep breath, and set off.

The room smelled a little better. The Australian soap was still on, a posse of lithe teenagers romping in the sun while a barbeque cast a blue haze in the background. Violet was slumped in her chair, snoring a little. Ellis replaced the pot in the commode, shut the lid on it, then squatted in front of her, placed her hand on Violet's knee, and shook her gently.

The old lady was wearing a flannelette nightie with a pink bed jacket over the top and a pair of velvet slippers. Her ankles, swollen and purple, bulged over the sides – bad circulation, Ellis guessed – but her knee felt bony beneath the nightgown.

'Violet . . .?' said Ellis softly. 'Granny, it's Ellis come to see you.'

Violet's head jerked up. The bottom half of her face, minus its teeth, had caved in between nose and chin, but her eyes, wide open and peering shortsightedly at Ellis's face, were still blue, still beautiful.

'Hello, darling,' said Ellis gently. 'It's Ellis, Laura's daughter. I've come to see you.'

The old lady was still half asleep. Her sparse white hair was sticking up on end and her chin was wet with saliva. She stared in bewilderment for a moment. Then she leaned forward in her chair and snatched at Ellis's hand, gripping it so hard Ellis could feel her fingernails digging into the flesh of her palm.

'Nell?' she said. Her voice was high-pitched, breathless with astonishment. 'Nell, is it really you? Have you come to put things right?'

Chapter Twenty-Six

As she woke up, Violet began to sit straighter, pay attention. After a while Ellis managed to persuade her she
was not Nell but the old lady immediately assumed that
she must be a new carer and to begin with she resisted
stubbornly all Ellis's attempts to enlighten her. 'I like
you better than Norah,' she confided. 'You don't shout at
me all the time. Could I have a cup of tea, please?'

Norah, Ellis discovered when she entered the kitchen
at the back of the house, had cleared the shelves of practically everything. She had to go out to buy provisions,
including, since it was becoming increasingly clear that
she couldn't possibly leave the old lady on her own, a
toothbrush, toothpaste, soap, deodorant and a plug for
the basin upstairs. On her return she had to spend nearly
half an hour clearing up the mess Norah had left before
she could make the tea. But at least the phone, black
Bakelite with a frayed canvas flex, which sat on the small
table by the front door, was still working. Just after she
got back from the shops it rang, an aggressive-sounding
female from the Bettacare Home Agency, demanding to
know whether or not Mrs Palmer would be requiring a
carer this evening, 'since you sent Norah packing without a moment's notice'.

'No,' said Ellis, 'Mrs Palmer will not be requiring a

carer this evening, nor tomorrow, nor ever again. And if you could see the state of this place, you'd know why.'

For a brief moment after she'd slammed the phone down she felt good, but her triumph was followed swiftly by a wave of pure terror, that she was now responsible for the old lady still sitting, staring vacantly at the telly in the sitting room with her glasses on and her teeth out. Reminded by the 'sold' sticker she could see from the window that Violet must be imminently moving, and recalling Norah's remark about her going into a home, Ellis got the estate agent's number from the board and asked to speak to whoever was handling the sale of 14 Lyford Road.

The girl seemed pleased when Ellis explained that she was Violet's granddaughter. 'Oh, I'm *so* glad,' she said. 'She's a lovely old girl, and they really haven't been looking after her as they should, you know. Actually, I hope you won't think I'm too pushy, but it was me locked all the doors. This woman she's had the past few weeks, she'd been helping herself to a couple of knick-knacks practically every time she came. That particular agency doesn't charge as much as some of the others, and I don't think they pay their staff too well – but I suppose it must be a pretty thankless task mustn't it, looking after old folk? Difficult to get the right sort of people for the job. So, what can I do for you?'

'I need to know when completion takes place,' explained Ellis. 'The place still seems to be full of furniture, and if she's not moving for another month or so I may have to make arrangements to stay a bit longer.'

'Oh, no!' The girl sounded cheerful, knowledgeable. 'She's moving any minute, hang on I'll just look up the exact . . .'

Ellis waited.

'I say,' came the girl again, 'I don't think I introduced myself, did I? Terrible scatterbrain, I'm afraid . . . Janice, Janice Wainwright. I've seen quite a lot of your gran over the last couple of months, what with showing people round and everything. It's been one of those sales – lots of interest but no serious offers for ages, then two buyers in a row, both of whom were in chains and had to pull out at the last minute – so one way and another, I've got to know your gran pretty well. We hit it off right away. I remind her of her daughter, she says – I gather Violet and your mum don't talk; sad, isn't it? So, anyway . . . look, I've just had a thought. Why don't I drop round on my way home? It's not far out of my way and it'll be easier to explain what's going on in person. Between you and me, I've been a bit worried about your gran – she's gone downhill since the stroke and I have my doubts whether that so-called carer has been feeding her properly since she came out of hospital.' She paused, briefly, for breath, then forged on, leaving Ellis struggling to keep up. Stroke? What stroke? Hospital? What hospital? Why hadn't anyone contacted William and Laura? Weren't next of kin supposed to be informed about such things? Had the rift between Laura and Violet really gone that far?

'Look, don't mind me,' Janice was saying. 'Talk the hind legs off a donkey, my mum says.' The giggle which came down the line was infectious, and Ellis laughed too, immensely cheered by the thought that this jolly, garrulous person had been keeping an eye on Violet. 'So how about it? I'll bring all the paperwork round, so you can see what's going on. Be there in about an hour, OK?'

'Wonderful,' said Ellis. 'I'm sure Violet—' It was going to take some getting used to, this. Like *Hawley*, *Ware*, *Smith*, like Nell and Laurence, Violet was no longer just a character in a story. 'I'm sure my grandmother will be delighted to see you.'

She made the old lady an omelette for her tea, and once Violet was reunited with her teeth she ate it with relish, then polished off three slices of bread and butter and a large bowlful of ice-cream. Her left hand was useless – Ellis had to cut the food up before she could manage it – but the meal seemed to energise her, and Ellis wondered if Janice was right about the carer not feeding her properly. She helped her use the commode and washed her face and hands. As she went to rinse the flannel, Violet grabbed suddenly at her wrist.

'Thank you *so* much, dear,' she said. 'That feels *wonderful*,' and she smiled for the first time since Ellis's arrival.

When she smiled she looked twenty years younger. Her skin was pink and white, remarkably unlined, and for the first time, despite the glasses and the rather flashy false teeth, Ellis could see where Laura had got her looks from.

Janice arrived as she was tidying away the plates. A lissom blonde in a neat business suit, she was as talkative in person as she was on the phone and she brought with her a pile of papers, which she dropped on the hall table on her way to the sitting room to greet Violet. She sat with her for nearly twenty minutes, chatting inconsequentially, while Ellis washed up and made Violet another cup of tea, and when she finally rose, kissed Violet's cheek and left the room, Violet looked completely crestfallen. Ellis followed Janice out into the hall and closed the door quietly behind her.

'Kitchen, I think,' said Janice, 'don't you? Wouldn't want Vi to think we were talking about her behind her back, would we?'

Violet was moving the following week. As Janice prattled her way through three cups of coffee and a packet of custard creams, it became clear that this jolly young woman was at least partially responsible not only for the sale of Violet's house, but for arranging the auction firm who were coming in to clear the house and the removal company as well. She had even, it transpired when she produced the book from the depths of her capacious handbag, been cashing Violet's pension for her every couple of weeks, 'plus she's got an attendance allowance now, by the way – jolly handy to pay for the carers.' When Ellis, astonished by such generosity, tried to thank her, Janice dismissed her with a casual wave of the hand.

'Course, she's done a lot of it by herself,' she continued. 'Vi, I mean. She found the retirement place on her own – I just ran her over to look at it, that's all. And she dealt with the auction people like a real pro, you should have seen her.' She rose to refill the kettle. 'More coffee? Sorry, taking over a bit, aren't I? Incurably bossy, I'm afraid. You'll see if you look around, practically all the furniture has little red stickers on, so they know what to take. It was probably the strain of it all, showing punters round, strangers going through her private things, that brought on the stroke. I don't think she's used to dealing with so many people.'

She leaned over Ellis's shoulder and shuffled the pile of paperwork, dragged out a glossy brochure. 'This is where she's going: twenty-two Britannia Court. It's just off the other end of the high street, nice little complex, well designed. They've got twenty-four-hour cover if you're taken ill too, not like some of these set-ups where the warden only works nine to five. She's chosen the furniture for it and everything, did that before the stroke, and it's being delivered this week. Still, it's going to be a shock to her system just the same, a two-bedroom flat after this place. She's lived here all her life, you know, – sorry, you must think I'm dreadfully nosy, but once Vi's started it's hard to stop her – except for a year during the war. So sad, that – I practically cried when she told me – left London in nineteen forty as a new bride and less than six months later her husband – Spitfire pilot, you know, dead glam, that's him in the picture on the chest of drawers – was shot down over the Channel leaving her pregnant with – sorry, keep forgetting, you must know all about this – your mum it was, wasn't it? So there she was, her husband dead and her heavily pregnant in the middle of a war. Just *tragic*, don't you think?'

The kettle boiled and Janice whisked the cups from the table, spooned coffee, added sugar. 'So, of course, as soon as your mum was born she came running straight back home, never mind the bombs, couldn't bear to stay in . . . um . . .'

Ellis cleared her throat. 'Suffolk,' she said.

'Where?'

'Suffolk,' repeated Ellis. Weird, hearing about her own grandmother from a complete stranger. 'My mother was born in Suffolk. Her name's Laura.'

'Mmm.' Janice brought the cups back to the table and plonked herself down again. 'Ridiculous, isn't it, that after all that they should end up not speaking to each other.'

Ellis sipped at her coffee, rather strong and very sweet. Not as ridiculous as this, she thought, that after years of being stonewalled by her own mother, she should be sitting here in her grandmother's kitchen listening to this young woman, with her irrepressibly cheerful personality and her infectious giggle, talk blithely about her family as if she'd known them intimately for years.

'Why?' she asked.

'Why did they stop speaking?' Janice shrugged. 'Didn't your mum tell you? Something to do with an unsuitable boyfriend, Vi said, well, not so much unsuitable, as already engaged to somebody else – and your mum getting herself pregnant and wrecking the happy couple's wedding . . .' She examined Ellis with unabashed interest. 'Mind you, the rules were different in those days, weren't they, I mean, it really mattered, didn't it, if you got involved with someone you shouldn't? 'Course *my* mum was in on the swinging sixties and she had a *whale* of a time, but she says *her* mum used to lecture her all the time. It was practically a mortal sin back then, according to Mum, to sleep with a bloke who wasn't your husband, and of course getting pregnant would have been the ultimate, wouldn't it? Daft really, when you think how we take that sort of thing for granted these days. I mean, look at you, how far gone are you, three months? Four? and not a wedding ring in sight—' She clapped her hand over her mouth, blushed with embarrassment. 'Oh Lord, look, I'm terribly sorry, I didn't mean – after all, plenty of women don't wear a ring these days. That is, well, you probably aren't even preg— Oh gawd, *hark* at me!'

Unexpectedly, Ellis found herself roaring with laughter at the girl's refreshingly tactless candour. 'Yes,' she reassured her when she could speak, 'you're a very observant girl. In five months' time I shall indeed be a single parent. Janice, about my mother—'

'I'm really, really sorry.' Still pink with embarrassment, Janice rose hurriedly from the table, collected the coffee cups and dumped them in the sink. 'Foot-in-mouth disease, I'm afraid.' She came back to the table, sifted through the pile of papers again. 'Look, I'd better go. Mum'll be wondering where I've got to. The auction chap's coming on Friday to take away the stuff that's going in the sale – it's all marked already as I've said, and he's ever so nice so you don't need to worry – and the removal man comes on Monday to pack the rest. Vi's not taking much, of course, they're not very big, these retirement flats, so he should be able to do it all in a morning. I told her I'd pop in on Thursday to help her sort out her personal bits and pieces.' She grinned. 'It'll be nice to have some company actually, and Vi'll be pleased to have an extra pair of hands – that's if you don't mind me butting in on your territory of course . . .'

By the time Janice waved a merry goodbye and bounced off down the path nearly an hour later, Ellis's head was spinning. Violet, at Janice's suggestion, had handed over the house keys by then, registered Ellis's name, if not the family connection, and managed to get herself out of her chair to use the commode unassisted. She apologised frequently for being such a trouble, thanked Ellis effusively for her ministrations, then promptly fell asleep in her chair with her teeth still in and her glasses teetering precariously on the end of her nose. Ellis found it hard to believe that she could ever have fallen out with anyone, let alone so violently as to not speak to them for over thirty years. Except that, if Janice's version was correct, Laura had done the one thing Violet would find impossible to forgive.

If Janice was to be believed, Laura had stolen another woman's man, by deliberately getting pregnant with his child.

Having once allowed her tongue to run away with her, Janice had clammed up completely. It was not up to her, she said when Ellis begged her to finish what she had so tantalisingly started, to talk about Ellis's mother behind her back – 'I shouldn't like it if you were to do it to *my* mum' – and all Ellis's pleas for more information fell on deaf ears. 'Ask Vi,' was all Janice would say, 'I'm sure she'll tell you, once she's grasped who you are.'

The old lady dozed, off and on, for most of the evening. Ellis left the television burbling in case the sudden silence woke her, then took the keys, and went exploring. It's all right, she told herself as she climbed the stairs to the quiet, stuffy landing. It's not prying, I'm family. Family? The pleasure was swiftly overtaken by other, more conflicting emotions.

It was like touring a museum, a museum long since abandoned, where no one dusted, no one cleaned, and no one ever came to look at the exhibits. The furniture, solid, old-fashioned pieces with clumsy handles and ugly mouldings, the faded curtains and worn Axminster carpets, the satin eiderdowns and ruched, bobbled lampshades, were a microcosm of another age. The paintwork was brown and cream, the sprigged wallpaper yellow with age and stained with green where the rain had sneaked through the neglected roof and trickled down the walls. The light switches were brown, round and fat, and they made a loud snapping noise when she depressed them; the flexes were grey and frayed like the telephone cable downstairs. The rooms were stiflingly hot and oppressively tidy, and after a while Ellis found herself tiptoeing, feeling not like family but more like a sneak thief, come to steal away Violet's most intimate secrets.

She started with the bay-windowed bedroom above Violet's sitting room. The double bed, with its mahogany head- and footboards and its embroidered eiderdown, was as perfectly neat as if its owner had just that moment finished making it, and the dressing table, draped with a dusty frilled valance, was as tidy as the bed, every pot of cream, every bottle of perfume, every pill-pot set out in regimented rows, each at a regular distance from its neighbour like soldiers on a parade ground; when Ellis lifted a jar of cold cream it left a perfect round imprint in the dust. The brush-and-comb set, each piece engraved on its silver back with a swirling *AC* (what did the A stand for – Amelia? Alice, Ariadne? Or were the brushes Pa's? – Arthur, Albert, Anthony?), was lined up precisely with the edge of the mirror and the edge of the dressing table. The spider's web stretched across the corner of the mirror seemed jarringly inapposite and when Ellis stood up, she found herself realigning the stool with the edge of the dressing table, lest it spoil the perfect symmetry of the room.

The wardrobe was as obsessively tidy as the dressing table – hat boxes, shoes, scarves all lined up with military precision; frocks, suits, coats, a moulting fox fur hung in strictly ascending order from longest to shortest. When Ellis moved across the landing to the other front bedroom – Pa's, she realised, when she opened the wardrobe – it was the same: brogues standing to attention on shoe trees, ties hung so every point was level, detachable collars and cuffs curled in boxes, tweed winter suits one end, wool pinstripes the other, day shirts, evening shirts – every item as regimented as if they had been measured with set square and ruler. It seemed like an affront even to breathe on them.

The third bedroom was Violet's. The atmosphere in here was less oppressive, and small touches suggested a more recent occupation, a more relaxed regimen. There was a book beside the bed, bits and pieces in the cut-glass tray on the dressing table – kirby grips, a lipstick, worn down at one side, a single, clip-on earring and a pink-stained powder puff; a quilted nylon housecoat hung on the back of the door. There was a silver-framed photograph on the chest of drawers, facing the bed so Violet could see it just by turning her head. Ellis picked it up and peered at it.

It was hard to make out the details; she switched on the bedside lamp.

'Oh . . .!'

It was a portrait, black and white, fading at the edges to sepia, of a young man. He was in uniform; a pair of wings and a row of coloured ribbons decorated his left breast and he was holding a cap between his hands. He was rather good-looking, in an old-fashioned sort of way, but his expression was distracted, distant, the face of a dreamer, and Ellis knew, without any shadow of a doubt, who she was looking at. This was Laurence Palmer. This was her grandfather, the man who had once owned Malletts, who had fathered two children in the middle of a war, then died before either of them was born, leaving a legacy of betrayal and bitterness which had lasted for over half a century . . .

She half expected the glass to hum beneath her fingers, but she couldn't feel anything; there were no restless ghosts here, at least not for her. Ellis traced the line of her grandfather's chin, ran her fingers across his steadily gazing eyes. If there's a place you haunt, she thought, it's that tiny cottage in Suffolk, but Violet still clings to your memory – why else keep your photograph on display, not just up here, but downstairs on the chest of drawers too? Yet for thirty-five years Violet has been estranged from her daughter, the one thing you and she made together. Why?

She chose the small room at the back to sleep in; it looked out onto the lush green garden behind number 14's barren yard, a welcome reminder that there were other people out there, ordinary people leading ordinary, untidy lives. Most of the furniture from this room had been moved downstairs, leaving only a single bed, a chest of drawers and a dressing table, both empty except for neatly folded lining paper. Like the other bedrooms, it was immaculately tidy, if rather dusty, but there was no clue as to who had once occupied that narrow bed. Ellis changed the sheets, taking clean linen from the chest on the landing, then went back downstairs to check on Violet.

The sitting-room light was off, but the nine o'clock news was on and the studio backdrop cast a flickering blue light on the old lady's face. She appeared to be asleep, but when Ellis pulled up a dining chair and sat down beside her she opened her eyes and smiled. Ellis could see Anna Ford reflected in miniature on her spectacles.

'Nell,' said Violet. 'Where have you been?' She was still half asleep. She patted Ellis's hand, sighed. 'You and I were good friends once, weren't we?' she said. She turned away, so her glasses glinted yellow in the glow of the street lamp outside, then back, peering in the half-light. 'I should have stayed, shouldn't I? But I wasn't feeling generous. I was so angry all I could think of was getting as far away from you as possible. But then Ma took over, as if I were a child again, and I was too weak to resist her. Perhaps if you'd been there . . . if I'd been stronger, stood up to her, my Laura might not have . . .'

Ellis made no attempt to remind the old lady who she was. She felt oddly detached, calm, almost peaceful. This was what Nell had sent her here for, to listen. If – when – she needed to do something she would be told, but in the meantime it was not up to her to manipulate events. Everything would become clear in time, if she was patient.

'Can you imagine how I felt?' Violet's eyes were watering behind the thick lenses, and her left hand trem-

bled in her lap. 'I couldn't forgive you. It was too much
to ask. I had to protect my baby . . .' She searched Ellis's
face, looking for some point of recognition, suddenly
uncertain. 'You were always so much *stronger* than me. If
I'd stayed you'd have taken her away from me, just like
you took Laurie.' Her hands scrabbled in her lap, the
right struggling to still the left. 'Although you did try to
warn me, didn't you? You tried to tell me what was happening right at the beginning, but I didn't listen . . .'

The words came to Ellis ready made. 'She tried to do
the right thing, dear. She tried to leave before it started.
She didn't plan for it to happen.'

'And I persuaded you to stay.' Violet shook her head.
'No, I sent Laurie to persuade you. That was the first
time, wasn't it, the first time he was unfaithful to me? I
never was very clever, was I, Nell?'

A tear slid from beneath her glasses and trickled
down her cheek. Ellis reached across to take the old
lady's trembling hands. 'It wasn't meant,' she said. 'They
didn't mean to hurt you, dear.'

Violet's hands fluttered like captive birds. The tear
reached her chin and was followed by another. They
joined, hung for a second in a groove of soft flesh, then
dripped onto her bed jacket. 'You did though,' she whispered. 'Oh, you *did*. And you hurt Laura too. My lovely
girl . . .'

The light from the television flared briefly, illuminating their faces. Violet's expression changed. 'You're not
Nell!' she said sharply. 'Who are you?'

'I told you, dear.' Ellis tightened her grip on the old
lady's hands. 'I'm Ellis. Laura's daughter, remember?
Nell sent me.' The words came easily, without thought.
'She wants to put things right.'

'Ellis?' Violet was becoming confused again. 'Are you
sorry, Nell? Do you want to make up? Maybe if we . . .

Laura's daughter, did you say . . .?' Ellis could see the battle going on as the old lady struggled to focus her failing memory. 'No. There must be some mistake. You can't be Laura's daughter. Laura looks like me. You must be Nell's . . .'

'No,' said Ellis gently. 'Nell had a boy, remember?'

'Did she?' Violet looked bewildered. 'I remember,' she said uncertainly. 'Dr Hills was there. And Marion . . . why didn't Marion tell me what was going on? Why didn't she stop it?' She was muddling past and present, talking to Nell again. 'You paid though, didn't you? You lost them both in the end, Laurie and . . . and . . .'

The tears welled, slithering in glistening furrows down her cheeks. The old lady fixed her swimming eyes on Ellis's face. 'What did you do with him?' she begged. 'No, you're not Nell, are you? You're Laura's daughter . . . I was so sure she'd be like Laurie, you know. But he put all of himself into his boy, didn't he, Nell? I should have had them both. *I would* have had them both, if you hadn't taken them away . . . Such a pretty child, my Laura . . .'

Ellis cleared her throat. 'Laura's very unhappy,' she said.

Violet's mouth quivered and her hands struggled to escape from Ellis's grasp. Ellis released her, afraid of breaking the fragile bones.

'All over again,' said Violet plaintively. 'It was just like it was happening all over again. I told her it must stop but she took no notice. I told her I couldn't bear it. I called her a— I should never have done that. But, *oh*, that letter . . .'

She sagged so suddenly in her chair that Ellis thought she must have fainted, or worse, had another stroke. 'Violet?' she begged, rubbing the old lady's hand to revive her. 'Violet, whatever's the matter?'

Violet blinked at her. She looked exhausted, shrunken, a bag of bones rattling around inside a pile of old clothes. 'She wouldn't come home,' she said. 'And she wouldn't answer the phone. So I had to write, but after I'd done it I wished I hadn't. She wrote back. Words . . . written down, they poison everything. Spoken, you can take them back, pretend you misheard, change their meaning, forget them, but once they're down there on the page in black and white . . .'

Ellis reached across to the table for tissues and wiped the old lady's tears, taking off her glasses and dabbing at her cheeks. 'If ever you get angry with someone,' Violet continued, 'whatever you do, don't write it down. You can't get rid of it, can't take it back . . . I'm sorry dear, I need to go to the toilet.'

As she lifted her grandmother's nightie, guided her hands so she could grip the arms of the commode, settled her down on the seat, Ellis remembered Joe's angry note, scrawled in black ink on the back of William's sketched plans for the lavender garden: *Next time you call, I shan't be listening*, and was filled with aching sadness.

'I should never have brought Laura back to this house,' said Violet the following evening. Ellis had spent the day cleaning. She had changed the old lady's bed, and her nightie, got her supper. Then she had dealt with the commode, washed her hands for her, read to her, until it grew too dark to see, from a library book she'd found on the table, a Mills and Boon romance, soothing, comforting, with a satisfyingly happy dénouement, and sat with her through an evening's small-screen entertainment. 'I expect you'll be off soon, won't you?' Violet had asked at one point, confusing Ellis with the carer again. 'Norah always goes as soon as she's given me my tea.' When

Ellis had assured her she was not going anywhere she seemed pleased.

'I should have stayed in Suffolk,' she said now. 'I should have taken the risk, even if it meant losing her . . .' She lapsed into silence for a moment, distracted by the film showing on the television, flashes and bangs, men running, gunshots. 'It was Marion's fault, trying to patch things up between me and Nell with that will. She knew I wouldn't want the Dower House, so she left it to Laura, on condition that she live in it for six months. She thought I'd go too, that Laura would persuade me, but I couldn't bear to go back. Laura was curious of course, and longing to be independent. She rang me when she first went to see the place, not a hint of what was going on, just what a nice man the solicitor was, how helpful he was, and all the time . . . Then later on, when we'd stopped talking, she wrote me a letter, so defiant, so *angry* . . . Of course she knew what she was doing was wrong, but it made her feel better, blaming me – I'd been stifling her for years, she said; living in this house had been like being in prison, he was her passport to freedom and she wouldn't give him up. Then when the scandal broke she said I didn't love her or I would take her side. She couldn't understand why I was so upset by what she'd done – why should she? She didn't know what it was like, being on the receiving end, never gave a thought to the other woman, but *I* knew how she was feeling, it was like going through it all over again . . .' She stopped, closed her eyes. 'She was a nice girl. Margaret, her name was, Margaret Hargreaves. She came all the way up to London to see me, to beg me to stop Laura taking him away from her. They'd been engaged for over five years, she told me. They were getting married the following week. The invitations had been sent, the cake ordered. What was she supposed to do with the bridesmaids' dresses? she asked me, as if *I* would know the answer. I didn't know what to do about anything – all my life someone else had made my decisions for me: Ma, Nell, Laurie, Marion. And that poor girl thought I could help her hang on to her man. I couldn't even hang on to my own man, so how could I stop my daughter stealing hers? I just made things worse. And then Ma got involved. I should've stood up to her, told her not to interfere . . . But it was too late – Laura was pregnant by then, just like Nell. She did it quite deliberately, she admitted as much in that awful letter . . . and she was never going to give him up. He was her passport to freedom . . .'

Ellis stared unseeing at the flickering television, trying to piece together the disjointed narrative. William – her father – had belonged to another woman. And her mother had stolen him, using the oldest trick in the book. She had always thought her parents' marriage a somewhat one-sided affair, but she could never have imagined this. She had always taken for granted her father's loyalty, his honesty, his integrity, but the William Violet was talking about had sired a child by one woman while still engaged to another, then abandoned a relationship of five years' standing only days before his wedding. And Laura had married William, not because she loved him, but in order to escape the suffocating atmosphere in which she had grown up.

All the comforting assumptions Ellis had built around her father – had they been based on nothing more than wishful thinking? Had she built him, against his true character, into a hero simply because she needed someone to look up to?

She stretched her stiff legs, and moved across to the window to draw the curtains, bending over Violet's chair as she passed to stroke the fine white hair from the old lady's forehead. The film had moved on to a dark interior, pale, ugly faces confronting each other and menacing, atmospheric music playing in the background; she could barely make out her grandmother's features. When she turned on the light it would break the spell, end the revelations. 'Violet,' she said gently, 'it's time for bed now, dear. Would you like a cup of Ovaltine before you get ready?'

She slept badly that night, her rest punctuated by dreams like the ones she had had as a small child. She had had nightmares then, of being abandoned by her mother at train stations or on beaches, crying for her in supermarkets and at school gates. Now, it was her father for whom she cried, her father who walked away as she reached out her arms . . .

The following morning, after she had settled Violet in her chair with her breakfast, she left her sipping her tea and went to ring her father from the phone in the hall.

'What's up, poppet?' demanded William. 'Where are you?'

His voice was just as it had always been. 'I'm at Rosemount,' said Ellis. 'Dad, I've found her.'

'Violet?' William sounded stunned. 'Good Lord! Look, poppet, are you sure you're doing the right thing?'

'Dad, I almost missed her!' It was harder to imagine in daylight, William abandoning his fiancée only days before the wedding . . . 'Another week and she'd have been gone. She's been ill, Dad. This lovely girl's been keeping an eye on her—'

'Slow down, poppet—'

'I've got to stay,' said Ellis. Now was not the moment to demand his side of the story. She couldn't do it over the phone, she needed to see his face when she confronted him, reassure herself that the man who had been the one reliable source of affection in her life for so many years was still who she had always thought he was. 'I can't leave her now, she needs me. Will you explain to Mum for me? Tell her something's come up.' And what about Laura? Deliberately getting pregnant to entice William away from – what was her name? – Margaret Hargreaves? 'I'm sorry to dump this in your lap just when you're in the middle of the new garden and everything—'

'Listen pet, about the garden. I ought to tell you—'

'Dad . . .' It was hard, not being sure of him any more, and it might be a week before she could hear his side of the story. 'Violet's been talking. She said – she told me about Margaret, and she said Mum—'

'Poppet—' William sounded flustered now and Ellis's apprehension grew. Her father was the rock on which her life was built. With Joe gone, who else did she have? 'I told you not to jump to conclusions. Two sides to every story, remember? It's so easy to apportion blame—'

Ellis heard a noise from the sitting room, metal clattering against china, then a thud. She had left Violet with a bowl of cereal. 'Dad,' she said, 'I think Violet's spilled her cornflakes. I've got to go. I'll phone you tomorrow.'

'Ellis, before you go. About the lavender garden. I ought to tell you—'

'Bye, Dad,' said Ellis, then, as much for her own benefit as for her father's, 'I love you.'

The phone clunked heavily onto its rest and she stood for a moment, her hand resting on the receiver. Uncovering the past was changing the present; all the constants she had taken for granted were suddenly no longer constant, all the assumptions she had made about her parents, the picture she had formed of their marriage, their relationship with each other and with her, had been made in the dark. Standing in Violet's dim, dingy hall, she felt a moment of stark terror. Throughout her solitary childhood William had been the one person she could rely on. Until Joe came along to turn her world upside down he had been the most important person in her life. What if he was not who she thought he was?

The idea was too frightening to contemplate. Pushing it away, she took a deep breath and went back to Violet. Spilt milk; she could manage that. No use crying over spilt milk . . .

Chapter Twenty-Seven

Over the next few days Violet grew stronger, more aware of what was going on. She began to do more for herself, getting washed and dressed in the morning, moving around the cramped sitting room. She was as pleased as a small child when Ellis praised her progress, blushed with pleasure when told how much better she was looking.

Ellis was doing things she had never done before: cleaning her grandmother's teeth for her, brushing her hair, cutting her food into easily chewable morsels and doling out her pills, emptying the commode and, in the absence of a washing machine, washing the old lady's vests and knickers by hand. She washed her face and hands too, under her arms and between her legs, and Violet tolerated the invasion of her privacy with sweet resignation, but it was unlike anything Ellis had experienced before, this physical intimacy with a woman she had known for less than a week. As the days passed her feelings for the old lady grew extraordinarily tender. Until now she had seen Violet only through Nell's eyes; now, her perspective was altered. Washing the old lady's hair, bathing her swollen feet in warm water, reading aloud to her from her favourite, romantic fiction, Ellis's tenuous feelings for her grandmother began to grow into genuine love.

Violet seemed to reciprocate. The smile with which she greeted Ellis's appearance each morning, the sigh of pleasure as Ellis brushed her hair or wiped her mouth with a cool flannel, freshening her up after breakfast, the hand she held out as Ellis brought her a cup of tea. Ellis was not positive that her grandmother knew *why* there was a bond between them, but she was absolutely certain that Violet recognised, and appreciated, its existence. The mutual pleasure their growing closeness brought was one of the most profoundly satisfying experiences of Ellis's life.

Sometimes the old lady talked to Ellis, sometimes she talked to herself, turning over the past and offering up missing pieces of the puzzle for Ellis to slot into place. It was clear that more than twenty years after her death Ma Carter still dominated her younger daughter. How grim it must have been, Ellis guessed, living with Ma's obsessive tidiness, her petty rules and regulations, her domineering ways, her moods. As Violet rambled, flitting from memory to memory, Ellis learned about Pa, his ineffectual attempts to stand up to his wife, his patience, his self-effacement, the only defence he had against the onslaught of Ma's overpowering personality, began to understand what it must have been like for Violet, bringing Laura back to this silent, proper house, how Laura – 'such a good, biddable child, everybody said so' – could have come to build up such a store of resentment.

'I should have stayed in Suffolk,' Violet told her again and again. 'I should have taken the risk. Nell and I were brought up in this house – I should have known Ma was too set in her ways to change.'

'Of course,' she said on the third morning, watching Ellis as she perched precariously on a dining chair to spray the bay window with Windolene, 'it's so different now, isn't it? In my day children were seen and not heard, we did as our parents told us whether we agreed with them or not. It was very frightening, getting married, leaving home. When Laurie took me to Suffolk on our honeymoon it was the first time I'd ever been away from Lyford Road. He was wonderful, so gentle. If I'd had to start married life at the Hall I'd have died of fright.' She watched Ellis clamber down and start on the lower panes. 'But then, if I'd been at the Hall, I wouldn't have needed Nell to keep me company, would I . . .?

'It should have been Nell,' she said, as she basked in the newly liberated sunshine while Ellis did up the buttons on her blouse, because her stroke-crippled hands couldn't manage them. 'It should have been Nell, nursing Ma when she got old. I was the pretty one, the one who was going to have a life of my own. But Ma would never have taken her back after . . . you know . . . even if she'd been prepared to come. The day I brought Laura home Ma cleared out Nell's room, packed up every single thing that belonged to her and burned it all, books, clothes, everything. And I joined in, I helped her. I enjoyed it; obliterating every trace of Nell from the house made me feel better, as if I was in charge at last. I even went through the photographs, painted Nell out of every last one, as if I could paint her out of existence. I never told Ma about Nell and . . . you know, though; she went to her grave thinking it was that poor soldier who was responsible. It was the disgrace she couldn't forgive, the shame, the immorality . . .'

That conversation, like their first, ended in tears, and afterwards Ellis sat with her grandmother for over an hour, holding her hand until she fell asleep, exhausted by her memories.

She found the photographs, lined up with inch-perfect

precision on the top of the upright piano in the dining room, wedding photos, holiday snaps, Violet, neat and sweet in her school uniform, Pa, standing in the doorway of his drapery store – *Geo. Carter, Draper and Haberdasher* – in a dark, narrow suit and a stiff collar, clutching his lapels and staring woodenly at the camera, a spare, plain man with long, gangling arms and legs, a beak-like nose and a mild, put-upon expression. In Pa's faded image, Ellis confronted for the first time the source from which her own looks had sprung, and found herself returning to his face again and again, drawn by the pull of a kinship unbroken through four generations.

The A, engraved on Ma's hairbrushes and embroidered onto her handkerchiefs, stood for Angela; Ellis found the name, inscribed in brown copperplate, on one of the photos. Here she was the young bride, standing pretty and prim next to a solemn, moustachioed Pa, there the mature, handsome matriarch at Laurence and Violet's wedding, lined up with the happy couple in front of a city-grimed church porch. Laurence's parents were in that one, Gerald and Marion Palmer, he hauntingly like his son, as handsome as Nell had described him, she, dwarfed by her husband's imposing height, turning her head to watch her son and his new wife, her misgivings about the enterprise written large upon her homely features. And right at the front, tall, gawky, her cloud of pale hair barely confined beneath an unflattering hat and wearing a shapeless dark suit, was Nell. Ellis knew it was Nell, because her face had been painted out and she looked like the blurred ghost in her dream. Ma's age sat lightly upon her – the genes were clearly strong on the distaff side of the family – but as she grew older her meanness and her small-minded pettiness began to show in the sour, downturned lines of her mouth, the frown-mark between her eyes and the aggressive set of her chin.

There were no photographs of Laura though, not one. Had Ma removed them? Ellis wondered, or was it Violet who had obliterated her daughter, as she had once obliterated Nell?

She didn't ask, but she dreamed again that night, a muddled uneasy nightmare of blanked out faces and whispering, shadowy figures, all of whom she recognised, but did not know.

'He belonged to another woman,' reiterated Violet as Ellis sat beside her the next day, cutting her long, ragged fingernails. 'But Laura wouldn't give him up, wouldn't give in.' Her hands fluttered within Ellis's grasp, making it difficult to trim the hard, yellowed nails. 'And what is a man to do, when a woman tells him she's carrying his child?'

'I should have fought for him,' she said, as they sat drinking tea on the Thursday, waiting for Janice to arrive. 'If I'd fought harder I might have managed to hang on to him. But I didn't lift a finger. When I found Nell's handkerchief in his pocket . . .' Ellis's heart skipped a beat. 'I washed it, ironed it, and put it back. And the way they were with each other, always so tense . . . his pipe, lying in the hearth at Malletts. Pipe smoke smells quite different from cigarette smoke, you know . . .' She examined Ellis's face, searching for something, something of herself, maybe. 'I was so much prettier than her. You should have seen me when I was twenty, I was beautiful, everyone said so, I could have had anybody. But it didn't do me any good in the end. In the end it wasn't looks that counted, it was . . . I don't know. I still don't know. What was it?' she pleaded, still wanting, after more than fifty years, to understand.

A peculiar chemistry, Nell had called it in her journal. But how to explain to Violet, who had spent more than half a century living with the consequences of that chemistry, that it wouldn't have mattered what she did, she would never have won Laurence back, because what he had found with Nell was too strong to fight . . .

Janice came soon after, and Ellis left her sitting with Violet while she went shopping. It felt strange, passing people on the street, waiting for the traffic so she could cross the road. Her head was full of the past, her mind a jumble of half-assimilated facts and feelings. She bought underwear, a couple of T-shirts, extra-large, and a pair of men's jeans (two sizes bigger than usual to accommodate her expanding waistline), then hurried back, anxious to make sure Violet was all right.

She found them both in the kitchen. Violet was sitting at the table and Janice was emptying the cupboards so Violet could decide what she was keeping and what was to go to auction. Already the table was covered with tea-sets, coffee-sets, plates, jugs. Janice hefted a cut-glass fruit bowl onto the draining board with one hand and waved a greeting to Ellis with the other.

'Vi's being absolutely ruthless,' she said. 'Are you quite sure, Vi, that you won't change your mind about that coffee set? You can't get it back once it's gone.' She poked her head round the cupboard door, enlisting Ellis's support. 'You try. I keep telling her she'll regret it if she gives away all this stuff, but she won't listen.'

Ellis bent to kiss the top of her grandmother's head. A few days ago the old lady had stunk of excrement and stale urine; now she smelled of talcum and shampoo. 'Well, darling?' she said, sliding into the chair next to Violet's. 'Janice is right, you know.'

Violet's eyes were bright and her cheeks were flushed. 'Ellis, dear!' She reached out to clutch Ellis's hand. 'You have no idea what fun I'm having!' She beamed, showing pearly white teeth and shiny pink plastic gums. 'If I'd only had you two to help me I would have done this years ago.' She leaned confidingly across the table. 'Ma would never have allowed—' She stopped, glanced nervously around the kitchen, then unexpectedly giggled, placing her hand over her mouth like a mischievous little girl. She made Janice giggle too, and the two of them were infectious. Ellis joined in, until all three of them were roaring with uninhibited laughter and Violet's hands began to shake so much she knocked a pretty flower-patterned saucer off the table. That sobered the two younger women up a bit, but Violet, having stared in surprise at the shards of china littering the floor, reached deliberately across to the pile of crockery, picked up a blue and white striped cup, and flung it down to join the saucer.

The three women contemplated the mess. And then Violet said, in tones of complete satisfaction, 'You have no idea how much I enjoyed that.'

By one o'clock Violet was visibly wilting, unused to so much excitement. Ellis made sandwiches, then settled her down for a nap, pulled the curtains and left her to sleep. She was glad of the chance to be alone. The sense of unreality persisted and she needed to talk to her father, get things into perspective. She made herself a cup of coffee, giving Violet time to drop off, then rang The Herb Garden.

William picked up the phone almost immediately. 'I've been worried to death about you, pet! Are you all right?'

He sounded tired, anxious, but he still sounded like William. Ellis leaned against the hall table, weak-kneed with relief.

'I'm fine. Dad, I . . .' How to put it? How to tell him what she was feeling, when she wasn't sure herself? 'Dad, I've been—'

'Yes pet, of course you have. Look, I know it must seem pretty bad.' Ellis could hear his breathing, quick, nervous. 'I wish you'd come home, poppet. I've told your mum what's going on, I thought it best, but she says . . . Oh dear. Ellis, won't you come home so we can talk about this properly?'

'Dad?'

'Yes, poppet?'

'Do you regret marrying Mum?' blurted Ellis.

A long, long silence, then, 'No. No, I regret the hurt we caused other people, not least my parents, who were so shamed by my behaviour that they had to leave the district altogether.' Another pause, an audible sigh. 'Can't speak for your mother, of course.'

'Why?' asked Ellis. All those years of discontent, all the petty resentments, the snapping and snarling, the contempt for everything William did. 'Why did she marry you in the first place? Why go to all the trouble of taking you away from another woman if she didn't love you?'

It wasn't what she had meant to say at all. When her father spoke again she could hear the distress in his voice.

'Well . . .' he said. 'Disappointment is a powerful thing, pet. I don't think it's that she didn't love me, it's just that she had . . . well, *expectations* I suppose you'd call them, which, as it happened, I couldn't fulfil. Nobody's fault, just the way things worked out. Ellis, I wish you'd come home. There's something I have to—'

He broke off in mid-sentence, and Ellis could hear him talking over his shoulder, a burble of sound. He was right, it was no good trying to discuss on the phone a subject they'd been avoiding for so long. She needed to see him face to face, remind herself that however badly he had behaved before she was born he was still the same father she had loved all her life.

'Dad?' she began.

'Yes, poppet?'

'Do you love me?'

'Yes, poppet, of *course* I do.'

'Thanks.' Ellis felt her eyes prickle with tears. 'Dad . . .'

'Yes, pet?' William's voice was unsteady, quavering.

The words came suddenly, tumbling out of her mouth in a flurry of unstoppable emotion. 'You should see her, Dad. She's so *little*, so *frail*. I *love* her, Dad, like I love you, you know? As if I've known her all my life. And I feel so protective of her, so guilty that it took me all this time to get here. She talks about the past as if she's just been waiting for me to get here so she could tell me – I can't leave her till I've seen her properly settled.'

'If that's what you want to do, poppet,' said William. 'But before you go, there's something I have to know. You didn't give me an answer the other day and it's been worrying me to death.'

'What?'

'Your young man.' A long, heavy-breathing silence, then, all in a rush, 'Did you – do you – love him?'

The sun came out, bathing the hall in rose-pink light as it flooded through the fanlight above the door. Ellis could feel the heat on her face, the smooth, heavy weight of the receiver in her hand, the edge of the table pressing against her hip. She could feel the swelling in her abdomen where her baby was lying. She laid her free hand on it. 'Yes,' she said. 'Yes, I did – I do.'

'Ah,' said William. 'Right then.'

They spent the afternoon going through the rest of the downstairs rooms. Violet, the prospect of leaving seemingly giving her a new zest for life, insisted upon overseeing everything, but the two younger women set the pace, breaking frequently for tea, coffee, biscuits,

manhandling a small but comfortable armchair Janice
found in the back parlour from one room to the next so
Violet could direct operations without having to stand.
Janice left just after five, and the house seemed awfully
quiet after she'd gone.

They ate their supper in the sitting room, watching
Neighbours with the window open and a gentle breeze
cooling their faces.

'We've just time before *EastEnders* starts to do a bit
upstairs,' said Violet as she polished off the last of her
instant chicken pie.

The old lady was strangely fired up, almost feverish,
and she had surely done enough for one day. 'We can
start early tomorrow,' said Ellis. 'There's no great rush.'

Violet insisted. 'I want to *finish* it,' she said. 'I've been
putting it off for more than thirty years, and I don't want
to waste another minute.'

She was triumphant when she reached the landing –
this was the first time she had risked the stairs since her
stroke – but she had to rest for a moment, holding on to
the newel post. As Ellis came up behind her she said
over her shoulder, 'I'd forgotten how *dead* it all is up
here.'

She wanted nothing of Ma's, waving every item Ellis
showed her away as if she found it painful even to look
at it, but Pa's things, his ivory-backed hairbrush, his
bowler hat, his walking cane, polished golden wood
with a silver band below the handgrip, brought a flood
of reminiscences – the texture of his Sunday suit when
she took his arm on the way to church, the smell of cigarette smoke and hair oil which always hung about him,
the bristle of his moustache against her cheek when he
took her on his knee to kiss her goodnight. 'Nell was his
favourite though,' said Violet. 'She was so quick, so
clever . . .' Her blue eyes hazed, focusing on another

time, another face. 'Nell took after Pa, I took after Ma . . .' She sighed heavily. 'And Laura took after me.'

She looked so small, so fragile, perched on a hard chair in the middle of Pa's bedroom carpet. 'If I brought Laura to see you,' suggested Ellis tentatively, 'if I could persuade her to come, would you . . .?'

Violet raised her head and stared at her. 'Would you?' she asked. 'Could you? Do you really think—? Oh, *yes*!'

She wanted nothing from her own room except the photograph of her dead husband. When Ellis offered to go through the cupboards, she shook her head and said fiercely, 'You can burn the lot for all I care. I don't want any of it,' and she was reluctant to enter the back bedroom, the one Ellis was using, at all.

'This was Nell's room,' she said. 'And then Laura's. Ma cleared it out when Laura . . .'

She didn't say anything else, but Ellis understood – Laura had been consigned, like her aunt before her, to the dustbin, leaving behind an anonymous space, no scent of her clothes, no hint of her likes and dislikes, no reminder of her childhood enthusiasms, no photographs to remind Violet of her only daughter's transgression.

'Was this what you wanted?' she asked, waving a hand at the neat, impersonal room. 'Was this what you intended?'

Violet's eyes filled with tears. Magnified by the thick lenses of her spectacles, they welled over and spilled down her cheeks. 'No,' she whispered, 'no, of *course* it wasn't.' It took her nearly an hour to recover, and Ellis cursed herself for her insensitivity.

The auction people came as promised on the Friday. They took away all the pieces marked with red stickers, including the cumbersome wardrobe, emptied before they arrived, and the heavy round table, from Violet's sitting room.

'I'm making a fresh start,' Violet announced when Ellis queried the decision. 'My bank manager tells me I shall be quite well off when this house is sold. The new furniture's being delivered . . .' Her brow furrowed momentarily. 'So annoying, not being able to remember . . . Anyway, the warden's going to let them in. It's all done out already, you know, carpets, curtains, I've even got a washing machine, though I doubt I shall ever use it. So complicated, these modern appliances . . . Janice helped me with the furniture, but that was before the stroke, and I really can't remember now exactly what we bought.' She giggled delightfully. 'It'll be a nice surprise, won't it?'

She turned to the grey-coated removal men, waiting patiently to get on. 'This is my granddaughter, you know,' she said. 'Such a good girl, looking after me.'

Ellis tried to remember Laura calling her a good girl in that tone of voice, so warm, so affectionate, and couldn't. She missed Joe suddenly, wondered where he was, whether he had managed to put things right with the university, mended fences with his mum. Why should she miss him so much more than usual, she wondered, just because an old lady she had never met until a week ago was moving house? The place seemed eerily silent and empty when the men had gone and the sitting room was lighter, brighter for the removal of most of its furniture. Violet had retained only the essentials: the chest of drawers in which she kept her personal bits and pieces, the big wing chair, the commode, the bed and the all-important television. 'Just look at all this space,' the old lady remarked with satisfaction when Ellis settled her down for her rest after lunch, switching on the news so she could doze in front of it. 'Isn't it *marvellous*!'

Ellis wandered from room to room, her feet making no sound on the worn carpets. The rooms looked bigger, less gloomy, without all that heavy furniture. You could begin to see the possibilities now, despite the neglect the place had suffered. Untouched for over thirty years, unmodernised, Ellis guessed, since it was built, most of the original Edwardian features – plaster ceiling roses, embossed cast-iron grates, panelled doors, glass light-fittings – were still intact, just begging for someone to restore them. She wandered into Ma's bedroom, where for the first time in years the sun was pouring in through the uncurtained window, illuminating the dreary carpet and casting its unforgiving light on the faded wallpaper, squares and oblongs of brighter pattern marking the places where the wardrobe, the bed and the chest of drawers had stood. Violet had lived here practically all her life, yet she couldn't wait to leave. It shouldn't be like this, thought Ellis, watching the dust motes dancing in the draught she had created. Violet grew up in this house, brought her child back here as a young widow. Yet it doesn't feel like a house in which children have ever lived.

She was reminded of her own childhood. She had been an untidy child, and clumsy too, unable, as very bright children often are, to organise either her limbs or her possessions, her brain moving too fast for her physical self to keep up. It had driven Laura to distraction – lost fountain pens, missing homework books, dropped socks, torn shirts. Was it here that Laura had learned her intolerance of untidiness, her need for order? 'I won't be like you,' Ellis announced, her voice echoing in the empty room, 'I won't make the same mistakes.' She tapped her stomach, felt, just for a second, a faint answering tap from within, then turned and left the room, shutting the door carefully behind her.

There was no disguising her pregnancy now. Looking

down at herself, she wondered how Laura could have missed the signs and for the first time acknowledged the anger that had been bubbling beneath the surface all week. Was her mother really so unobservant, or did she simply not care enough to take an interest? She could have come round to see her after Joe broke the news, she had had the opportunity if she'd really wanted to. She could have made sure, for that matter, whether Ellis actually wanted to see him before sending him round to confront her. Thinking of Violet, asleep under her candlewick bedspread downstairs, Ellis felt a rush of affection the like of which she had never felt for her mother in her whole life, and her resentment increased. She should feel more for her mother. But love requires reciprocation to thrive, withers if it is not accepted and returned. What a bloody idiot she had been, to throw away what she had with Joe . . .

Was she in danger of becoming like Laura? she wondered. Was there a pattern, a lesson to be learned from Ma and Pa Carter, from poor Violet, whose life had been blighted not only by her unfaithful husband but by her inability to move on, whose relationship with her daughter had been fatally undermined by her subservience to her mother?

Only now, at the age of seventy-five, had Violet plucked up the courage to break free. What if she had stayed in Suffolk? What if she had mended fences with Nell? What if she had learned from Marion, goodhearted, generous Marion, how to look after her child? Would Laura, growing up in Suffolk surrounded by people who loved her, have learned how to give affection, instead of merely receiving it with such indifferent grace? And Marion – with a granddaughter to fuss over, would she have found the heart to carry on, a reason to keep the estate going? What if? What if . . .?

One day, she thought, her own daughter would grow up. She would leave home, make her own life, start her own family. Standing on her grandmother's empty landing listening to the silence, Ellis suddenly saw her own future with appalling clarity. William was in his sixties. By the time her daughter was twenty he would be over eighty, if he was still around. And it was too late to change her mind about Joe. She had sent him away, and she didn't have a clue how to get him back.

Was she destined, like Violet, to become a lonely old woman, relying on the kindness of strangers, with nothing to look forward to except death?

The district nurse came on the Monday morning, turning up on the doorstep just as the removal van arrived. She was plump, apologetic, and in a tearing hurry. 'Sorry dear,' she apologised to Violet, 'should have popped in last week but I'm three staff short at the moment, I've got two more off sick, and the powers that be've just increased my caseload again.' Then, to Ellis, 'You must be the carer. Glad I caught you. Everything all right?'

'Yes,' said Ellis. 'Everything's fine. Violet's coming on splendidly, aren't you, darling?'

Violet beamed. 'This is my granddaughter,' she said to the nurse. 'She's been absolutely marvellous.'

The nurse glanced from one to the other and nodded approvingly. She was here to take Violet's blood pressure, she said, and some samples, blood first 'to check they've got the Warfarin dose right', then urine. She listened to the old lady's heart, shone a light into her eyes, filled in her co-ag levels in a little book.

'Astonishing,' she told Ellis as she said goodbye on the doorstep. 'Remarkable improvement since last time I saw her.' She lowered her voice confidentially. 'Between you and me, it wasn't the stroke that was worrying me.

It was very minor and it's hardly affected her physically at all. It was her state of mind that was dragging her down; she'd given up on herself. It's crucial, you know, with old people, that they *want* to get better, otherwise . . . well, you can imagine. I'd visit more often, but nowadays there just isn't the time. In the old days it was part of the job to sit and chat – now if you stop for a gossip you're neglecting some other poor soul.' She patted Ellis's hand, glanced at her stomach. 'We all need to feel loved and wanted, don't we? This your first then? Hubby must be thrilled!'

The removal man was there for under three hours. He packed the crockery, the kitchen utensils, the remaining furniture, odds and ends, then set off, leaving Ellis and Violet to follow more slowly. The old lady didn't stop smiling from the moment he arrived to the moment he left.

'They've got children, you know, the people who've bought it,' she said as their taxi pulled away from the kerb. 'Two little girls.'

'Good.' Ellis turned to look back at number 14, already receding into the distance. 'They'll bring it to life, you'll see. They'll redecorate, open the windows, blow away the cobwebs. Their kids'll roar along the passages, slide down the bannisters.'

'We were never allowed to make a noise in the house,' said Violet. 'Ma couldn't abide noisy children.'

Number 22 Britannia Court was on the ground floor. The sitting room faced south across communal gardens, and when they walked in the sun was pouring through the french windows. When Ellis flung the doors wide to let in some fresh air the room filled with the scent of roses.

Violet's new furniture had already been delivered, all pink and turquoise Dralon and pale peach-coloured wood, not to Ellis's taste at all but Violet was thrilled with it. 'Do you know,' she said proudly, 'it's the first time in my entire life I've chosen something by myself. Isn't it all *gorgeous*?' Despite her reservations about the *pinkness* of it all, Ellis could see what a wonderfully revivifying, almost rejuvenating effect this light, airy flat, with its big windows, its sunny aspect and its fluffy femininity, was having on her grandmother. 'So *pretty*, don't you think, dear?' the old lady said at least half a dozen times during that day.

Ellis spent the afternoon making up beds, putting away crockery, rearranging the furniture, and after an early supper of soup and scrambled eggs she joined Violet in front of the television to watch *Coronation Street*. By the time the advertisements came on Violet was fast asleep.

Ellis was growing more optimistic about her grandmother, hopeful that the improvement she had seen since her arrival at Rosemount would continue now the old lady was comfortably settled. The complex was new, still only half occupied, but the residents came from a generation reared to serve others, and a steady trickle of women had called round during the day to introduce themselves and offer help. Within an hour of her arrival Violet had been invited to two coffee mornings, a cake sale in aid of the Cats' Protection League and a residents' meeting at which the possibility of ballroom dancing lessons was to be discussed.

The following morning, though, her grandmother was confused again, muddling Ellis up with Nell, bewildered by the unfamiliar view from her bedroom window, the strange furniture in the sitting room, her left hand more shaky than Ellis had seen it since that first day at Rosemount. It's only temporary, Ellis reassured herself as she helped the old lady to the bathroom. She's tired, that's all.

She was better once she'd had some breakfast, remembering where she was, recognising Ellis and begging her, 'Take no notice of me, dear. I'm just a silly old woman.' Her temporary lapse was a timely reminder, though, that there was no miracle cure for old age. She was going to need help if she was to stay in her own home. Ellis persuaded her grandmother to write a rather shaky letter authorising her to enquire into her financial affairs, then set off to see her accountant.

There was a healthy balance in Violet's current account and various investments, mostly in Treasury stock, swelled her income every six months. Her capital was substantial, a consequence of Pa's shrewd business acumen, the accountant explained, and the sale of Rosemount for considerably more than the purchase of Number 22 had further increased the old lady's financial security. Encouraged by the confirmation that her grandmother could afford the best available, Ellis set off on a tour of the local care agencies, comparing charges, checking references, visiting premises. When she was satisfied she had found the one most suited to Violet's needs she booked them to start the following week, three times a day, seven days a week. They would take care of the old lady's laundry, do her shopping and make sure she got three decent meals a day.

By the end of the week the flat was beginning to look like home. Ellis had sorted out the kitchen, filled the cabinet in the sitting room with the prettiest pieces of china, placed flowers on the table, put out the few knick-knacks Violet had brought with her.

There weren't many photographs – Laurence in his uniform, Violet at her confirmation, looking wonderfully pretty in a white dress with a wide sash and a garland of flowers in her hair, and one taken on her wedding day, cheek to cheek with Laurence and smiling beatifically for the camera. She had kept Pa, posing outside his drapery shop, and that was all.

'No dear,' she'd said, when Ellis had queried her unexpected determination to be rid of the rest. 'I'd never be able to make a fresh start with Ma watching me all the time.'

'Darling, it's time I went home,' said Ellis. 'I haven't even got a spare pair of shoes with me, and I have a living to earn.' She was squatting on her haunches beside Violet, who was sitting in her chair by the open window. The television was on as usual and Violet was half-watching a discussion programme about divorce. 'I'll be back to see you very soon, and I'll phone you as often as I can, I promise.

Violet blinked at her from behind her glasses, her mind still on the telly. 'It must be difficult,' she said, 'not having any rules to go by.' She cocked her head on one side, thinking about it. 'Anything goes these days, doesn't it? Look at *EastEnders*, and even *Coronation Street* these days. Ellis, who had seen *EastEnders* no more than half a dozen times in her life, had no idea what she was talking about. 'When your baby comes, you will bring it to see me, won't you, dear?'

'What?' Ellis had deliberately not mentioned her pregnancy, in case she shocked her grandmother 'How did you know about the baby?'

The faintest ghost of a smile crossed Violet's face. 'I may be old, young lady,' she said. 'And I may not be very clever. But I'm not blind.'

Chapter Twenty-Eight

It was hard leaving the old lady – too hard, Ellis discovered, to do immediately. She stayed another day, and then another. She found excuses, helping her grandmother sort the backlog of bills which had built up since her stroke, making sure the carers knew what was required of them before she let them loose on their own. But as two weeks stretched into three, Ellis knew she must make the break. Since her arrival she had been managing with two pairs of jeans, one of which would no longer fasten at the waist, and a couple of cheap T-shirts.

'Your mother's taking it very badly,' William told her every time she phoned. 'Are you all right, poppet?' he asked constantly, looking for reassurance that she wasn't passing judgement, taking sides, making herself miserable. Ellis longed increasingly for the solitude of Malletts and she was anxious to put things right with her mother, yet she was torn, held captive by Violet's need of her, painfully aware of how fragile the old lady was, how little time she might have left to enjoy what they had so recently found together.

In the end Violet made the decision for her. She was grateful for everything Ellis had done, she said. 'So kind, so very, very kind, dear, *dear* Ellis, but it's time you got on with your own life.'

So Ellis left the following afternoon, stripping her bed before she left, and setting the washing machine going, then collecting her few bits and pieces into a carrier bag. The carer would arrive in a couple of hours, to give the old lady her tea. She had already been entrusted with Violet's pension book, had refused Ellis's offer of payment at the end of her first session – 'Oh no, miss, the agency deals with all that!' – and been instructed to get in touch via William if she was even slightly concerned about Violet's state of health. The resident warden would be on hand in case of emergencies and Ellis was no longer worried that her grandmother might not be able to cope. She had promised to visit regularly.

'Don't you worry about me, dear,' said Violet when she went to say goodbye. 'I'll be fine.' She turned her head to look out at the garden. 'It's so *nice* here, so bright and pretty. I should have done this years ago. You won't forget . . .?' Her voice trailed away and she laid her bony hand over Ellis's. Ellis could feel it trembling, a reminder of the old lady's approaching mortality. 'I mean, about Laura . . .?' She patted Ellis's hand, then released her. 'Next time you come you must bring your young man to see me. I should like that. And Ellis dear . . .'

'Yes, darling?'

'Just one more thing.' The old lady's eyes were blurred, the blue of the irises surrounded by a milky white halo. 'There's a shoebox in the bottom of the cupboard in my bedroom. I want you to have it.'

'What, darling?'

'The brown one . . . or is it the green? No, that's . . . Oh dear, so *tiresome*, not being able to remember.'

The brown one slipped from Ellis's hand as she was taking it out of the cupboard, and a pile of letters scattered on the floor. She knew when she picked them up what they were.

Show Nell this letter and tell her I hope she is not too sad.

All those letters, addressed to one sister, meant for the other, yet still Violet had kept them for over half a century. What a waste, thought Ellis, what a terrible waste. Replacing the neatly folded missives in the box she glanced across at Laurence, gazing dreamily into the distance from the photo by Violet's bed. Keep an eye on her for me, she told him silently. You owe her that, don't you think?

'This one,' said Violet, holding out the green one. 'I want you to have it.' She hesitated. 'Only, would you . . . could you do something for me in return, dear?'

'Of course,' said Ellis. 'Whatever you want, darling, you have only to ask.'

'I should so like to know . . .' Violet's eyes filled suddenly with tears. 'I should *so* like to know what happened to the boy . . .'

Chapter Twenty-Nine

Ellis walked slowly along the high street, carrying the bag with her spare clothes. She passed the estate agents where Janice worked but she didn't go in. She caught a bus, then another, and only when she was finally settled on the Ipswich train, seated by the window in a half-empty carriage, did she lift the green shoebox onto the table in front of her and run a fingernail along the Sellotaped edge.

The smell brought it all back to her; it smelled like Nell's journal, damp, musty, fusty. It smelled of the past.

It was full to the brim with photographs, curled at the edges, torn, cracked, faded; some were even stuck together, welded fast by close proximity and lack of air. Ellis stared at the images in astonishment. Here were the missing pictures of her mother, squirrelled away by Violet lest Ma find and destroy the only reminders she had left of the daughter who had disowned her.

There were dozens of them: Laura's christening; her first halting steps, holding her mother's hand; building sandcastles on the beach, Pa in a collarless shirt and braces with his trousers rolled up to his calves watching fondly while Laura, her face ferocious with concentration, patted a small bucket with an even smaller spade. As she grew older Laura grew more like Violet. There were photographs of the two of them, of all three, Ma, Violet and Laura, three generations of beautiful women, Laura tipping her head, flirting with the camera while Ma stood stiffly to attention and Violet gazed at her feet. There were dozens of family portraits, Violet and Laura, Ma and Pa – Angela and George, real people, with real names. And right at the bottom, beneath a badly crazed photo of Laura looking sulky and rebellious in ballet costume and ringlets, was a tiny black and white picture of a young Violet. Beside her, her arm linked affectionately through Violet's, her head turned slightly away as if she were uncomfortable with the scrutiny of the lens, stood—

'Oh . . .' said Ellis out loud, startling the elderly woman dozing opposite.

The likeness to Pa was unmistakeable. How it had come to be here, in the midst of Violet's secret hoard, Ellis had no idea. Maybe it had been missed during Ma's purge. Or perhaps it had lain hidden, fallen unnoticed from the back of an album as Violet hastily hid her daughter's image from Ma's destruction. Or had Violet kept it deliberately, a last poignant reminder of the sister who had once been her best friend?

The train slowed, and all around her people began to rise, collecting jackets and bags, fumbling in the overhead lockers for umbrellas and briefcases. Ellis sat on, staring at the faded image in her hand. She knew her, this plain woman, with her hawk-like nose and untidy hair, her fierce, intelligent gaze – *really* knew her, not just her history, her family tree, but the woman herself, how she felt deep inside, her fears, her hopes, her longings . . . This, at last, was Nell Carter.

It was only the guard, dropping his ticket-puncher by her foot as he strode past, who caused Ellis to glance up. The train had stopped, and everyone else had already disembarked. Hastily, she dropped the picture back into the box, grabbed her things, and left the train.

She drove slowly out of the station car park, then on into the country, enjoying the breeze on her face, glancing every now and then at the box lying on the passenger seat beside her. Her daughter was fluttering like a captive moth beneath her skin. She had wanted a history to give her; now, most of it was clear. It was not a very uplifting history, not a past, or a family, to be proud of. She would have to explain her own decisions too, Joe's absence from her life. Would her child blame her for sending him away?

Thinking about Joe made her miss him all over again. It's a funny thing, love – that sudden rush of tenderness, that longing to see one particular face, hear one special voice, above all others. Why does missing someone you love make you ache so, as if separation were a solid physical ailment?

She drove straight back to Malletts; she needed time alone before she faced her father and she was far from ready to confront Laura. But as she turned off the road and began to bump along the drift her spirits rose, and as the glade opened out in front of her she brought the car to a halt, sat back in her seat, and actually smiled. Regardless of what had happened here, this was home, as her city flat had never been.

She left the car under the trees and strolled across the clearing, noting the colour of the grass, paler than when she'd left, baked dry and brittle by weeks of unbroken sunshine. The sky was overcast now though – the forecast was for rain later tonight – and the air in the glade was still, the leaves hanging lifeless on the trees. As she neared the cottage a pigeon flew past her and landed clumsily in the lilac tree, which swayed and dipped beneath its weight. She made a mental note to bring in the deckchair before it got soaked.

Inside it was cool, silent. Ellis stood in the hall, resisting the temptation to touch the wall, reminding herself that there were no such things as ghosts. There was no smell of smoke, no whisper of approbation from Nell for her efforts over the past three weeks. What did you expect? she mocked herself as she pushed open the sitting-room door. Rattling chains? telekinesis? a manifestation? Nell was still there though, she could *feel* her, an invisible, inaudible presence all around her.

The journal was still where she had left it, but she let it lie; there were other, more urgent tasks to be completed first. She ran a bath and while it was filling she threw out all the food she had left in the fridge when she departed so abruptly for London. She made a shopping list, found a tin of soup, then unlocked the back door, got bread from the freezer and left it on the draining board to defrost while she soaked in the tub. Then she returned to the bathroom. She washed her hair, then settled back and let the hot water ease the ache in her bones, if not the one in her heart. When she came to the room was dark and the steamed-up bathroom window had turned a menacing blue-black. As she climbed out onto the bathmat Ellis heard the first faint rumbles of distant thunder.

She was over twenty weeks pregnant now, and her stomach was noticeably swollen, cobwebbed beneath the skin with faint blue veins. A brown tramline had appeared, running from her belly button to her crotch, and she traced its path with her finger, following the curve of her abdomen. As if in answer to her knock her moth-like daughter fluttered against her hand. She was already fully formed, all her limbs and internal organs in place, and Ellis was overwhelmed by that same warmth she had begun to feel this last fortnight for her grandmother. She hung the towel over the rail and stared long and hard at her misty reflection. 'Face it,' she said, 'you've made a mistake. You were wrong, sending Joe away.'

Next time you call I shan't be listening. How do you make someone listen if they no longer want to hear?

I'll go and see Dad, she decided, as she dressed in a clean shirt and an old pair of baggy tracksuit bottoms. Dad'll make me feel better.

Chapter Thirty

It was after five when she turned into The Herb Garden car park, but it was still crowded. The far end had been coned off, and behind the ropes a man on a fork-lift was unloading a pallet stacked with bricks from a flatbed lorry, while another leaned against the cab directing him. A huge pile of topsoil had been dumped where William usually parked his car, ready to fill the new beds. Ellis was puzzled by the bricks – she couldn't remember any brickwork on the plans William had drawn up for the lavender garden – and surprised by how far the project had moved forward since she had last been here. It was unlike William to move so fast, especially as he hadn't even finalised his plans when she went away.

She swung her car into the only gap left and switched off the engine. A Dial-a-Ride bus which had just arrived with a party of disabled garden enthusiasts, was dis- gorging its passengers by the garden entrance. It was a regular tour, one that William usually liked to take charge of personally, and the driver had parked at an angle as near as he could get, blocking half a dozen park- ing spaces. A man in a wheelchair was being lowered by hydraulic lift to the ground. Searching for her father's burly figure amongst the throng, Ellis caught a brief glimpse of his bald head on the far side of the lorry. He was poring over a blueprint, discussing the layout with a third man, obscured behind the lorry. William was gesticulating with one hand, scratching his bald head and nodding vigorously. Ellis, watching him while she waited for the bus to unload, decided not to interrupt and followed on behind the last wheelchair into The Herb Garden.

This was how it always was during the summer – seething with customers strolling the paths, bending close to read the labels, lifting pots to examine the plants more closely, discussing the relative merits of one variety against another. Ellis could see them in the Orangery, wandering round the display shelves with their wire baskets, turning seed packets, riffling through cards, choosing cut flowers, queuing at the check-out with armfuls of fuchsias. Above the rumble of trolley wheels on the concrete paths she could hear a hum of conversation and the lazy drone of bumblebees industriously pollinating the merchandise.

The staff – 'my kids', as William called them – were busy everywhere. Most of them were young, and those Ellis had got to know over the years had all been bright, capable. But the best, the most promising, rarely stayed for long. It wasn't that they didn't enjoy working for William – he was an amiable employer, insisting they all call him Bill, sharing a joke, mucking in with the mundane tasks when necessary – it was just that after a while they got tired of doing a dead-end job and moved on to better things. The tasks William set them to do, watering, tidying, filling shelves, sterilising propagators, operating the tills, were neither particularly skilled nor terribly well paid. Ellis was convinced that some of the brighter assistants William had had over the years would have been perfectly capable of taking some of the load off his shoulders, if only he'd been willing to take the time and trouble to train them. But no, they had to have the instinct for it, he insisted, if they didn't pick up the art of growing herbs almost by osmosis, he was not prepared even to consider them. It was the only subject upon which he was totally immovable, stubborn to the point of pigheadedness.

Ellis threaded her way through the crowds towards the fountain, then turned left along the central walkway, making for her father's office. The air inside the high brick walls was hot and heavy, and the clouds overhead had darkened to a deep, ominous indigo. The electricity was palpable and the distant rumbles of thunder were becoming louder. As Ellis reached the office door a flash of lightning turned everything momentarily blue and the strolling crowds found a new urgency, speeding up along the paths and turning their faces uneasily to the menacing sky. People were on the move along every path, and behind the noise – shoes pattering on stone, the burbling fountain, rumbling trolleys – a strange silence had descended as if the garden were holding its breath, waiting for the coming storm. The air felt almost solid, thick with incipient rain.

There was another flash of lightning and a couple cantered past, towing a trolley behind them. The noise of its wheels was drowned out by a clap of thunder and Ellis felt the power of it from her shoulder, leaning against the doorjamb, to her feet. The paths were almost empty now and she could just pick out the faces of sheltering customers at the far end of the garden, pale and out of focus behind the glass windows of the Orangery. A lone woman in a wheelchair was racing past the fountain. She had spurned an offer of help from a passing stranger and was propelling the wheels with her hands, arms pumping like a competitor in the disabled Olympics, forcing her chair forward faster than she could have walked. As she approached, rubber wheels squealing on the concrete path, the Orangery door was opened and willing hands reached out to manoeuvre her inside. There was a faint burst of applause and Ellis heard the woman's laughter, carrying on the still air almost two hundred yards to where she stood.

The rain came suddenly, as if someone had turned on a giant sprinkler, and the temperature plummeted. Within a couple of minutes it dropped ten degrees and Ellis began to feel cold. She stayed for a moment, watching the rain splashing onto the paths, bending the leaves of the plants, turning the soil black with water, then ducked into the stuffy office and stood listening to it drumming above her head, splashing, dribbling, gurgling, dripping, as puddles formed on the path outside the window. There was another flash of lightning. It occurred to Ellis that William must be getting soaked. A cup of tea, she thought; that'll warm him up.

She heard him coming, heavy footsteps outside the door, a burst of hearty laughter, then shaking, stamping, more laughter. She was pouring water into the mugs when he appeared in the doorway, trailed by the two men she had seen earlier.

'Ellis!' William greeted her. 'I wasn't expecting you till tomorrow, poppet. What a wonderful surprise!'

His face was dirty, like a small boy who has been dabbling illicitly in the soil; his shoulders and the top of his bald head were soaking wet. He held out his arms, beaming, and Ellis put the kettle down, then stood with her face pressed to his barrel chest, imbibing the familiar smell of earth and fresh air, and sighing with relief. Seeing his face again, she knew it was going to be OK; whatever William had done in the past, he was still the same man she had loved all her life. She stood on tiptoe and planted a smacking kiss on his cheek.

'Hello, you,' she said. 'It's nice to be back.'

William's companions, brawny, cheerful youths in hard hats, dirty jeans and ragged T-shirts, were clearly, despite the dark, leathery look of men who spend their working lives out of doors, brickies rather than horticulturalists. One of them had a thick smear of cement adhering to his leg, and their hands were streaked with grey dust; when they removed their hard hats more grime drifted from their hair. They were here to help lay the paths, William explained as Ellis swilled out dirty cups and made more tea.

'Paths?'

'Mmm.' William sat down at his desk, wriggling awkwardly to get his hand into the back pocket of his moleskin trousers. 'Brick paths, herringbone pattern, with lavender hedges in between. We've found the perfect bricks, got them secondhand from a reclamation place over Cambridge way, lovely mellow pink, very hardwearing. Just come and look at this, pet!' He extracted a folded plan from his pocket and spread it on the crowded desk, beckoned Ellis to come closer. 'Isn't it terrific?' The brickies, who had clearly heard it all before, moved away to lounge in the doorway, peering out at the torrential rain lashing the now empty garden.

Ellis brought her tea and peered over William's shoulder. It was a colour sketch, more sophisticated than any of the previous roughs she had seen, a pattern of interlocked geometric shapes, narrow pathways separating the lavender beds, each variety's name scribbled in William's untidy handwriting beside its position in the layout, *Lavandula* this, *Lavandula* that, each group of plants shaded in with the appropriate colour. 'It's brilliant!' enthused William, clapping his dirty hands and showering the desk with soil. 'It's a maze, see? With brick paths between the hedges to draw the punters in. We're planting in blocks of colour, starting at the outside with the deepest purples – this one's "Hidcote Twickel Purple", see? – then graduating through the mauves – "Royal Purple", "Grappenhall", then "Munstead", I think, but I haven't quite made up my mind yet – and on to the blues and pinks – this one's "Miss Katherine", *wonderful* fragrance, *fabulous* colour, had to buy it in specially from Norfolk Lavender up at Heacham – with the "alba" – the white – nearest the centre. It's designed to stretch the imagination a bit – you have to follow the colours from dark to light in order to get to the middle and there'll be lots of red herrings, like this path here.' He stabbed a thick finger at a dead end. 'You pass the clue here.' Another stab, another dirty fingermark. 'See? Look, here's a "Munstead", then "Lodden Pink", then another "Munstead", a block of pink between two mauves, which tells you you're on the wrong track. And all the time you're following the trail you're paying attention to the plants, really looking at what you're passing through. We're having a postcard made for it, with a colour photo of the different varieties on the front, so even when they're not in flower you can play the game by reading the names on the plates. I'm just so thrilled with it, poppet. It's absolutely spot on what I wanted. Lavender's the ideal plant for a low-growing hedge, of course, and it echoes the knot-garden theme too, the same sort of medieval feel. Did you know mazes have been around since Roman times? And lavender's been grown in this country since way back in the sixteenth century. It couldn't be better!' He tipped his chair and grinned up at her. 'Well?' he asked eagerly. 'What do you think?'

'I think it's a wonderful idea,' said Ellis. 'Did you dream it up all by yourself?'

'No, I . . . Er . . .,' William coughed. 'Um . . . had a bit of help on that one, pet.'

He looked uncomfortable suddenly, evasive, almost shifty, Ellis thought. His chair thudded heavily back onto the floor and he peered around the room, avoiding her gaze.

'Now where did I put my tea?'

'Here.'

Ellis rescued his mug from beneath the plan and held it out. The rain was slowing outside, the noise above their heads diminishing, the sky, framed by the window above William's desk, was growing lighter as the clouds moved away. The brickies had finished their tea and they were getting restless. 'Right, Bill,' said one of them, moving back into the room to dump his mug on the dresser. 'Seems to be easing up. We'll be getting on, OK?'

William twisted in his chair, nodded, raised a hand. 'With you in a tick,' he said. Then he turned back to his tea, sipping with one hand and smoothing his plan with the other.

'Dad?' said Ellis. 'You didn't answer my question.'

William's big shoulders lifted awkwardly. 'What question was that, pet?'

'How did you come up with the idea for the maze?'

'Um . . .' William clutched his tea to his chest. 'We must talk, pet,' he said. 'I've been trying to talk to you for over a fortnight now, but every time I—'

'Dad,' protested Ellis. 'You *know* why that was. I explained at the beginning that it wasn't something I wanted to talk about on the phone. It's been difficult enough, the shock of finding out about you and Mum—'

William silenced her with a wave of his hand. 'No no, pet, that wasn't what I meant at all. What I've been trying to tell you is . . . Oh Lord, this is difficult. I didn't mean it to happen like this, I swear I didn't, but it wasn't till after we'd got chatting that I realised who he was, and you did say when I asked you that—'

'Didn't mean what to happen?'

William winced visibly. 'What I'm trying to say is, I didn't know who he was until after—'

'Bill, can you spare a minute?'

Ellis froze, her mug of tea poised halfway to her mouth. She couldn't see his face clearly – the sun had come out and it was pouring through the open doorway behind him – but she knew instantly who it was, knew by the way he stood, the set of his shoulders, the unmistakeable timbre of his voice. He was wet, his hair slick with water and his blue T-shirt stained black by the rain. Her heart began to pound and she felt that same aching longing she had experienced less than half an hour ago at Malletts. But the almost delirious pleasure was overlaid with astonishment, apprehension. How had he got here? What was he up to? Why was Joe Leavis standing in the doorway of William's office, calling her father by his christian name as if – as if he *worked* for him?

'Ah . . .' said William. 'I was just about to tell you about that, poppet.'

Ellis could hear the water dripping from the gutter outside the window, the cement mixer starting up on the other side of the wall, the faint sound of a car revving in the car park.

'Dad—'

'Um . . .' said William.

'Dad, what is going on?'

The customers were venturing out again now the rain had passed. Ellis could hear the smack of shoes on wet concrete, a flowerpot banging against a trolley. Joe shifted a little, moving out of the sunlight.

'That's what I've been trying to tell you, poppet.' William wriggled uncomfortably in his chair. Ellis could hear it creaking beneath his weight, but she didn't look; she couldn't take her eyes off Joe.

Joe stared back. Just for a second his face registered shock – clearly he had had no more expectation of seeing her than she had had of meeting him – but he quickly adjusted his expression; he straightened up, shoved his hands deep into his jeans' pockets, gave a shrug of his shoulders. His mouth – oh, that *mouth*, thought Ellis, remembering the taste of it, the way it lifted when he smiled – straightened into a thin, defensive line. Ellis could feel his animosity from the other side of the room, coming at her in waves. Don't you dare, his look said, don't you *dare* challenge my right to be here.

'Sorry to interrupt, Bill,' he said, calmly beginning his sentence again, 'but the digger's just arrived. The lads need to know how deep you want the trenches for the topsoil.'

'Right, son,' said William. 'I'll be with you in a minute. Just bear with me while I . . .'

He lumbered to his feet, slopping milky tea down his hand, and his head found the naked lightbulb hanging from the ceiling. The light swung crazily back and forth, throwing wild animated shadows across the walls with each arc. William's face was puckered with embarrassment, and Ellis could feel herself blushing, like a teenage girl unexpectedly confronted by the object of her adolescent fantasies. She leaned against the desk, needing support, and clutched her mug of tea between her hands. Joe sounded totally in control, appeared, once that initial moment of shock had passed, to be completely in command of himself. Only his eyes gave him away. They never wavered from her face, never blinked. All the time he was talking to William he stared at her, and his steady, hostile scrutiny made her skin tingle; she couldn't move, couldn't look away. It was William who came to her rescue, stepping between them like a teacher separating sparring children in the playground.

'There's something I've got to sort out with Ellis,' he said.

'Right,' said Joe, and turning abruptly on his heel he strode out into the sunshine without looking back.

When William turned to face her, jingling the change in his pockets, he looked so sheepish, so guiltily hang-dog, that Ellis, lightheaded with shock, burst into slightly hysterical laughter.

William's expression lightened a little. 'Not too mad with me then, poppet?' he enquired hopefully.

'Absolutely bloody furious,' said Ellis. 'What on earth do you think you're playing at?'

William bent to rummage in the dresser for the biscuit tin. 'Look pet . . .' He retrieved it, held it out. 'Rich Tea?'

'No,' said Ellis. 'Dad, what did you think you were trying to do?'

'I know.' William raised a hand, still clutching the tin lid. 'You don't need to tell me. I'm an interfering old man. But it wasn't intentional, poppet, truly it wasn't. He turned up out of the blue the day you left for London. You know what trouble I've been having with the plans for the lavender garden, couldn't get them right at all. I'd been standing there for an hour, staring at the site waiting for inspiration and getting more and more disheartened. So when he asked me what I was going to do with it . . .'

Ellis could imagine it. William would talk gardens for hours on end, with anyone who was prepared to listen. Joe had only to go along with him, show an interest . . .

'How could I send him away?' pleaded William spreading his arms apologetically. 'I had to take him on, pet. I've never come across anyone with such a feel for garden design. It's astonishing, amazing. Your Joe is a remarkably talented young man.'

Her Joe? Ellis gazed in perplexity at her father's

luminously enthusiastic face. Her Joe's talent wasn't for garden design. Her Joe's talent was for quoting poetry at inopportune moments. Her Joe's talent was for making her laugh, for making love, making her happy. And miserable.

'Dad,' she said wearily. 'I've told you, he is not my Joe any more. It's over, finished. You saw the way he looked at me just now. How *could* you take him on without asking me?'

William slumped back into his chair and bent over the biscuit tin. 'He said you wouldn't care,' he mumbled into the rich teas. 'He said as far as you were concerned what he did with his life was no longer an issue—'

'No longer an issue?' Ellis's temper was rising again. 'Do you realise what you've done? I thought when he came to see me at Malletts that I'd managed to change his mind, persuaded him to go back. And now I find that my father – my *own father* – has set him up as a bloody gardener! He's thrown up his place at university! You couldn't have done any better if I'd asked you to ruin his life!'

'You seem to forget, poppet,' said William quietly, 'that I've been a bloody gardener for thirty-five years.'

He looked as he did when Laura was nagging him, hurt, bewildered, confused. Ellis dumped her tea on the dresser and flung her arms round his neck.

'Oh, Dad, I'm sorry,' she begged. 'You *know* I didn't mean it like that. It's just that Joe could have done *anything*. You have no idea how clever he is – he could have been whatever he wanted, and he's just thrown it all away!'

William gently prised her loose. 'Sit down, poppet,' he said. 'That talk you wanted, face to face, you said. It's time we sorted out a few things.'

They were interrupted by Julie, coming to check

whether William wanted to take the disabled party round now the rain had stopped. 'No,' said William, 'get Pete to do it, would you, Jules?' so Ellis knew it was serious. Then he made more tea, and settled down in his chair while Ellis perched on the desk. 'So,' he said, tipping his chair back and gazing at the ceiling. 'You think I've wasted my life, do you, pet?'

Ellis was wishing she had never started this conversation. 'No, of course I don't!'

'Then why is Joe wasting his life by coming to work for me?'

'Because . . .' How to explain? How to make her father understand without hurting his feelings? 'Because Joe's not *like* you. He's got a first-class mind—'

William chuckled suddenly. 'Whereas I have a third-class mind—'

'Oh, *Dad*.' Ellis lowered her mug to the desk and rubbed at her face. She was handling this badly. 'You know what I mean. You're absolutely brilliant at what you do. Joe's talents lie in a different direction, that's all. He's a straight-A student, exceptionally gifted – academically, there's no limit to what he can achieve. Harriet says the papers he turned in during his first two terms were quite simply outstanding. That doesn't take away from what you do, it doesn't mean he's better than you, it just means—'

'So, let's get this straight, poppet. What you're saying is that you do not consider being a gardener sufficiently stimulating – intellectually stimulating, that is – to be a suitable occupation for your Joe?'

'No,' protested Ellis. 'I'm not saying any such thing. Of *course* it's a suitable occupation for an intelligent . . . it's just . . . it's just that I wanted Joe to . . .' She stopped. Every time she opened her mouth she made it worse.

'Quite,' said William. His tone was heavily ironic.

'Ellis, did Violet tell you how your mother and I met?'

'Yes,' said Ellis. 'Well, sort of. She didn't go into much detail. You were working in a solicitor's office or something.'

'Mmm.' William helped himself to another biscuit, munched on it in silence for a while, then took a gulp of tea and set the mug carefully down on his desk. 'I was indeed working in a solicitor's office. But did Violet also tell you that the law firm I was working for was one of the most prestigious in East Anglia? Did she happen to mention in passing that I had just been invited to become a senior partner, the youngest they'd ever had? Did she let slip that I was – still am for that matter – a Cambridge graduate, with a first class honours degree?' Ellis opened her mouth, then shut it again, speechless. William took another biscuit, another gulp of tea, contemplated the ceiling. 'Did she tell you that I was, not to put too fine a point on it, what in common parlance you might call a . . .' Another mouthful of biscuit, another gulp of tea. 'A bit of a whiz-kid?'

William? Dear, kind, bumbling, untidy William? With his fondness for dunking biscuits, his gentle, self-deprecating sense of humour? William, with his love of the outdoors, his predilection for getting his hands dirty? William a *whiz-kid*? Senior partner in a successful law firm, a sharp operator in a business suit? Ellis, swallowing, choked on her tea.

William chuckled. 'Pretty far-fetched, huh?' he said. 'But true, cross my heart. What you've got to stop doing, poppet, is assuming that everyone else wants the same things you do.'

Ellis wiped the tea from her chin. 'I don't!' she said, then, uncertainly, 'Do I?' William eyed her quizzically from beneath his bushy eyebrows. 'I do, don't I?' She reached across the desk and took a biscuit, then settled back, leaning against the wall and swinging her legs, drumming her heels on the desk drawers as she had when she was a little girl and William had had to lift her up because she was too small to climb up by herself. It had got them both into trouble more times than she could count; every time William brought her up to The Herb Garden she came home with mud on her shoes and a dirty face and made her mother mad. 'Am I an appalling intellectual snob?'

William chuckled again. 'Absolutely dreadful, pet,' he said equably. 'But at least if you recognise the problem you can do something about it.'

'Have you really got a First?'

'Mmm-hmm.' William was teasing now. 'Does it shock you, poppet, that I've been wasting my talents all these years?'

'Yes. No. I don't know.' Ellis shook her head, confused. 'I still don't know all of the story. Violet said it was Marion who brought you and Mum together, is that right?'

William nodded. 'Wasn't what she'd intended,' he said, 'but yes, she did.'

'Go on.' Ellis lifted her right leg and plonked her foot down on a pile of invoices, wrapping her hands round her ankle and resting her chin on her knee. 'Tell me, Dad. I've been in the dark my whole life. Tell me how you and Mum met, how you fell in love. Then maybe I'll understand.'

Chapter Thirty-One

'Did you know her well?' Ellis began. Marion, I mean.'

'Lady P? No, not well, exactly. Though I suppose I got to know her as well as one can in such a short time.'

'How short?'

'Um . . . She first came to see me at the end of nineteen fifty-seven. She'd just discovered her husband was dying, and she wanted to update her will. She was anxious to heal a rift, she told me –' William pulled a wry face. 'Runs in the family, huh? – between Nell and Violet, and she didn't know how to go about it. Then, after Sir Gerald's death, we sat down and discussed the options.'

'Which were?'

'Well . . .' William hesitated, old habits dying hard, then shrugged, and plunged on. 'The Palmer estates went bankrupt in the late forties, and when Lady Palmer first came to see me she and Sir Gerald were already leading separate lives. After Sir Gerald's death his flat in Albany was sold to buy her an annuity, but that was going to die with her, so the only asset she had was the Dower House. Her thought was, if she could get Violet back to Suffolk, bring her and your great-aunt Nell face to face, they might be able to sort out their differences. She was adamant that Violet wouldn't be tempted by the Dower House herself – too many sad associations she said – but she thought if Laura could be persuaded to move to Suffolk then Violet might just come too.' He reached into the biscuit tin. 'She was a terrible bossy-boots, your great-grandma, couldn't get out of the habit of acting like the lady of the manor long after there had ceased to be a manor to be lady of. But she was a character, and by the time she died I'd got rather fond of her. She drank a fair bit too, and years of living on her own at the Dower House had made her a little eccentric, to put it mildly. She got it into her head that I was the only one in the firm who was competent to handle her affairs and refused to deal with anyone else, yet she started off treating me like a head-gardener or a butler, called me "Jones" as if I were one of her flunkies.' He chuckled. 'I soon put a stop to that, of course. I think I was the first person, apart from Nell, who'd ever had the nerve to stand up to her. "I like you," she said to me once; "You speak your mind, none of this namby-pamby nonsense about the customer always being right." We got on like a house on fire after that. Did Violet tell you, pet, that she took your mum back to London less than forty-eight hours after she was born, and that poor Lady P never set eyes on her granddaughter again?'

Ellis shook her head. 'Dad,' she said, 'when I spoke to you on the phone you said, "Disappointment is a powerful thing." What did you mean?'

William's gaze drifted to the ceiling again. 'How d'you think *you'd* feel, poppet? When your mother and I first met I was an up and coming lawyer, a man who was going places. She was very young, very innocent, terribly over-protected, and I think she was flattered that I . . .' He grimaced, then continued. 'She didn't know what she was up against, and by the time she found out, it was too late. She was already . . . well . . . you were already on the way.'

'I don't understand,' said Ellis. 'What *was* she up against?'

'Margaret, my fiancée.'

'Ah,' said Ellis. 'Violet told me about Margaret.'

'Maggie and I had been engaged for over five years.'
Ellis nodded. 'Violet told me.'

'Uh-huh.' William glanced briefly at her, then went back to his contemplation of the ceiling. 'Well, Maggie and I grew up together. Our mothers did meals-on-wheels, our fathers were in the same regiment during the war, we attended the same church. As far back as I can remember it had been taken for granted that we'd get married, sort of a natural progression. We were very fond of one another—'

'But?' prompted Ellis.

'It was all very cosy.' William rocked his chair, which squeaked in protest. 'Maggie's father, Henry Hargreaves, was my employer. The plan was for him to retire on our wedding day – he'd been grooming me for over six years to succeed him. My senior partnership was his wedding present to Maggie.'

'And when you told him you weren't going to marry Margaret . . .?'

William's chair rocked back and forth, groaning. 'He threw me out, sacked me on the spot. And he informed me, rather forcefully, that he would make sure I never worked as a lawyer ever again.'

'Oh,' said Ellis.

'He was as good as his word too.' The chair came to rest with a thud. 'He was a highly respected man, connections throughout the legal profession. Within a month I was not only unemployed, I was unemployable—'

'And Nell took you on when no one else would give you a job.'

'Yup.' William tugged ruefully at his eyebrow. 'You

can see, can't you, how hard it was on your mother? She thought she was getting a high-flying lawyer and what she got was a pariah. Maggie was well liked in the district, and her father made quite sure the word got around – what I'd done to her. When we moved into the Dower House the whole village sent us to Coventry and every time Laura walked down the village street she ran the gauntlet – twitching curtains, whispering, gossiping, pointing the finger. Instead of the comfortable life she'd been expecting, here she was, camping in that tiny house with no money, no friends, married to a—' He glanced quizzically at Ellis from beneath his brows. 'A bloody gardener.'

Ellis grimaced at him, accepting the implied rebuke. 'Poor Mum. Poor you—'

'Poor me?' William lumbered to his feet and began folding up his plans. 'You don't need to feel sorry for me, pet. It would never have worked with me and Maggie. She's as happy as Larry now, married to an accountant, three nice kids. He's a splendid chap, much steadier than me, can't do enough for her. They're comfortably off, got a big house in town—'

'And you?'

'Me?' William chuckled. 'What more could a man want, poppet – a beautiful wife, a clever daughter, a nice house, all this . . .' He waved a hand at the battered dresser, figuratively embracing his beloved garden. 'A granddaughter on the way. I'm the luckiest man in the world, poppet.'

His mood changed, and he frowned. 'But I do seem to have landed us in the most almighty pickle. I've been trying to work out a way of getting round your mum, but so far I've got nowhere. Would you – I mean, do you think you could go and see her soon? Explain to her why all this was so important to you?'

'Yes,' said Ellis. 'Yes, of course. Dad, I'm sorry I've got you into so much trouble.'

William regarded her solemnly from beneath his eyebrows. 'Now, about your Joe . . .?'

'Just leave it, Dad,' said Ellis. 'There's nothing you can do about me and Joe. He thinks – I told him – that I got pregnant deliberately, and I don't think he'll ever forgive me.'

The puzzle was almost solved now, most of the pieces slotted into place. She would never know it all, but there was still one piece she *had* to find.

William walked her as far as the fountain and she kissed him goodbye at the crossroads. The disabled party had congregated there, blocking the path with their wheelchairs, and William's passion for his herbs was taking over, drawing him into their midst. She walked slowly away from him along paths steaming in the sun.

'Go and see your mother,' he called after her. 'Please?'

The evening was still calm, but there was a dark smudge along the skyline to the west denoting more rain and cooler temperatures on the way. Ellis made a detour to the Orangery to buy a bag of coal, added a bundle of kindling and a box of candles, then chatted briefly to the cashier, who recognised her from a previous visit. Tonight, she thought, she would light a fire, treat herself to a candlelit dinner for one. Then she would sit by the range and finish reading her great-aunt's journal. She had promised Violet she would find out where Nell's lost boy had gone, and only Nell could tell her.

She plodded towards the exit, balancing the kindling precariously on the bag of coal and mulling over what William had told her. It all made sense – Laura must have seen in William a means of escape from Lyford

Road, the key to affluent, comfortable independence. He was an older man, about to become the senior partner in a highly respected law firm; how glamorous he must have seemed, how exciting. What had Laura envisaged, Ellis wondered, when she set out to steal him from his fiancée? Had she imagined an elegant town-house in Woodbridge? Diamond rings, exotic holidays, a place of importance within the local community? Had she fallen so thoroughly in love with William's position that she'd failed altogether to notice the man himself?

She lugged the coal across the gravel and tumbled it into the boot, then turned to face the car park, running her eyes along the remaining cars.

It was almost six now and the wide space was nearly empty. The other two men were still at work but Joe's tatty Fiesta wasn't there. She slammed the boot shut, then walked across to the coned-off area.

One of the brickies had just climbed down from the cab of his JCB. 'Sorry, love,' he said. 'You've just missed him. Took off like a scalded ferret ten minutes ago.'

'Oh,' said Ellis. 'Right. Thanks.'

'No sweat. Urgent was it?'

'Yes,' said Ellis. 'No. That is, I . . .'

What was the point of pursuing him? she thought. If he'd gone, it was because he didn't want to see her. It is easy for a plain woman to lose her confidence, easy to believe that any interest shown in her must, by definition, be transient. I've blown it, baby, she told her daughter as she swung her car out of the car park and pointed it towards the Dower House. Sorry.

Where did she go from here? she wondered. She hadn't touched her treatise for weeks, couldn't work up any enthusiasm for the research which still needed to be done, couldn't even concentrate on what she had already done. Until she had finished reading Nell's journal, sorted the past out once and for all, she was not going to be able to put her mind to anything else. She would have some supper when she got home, then she would light a fire and finish the journal.

But first, she must go and see her mother.

Chapter Thirty-Two

Laura was waiting for her. She opened the door and stared at her coldly, then led the way along the passage from the hall without a word. She was as beautiful as ever, sweet-smelling, perfectly made-up, but, following her along the passage to the kitchen, it occurred to Ellis that for all their shared holidays, for all the effort she had made over the past few years to get closer to her mother, she had no more idea what went on behind that immaculate façade than she had had thirty years ago.

If she had hoped for a swift reconciliation, she was disappointed. 'How *could* you?' Laura began the minute they reached the kitchen. 'How *could* you go behind my back like that, when I *specifically* said I didn't want you raking up the past?'

Ellis sank into the nearest chair. 'Mum,' she began. 'I tried to ask you the other day but you didn't give me a chance—'

'*And* I had to find out about your pregnancy from a complete stranger!' continued Laura. 'How do you think that made me feel? Even your *father* knew before I did!'

'Mum . . .'

'And now you think you know all there is to know about the whole thing. You've made your judgements, passed sentence, condemned me as the villain of the piece, just like all the other gossips in this village!'

'No!' began Ellis. 'That's not fair! How many times have I *asked* you to tell me your side of the story?'

Laura banged the kettle from its rest, stuck it under the tap and filled it, slammed it back and flipped the switch. 'How *could* you?' she said again.

'Mum . . .' Ellis tried again. 'I'm not blaming you for anything, I'm trying to put things right. If you'll just calm down, we can sort it out, I know we can.'

Laura stood by the kettle, fingernails drumming on the tiled worktop, mouth pursed into a tight angry line, and Ellis talked. She told her about Joe, how she had tried, and failed, to tell her about the baby the last time she had been here. She apologised, haltingly, explained why she needed to know where she came from, so she could put herself and her coming child into some sort of context. She got the impression that Laura wasn't listening to a single word.

'And I suppose my mother told you what a wicked woman I am? How I deliberately set out to wreck your father's engagement?'

'Mum—'

'She doesn't know *anything* about what happened. It was your father who made all the running. I didn't even know he was engaged when we first met.'

She was angry, bitter. None of it was her fault. She was a victim of her upbringing, of her mother's callous disregard of her feelings, of William's stubborn refusal to leave Suffolk after the scandal broke. 'We could have gone to London,' she said. 'We could have gone anywhere. He was highly qualified; he could have got work where no one knew him. He could have been *somebody*.' Violet fared no better. 'She was my *mother*. She should have supported me, stood by me, but she never did, not once. All through my childhood, Grandma's word was law. It was Grandma who decided what time I should be in at night, what clothes I should wear, where I should go to school, how I should do my hair.' She slammed cups, clattered plates. 'You have no idea how desperate I was to escape from that house!' She yanked at the chair opposite Ellis's, plonked herself down, leaned across the table. 'You are so *lucky*!'

'Lucky?' queried Ellis. 'How do you mean, lucky?'

'Nowadays,' Laura continued, ignoring the interruption, 'nobody would think twice about what I did.'

The kettle boiled and switched itself off. Laura went to make coffee, banging cupboard doors and rattling spoons.

'When I was twenty,' she said, flinging the words angrily over her shoulder as she poured boiling water into the cafetière, 'sex before marriage, living together, simply wasn't an option. You didn't find out whether – *if* – you were compatible until it was too late. And once you'd committed yourself you were expected to get on with it, make the best of a bad job.' She banged the kettle back on its rest, threw the teaspoons into the saucers. 'Nowadays people change their partners almost as casually as they change their cars. No,' she corrected herself. 'No, *more* casually than they change their cars.' She snorted, loud and unladylike, startlingly out of character. 'Nineteen sixty it was when I met your father. You've heard of the swinging sixties, I suppose? Free love, let it all hang out. A myth. It was all a myth. Oh, it might have been like that for a few arty-crafty students in London, but for the vast majority of us the permissive society was just something we read about in the papers. The reality was no sex before marriage. You saved yourself for your wedding night; adultery was practically a mortal sin.' She found the sugar and dumped it on the table, sat down again. 'I knew nothing about contraception, and of course no doctor would prescribe to an unmarried woman. But you . . .' An angry stab of the finger. '*You* can decide to have a baby out of wedlock and the state will step in and support you. Your generation take it for granted that you have the right to run your lives however you choose. You can have your two-point-four-children and still go out to work, you can divorce your husband if he doesn't suit, do without a husband altogether if you want—'

'Mum,' begged Ellis, but there was no stopping her now.

'But in those days once you'd got a ring on your finger you were stuck with it. It was the man who went out to work, the woman who stayed at home and looked after the children, kept the house, and herself, nice for her husband. And nobody ever warned you. Nobody ever said how *dreary* it would be . . .'

There was more, much more, railing against the ignorance that had led to her pregnancy in the first place and which had then forced her to marry William; it was almost as if, thought Ellis, Laura was blaming *her* for the lack of contraceptive advice available in 1960. After a while she stopped trying to intervene and just sat in silence, as her mother poured out all the spleen collected over thirty years of an unhappy marriage. And when her mother began to cry with self-pity, giving her the chance at last to offer understanding, sympathy, even forgiveness, Ellis discovered she had absolutely nothing to say. It was only afterwards, as she walked out to her car, that she realised: in all the talk, her mother had never once asked how Violet was . . .

It would have been better, she thought sadly as she drove back through the village, to have left well alone, to have preserved intact the polite veneer of familial affection she and her mother had built up over the years. Now, nothing would ever be the same again; too much had been said, too many raw nerves exposed. She doubted if she would ever know whether she had been conceived through love or ambition, whether accidentally or on purpose, or even who had pursued whom. Was it Laura who had thrown her cap at William, or was it William, already having doubts about his approaching marriage, who had fallen for Laura's beautiful face and allowed his emotions to override his loyalty to his fiancée? Waiting at the bottom of the hill for the traffic passing on the main road, Ellis remembered all those times when she had failed so miserably to please her mother, the lack of warmth she had sensed all through her childhood, and dropped her head onto the steering wheel, overwhelmed by another wave of loneliness. Whatever the rights and wrongs of her parents' marriage, one thing was clear. Except as a means to an end, her mother had never wanted her at all.

It was well after seven by the time she turned off the road and bumped along the drift. The glade was cooler now, and the cottage was dark and peaceful. Ellis waded out through the damp grass to rescue the deckchair from behind the lilac tree and carried it round the back of the house to store it alongside the freezer in the privy. Then she set about making herself some supper.

By the time she sat down to eat a hastily cobbled-together stew it was nearly eight o'clock and Ellis had lost her appetite, as well as the candles. Outside, the sky was growing ominous again, towering black clouds tracking across from the west, their undersides painted dramatically scarlet by the setting sun, and the sitting room was getting darker. She pushed her plate away, and tidied up the remains of her meal, but she couldn't find the candles – she must have left them on the counter in the Orangery.

She had never laid a fire before – the fireplaces at the Dower House had been blocked up when the central heating was put in in the early seventies because Laura couldn't stand the mess. 'See?' she would cry whenever William summoned the courage to light a fire, 'Dust everywhere!' and 'Just look at this grease!' she would complain, sweeping her index finger along the mantel-piece and puckering her elegant nose with distaste. By the time Ellis turned ten the crackle of a real fire was just a distant memory.

She knelt in front of the hearth and stared helplessly at the cast-iron grate. The range had been carefully reno-vated, the crumbling brick chimney lined, the ovens re-blacked, the corroded brass knobs and the drying rail replaced. She laid her hand on the left-hand oven; the metal was cold to the touch. It had been here over a hun-dred years, the sole source of heat for generations of solitary countrymen. Mallett, the first tenant, had warmed his hands at this fire, hung his blackened pot over the flames to cook his rabbit stew. Laurence Palmer had browned toast here, and Nell Carter had boiled the water for her morning tea in a kettle suspended from the idle-back tilter, still hanging from its hinged bracket at the left-hand side of the opening. Ellis hooked her fin-ger over the bar, mimicking the action of a tipping kettle – so simple, yet so clever – then reached across and shook out a sheet of newspaper. A twist of paper here, Nell murmured in her ear. A twist of paper there. Now the kindling. Place the sticks so, this across here, that across there. Now some coal. Ellis dragged the bag towards her and peered at the black, shiny nuggets inside. That's it, Nell guided, a lump here, a lump there, build it up towards the centre. Don't forget to leave some gaps, without a draught the fire won't draw. Ellis sat back and inspected her work, then struck a match and held it out.

The newspaper caught, turned red, glowed; a tiny yellow flame licked along its edge. Ellis moved on to the next twist of paper, waited for it to catch, then dropped the match before it could burn her fingers and struck another. Three – four – five. Five yellow flames now, licking up through the kindling, blackening the wood, curling round the gleaming lumps of coal. Ellis took a deep, sulphurous breath and a sudden gust of smoke billowed towards her, making her cough. The chimney's cold, Nell suggested, the fire won't draw until it's heated up. She moved to one side and watched the swirls of smoke. She could feel the heat now, hear the metal groaning. The room was full of shadows; it would be easy to believe in ghosts. She rose from the hearth and dusted her knees. As she dropped the matches on the table she heard the sound of more distant thunder.

The storm rumbled across the valley. Peering out into the glade Ellis could see the lightning flashes making livid skeletons of trunk and branch. The rain was flattening the grass, rattling a tattoo against the sitting-room window.

This, she thought, watching the flames leap behind the bars of the grate, was how it must have been when Nell lived here, the crackle and hiss, the smell of damp coal and woodsmoke, the increasing heat. The walls flickered, flushing rose pink as the flames rose, then fading into grey as they fell. With each blue flash, black shadows leapt behind the piles of books still lying on the floor.

The kindling was almost spent now, the coals glowing red. Ellis picked lumps of coal, placed them carefully on the pyramid she had already built up, then rattled the poker between the bars of the grate, sending glowing ash floating down to the battered pan beneath; the draught increased and the flames began to spurt again. She dusted her hands together, congratulating herself, then shook her head at her own whimsy. Ridiculous, taking advice from a woman thirty years dead on how to lay a fire. A sudden, ferocious clap of thunder, sounding almost directly above her head, made her yelp with surprise.

The storm rolled on. As Ellis moved around the room her own shape followed her across the wall like a shadow-puppet show. The room was getting warm now, cosy. She pulled the curtains, shutting out the night. It was almost half-past eight – now would be a good time to finish Nell's journal.

She went to switch on the light. Nothing. She opened the door and tried the switch in the hall. Nothing. She checked the kitchen, then the mains box in the study. None of the fuses had tripped, so it must be an external fault. She returned to the hall and opened the front door, then stepped out into the porch and peered across the glade at the trees lining the drift to see if there were any lights visible across the valley. Nothing. It was cold out here, and the air was scented with rain and wet grass. Ellis stood for a moment, listening to the water dripping from the thatch, then shut the door and went back to the sitting room.

It was too dark to read. She skirted the table, running her finger across Nell's journal as she passed, then settled down by the fire, tucking her legs up and resting her chin in her hand. What had happened to Nell's missing son? Where had Nell sent him? He couldn't have gone to her cousin Molly – if he had, Violet would have known, might even have stayed in touch. Perhaps he had gone to a local orphanage, been adopted by complete strangers, grown up in Dr Barnardo's? He could be living just down the road for all Ellis knew, or thousands of miles away. He could be the father of six grown-up children; he could be dead.

Unable to settle, she rose and fumbled her way in the semi-darkness to the kitchen. She would find a saucepan, she thought, boil some water on the range for a cup of coffee.

It was lighter in the kitchen. The weather front was moving on and the clouds were breaking up to the west, ragged black stragglers hurrying across the sky, leaving a strip of blue along the top of the tree line, tinged with pink where the sun was sinking below the horizon. Ellis washed up her supper dishes, then fumbled in the drawer for a tea-towel and dried up, staring out at the shadowy glade. She could see the privy from where she stood, and the trees behind it, silhouetted against the sky. 'Joe?' she said out loud. 'Where are you?' She leaned against the sink and watched the strip of blue spread. 'Joe? Are you listening?'

By the time she had put away the last spoon and hung the tea-towel on the hook behind the door the sky was turning black and the first stars were appearing. She could no longer see her watch, and she'd gone off the idea of coffee. She tried the switch on her way back to the sitting room, but the electricity was still off. The room was warm, dark, welcoming. She would sit for a while before bed, she decided; she was too restless to go up yet.

The fire was getting low. She knelt in front of the hearth and picked more coal out of the bag. She must get a proper scuttle, she thought, and a proper kettle to go on the hob, in case this happened again. How stupid, to buy candles and then leave them behind. She stood up and dusted her knees.

The clattering door latch caught her by surprise. When she turned Joe was standing in the doorway.

For one crazy second she thought he must have heard her calling. She stared at him, heart thumping, breath coming too quickly. He was holding a box of candles, and a Herb Garden carrier bag.

'You left these at the cash desk,' he said, holding out the candles. 'Bill thought you might need them.'

'Oh.' Ellis gulped. 'Thanks.'

He moved slowly into the room, avoiding the piles of books still littering the floor. Ellis watched him.

'You must've been working late.' Her voice sounded shrill in her ears, breathless.

'Yeah. We're still trying to decide what to put at the middle of the maze. We didn't finish till after eight.' He tried the light switch, lifting his feet to avoid a jumble of books which had tipped sideways across his path. 'Funny,' he said, 'there don't seem to be any power cuts anywhere else. Have you checked the mains?'

'Yes,' said Ellis. 'There's nothing wrong with it.'

'Oh. Got any candlesticks?'

'Yes,' said Ellis, 'but I'm not sure where I've put them . . .'

He shrugged; she watched his shoulders lift and fall, darker shadows against the shadowy wall. 'If you could find me a couple of plates then?'

'Yes,' said Ellis. 'Yes, of course. I'll see what I can rustle up.' She made for the kitchen, then stood in the dark, gripping the sink and staring out of the window listening to the blood pounding in her ears. The first stars were glittering above the privy roof and she could pick out the Plough. The shadows beneath the trees were black and sharp-edged – there must be a moon.

I called him, she thought, astonished. I called him, and he came. What do I do now?

She found a couple of saucers. They rattled against each other as she took them out because her hands were shaking rather badly. She carried them back to the sitting room.

'Thanks.'

He held out his hand and she thrust the saucers at him, then backed away, hugging herself awkwardly.

'Matches?'

'On the table somewhere.'

She moved towards the comforting warmth of the fire, then stood with her back to the range, watching him. She could feel the heat on her legs, smell the ash dripping into the hearth.

Joe was feeling with his hands, searching for the matches. He dislodged a pile of papers, grabbed them just before they slid off the table, and moved them to the floor. He found the matches, shook the box, then cleared a wide space round the saucers, setting a precarious stack of books and Nell's journal to one side. Then he picked up a candle and struck a match.

The flame flared and he touched it to the wick. His face was all sharp angles in the yellow light, the frown of concentration a black slash between his eyes. He tipped the candle sideways, letting it run onto the saucer, then stuck it into the molten wax and held it until it was set. Then he repeated the procedure.

'There,' he said, replacing the matches and standing back. 'That'll do you till the power comes back on.'

'Thanks,' said Ellis. There was an awkward silence. 'I didn't hear your car,' she offered, stretching the moment, hanging on to him.

'Didn't use it.' He was standing with his back to her, watching the candles as they dipped and swayed in the draught from the door.

'How did you get here then?'

'I walked.' He shifted from one foot to the other. 'I like walking after rain. Smells good.'

It was a long way to walk from The Herb Garden, a dangerous road in the dark. 'Shouldn't you have brought a torch?' asked Ellis. 'People drive so fast along that road—'

'I didn't come along the road,' he said. 'There's a track through the woods.'

'Where?' Ellis was astonished. 'I looked for that path the other day, and I couldn't find any trace of it at all.'

'Badger trail,' he said dismissively. 'Lot of footpaths start life as badger trails. They like to get from A to B without a fuss, badgers.' He shoved his hands in his pockets, shuffled his feet again. 'Better be on my way.'

'Yes,' said Ellis. 'Thank you.' He moved away towards the door, placed his hand on the latch. 'Don't go,' she blurted.

He stopped, his hand still resting on the latch. 'I told you,' he began. 'I told you—'

'I know.' Ellis took a hesitant step towards him, then another. She wanted to touch him, wrap her arms round him and stop him leaving. 'But you walked all the way here just to bring me some candles—'

'Bill asked me to. He was late for his supper.' He lifted the latch. The door creaked and the candles on the table leaned away from the swirl of cold air. 'Bye,' he said.

'Are you going to go on working for my father?'

Another shrug, cool, dismissive. 'Dunno. Shouldn't think so. I'm only helping out while he sets up the lavender garden. He'll have no trouble replacing me.'

'Yes he will.'

'No, he won't.' The laconic façade slipped momentarily. 'It's no big deal, finding a bloody gardener.'

It was the same phrase Ellis had used to her father,

only three hours earlier. 'Why did you give it all up?' she asked.

'What?'

'Your degree. University. Why did you give it up?'

His face was inscrutable, unreadable. I don't know you, thought Ellis, panicking. I love you, but I don't know you at all.

He let go of the latch and turned back to face her. 'What did your childhood smell of?' he asked unexpectedly. 'When you think of growing up, what do you smell?'

'I don't know.' Ellis's legs were giving way. She moved across to the table, then sat down and stared up at him. He came back into the room and sat down opposite her. The flickering candlelight changed the contours of his face, made his cropped hair look spiky, bristly. Ellis longed to reach across the table and touch, run her fingers through it to feel its new texture.

'Well?' he asked, impatient, restless, clearly longing to be gone.

'I don't know. I've never thought about it before.' She frowned, then suddenly remembered her bedroom at the Dower House, revising for exams. 'Beeswax,' she said. 'It smelled of beeswax polish, and vinegar.'

Laura used to blitz her room every day. She moved her books, piled in organised chaos on the desk, closed them up and put them away, losing Ellis's page because she needed to polish the furniture and they were in the way. She wiped the windows with vinegar to get rid of the smears and sometimes when Ellis went to the bathroom the smell of bleach was so strong it brought tears to her eyes. 'Bleach,' she added. 'Polish and vinegar and bleach and disinfectant.'

'Mine smelled of geraniums,' said Joe. He picked up a felt-tip pen and began to play with it, pulling the lid off, then putting it back, twisting it between his fingers. 'Pelargoniums and paraffin. It's a . . . *thick* sort of smell, geranium, coats your nose, hangs about.'

Ellis nodded. She knew what he meant – William had given her a geranium for her birthday once, an attempt to interest her in flowers. She had put it on her windowsill, then forgotten to water it. It had died.

'My dad was a brickie,' Joe was saying. 'Started out on the lump when he was fifteen, as a hod-carrier. But he was a quick learner, did well for himself – by the time he died he had his own business, something to pass on. My brothers run it now.' He examined the pen, turning it over and over between his hands. 'But it was a struggle to begin with. When he first went out on his own he was pushed to make ends meet, wife and five kids under fifteen to support.' The pen flicked between his fingers, twisting and twirling. 'First big contract he got he bought a house. Tumbledown cottage in a village just outside Middlesbrough, three bedrooms and a boxroom, downstairs bathroom.' He pulled a piece of paper towards him, took the cap from the pen, and began to doodle. Ellis watched him, mesmerised by the shades of expression flitting across his face, the black squiggles emerging on the page. 'We were stacked up to the rafters, five kids and two adults all squeezed in together. It's noisy, in a big family, nowhere to go, no place to be on your own, be quiet. We had this lean-to out the back, halfway between a porch and a greenhouse.' His accent grew stronger as he talked, his Yorkshire lilt more marked. 'Dad built it, somewhere to go to get away from the noise. It wasn't too grand, he couldn't afford anything posh, just a bit of glass and wood tacked on the end of the kitchen with a corrogated plastic roof that sounded like a bucketful of pebbles when it rained. He didn't do much with it for ages, just used it as a place to keep his workboots, tacked up a couple of planks for a workbench so he could mend our bikes or do a bit of carpentry. But then one year our Katie bought him a red geranium for his birthday – there wasn't much money to go round that year so she couldn't afford anything else. The only place there was enough space to put it was the lean-to.'

He glanced up from his doodling, but Ellis was under no illusion; the slow, affectionate smile that spread across his face was not meant for her. 'Once he'd started there was no stopping him, he was hooked right from the start. He was a city kid, Dad, grew up in a high-rise on a sink estate, not even a balcony. Growing flowers was for cissies where he came from. Leeks, maybe, on the allotment, but grown men didn't grow flowers.' The candle dipped, and Joe glanced up again, then went back to his doodling, still talking to himself. 'I used to sit and watch him for hours. He let me in because I was quiet, I didn't talk at him like the others. He'd sit on his stool taking cuttings, sowing seeds, potting up. It took over all his spare time, summer and winter, drove Mam demented. By the time he died, she'd not had a holiday for ten years – he wouldn't go away because he couldn't bear to leave his bloody pelargoniums.'

'Just like my father,' said Ellis.

'Yeah.' He nodded, acknowledging her presence at last. 'Just like your father. Anyway, from that first plant it just grew and grew. He put up extra shelves, till there was hardly any room to walk down the middle and he filled them top to bottom with geraniums – red, white, pink, lilac, orange, single, double. Every time you went out back, every time you brushed against a leaf, that smell would hit you. I used to watch him taking cuttings. Great ham-fisted bloke he was, my dad, but watching him take a geranium cutting was like watching a man doing fine embroidery. He had this paraffin stove going twenty-four hours a day during the winter, to keep the frost off his precious flowers, and when you opened the door the fumes – geraniums, paraffin, compost, damp – were overpowering. I used to sneak in there sometimes while he was at work, sit on his stool and rub the leaves.' He smiled again, at something invisible in the shadows. 'While the other kids down our way were sniffing glue I were sniffing geraniums.'

The fire began to crackle and spit. Joe rose and moved across to feed it, confident with an open fire in a way that Ellis had not yet learned to be. 'All my brothers and sisters are married,' he went on, talking as he worked. 'I'm the baby. My brothers run the family business, one of my sisters is a hairdresser, goes round in a van giving old ladies blue rinses, and the other works part-time in Marks and Sparks. Between them all they've got nine kids, and another on the way.' He knelt, lowered the poker to the hearth and held out his hands to the heat, flexing his fingers. 'I was the bright one, the one who was going to set the world on fire. Mam were dead proud when I got the scholarship. She had big plans for me, big hopes. And I went along with it. I wanted to please her, make her proud of me . . . University. Just the word was enough to put a smile on her face. "My son's going to the university," she used to tell her friends when I were a kid. "My son's going be a lawyer, a doctor, an architect."' He wiped his hands on his jeans, leaving a streak of coal dust. '"My son's going to be a clever-dick."'

'Joe—' began Ellis, but he cut her off with a chop of his hand.

'I don't want to be a clever-dick. Yeah, I thought I did – you don't know till you try, do you? Dad were always teasing me when I was a kid, said I were soft in the head. I used to quote poetry all the time, never had my head out of a book. Got some stick at school for it, till I got tall enough to thump 'em. I thought university would be different till I got there, and then I found it was just like being back at school, with the added extra of too much beer and a wider choice of girls to shag behind the bike sheds.' He straightened up and dusted himself down, then stood with his back to her, staring down at the fire. 'I'd already done the shagging behind the bike sheds bit, got it out of my system long before I left school. I stayed because you were there, not for any other reason.'

Included at last, Ellis felt a rush of pleasure, but his attention was quickly withdrawn. 'What Mam can't grasp is that it's not what I want to do with my life. There must be thousands out there waiting to take my place.' He waved a hand at the darkened window, moved back across the room towards her. He looked terribly serious, terribly young. 'But now . . . now I know what I want to do. Bill reminds me—' He sat down heavily at the table and gazed at the doodles he had made. 'Bill reminds me of when I were a kid, watching my dad propagating his geraniums.' He raised his head and looked straight at her, bridging, for a brief moment, the gulf between them. 'I envy you,' he said. 'I've seen you working on your lecture notes, I've seen the look that comes over your face. Your dad gets it with his plants, total concentration, total involvement and I can get it too. I walked round The Herb Garden the other night, and the smells, the shapes, the textures, they made me want to—' He clenched his fists suddenly, thumped the table, making the candle-flames leap and jiggle, then flushed, blinked, and folded his arms, as if to keep them under control. 'I'd better go.'

He had withdrawn again, Ellis could see it in his face,

feel it in the atmosphere. Despite the fire, and the yellow glow of the candles, she shivered. She had lost him; he had gone somewhere she couldn't reach him, stopped listening. For too long she had been repeating a message he didn't want to hear and now it was the only message he could understand.

She wanted to say, 'I was wrong,' but the words stuck in her throat. 'You're so very British,' Joe had teased her at the beginning, when she had stumblingly tried to tell him how she felt about him, 'a typical tight-arsed, tight-lipped, middle-class British spinster. Say after me: I – love – you. See? Easy huh?' Now, when she needed to tell him that she loved him, she found her tongue cleaving to the roof of her mouth.

He reached down, swung the carrier bag, still weighted with its contents, onto the table. 'Almost forgot,' he said. 'Bill sent this for you. Said to tell you he'd salvaged it from the fire and would you like it?' He glanced at his watch, then rose, his chair scraping loudly across the flagstones. 'I must go. My landlady'll get the hump if I'm late in.'

'What will you do?' asked Ellis.

'I've enrolled at evening classes.' He made for the door. 'To study horticulture.' He moved out into the pitch-black of the hall.

He was going, really going this time. Ellis raised her voice in desperation. 'Joe?'

He reappeared in the doorway, frowning. 'What?'

'You heard me,' she challenged him. 'I called you and you heard me.'

'Of course I heard you.' He refused to rise to the bait. 'I'm not deaf.'

'Joe . . .' she pleaded.

'Yeah?' He leaned against the door jamb, waiting.

Ellis swallowed hard. 'Take care.'

'Uh-huh. See you around.' He turned away, then back. 'You didn't tell me,' he said. 'That's what does my head in. You didn't tell me.' Then the latch clattered, and he was gone.

Ellis stayed where she was, glued to her chair. If she had any guts at all, it occurred to her, she would go after him, beg him to stay. She reached across to the carrier bag he had left on the table and drew out the contents, then sat back and stared.

It was a model aeroplane, made of some light wood, with fabric wings, and complicated struts such as a dexterous schoolboy might build. When she reached across and touched it with the tip of her finger it vibrated against her skin.

This was the aeroplane Nell had seen the first time she went to Malletts. This was the aeroplane she had moved upstairs in the autumn of 1941 to make space for her young plants. Ellis leaned across to retrieve Nell's journal and ran her hand over its battered cover; she could have sworn it hummed quietly against her palm. 'What now?' she asked. 'What should I do, Nell?'

She peered at her watch; well after ten. How long had she been sitting? The candles were burning low and so was the fire. She lifted the little aeroplane and carried it carefully across to the window, then parted the curtains and laid it down gently next to the Tiffany lamp, where it tipped slowly onto its starboard wing.

'Maybe if I sleep on it?' she said, and, as if at some invisible cue, the candles dipped and died. There must be a draught, thought Ellis, puzzled by the sudden plunge into darkness; Joe must have forgotten to shut the front door properly.

As she leaned over to snuff the glowing wicks between finger and thumb, the Tiffany lamp blazed suddenly into life. Ellis stood for a moment, blinking in the light, then nodded. Nell had made the decision for her. She banked up the fire, put the kettle on, made a cup of coffee. Then she went back to the table, scooped up Nell's journal, and took it across to her armchair. She leafed through the pages, stopping here and there to remind herself. It was like being enveloped in an ancient, musty cocoon, opening a door into some long-closed secret room.

She found her place, re-read the telegram: ... *REGRET TO INFORM YOU THAT YOUR HUSBAND ACTING SQUADRON LEADER LAURENCE PALMER DFC*. . .

Then she turned the page, and settled down to read.

Chapter Thirty-Three

The letter that followed the telegram offered *sincere sympathy with you in your present anxiety*, and a slim hope that Laurence might still be alive. Marion was determinedly optimistic – he might be a prisoner of war, she told Nell, or hiding out in France; he could be injured, or washed up on a beach somewhere, suffering from amnesia. Nell said nothing to disillusion her, but she knew better. The sadness was giving way to anger, furious, white-hot rage, that Laurence could have done this to her after all he had promised.

Four days after the letter a second telegram arrived, then another letter; Laurence's burning aircraft had been witnessed going down over the North Sea.

The Air Council, the second letter said, *desire me to express their profound sympathy with you in your bereavement*, and Marion brought it, as she had brought all the others, to show Nell, then took it away again, as she had all the others, lest Violet notice its absence. 'Not that there's much chance of that. She's incapable of noticing anything much just now.'

Over the past few days the little woman had lost all her bounce, all her pugnacity. It was she who had found Nell's handkerchief, lying in the long grass at the entrance to the drift where it had fallen from Laurence's pocket as he cranked his car engine in the fog. When Marion gave it back Nell wished she had left it lying, because holding it in her hand she knew immediately exactly how Laurence had died, and the anger, which had begun to lessen a little, rose again and threatened to choke her.

He wouldn't have noticed his loss straightaway. Only when he reported for duty would he have checked his pockets, and it would have been too late by then. He had gone flying without his mascot, knowing he was no longer safe, that this time he had everything to lose. It was his terror Nell had felt when she woke in the early hours, his fear she had endured during those last few moments of his life. Without his lucky mascot he had burned like that nineteen-year-old mechanic, engulfed in 100-octane fuel, skinned alive and screaming like a cornered fox.

It wouldn't have taken long, just the few seconds it took his aeroplane to spiral down into the sea, but death must have seemed like sweet relief by the time he hit the water. Staring down at that small square of embroidered cotton, neatly folded and still damp with dew, Nell could hear the hiss as the flames were extinguished, feel his pain as the salt water licked at his flayed skin; closing her eyes she could smell his raw flesh, roasting like Charlie Bewson's pigs, in the cramped cockpit of his burning Spitfire. During those last few seconds, as he was dragged down beneath the waves into the cold and the dark, he had finally given up the struggle; he had stopped fighting, drifted away from her. When Marion, in a half-hearted effort to cheer her up, brought her a small joint of meat she had to throw it away, because the very smell of it made her feel sick.

How could you do this to me? she railed at him in her journal. *How could you leave me all alone?*

Only a few more days to go now, to the birth of her son. It should have been a comfort, but what had so recently been a source of shared delight now seemed just a burden, one of which Nell longed, perversely, to be rid.

Marion, solicitous as ever, checked on her every day, 'Just in case.' Each time she came she brought something: talcum powder and zinc cream, soap, gripe-water, a pile of threadbare nappies, cod-liver oil and a bag full of yellowing baby clothes she had rescued from the attic at the Hall. She brought extra towels, even a wicker cot, smuggled up after dark in her car. She was distracted though, worn down by her own loss, and by Violet's problems – Dr Hills was worried about the poor girl's swollen ankles, she told Nell, and the headaches, which grew worse every day. Since the confirmation of Laurence's death Violet's lethargy had given way to an almost hysterical desperation, heartbreaking to see, she said, watching Nell out of the corner of her eye for any evidence that she too might be in imminent danger of physical or mental collapse.

She was clearly puzzled by Nell's lack of overt grief, but Nell couldn't bring herself to care much. The anger left no room for any other emotions. She was no longer concerned about the future, about the baby and what she must do when it came; all she could feel was cold, gut-wrenching fury. How could Laurence have been so careless? How could he have been so *stupid*?

Marion didn't ask about her plans. She looked dreadful, old, haggard, grim. Gerald, she said, not even attempting to disguise her bitterness, was still in London. She had not seen him since the news came about Laurence, had spoken to him only once on the telephone. Sometimes she was noticeably drunk when she came, slurring her words and moving unsteadily about the room, bumping into the furniture. She blamed herself for Laurence's death – if she hadn't quarrelled with him, if she hadn't been so determined to get her own way, it wouldn't have happened; she was an interfering old woman and she was being punished for her sins. She blamed Nell – if she hadn't lured him away from Violet, if he hadn't come home that last time, 'if he'd never met either of you bloody Carter girls . . .' Sometimes she even blamed Laurence, but Nell paid no attention to her ramblings. Violet's troubles, Marion's self-flagellation were none of her concern. Everyone is entitled to choose their own route to perdition, she thought, watching dry-eyed and ice-cold as Marion lurched on her way after one particularly drunken visit; who was she to criticise the way Marion had chosen?

Laurence's will was short, and straightforward. Made months ago, back in the spring when the primroses were blooming, it left all his worldly possessions – the cottage, its contents, and a small sum of money – to Nell. Marion, practically speechless with indignation, brought the news a week after his death.

It was late, Nell was on her way to bed and she let her in reluctantly. 'Violet doesn't know,' said Marion, gulping whisky as she sat in her usual place by the fire. 'I haven't shown her the will and I'm not going to. All she needs to know is that her child . . .' glaring furiously at Nell with red, alcohol-rimed eyes, '*her* child, will inherit the estate. This . . .' waving the document violently under Nell's nose, '*this* could tip her over the edge completely.' Nell nodded her agreement, then sat on after Marion had left, staring into the fire and wondering why it mattered, now that Laurence wasn't coming home.

You're the strong one, she reminded herself. You're the one who was going to strike out on your own, put all this behind you and start again, remember? She prodded the fire, sending showers of sparks leaping up the chimney. That was before though. Before the prospect of happiness was dangled in front of me, before promises were made and given, before we were together. She dropped the poker in the hearth, then rose from her chair and wandered across the room, making for her bed and the oblivion of sleep. Extinguishing the oil lamp, she felt her way to the window to take down the blackout, then stood for a moment listening. It was raining, the drops pattering onto the ground beneath the eaves, and she leaned forward, placing her hands on the sill to listen.

She felt it only for a moment and it was so faint that as soon as she concentrated on it, it disappeared. She spread her fingers and stood motionless, holding her breath, but there was nothing there, just the cold stone against her skin. Think about something else, she told herself, something unconnected, anything will do – what shall I have for breakfast tomorrow? Will there be a frost tonight? Should I visit the bumby before I go to bed?

Sometimes, her uncle had told her when she was a child, when the sky is clear and the Milky Way is visible, it is better to look not directly at the haze but to one side of it – that way you can pick out the individual stars more distinctly, sidling up to them obliquely and taking them by surprise. Concentrating with all the strength she could muster on what she had in the larder, Nell felt the vibration increase beneath her fingers, and she knew then that she must stay. Marion would not approve, but that didn't matter. What mattered was that while she was here, Laurence was still with her.

As she climbed the stairs to bed she felt the baby move. She stopped short in the bedroom doorway and spread her hands on her swollen belly. What am I going to do about this though? she challenged him silently. What in God's name am I going to do about our son?

Chapter Thirty-Four

Nell was in the garden when the first twinges came, clumsily tidying up the herb beds. She didn't recognise the symptoms to start with, brief stabs of pain low down, starting in her back then moving round to the front. But as they increased, both in frequency and intensity, it became obvious what they meant. She felt neither fear nor elation at the prospect of her pregnancy drawing to an end. The anger was fading, turning gradually to a stony acceptance of her situation, as if from feeling too much she had lost her capacity to feel anything at all, and she carried on with what she was doing – the twinges, which went on for most of the day, were perfectly tolerable as long as she didn't give in to them. It was not until later, after she had fixed the blackout and lit the lamp, peeled potatoes and chopped cabbage for her frugal supper, that she began to grow nervous, began to long for Marion, someone, *anyone*, to appear. By eight o'clock she was taking short, panicky breaths, marching back and forth, groaning out loud and wondering what she would do if no one came to help her. By the time Marion arrived just after ten, her waters had already broken and she was hunched up in the leather armchair by the fire, ashen-faced, exhausted, rocking backwards and forwards and grunting like an animal.

'You can't give birth down here,' said Marion, breathing whisky fumes into her face as she bent to examine her. 'We must get you upstairs to bed.'

'No!' Nell gripped the chair arms and shook her head. 'Here. I want to stay here, in front of the fire.'

'Don't be stubborn, you'll be much more comfortable in bed.'

Nell grimaced as another contraction rippled across her stomach. 'I'm not moving.'

'Of course you are!'

'No, I'm not!'

Marion tutted with exasperation. 'I haven't time for your temper tantrums. Poor Violet's just gone into labour and she's in a terrible state. The only reason I've left her is because Dr Hills is with her. You couldn't have picked a more inconvenient time frankly—'

'*Inconvenient?*' Nell scowled. Now that Marion was here she didn't want her. 'Why don't you go away then?' she snarled. 'Why don't you go back to Violet and leave me alone?'

Marion snorted. 'Don't be so damn silly. Dr Hills has delivered hundreds of babies. He's perfectly capable of managing Violet. Of *course* I won't leave you.'

She fetched blankets from the bedroom, and pillows to put behind Nell's back. She brought towels, moistened a flannel to bathe the sweat from Nell's forehead and moved the rocking chair so she could sit beside her. Then she put the kettle on and settled down, whisky in hand, to wait.

They sat for three hours, Nell panting and gasping with every contraction, Marion drinking steadily and talking, about nothing in particular to begin with, then, as her state of inebriation increased, about her husband, absent as usual, about his mistress, about Laurence, fuelling the revelations tumbling unstoppably from her mouth with constant slurps of whisky. Towards the end of their vigil she grew maudlin, sentimental and accusatory by turns.

'He was so handsome,' she said, reminiscing about her wayward husband. 'He could have had any woman he wanted. But he chose me.'

Nell sucked her breath in and counted to ten, biting her lip until the contraction passed. They were coming every two minutes now.

' 'Course he only wanted me for my money . . . never made any secret of it. But I could've made him like me well enough if *she* hadn't got in the way.'

'She?'

'Pretty, dainty, la-di-da upper-class tart . . .' More whisky, a drunken shake of Nell's arm. 'He's with her you know, this very minute. Women like us . . .' tapping her nose and leaning close, '*plain* women, how are we supposed to compete? Eh? Eh? How are we supposed to hang on to our men when women like that . . .' She settled back in her chair, glared. 'Except for you, of course . . .'

Nell clenched her jaw, not listening. Why had nobody warned her how much it was going to *hurt*?

Marion leaned across, screwing up her eyes in an effort to focus. 'You should've married him. You should've married him when you had the chance – you could've saved Violet all this misery. Why didn't you marry him when you had the chance?'

'I've told you—' Another contraction, sharper than the last. Nell closed her eyes, concentrating on breathing. 'Because he was seduced by Violet's beautiful face before I ever met him.'

'Then why didn't you leave him alone?'

'Because he wouldn't let me. Because I couldn't help myself.'

'You could've saved him.'

They'd had this conversation a dozen times since Laurence's death. Marion reached for the whisky bottle, then swayed forward to examine Nell's perspiring face. 'How're you doing?'

'Not too good.' Nell was rocking back and forth, groaning. 'Marion, could you pour me a whisky?'

'Good idea.' Marion staggered to her feet. 'Should've thought of it m'self.' She meandered across the room to the corner cupboard, brought back another tumbler and filled it half full of Johnnie Walker, then held out the glass, moving with exaggerated care lest it spill. Nell took it gratefully and breathed in the fumes, then doubled up again. Marion heaved herself unsteadily out of her chair, grabbed the glass and dumped it in the hearth.

'I think it's time,' she said, rolling up her sleeves.

Chapter Thirty-Five

It was all over by three o'clock, and Nell was done in. She could hear Marion talking as she cut the cord and cleaned the baby up, but it was like listening under water; the words didn't make any sense. She didn't want the mewling bundle Marion placed in her arms, would have pushed it away if she hadn't been too weak to argue. Its pink, angry face bore no resemblance to Laurence, and she felt no rush of maternal love, could find no pleasure in the knowledge that this was Laurence's child.

She balanced the tiny scrap, wrapped by Marion in a soft woollen shawl, awkwardly in the crook of her left arm and reached out to touch the wall with her right; it was dead, cold and unresponsive. Like Laurence, she thought, staring down into her child's eyes – not blue, not brown, not anything. 'I don't want this,' she said, turning her face away.

Marion tutted at her. 'Don't be ridiculous. You'll feel different after the first feed. Maternal instinct – never fails, you'll see.' Nell was vaguely aware of her bustling around in the shadows, but she felt, rather than saw, the wicker cot appear beside her. The bundle was lifted and her left arm, relieved of its burden, felt suddenly light. Marion was talking again, close to her ear, breathing whisky fumes. 'Maternal instinct, you'll see. Now go to sleep while you can. I'll be back as soon as . . . ' Nell's eyes closed and she slept.

She woke to the sun on her face and the sound of a baby crying. She opened her eyes and frowned at the ceiling, wishing someone would make it stop so she could sleep in peace. She was lying on her back on the rag rug in front of the dying fire, swaddled in a nest of blankets and pillows. When she struggled up onto one elbow the movement pulled at her sore stomach and she grimaced with pain.

The child's face was invisible. All she could see was a tiny foot, kicking above the edge of the cot Marion had placed by her head. She stared at it, waiting to feel Marion's maternal instinct, but nothing came, except irritation that it would not stop crying.

It must need feeding, she thought. Babies need constant feeding, don't they? And I must change its nappy. Marion had shown her how to do that the previous week, making her fold and refold the threadbare squares of cotton towelling over and over, mocking her incompetence when she got it wrong. She struggled to sit up, every muscle aching, then reached out to touch the wall again. Still dead; just when she needed him most, Laurence had deserted her. She closed her eyes and lay back against the pillows, trying to blank out the increasingly strident wails coming from the cot. Then she took a deep breath, rubbed at her face with both hands. 'This won't do,' she said fiercely. 'Get up. Get up and deal with it.'

She did. She stood upright, went to bend over the cot. She could feel the blood, soaking into the sanitary towel Marion had clamped between her legs after the birth, smell the stinking nappy about which the child was complaining so vociferously. She cleaned up the mess, changed the nappy, and her own towel. Soon, she told herself as she poured Jeyes' Fluid into the galvanised bucket Marion had provided for the purpose and dropped the soiled nappy into it, the maternal instinct will come soon.

It didn't. She settled herself in the rocking chair and stared fixedly out of the window at the turning trees while the baby mewled and grizzled at her nipple. After a while, when the wails of hunger became too loud to ignore, she took hold of her breast and squeezed until a few drops of liquid appeared, then thrust her nipple at the red, open mouth in the hope that the taste would encourage the suckling instinct. The child nuzzled and dribbled and she allowed her thoughts to drift. Ernie had offered to show her how to make sloe gin, and there was bullace to be picked, blackberry jam to be made . . . The baby slipped from her nipple and began to yell. Nell gritted her teeth, took hold of her breast and tried again. Soon, she reassured herself, attempting to stem the mounting panic, soon I must begin to feel something. You are Laurence's child, made of him and me. So I *must* love you, mustn't I? Still she felt nothing, just a dull, dead acceptance of the physical tasks she must perform, a grudging acknowledgement of what must be done to keep the poor mite alive.

As the hours passed, the situation deteriorated. Nell could not produce more than a few measly drops of milk, though she squeezed till her nipples were raw and painful to touch. The cottage walls remained cold and dead and her panic grew. One of her earliest memories was of Ma feeding Violet from a glass bottle, testing the milk on the back of her hand to make sure the temperature was right. Maybe that was what she should be doing now, she thought, since she appeared to be incapable of providing milk naturally, but Marion had made no provision for a baby who would not feed, a mother who could not produce milk. Is this what the future holds? she wondered as she trudged to and fro across the sitting room, attempting to soothe her fractious charge, trapped here for ever with this howling banshee? It was almost forty-eight hours, an endless waking nightmare of failed attempts to get the child to suckle, before she heard the clatter of the latch and Marion's familiar step in the hall; the relief was exquisite, overwhelming.

'Thank God,' she exclaimed, meeting the little woman at the door. 'Where have you *been* all this time?'

Marion shook her head. 'Don't ask.' She was hollow-eyed, grey with fatigue. 'You have to come. Violet needs you.' Her voice was hoarse and she passed a hand across her eyes as she spoke, swayed.

'What's happened?' asked Nell, alarmed. 'Is Violet all right?'

'Yes,' said Marion brusquely. 'Yes, of course she is. You'll need to wrap the baby up warm. It's cold outside. Hurry up.'

Nell turned away. She settled the baby in the cot, squatted for a moment staring down at the red, angry face, the tiny fists punching the air. 'I'm sorry,' she whispered. 'This is my fault. You'll be all right now – Marion's here.'

Marion took over while Nell banked up the fire and extinguished the lamp, then led the way to the Morris, parked on the other side of the clearing beneath the trees. Nell could feel the wet soaking into the hems of her hastily donned trousers and the child complained all the way. It was the first time, she realised, as she climbed stiffly into the passenger seat, that she had left Malletts in over six months.

Everything ached, arms, legs, stomach, breasts. She longed for sleep; even the oblivion of death might be preferable to this limbo, this soul-deadening nothingness. Marion sat in grim-faced silence, concentrating on her driving. Despite her reassuring words it was obvious that something was seriously wrong with Violet. Whatever it was, thought Nell, it was all her fault; right from the beginning everything had been her fault.

She stared out of the window at the passing countryside, no longer familiar after six months hidden away at Malletts. The moon was nearly full, hanging low in the sky behind thin scudding clouds, and the car was cold. At least the baby was quiet though, soothed by the burbling of the engine and the hum of the wheels on the tarmac.

Marion turned in through the imposing gates, then drove slowly past the rows of army lorries parked on the grass, winding down her window to bark a greeting at the soldier standing to attention on the far side of the cattlegrid. Nell could see the lines of tents stretching up the sloping lawn towards the house, row upon row of black triangles against the navy-blue sky, could smell the tobacco smoke drifting from the sentry's hut. The gravel drive curved right along the imposing façade, then branched off through a tall archway to the courtyard at the back of the house where Marion drew up at last outside the narrow, unprepossessing entrance to the servants' quarters. Then she led Nell, blinking in the dazzle of the first electric light she had seen for months, along a wide corridor with scuffed grey-painted walls, past a cavernous, cabbage-smelling kitchen, to the foot of a dark, winding wooden staircase.

As they began to climb Nell heard a sudden burst of laughter, and the sound of heavy footsteps filtered through the green baize door they had just passed.

Marion paused. 'Officers' mess,' she said, snorting contemptuously. 'Mess being the operative word in the drawing room. God knows what sort of state the place'll be in by the time I get it back.'

They trudged on up towards the first floor, turned left on the landing, then carried on along another, narrower corridor with doors opening off the right and tall windows overlooking the courtyard below to the left. The blackout curtains were undrawn here and their passage was guided only by the moonlight pouring through the glass. The baby was asleep at last, snuffling and mewing like a small animal, and the weight tugged at Nell's arm muscles, made her shoulders ache. She could feel the blood soaking through the sanitary towel to trickle down her legs inside her trousers and she longed to put her burden down, turn aside, find a bed and sleep. Marion ploughed doggedly on, glancing back every now and then to make sure she was still following.

They had hardly spoken in the car, awkward with each other like neighbours who meet suddenly out of context and discover that the only thing they have in common is their proximity. When Nell had ventured into the silence that the baby would not feed, Marion had merely grunted and driven on, staring fixedly ahead into the gloom. So curt, so distracted was she, that Nell had wondered whether the little woman had heard a single word she said.

They reached another staircase, shorter this time, six steps up, then two down and passed through another door into the heart of the house. Marion snapped a switch and Nell closed her eyes, blinded by the light.

'Bearing up?' asked Marion. 'Like a rabbit warren, this part of the house, but we're nearly there now.' Then she was off again, not waiting this time, along another passage, wider than the last, with doors on both sides this time. There was carpet here, threadbare runners stretching into the distance, and pictures on the walls, too grand for their surroundings, sombre, handsome portraits of men and women, landscapes, children, family pets. Now and then, catching a faint echo of Laurence, Nell would slow, glancing from the pale, impassive face in the painting to the child she carried in her arms, searching for a connection that might trigger her emotions. There was nothing there though, just a blank space where her feelings ought to be, and the panic was rising, setting her heart thudding behind her breastbone in time with her hurrying footsteps. What if this is it? she wondered. What if this is all there's ever going to be, this black hole, this *emptiness*?

Marion had stopped. She turned briefly, making sure Nell was still there, then knocked on the heavy oak door in front of her. There was a shuffling from within and the door was opened. A male face peered at them through the gap. Behind him Nell could see a high-ceilinged bedroom, sparsely furnished with a washstand, a cheap, battered chest of drawers and a high narrow single bed – a maid's room, she guessed, taking in the portrait of the Virgin above the sagging bed and the chipped enamel chamberpot poking from beneath it. The floorboards were bare and her outdoor shoes clattered loudly after the silent walk along the carpeted corridor.

The man who had ushered them into the room was young, no more than thirty-five. He was very nervous too; his left eye twitched constantly so he seemed to be winking. 'Lady Palmer,' he began, 'I've been thinking—'

Marion dismissed him with a chop of her pudgy hand. 'Don't be difficult,' she said. 'It's all decided. Eleanor, dear, you know Dr Hills, don't you?'

Nell nodded obediently. She had seen him now and then, months – years – ago, when she still lived in the

real world, before Laurence, before Malletts, before . . .
She shifted the weight in her aching arms, glanced
down at the small face . . . before *this*. She had paid him
little attention as he went about his rounds in the village, a tall, gaunt man with a permanent frown of
worry between his brows and a weak, receding chin.
She nodded a silent greeting and he nodded back, then
looked away; his obvious discomfort brought Nell up
short. What must she look like to the outside world?
The woman who had stolen her sister's husband and
who now had the brazen nerve to bring her illegitimate child under the same roof as that sister. She felt
the colour rise in her cheeks and lowered her head,
shamed all over again as she had been at the beginning.

'How is Violet doing?' Marion was saying. 'And have
you, er . . .?'

Dr Hills swallowed, his Adam's apple bobbing above
his collar. 'Yes,' he said. 'She's not too good, I'm afraid.
Physically, of course, she'll recover, but mentally—'

'Yes, well,' said Marion briskly, cutting him off in mid-
sentence. 'That's what we're here for, isn't it?'

At her command, Dr Hills took the baby across to the
bed, stripped the shawl away and examined everything,
bending tiny arms and legs, offering a finger to test the
strength of the child's grip, peering into eyes and mouth.
His hands shook with nerves.

'A strong healthy baby,' he announced at last, address-
ing Marion over the wails of the newly awakened infant.
'A little dehydrated, but we can soon put that right . . .
How is our mother doing?' His eyes met Nell's briefly,
and she was puzzled to see there not the distaste she
expected, but rather pity, sympathy.

He turned away, drawing Marion with him into the
furthest corner of the room, then whispered urgently in

her ear. Marion nodded, shook her head, said, 'No!' then moved briskly away from him, cutting the conversation short.

The baby was roaring, wide awake, hungry, thirsty. It was over two days now since Nell had given birth, far too long for a newborn to go without its mother's milk. Dr Hills took charge, pouring water from the jug on the washstand and wetting his fingers, then dabbing at the red, bawling mouth. Watching him, the only emotion Nell felt was relief, that the responsibility had been taken out of her hands.

'Come along,' said Marion, 'it's time this child was fed,' and she led the way out of the room and along the corridor again. Dr Hills handed Nell's baby back, but he stayed where he was. It was not until long afterwards, when it was all over, that Nell realised why. He wanted nothing to do with what was about to happen. If he knew nothing about it, he couldn't be held accountable.

The room to which Marion led her was bigger than the one they had just left – a housekeeper's room, guessed Nell, or maybe a governess's. A single lamp with a tasselled silk shade was burning on the bedside table and the scene was bathed in soft yellow light: a double bed, a narrow chest, on which sat a jug of water, a Turkey carpet. A blackout curtain stretched across one wall, concealing a wide window, and a fire burned in the grate. It was warm, almost too warm after the chilly corridor. Nell was swept once again by an overpowering need to sleep.

Violet was propped against a pile of feather pillows with her head tilted to one side and her eyes closed. She looked frail, thin – as if one puff of wind would blow her away, thought Nell – and there were black rings under her eyes, dark hollows beneath her cheekbones; she looked like a drowned Ophelia, pale, ethereal, her hair spread about her in a golden, angelic halo. Pausing in the doorway, Nell wondered how she could have been so stupid. How could she ever have thought Laurence might leave Violet for her? How could she ever have thought she might make a life with him, take him away from her poor, innocent sister? She stood stock-still, tongue-tied with guilt and sorrow.

It was the baby, mewling with hunger, who woke Violet. Her eyes flew open, her face lit up, and for a moment she looked like the girl Nell had known all her life: the radiant young woman bursting into the sitting room on her twenty-first birthday to announce that she had met the man she was going to marry, the beautiful bride, whirling gracefully round a hotel ballroom on her wedding day, the glowing wife, dancing her feet sore with her dashing fighter-pilot husband, the focus of admiration for every male under the age of sixty at the New Year party in the village hall. Marion leaned over the bed and murmured in her ear. Violet turned her head towards Nell and the glorious smile faded into misery.

Nell went cold. There was no cot in the room, no sound but that which her own child was making.

'Violet?' she began. 'Violet, where's your . . .?'

Marion passed her, making for the door. Nell felt her hand on her arm as she went, squeezing, and pleaded silently, Please don't leave me here alone. Marion was wearing that same expression, that same look of pity and embarrassment she had seen just now on Dr Hills' face. Nell felt her hand in the small of her back, pushing her gently towards the bed, then heard the door close behind her.

She took a deep breath. 'Hello, Violet dear,' she said. 'It's me . . .'

Afterwards Nell could never remember exactly what

was said. But standing by the bed, meeting her sister's gaze for the first time in almost six months, she was sure, without any shadow of a doubt, that Violet knew, and when Violet held out her arms she relinquished her baby without a second's hesitation; she felt as if she were acting out a role in a play, taking part in a pre-ordained ceremony, a service of atonement. She stepped back and watched as Violet slowly unbuttoned her nightgown and exposed her breast. The wailing stopped. The baby mewed like a kitten, spread a tiny hand across Violet's swollen breast, searched for a moment, then settled down and began to suck.

Nell's milk came in a great gush then, warm and wet against her heavy cotton shirt, and she had to bite back the howl of pain which rose in her throat. Here at last was a wound she could feel, a wound made all the more cruel for being self-inflicted.

It all made sense now – Dr Hills' sympathetic glances, Marion's parting squeeze. She had known from the beginning that there would be a price to pay. This was the reckoning. She had stolen Violet's husband, and now Violet was claiming her child. The milk, cooling rapidly, trickled down into the waistband of her trousers. She felt no resentment, just a deep, bottomless well of sadness, a weariness beyond anything she had ever known. When Violet began to cry, the tears coursing silently down her cheeks, dripping off her chin, making the baby blink as they splashed onto the tiny scrunched-up face, she knew it was all over.

'What . . .' began Violet. 'I mean, what is—'

'A girl,' said Nell. 'It's a girl.' Somehow, what came next seemed inevitable.

'What will you call her?' asked Nell gently.

'Laura,' said Violet. She raised her head. Her blue eyes

were brimming but her face was quite calm. 'I shall call her Laura . . . after her father.'

Marion was waiting in the corridor. She didn't say anything, just patted Nell's hand and nodded, as if she were a child who had performed well at some simple task. For once the smell of whisky was absent, but Marion's eyes, like Violet's, were full of tears, and she stumbled as she walked. She stopped at a door further along.

'There's one more thing I have to ask of you, my dear,' she said. 'It's for the best, you know. For everyone.' She fumbled in the pocket of her skirt, took out a handkerchief, blew her nose. 'It was never going to be any good,' she said. 'But then you knew that, didn't you?' Nell didn't answer. Never, she was thinking, such a long time, never . . .

The room into which Marion led her was long and narrow, lined from floor to ceiling with slatted shelves and stacked with linen, sheets, pillowcases, towels. There were no curtains, and the moon filled the room with ghostly blue light, cast black shadows on the floor. The tall sash window at the far end was wide open and the air was icy cold after Violet's warm bedroom. Nell's arms, burdened for so long, felt strangely light, and her fingers prickled with pins and needles.

'I'm so sorry,' said Marion. 'I'd do it myself, but I can't leave Violet – you've seen how she is.'

'Do what yourself?'

Marion turned away, fumbled with the pile of linen on the shelf, turned back, holding out her arms.

Nell looked down, choked. 'No,' she begged. 'No, Marion, don't ask me, please. I can't.'

'You must.' Marion raised her head; Nell caught the glint of her eyes in the moonlight. 'You're the only one who can do it.'

'No,' pleaded Nell again. 'Marion . . .'

'I shall never ask anything of you again,' said Marion, 'but this you *must* do.' She was implacable, unyielding. 'You owe it to your sister. To Laurence.'

Capitulating, Nell held out her arms and took the bundle Marion handed her, then turned slowly away.

'It's a boy,' said Marion as she reached the door.

Violet's stillborn baby was a boy.

Chapter Thirty-Six

There was no sound from Violet's bedroom, or from the other room where Dr Hills was presumably still hiding. There was no one on the stairs and no noise from the officers' mess on the other side of the green baize door. No one challenged Nell as she emerged into the open.

She half expected to be stopped as she crossed the yard – her feet sounded loud on the cobbles and she could see her own breath clouding in front of her as she walked – but nobody came. The tented camp was invisible from this side of the house, the sentry post nearly half a mile away.

The moon was hiding briefly behind a thin layer of scudding cloud and the air was damp. It was cold, and Nell shivered despite her heavy coat. She stared straight ahead, avoiding looking at the still, silent corpse in her arms. She had seen dead animals – working on her uncle's farm she had watched a pig being slaughtered, had seen the bodies of a hundred rats laid out in bloody rows after the terriers had finished with them. She had seen a cat too, its rear leg almost severed by the gin-trap into which it had strayed, its teeth bared in a grotesque grin and its front paws pointing at the sky. Her uncle had taken her to one side, explained about rigor mortis, and she had stored the information for future reference. So she knew when she tightened her grip, attempting to impart some warmth into the baby's body, that it was foolish to think she could stave off the inevitable.

On the other side of the courtyard was a wall and a door. She struggled one-handed to lift the heavy iron latch, then slid through and stood for a moment, getting her bearings. Behind and to her right the park stretched away towards the main drive. Ahead of her she could see sheep, settled for the night into indistinct huddles and to her left the woods began, running down the slope towards the river, the road and the railway. She set off, aiming roughly in the direction she thought Malletts must lie. Somewhere along that dark line was the path Ernie used, the narrow track along which Marion had come every other day for the past six months, bringing her provisions.

She picked her way carefully, watching her feet in the uncertain light, and a hundred yards from the house she began to make out another line, barring the way between her and the woods. As she drew nearer she saw that it was a high, red-brick wall, and she had to turn aside and follow it. As she came out the other side, the moon rode free of its covering and lit the scene from above, a pile of broken clay pots, an untidy bundle of fine netting, a wrought-iron gate. Nell moved closer and peered through the ornate curlicues into the garden beyond.

It was badly neglected, weed-strewn beds, matt-black holes here and there amongst the glinting glass of the Orangery. 'Oh . . .' whispered Nell, enchanted, 'will you just *look* at that . . .' and for a second, she forgot. She lifted the baby, glanced down at his face, gazed.

He was perfect. His skin glowed like marble in the moonlight, white, translucent, and he looked for all the world as if he were sleeping, slumbering peacefully in his mother's arms. He looked like Laurence. Nell's milk spurted again, hot against her cold, damp shirt. She felt a surge of tenderness, a wave of such hopeless, helpless longing it deprived her momentarily of the power to move. *This* is my child, she thought. *This* is the baby I carried all these months, the son I made with Laurence. She tightened her grip, drawing the tiny body closer, and stared through the gate at the moonlit garden. Years ago, when she was no more than ten years old, an aunt had given her *The Secret Garden* for Christmas. Reading it, she had become infused with excitement, and for weeks afterwards she had gone everywhere with her eyes wide open, searching for her own secret garden. Now . . .

She stood for nearly ten minutes, and she moved on reluctantly, stopping under the lee of the trees for one last look, then another. The glass of the Orangery roof glinted and glimmered above the black line of the wall, and, hypnotised by the magic of that abandoned garden, she touched the baby's cheek with her finger; he was not dead at all, but sleeping.

His skin was icy cold; it was no use. Nell turned her head again, gazing over her shoulder at the garden. I could find peace here, she thought. I could grow my herbs; I could stay where Laurence . . . where my son is.

She found the path by accident, heard a noise in the undergrowth and followed a badger as it snuffled along with its nose to the ground. The narrow track from which it had emerged was clearly visible beneath the trees, winding into the distance.

She walked on. She could hear scufflings and murmurings in the undergrowth, the rustling of leaves all around her, but she felt no fear. By the time she stumbled out into the grassy bowl of the glade, her son was already stiffening, and she could no longer pretend he was alive. She trudged across to the cottage, lifted the latch, then stood in the darkened hall wondering what to do next.

The sitting room was warm, the fire, banked up when she left, glowed red round the edges. Nell moved slowly across the room to the wicker basket which had held that other child – Violet's child – and laid her son down, tucking the shawl around his face to make him comfortable, even though he was long past feeling comfort or discomfort. Then she went to the table and lit the lamp.

The shadows flared against the walls and she blinked in the light. Her arms ached and her eyes stung, but there were things to be done before she could sleep. She took the lamp through to the storeroom and found the spade. She left the lamp sitting on the floor in the hall, opened the front door, and walked into the moonlit glade. As she passed she picked up the brown paper bag Ernie had left her, a dozen pink cyclamen corms.

It took her a long time; her stomach ached, and her back, and her energy was almost spent. She buried the boy deep, and marked the spot with the cyclamen corms. Then she pressed the loose soil down with her feet, and went back to the sitting room.

She folded the bloodstained blankets, picked up the pillows from the floor. Then she took her journal from the bread oven and sat by the fire to record what she had done. When she had finished, she extinguished the lamp and felt her way across the room to the window to take down the blackout. It was almost dawn – the digging had taken longer than she'd realised – and the pale light flooding into the room made her eyes water.

At the top of the stairs she paused and spread her hand on the wall. It was quiet. She stared straight ahead, focusing on the brass knob at the foot of the bed, but still nothing came. She moved across to the window and leaned on the sill. No one would ever hear about this night's work. In time, the tree above his resting place would give him shade and the cyclamen would mark his grave, but only she would ever know where her son was buried.

She was all alone now; she must make her own way. A vision came to her, of the walled garden, silent and serene in the moonlight, and she knew that she would get no more sleep tonight.

Tomorrow, she thought, tomorrow she would go and see Marion, to ask if she could have it for her own.

Chapter Thirty-Seven

Marion came the following day, driving up the drift in the Morris in broad daylight. She was hunched, bowed down as if in pain, and she couldn't meet Nell's eye. Violet was taking the baby back to London, she said – she had begged and pleaded with her to stay, but she was adamant.

'She says it's the best thing for all of us,' she told Nell, sipping whisky and staring morosely into the fire. 'She says she doesn't think she could bring the child up here with you – us – looking over her shoulder all the time. It'll be best for the baby, she says, less confusing, if she doesn't see us any more. Nell, dear, don't you think you should go back to London too? Not to your mother, of course, but you could find a room somewhere, work for your father. You never know, you might be able to change her mind—'

'No,' said Nell. She was seated at the table. She had been drawing up plans, making sketches. Early that morning she had retraced her steps, drawn back through the woods to the walled garden by a force she did not understand. She had followed the wall, moving stealthily like a burglar, then tried the wrought-iron gate and found it unlocked. Unable to resist, she had spent the ensuing hours pacing the gravel paths, taking measurements, scooping handfuls of soil into her hands and letting the grains trickle through her fingers, thinking, plotting, planning. By the time the sun rose over the horizon she had made up her mind.

'There's something I want to ask you,' she said now.

Marion sighed and topped up her whisky. 'What?'

'I want the kitchen garden.'

She was incapable of subtlety; her need was too urgent for politeness. 'I want the space for my herbs.' She rose from the table and crossed the room, sat down on the rocking chair, facing Marion. 'I shan't be able to pay you any rent to begin with, but once I start to sell my produce—'

Marion waved her glass. 'Why not?' she said. 'It's yours. Do what you like with it.' She transferred her whisky to her other hand, wiped her hand on her skirt. 'But what about the baby? How can you bear not to—?'

'He's here,' said Nell. 'My son is here, and so is Laurence. I can't leave them.'

Marion looked startled for a moment; then she shrugged, too tired to argue. 'So,' she said. 'That's that then, is it?'

She drained her whisky, placed the empty glass in the hearth and rose unsteadily to her feet. Her plain features were twisted with distress. 'No visits, Violet says. A clean break.' She drew herself up, took a deep breath, squared her shoulders. 'Just give me a couple of days, and I'll put the word round the village that you're back.' Her lower lip quivered, and she jutted out her chin, fighting the tears. 'Might as well keep up the charade to the bitter end, eh?'

She trudged across the room to the door. 'I wish *I* could feel him here,' she said as she disappeared into the hall.

Nell followed slowly in her wake, out of the sitting

room, out of the hall, and into the clearing. She watched her plod across the grass towards her car, saw the swirl of smoke rise from the Morris's exhaust. Of course, Marion didn't understand – how could she? She was not sure she understood herself. She had convinced herself that her child was a boy because deep down she had thought if she couldn't have Laurence then she could at least have his son. So all the love she should have felt for her living daughter had gone to Violet's dead son, and there seemed to be none left over. She turned back into the porch, shut the front door, then walked slowly across the sitting room to the bread oven. Maybe, she thought, as she lifted her journal out, maybe writing it down might help her make some sort of sense of it.

As she stepped backwards she caught her foot in the rag rug, and she had to reach out to steady herself against the wall. She felt him then, humming against her skin.

'Ah . . .' she murmured. 'So you're back.' She took the book to the table and opened it at a fresh page. She reached across for the ink and dipped her pen.

Where have you been? she wrote. *I've missed you.*

Chapter Thirty-Eight

Ellis turned the page but there wasn't any more. She closed the book, then moved across to the window and stared out into the clearing. The grave could be any-where – beneath the sycamore which leaned over the entrance to the drift, under the hawthorn near the pond; was it marked by the elder, laden with black, shiny berries, which shadowed the old privy? Tomorrow she would look for it.

She rested her hands on the stone sill. Somewhere away to her left an owl hooted and as she searched the tree-line a heavy-set badger moved warily out into the open. It raised its nose and sniffed the air, then ambled across the wide open space in front of the cottage. Its striped head was hunched between its shoulders and its short legs brushed the thick grass. Ellis marked the spot where it had emerged, between a pale-barked silver birch and a tangled mass of wild rose and bramble. Somewhere out there was the path along which Ernie had wheeled his bike, the path Marion had walked to check on Nell as she waited out her pregnancy. Somewhere out there was the route along which Joe had found his way a few hours ago, bringing her candles and a model aeroplane with fabric wings and complicated struts, such as a dexterous schoolboy might build . . .

Nothing was certain any more. Her grandmother was not her grandmother, but her great-aunt. Nell's son, her missing namesake, was not a son at all, but a daughter, Violet's niece, her own mother, and somewhere out there Violet's son was buried, his grave marked by a drift of pink cyclamen . . .

Drawn by a need, a compulsion over which she had no control, Ellis turned away from the window and walked out, out of the sitting room, out of the hall, through the porch and into the moonlit clearing. The grass soaked her shoes, and she shivered with cold, but she strode on through the long grass, her eyes fixed intently on the silver birch tree.

She could see it now, a narrow winding track, pale in the moonlight, stretching away into the distance. Somewhere on the other side of those trees, Joe was waiting for her. If anyone had asked how she knew she wouldn't have been able to tell them. Common sense told her he was long gone. But the smell of tobacco was strong in her nostrils, and as she'd passed through the porch the wall had sung.

She just knew.

She walked on, dreamy, light-headed, still not quite in the present, along the narrow track in the dark, her eyes fixed on the pin-prick of light at the far end where the woods ended and the parkland began. She felt no fear of the night-time rustlings all around her, noticed only peripherally the scratches inflicted by bramble and sloe as she passed, the leaves which caught in her hair and her clothes. She was intent on only one thing – stopping Joe from leaving.

His car was there when she emerged into the open, as she had known it would be, parked askew in the middle of the empty car park with its doors wide open and Joe's rucksack leaning against the rear wheel; the lights were on in The Herb Garden, and the wrought-iron gate was ajar. She felt no surprise, didn't think it odd that Joe should have a key, or that he should still be here more than four hours after he had left her, apparently for good. She was aware of her feet crunching on the gravel as she crossed the wide open space, of her wet tracksuit clinging to her legs, but she felt no connection with the noise, no discomfort from the damp.

The lights were on in the Orangery and she could see Joe's sleeping bag, rolled up on a striped garden lounger. Had William had been letting him sleep here? she wondered. Joe was squatting by the pond at the crossroads. He had his back to her and he was playing with the water, slashing a broken plant frond back and forth across the fountain, scattering showers of raindrops over the rippling water. He didn't hear her coming, didn't notice she was there until she stopped beside him and her shadow fell across his face. He jerked his head up, startled.

'I'm sorry,' she began, spreading her arms wide in a gesture of helplessness. 'Joe . . .'

He straightened up, slowly, deliberately, and stared at her. Ellis could hear the fountain burbling, feel its fine mist on her skin. Unnerved by his silence, she hung her head and just stood there, listening to the blood pumping through her veins. A jumble of pictures raced through her mind – the first time she set eyes on him, the night she let him into her flat, the first time they made love, their last meeting, flickering candles and firelight – images flashing before a drowning woman's eyes.

'Joe . . .' She took a clumsy, stumbling step towards him. '*Help* me. Don't make this any more difficult than it already is.' Joe stared stonily at her. 'I'm sorry,' she said. 'I was wrong. Stay with me.'

'Why?' he said. His voice was hoarse, angry.

'Because I'm asking you to. Because I'm going to have your child.'

'So? That wasn't *my* decision.'

'Nor mine.' She was begging now, pleading. 'It was an accident.'

'That's not what you—'

'I made a mistake.' She could hear her own voice, rising indignantly above the noise of the fountain. 'Haven't you ever made a mistake?'

'Yeah.' He turned his back and slashed the frond he was still holding across the rising jet, spraying glittering droplets in all directions. 'I trusted you.' The water ran down his arm, dripped like liquid mercury from his fingers. 'I thought . . .' He slashed at the fountain again and Ellis began to despair.

Look at him, she berated herself *Look* him straight in the eye and *make* him believe you. Make him look at *you*. Make him *see*. All that self-inflicted torture, teaching herself to look her students in the eye, to face the world with at least the veneer of confidence. What use was it unless she could make it work when it really mattered? '*Look* at me,' she demanded, grabbing at his arm and tugging him round to face her. She was past being reasonable, swept up, carried away, desperate.

'Why should I believe you?' he accused her.

Ellis caught the scent rising from the broken stem he was holding, sharp, lemony. It was southernwood, Maiden's Ruin, and it brought her up short, reminding her unexpectedly of Nell. The right words came then, without effort, as if they had been put into her head. They were part of a Rupert Brooke poem, the last few lines of the last verse. He had quoted them to her, long ago when they were newly lovers, and she had never forgotten them.

'"*For what they never told me of*,"' she began, '"*And what*

I never knew . . ."'

She caught him by surprise. She watched his face soften, saw the anger seeping away. Then she felt his hand, picking leaves from her hair, his fingers, ice-cold and still wet from the fountain, on her cheek. *'"It was that all the time, my love,"' he* recited with her, *'"Love would be merely . . . you."'*

In the silence that followed Ellis could hear the fountain, feel the drops of water from Joe's fingers trickling down her neck. And she could tell by the lift of his shoulders, the way he leaned to meet her mouth with his, that maybe, just maybe, it was going to be all right.

Chapter Thirty-Nine

It was snowing when her labour began. It had been snowing all night, thick heavy flakes which turned the ground white, blurred the branches of every tree, every bush, every blade of grass; when Joe waded out to see what the road was like Ellis was already prepared for the worst. The snow-plough had just been through, he told her on his return; it had piled half a ton of dirty snow across the entrance to the drift, and it was going to take him hours to clear it.

The system they had devised had been working well up till now – from Tuesday to Thursday Ellis worked at her city flat; she had moved her computer back to town, hooked up to the Internet, and she spent her mornings researching in the university library. The arrangement gave them both space – Ellis didn't have to feel guilty if she wanted to write until three in the morning and Joe could work late, or attend extra sessions at college, without feeling he must rush home to keep her company. She was thinking about going part-time next year, when she was due back from her sabbatical, so they could be together more; she had already organised day-care for after the baby's arrival.

Joe was living at the cottage full-time, working at The Herb Garden during the day and attending evening classes three nights a week at a horticultural college on the other side of Ipswich, learning as he went along. He had enrolled with the Open University to do A-level Biology, and his language when talking to William was becoming increasingly peppered with incomprehensible words like 'acuminate', 'bigeneric', 'dioecious', which Ellis had never heard of. He was learning about pest management, propagation, fertilisers, the treatment of fungal diseases; William was teaching him everything he knew and sometimes, in the face of his newly acquired knowledge, Ellis felt positively stupid.

The lavender garden was almost finished, only the centrepiece, on which Joe and William had still not decided, remaining unplanted. The two men had grown extraordinarily close over the past few months, almost too close for Ellis, still worried about the long-term future. She had never seen her father so animated, nor so optimistic about The Herb Garden's long-term survival.

She hadn't planned to be at Malletts for the birth. She was booked into the city hospital near her flat, due to be induced in three days' time – she was thirty-five years old, they had reminded her at her last check-up, she was already a week late, and with an older mother there was always the possibility of complications. Joe was taking a rare day off work so he could be there to hold her hand. He was trying hard, making all the right noises, but Ellis had been sleeping badly lately, worrying about what would happen when it was all over.

The baby was coming between them, getting in the way, causing tensions that had never been there before. Sometimes, as she lay wide awake in the small hours with Joe sleeping quietly beside her, Ellis wondered whether it might have been better if the pregnancy had been planned, if Joe had been included from the beginning. In her more clear-sighted moments she knew he would never have agreed to have a child at all if she had consulted him first.

He was trying too hard. He had accompanied her to pre-natal classes, and to the hospital, he had helped her choose the cot, followed her patiently round Mothercare while she mulled over Babygros, miniature duvets, carry-slings, changing-mats, approving her choices with a smile and a shrug. But all the time she had been aware that his heart wasn't in it, that he was doing it for her, because it was what *she* wanted.

She had been aware of the problem ever since their reconciliation. They had locked up that night, then walked back along the narrow trail to the cottage leaving Joe's car littered in the middle of the Herb Garden car park, and Joe had been at Malletts ever since. Already, in under five months, he had made dramatic changes; he had cleared the selfseeded ash trees and the brambles from the middle of the glade, dug a new vegetable patch; he had made a start on resurrecting the herb beds, planted a climbing rose beside the porch. Ellis was uncomfortably aware that if they ever split up he would find it almost more of a wrench to leave Malletts than she would but, 'For God's sake, Ellie,' he said when, restless and insecure, she confided her fears, 'nobody's going anywhere. Put a sock in it, will you?'

Since that night at The Herb Garden the balance between them had shifted – they were more equal now, no longer tutor and student, teacher and pupil – but it had taken time to re-establish their fragile partnership, rebuild the trust that had been so badly damaged. The pleasure Ellis took in their time together was immeasurable, but sometimes she felt as if they were avoiding the one issue they should be discussing, backing away from it because it threatened the very foundations of their relationship.

She had broached the subject that night at the cottage. They had just made love for the first time in almost two months, and they were lying, warm and sleepy, in Nell's big bed, as close as they had ever been. The window was open, and the air was cool, the sky just beginning to lighten with the onset of dawn. Joe's answer, when she asked him if he was pleased about the baby, had been typically forthright. 'I don't know,' he'd said. 'I'd not planned to become a father, at least, not for a while.' He'd paused, considering. 'At the moment all I can see is that I'll have to share you. I may not like that.' He'd apologised then, aware that he had said the wrong thing, attempting to soften the blow with soothing words. 'No, that's not what I mean. I've not got used to the idea yet, that's all. I'll feel differently when it comes. I can see it needs a father. Maybe when it's born—'

'She,' said Ellis. 'When *she is* born. It's a girl.'

She felt him shrug, dismissing the problem. 'OK, maybe when *she* is born, I'll feel differently. Will that do?'

'I suppose it'll have to. Joe?'

'Yeah?'

'I love you,' said Ellis.

He rolled over and tightened his grip. 'I love you too,' he said, and fell asleep.

Since then, watching him as she talked about her plans for their daughter, listening to him making what he thought were appropriately enthusiastic noises about their future as a family, it had dawned upon her that he was simply not ready for a child.

'I don't know,' he said with brutal candour, when she attacked him for a second time. 'At the moment I feel no . . . paternal instinct at all.' They were in the garden at Malletts at the time. Joe was clearing the thickets which had grown up around the pond and Ellis had just brought him a mug of coffee. He was leaning on his fork while he drank it. 'Don't worry,' he repeated. 'It'll be all right when it's born. It always is, isn't it?'

He had gone back to his digging, clearly relieved that the interrogation was at an end, but Ellis, remembering Nell's terror as she held her newborn daughter for the first time and that instinct failed to come, wished she hadn't asked the question.

'We must get you out straight away,' said Joe now, 'before the weather gets any worse.'

Ellis was touched by his palpable anxiety. 'Looks like you'll have to fly me out then,' she said, teasing him, 'or deliver the baby yourself.'

He frowned ferociously, not seeing the joke. 'Don't be daft. I'll phone the emergency services, get them to come and clear the entrance to the drift.' His face cleared. 'They can send a helicopter if necessary. Where's your phone?'

Another contraction gripped Ellis's stomach and she winced.

Joe squatted in front of her, his face pinched with concern. 'Where's the phone, Ellie? In your bag?'

It had seemed like a sensible alternative at the time. A phone had become essential, to keep in touch with Violet, but a land line to such an isolated spot would have been prohibitively expensive, the waiting time for installation far too long, so Ellis had bought a mobile instead. Over the past few months she had covered every other eventuality she could think of. She had got the builder to put a woodburning stove in the study, with a back-boiler to heat the hot water and a couple of radiators, so even in the event of a power-cut the baby would be warm; she had installed a coal-bunker outside the back door, stockpiled wood, bought a tumble-dryer.

But the phone, she remembered as Joe rifled anxiously through her bag, was recharging on the desk in her city flat, where she had put it the previous night. It might as well be on the moon, for all the use it was going to be.

'I'll walk,' said Joe. 'I'll walk over to The Herb Garden and use the phone there.' He had had a set of keys for months, ever since William first took him on while she was in London, the only one of William's employees to be so entrusted.

Another contraction. Ellis groaned. 'No,' she said when she could talk again. 'No, don't leave me. I want you here.'

'But I don't know anything about delivering babies!'

His voice was sharp; Ellis could hear the panic beneath the surface. 'So?' she said. 'Women have been having babies for hundreds of years . . .'

It was a while since Nell had made herself felt; the walls had been quiet since the night Ellis finished the journal and there had been no smell of tobacco. Now, suddenly, Ellis was aware of her presence, more strongly than she had been for months. 'I want you to make me up a bed,' she said. She felt calm now, in control. 'In front of the fire. I'll be fine, you'll see.'

While Joe brought blankets, pillows, his old sleeping bag, Ellis lay back in her chair, counting the minutes between contractions and mulling over the future. So many things were unresolved; Joe had been wonderful with Violet, striking up an instant rapport with her the first time Ellis took him to visit, showing himself willing, even eager to include her in their lives, but Laura was proving more difficult to placate. She was still refusing to meet the old lady, even on neutral ground, and although Violet was happy in her new home Ellis was painfully aware that the one thing she longed for, to be reconciled with the woman she had brought up as her own daughter, was so far proving impossible to arrange. Ellis was pinning all her hopes on this baby, hoping it would bring together as she had not been able to do. She hadn't found the dead boy's final resting place either, although she had searched the glade from end to end for some sign of the cyclamen with which Nell had marked his grave. Of course, the corms could have failed to thrive, been dug up by badgers, even crushed by the builder's lorries, but every time she phoned, every time she visited, Violet asked, and every time she was forced to disappoint her again.

She had kept Nell's secret to herself; she was not even sure whether Violet remembered exactly what had happened the night Laura was born, and it was not up to Ellis to remind her. She still thought of the old lady as her grandmother, still felt the tie of kinship she had felt before she knew the truth, and she saw no reason for that to change.

Another contraction, stronger this time. Joe was hovering in the doorway, torn between his instinct to get help, and his reluctance to leave her. She must give him something to do, she decided, keep him busy.

'Tea,' she suggested. 'Could you get me a cup of tea? And some toast would be nice.'

As he disappeared into the kitchen she reached across to touch the wall behind her head. It was quiet; no vibration, no faint humming beneath her fingers. 'Nearly there, Nell,' she murmured. 'Not long now.'

Eleanor Carter's great-grandson was born just before dawn, in the middle of a blizzard. By the time he emerged, yelling lustily, Ellis was too tired and battered to worry about what Joe might be feeling, but when her son – 'A *boy*? Are you *sure*?' – was placed, scarlet with rage and with a shock of thick black hair just like his father's, into her arms, she gazed at him through a mist of tears and felt all the maternal instinct she could possibly have wished for.

After Joe had delivered his own son, with quite astonishing efficiency, she had slept, lying by the fire as Nell had done more than half a century ago, too exhausted to stay awake a moment longer, and it wasn't until late in the afternoon, after Joe had flagged down a passing motorist to get help and the doctor had made it at last through the drifts to check all was well, that she finally began to pay attention.

It was the sound of a baby crying that woke her. Joe was seated at the table. He was holding his son in his arms, gazing down at his dark head, and Ellis could see a tiny hand, tightly gripping his curled finger. He was trying to soothe the child, rocking him gently back and forth, crooning, and his face was glowing, luminous with pride, delight, awe. Hearing her stir, he looked up.

'Hi,' he said. 'Ellie . . .' He lowered his head again, drawn back as if by a magnet to the baby he was holding in his arms. 'I can't believe . . .' He crossed the room to kneel beside her and leaned across to kiss her, taking care not to squeeze his son too hard. 'I think he's hungry,' he began, then, all in a rush, 'I didn't know, Ellie – why didn't you tell me I'd feel like this?'

His eyes were swimming with tears. Ellis took the baby, settled him comfortably in the crook of her arm, smiled up at Joe. 'Do you remember,' she asked him, 'the night you told me about your dad, about his geraniums?'

'Yeah.' Joe squatted in front of her, puzzled. 'What does that have to do with anything?'

'Everything,' said Ellis. 'Who would you be, do you suppose, if you weren't defined by your father?'

Her son was crying, hungry for his feed. When she looked up again, the sitting-room door was wide open, and Joe was missing.

It was twenty minutes before he returned. His shoes were covered in melting snow, and he was holding something in his hand. He knelt by Ellis's head and reached across to touch the baby's cheek. 'Look what I found,' he said, holding out his gift. 'They're under that lilac near the pond, dozens of them right in among the roots, must've been planted years ago when the tree was quite small. You could search for a month and you'd never notice them unless it snowed . . . They've given me an idea. It's exactly what we need, a lilac at the centre of the maze. A white one, what d'you reckon? Can't wait to tell Bill, it's perfect . . .'

Ellis took his offering in her free hand. Cyclamen, a single tiny rose-tinted bloom. *In time, the tree above his resting place will give him shade . . .* Of course, she should have guessed. She leaned back against the pillows and stared at the delicate petals, reminded poignantly of another time, another posy of flowers, picked more than half a century ago.

Her son was the first of a new generation. He would have a history as well as a future. He would break the deadlock, she was sure, he would reconcile Laura and Violet as Marion had once so disastrously failed to reconcile Violet and Nell. Ellis placed her hand, palm down, on the wall beside her and just for a moment she felt that familiar humming, caught a faint whiff of pipe-smoke. She spread her fingers, pressed harder, but there was nothing there, just cold, solid plaster. 'Is this what you wanted, Nell?' she murmured.

'What?' Joe was stretched out in the armchair on the other side of the fire, watching her. 'What did you say?'

'Nothing,' said Ellis. 'Nothing at all. I was just asking if you were all right.'

'Yeah.' Joe stretched his legs to the fire, then dropped his head back and closed his eyes. 'Yeah,' he repeated. A big smile spread across his face. 'I'm absolutely bloody wonderful!'

Chapter Forty

It was nearly three months before Ellis got round to disposing of Nell's journal. She and Joe had decided on the baby's name by then – Thomas William, after Joe's father and her own. Laura was coming round at last, beginning, grudgingly, to join in the general rejoicing; Violet was enchanted with her 'great-grandson', as both she and Ellis thought of him, and even Joe's mum had melted the first time she held her grandson in her arms. Joe was happier than she had ever seen him, and so was her father.

She waited until Joe was at work to dig the hole, strapping Thomas to her chest so her hands were free, and borrowing Joe's spade. She was careful not to dig too close to the lilac's roots in case she disturbed the grave, and when she had finished she carried the journal out, along with Laurence's aeroplane. It was as she was lowering the book into the hole that she found it, stuck between two pages right at the back in a fold of brown paper. The stems were bound with black thread, the flowers fanned across the page, a tiny posy of primroses pressed more than fifty years ago. The petals were faded, pale and milky, and when she tried to peel them from the paper they crumbled into dust and blew away. She lowered the journal gently into the hole and reached across for the little aeroplane.

As it passed, Thomas snatched at it. His plump fingers caught one of the struts and it pulled away from the fuselage. The canvas tore, then parted company with the frame. As Ellis gently uncurled her son's fingers from his prize, it disintegrated into matchwood and trickled down like rain onto the journal.

She knelt in the long grass, and shovelled the soil back. When she had finished she sat back on her heels and raised her face to the lilac tree. Already the trusses were set above her head. Another month and the buds would begin to open. She would pick a big bunch then, to take to Violet. She would tell her where the boy was buried, try again to persuade Laura to go and see the old lady.

'Is this what you wanted, Nell?' she asked, but no smell of tobacco came, no vibration disturbed the damp ground beneath her knees. She felt no sense of Nell's presence, only the chilly spring breeze stirring the branches above her head and Thomas kicking energetically against her ribs. Her grandmother was gone for good this time. Which was, thought Ellis, hitching her son closer as she made her way back through the wet grass to the warm sitting room, exactly as it should be.

Joe would be home soon. She smiled, and quickened her step.

STOATS AND WEASELS

Kitty Ray

Art school, 1964. Five disparate students – Emma, tall, red-haired and naïve; beautiful, manipulative Alison; pompous George; shy, gentle Bill; and Jay, a sardonic loner with no past – come together in 60s London, along with black-eyed Ricky, as beautiful as his sister Alison, but handicapped by dyslexia and a crippling stammer.

Jay is in love with Emma, but Emma is in love with Ricky. Alison is pursuing a married tutor – a Weasel if ever there was one. George thinks he has all the answers, but poor Bill hasn't even worked out the questions yet . . .

'A warm and perceptive novel' – *Choice*

A FINE RESTORATION

Kitty Ray

Interior designer Clementine Lee lives and works in London. With a job she loves, a stylish flat she has designed herself and a gently promising relationship with her boss, she has everything to look forward to – until, in the space of one traumatic week, she loses it all: her lover, her livelihood and the roof over her head.

Seeking solace in a return to the village where she grew up, she takes a post as a housekeeper to a Norfolk book dealer. But her new employer is a difficult man, as profoundly damaged as his crumbling Victorian mansion . . .

'Moving, funny and romantic' – Katie Fforde